DREADFUL PENNY: HAUNTED PAST

J. MATTHEW SAUNDERS

SAINT GEORGE'S PRESS

CONTENTS

DREADFUL PENNY

1.

Your secrets won't stay secrets forever. It doesn't matter if you're a member of the Rotary Club, a Little League coach, an upstanding man of God—even a deacon at the First Baptist Church of Greenville, S.C. You could be there among the pews every time those church doors are open, hands clasped and head bowed.

Pray all you want, the truth will come out.

Maybe you dipped your hand in the petty cash jar at work. Maybe you didn't give Uncle Sam his fair share of your wages. Maybe when you fell off that ladder you didn't break your leg like you told the nice lady from the insurance company. Or maybe you're just stepping out on your wife.

Sooner or later, someone's going to find out.

And then you'll have a decision to make.

———

Penelope slid the file across her desk toward the woman seated opposite. Mrs. Joyce Gaines, hands clasped in her lap, stared at the plain manila folder. She'd worn a simple blue dress to the meeting. Her only jewelry, besides her husband's momma's diamond on her left ring finger, was a string of pearls around her neck. Her makeup was tasteful, and you'd be hard pressed to find one strand of gray in her neatly permed hair. In other words, she looked exactly like you'd expect the wife of a deacon at the First Baptist Church to look.

Mrs. Gaines glanced up at Penelope, who just nodded. No words of comfort or sympathy. They never helped anyway.

The deacon's wife moved to pick up the folder. Her hands trembled. She hesitated, fingers hovering tantalizingly close to the truth. For a moment, Penelope thought she might actually refuse to look, that she would choose to stand up and walk out of the office. But Mrs. Gaines took a deep breath and bit into the apple.

As she studied the first photograph, a tear slipped down her cheek. Yes, that was definitely her husband Ronald. No, that wasn't their house, and no, she certainly wasn't the woman greeting him at the door with a kiss.

By the fifth photograph, the tears had stopped. Joyce Gaines set her jaw and narrowed her eyes, then picked her handbag up from the floor and stuffed the whole folder inside. She retrieved her checkbook and furiously scrawled out a check, which she placed on the desk as she stood.

"Thank you, Miss Drake," she said. "Please don't take this the wrong way, but I hope we never have to speak to one another again."

As soon as the deacon's wife left, Penelope buried her face in her hands. She took in several deep breaths, trying to calm herself down. It didn't work. She still wanted to throw up. She suspected giving people news that tore their lives apart was not a part of her job she'd ever get used to. She hoped she never did.

The front door bell startled her. Penelope went to answer, crossing the foyer of the old converted house. She found Zed McKay, her part-time assistant, standing on the porch.

"You're here early," she said as they walked back into her office.

Zed shrugged. "Couldn't sleep."

She shot him a sideways glance. "It's two-thirty in the afternoon."

He grinned. "Your point?"

"Most contributing members of society start the day a little earlier."

"I'm sorry. You must have me mistaken for someone else." Zed threw himself into the chair Joyce Gaines had recently vacated. "How did the meeting with the deacon's wife go?"

Penelope perched on the edge of her desk. "As well as you'd expect."

"Did you manage to keep your lunch down this time?"

Penelope grimaced. "Just barely. My stomach's been in knots all day."

"I'm glad that's not my job. I just get to do the fun parts."

"At least she reacted a lot better than the last one. No wailing, gnashing of teeth, or rending of garments this time. I have a feeling she's going to come out okay. I can't say the same for her husband."

Zed's smile faded. "Do you ever wonder how things get to that point?"

"What do you mean?"

"The point where you stop talking, where you stop listening, where you have to hire a private detective to follow your husband and find out what he's up to."

Penelope shook her head. "I stopped wondering that a long time ago."

"Makes you wonder. What is it about humans that we have to foul up everything so badly? Why are relationships so hard?"

Penelope cocked an eyebrow. "This isn't about Mrs. Gaines, is it? Whatever happened to that girl you were seeing? Annie was her name?"

Zed exhaled slowly. "We're not seeing each other anymore."

Penelope winced. "Oh. I'm sorry."

"Don't be. It didn't work out. That's all."

With his easy-going nature, Robert Redford good looks, and

blue eyes just a shade off from violet, Zed turned the head of every woman he passed. His relationships never lasted for very long, though. He wasn't in the habit of offering details as to why, and Penelope didn't push. She figured if he wanted to talk, he would.

"So, what was it you wanted to see me about?" Zed asked. "New case I'm assuming."

Penelope studied her feet rather than meet his gaze. "Not exactly. In fact, the opposite of that. With the Gaines case wrapped up and that job up in Asheville done, I don't have anything else."

Zed frowned. "Nothing at all? Not even a lost dog?"

She let out a chuckle. "Believe me, I'd take that right now."

"You haven't had that many cases this year."

Penelope picked up Mrs. Gaines' check and stared at it. "I know."

"What are you going to do?"

Zed sprawled nonchalantly across the chair. No paycheck for her meant no paycheck for him either, but he never seemed to worry about money.

A wave of annoyance overcame Penelope. "I suppose I'll starve, Zed."

He flinched. "That's not what I meant."

She sighed. "Sorry. I'm just a little anxious about things right now."

"Well, maybe things will turn around."

The telephone on Penelope's desk rang. They both stared at it.

"That's the phone," Zed said.

Two rings.

Penelope nodded. "I know."

Three rings.

"When was the last time it rang?"

Four rings.

"About a week ago."

Five rings.

"One of us should probably answer." Zed glanced in Penelope's direction. "And since you're the proprietress of the establishment ..."

"Right." She picked up the receiver, fully expecting to hear nothing but the dial tone, but to her surprise, the line remained connected.

"Drake Investigations," she said as pleasantly as she could muster.

"Penelope?" said a man on the other end of the line. "Penelope Drake?"

"Speaking."

"This is Ephraim Brown. I don't suppose you remember me."

An old friend of her father. When Penelope was younger, she went to pool parties and cookouts at the Browns' house. She and their son Bertram had gone to college together. Since then, the two families had drifted apart. She hadn't spoken to Ephraim Brown for several years. She didn't think he even attended her father's funeral. "Of course I remember you, Mr. Brown."

"Penelope, we ... we've had a situation at our house. A break-in. I'd like to employ your services. Would it be possible to meet with you, face to face?"

Penelope's heart leapt into her throat at the prospect of a paying case, but she bit her lip, knowing she had to say what she said next. "Mr. Brown, if someone broke into your house, you'd be better off calling the police. As much as I'd love to help, they're far better equipped to handle things like that."

There was an audible sigh on the other end of the line. "I have my reasons. Please, if you'll meet with me, I can explain. I'll pay double whatever your normal retainer is."

Penelope glanced at Zed, who wore a quizzical expression. Burglaries were definitely not her normal fare, but Ephraim Brown's "reasons" piqued her interest, not to mention it would be nice to have money to pay for food.

"Think of it as a favor to your father's old friend," Ephraim Brown added.

"When would you like to meet, Mr. Brown?"

It's just a meeting, Penelope told herself. No harm in that.

"Could you come by the house today?"

"Hold on a second while I check my calendar." Penelope paused and counted to ten. "I believe I have some time this afternoon around four. How does that work?"

"Perfect. You remember where we live, I hope?"

She rattled off the address.

"That's it," Ephraim Brown said. "Thank you. I truly appreciate your help handling this."

———

The Browns lived in an oversized brick Colonial on Crescent Avenue, nestled in among the other mansions, some of which dated back to before the Civil War. Giant maple trees shaded the yard, even in the bright afternoon sun. A fountain burbled in front amid a small formal garden.

"Fancy," Zed muttered as they walked up the brick pathway to the front door. "Old family. Hopefully they have old money."

Penelope rolled her eyes at his remark. "Oldish. As Greenville high society goes, they haven't been around that long, only three generations or so."

"How did they make their fortune?"

"Farm equipment."

Zed stopped. "You're joking."

Penelope glanced back as she continued up the steps to the front door. "Do I look like I'm joking? It's still how they make their money." She motioned for him to join her on the stoop. "Now come on, and remember your manners."

She rang the doorbell. No more than a few second passed before a man with a mane of white hair and a full beard opened the door.

Upon meeting Penelope's gaze, he broke into a warm smile. "Penelope, it's good to see you again." He offered his hand, but hesitated when he noticed Zed behind her. "And Mr. …"

"McKay," Zed offered.

"My assistant," Penelope added.

Zed held up the Polaroid camera on the strap around his neck.

Penelope took Ephraim Brown's still outstretched hand. "It's good to see you again, too, Mr. Brown."

"Please, it's Ephraim." He stepped aside and motioned for them to enter.

The house looked exactly as Penelope remembered. Directly in front of them, a set of stairs led to the second floor while a hallway extended straight back. The dining room, to the left of the entryway, boasted an antique table surrounded by eight chairs, all dark carved wood. A china cabinet spanned one entire wall, displaying plates and cups edged with tiny, painted pink roses. A crystal chandelier caught the light shining through the large picture window and threw rainbows onto the damask wallpaper.

To the right was the formal living room, crammed like the dining room with antiques—overstuffed, high-backed chairs, a settee, and lacquered tables all arranged around a brick fireplace with a faux oriental screen. Books lined built-in shelves, though Penelope had never seen anyone read any of them. Growing up, she'd been in awe of those two rooms. The idea that a house could be so big there were rooms that were never used amazed her. Almost as far back as she could remember, she and her dad had shared the apartment above the detective agency, the apartment where she lived alone now.

"I'm really sorry to hear about your father," Ephraim said. "He was a good man."

Penelope nodded. "Thank you. Yes, he was."

"I wanted to attend the funeral, but I had … other obligations."

Penelope held up a hand. "No need to explain. Everything was so sudden. No one really had time to prepare. Besides, Dad would have hated that we had a funeral at all. My grandmother insisted."

"Well, it must have been a difficult time for her, especially."

Ephraim shook his head. "I don't even want to imagine what it's like to have to bury your own child."

"Actually, she hates funerals, too. A waste of perfectly good flowers, she says, but she'd die herself before breaking with propriety."

Ephraim chuckled. "I do remember Mrs. Drake being a force to reckon with."

Penelope grinned. "She still is."

Zed cleared his throat. "I think Penelope takes after her."

Ephraim eyed him. "I've heard that." He turned back to Penelope. "At any rate, thank you for taking time to come over here."

Penelope jabbed an elbow in Zed's side. "Mr. … Ephraim, you said you had a break-in?"

He pointed down the hallway. "They came in through the back door. We just noticed it this morning. I can show you. I haven't let anyone touch the door or even go near it."

He led them toward the back of the house, past the kitchen and a family room much less formal than the two front rooms. Penelope had spent quite a few evenings there watching old movies on the giant leather sectional or playing on the foosball table, more luxuries she had always envied. The hallway ended at a door that stood ajar. Beyond, Penelope caught a glimpse of the patio, the kidney-shaped pool, and a green expanse of lawn.

She approached the door and knelt to examine the lock. "Looks like it was picked, pretty expertly, too."

Zed raised his camera and snapped a picture of the lock.

Penelope scanned the area around the door. "It rained yesterday. The ground would have been wet, but there aren't any footprints. I don't see any fingerprints either, although whoever did this probably wore gloves. If I had to guess, this wasn't his first rodeo." She looked back at Ephraim. "You didn't hear anything?"

"Nothing," he said.

Penelope stood. She traded glances with Zed, who was clearly thinking the same thing she was. Something about this break-in didn't add up.

"Have you been able to figure out what was taken?" she asked. "Your television and stereo are still here, I noticed. Is the silver accounted for? Mrs. Brown's jewelry? Any cash you have stashed away?"

Ephraim held up his hands. "That's just it. Nothing seems to have been taken at all."

"Is that why you don't want to go to the police?" Zed asked.

Ephraim drew his mouth into a thin line. "Not exactly."

Penelope studied Ephraim. He rubbed the back of his neck and chewed on his lower lip. She didn't need a degree in psychology to know he was debating what to say next. "Then what is it?" she prodded.

Ephraim sighed. "Penelope, as I'm sure you know, your father had a reputation for handling … unusual cases."

And there it was. The missing piece. Penelope gritted her teeth, wondering if she'd ever be out from under her father's shadow, but then she reminded herself that she was getting paid. "Are you saying something about this break-in is *unusual*?"

Ephraim beckoned to Zed. "Come here. You'll want to take a picture of this."

He opened the door wider. On the back, deep, rough gouges marred the wood where three symbols were carved. They looked like letters, but not from any alphabet Penelope had ever seen.

Zed snapped a Polaroid.

Penelope traced the curved lines with her finger, almost, but not quite, touching the surface of the door. "Do you know what they mean?"

Ephraim scratched his beard. "I was hoping you would."

Penelope studied the symbols. They seemed to stare back at her, with malice. "I'll have to do some research."

"Please," Ephraim said, "anything you can find out."

Penelope and Zed spent some time sweeping the rest of the house and the back yard for traces of the burglar before they took their leave. Penelope promised to get back in touch with Ephraim once she found out anything.

As she and Zed walked back to Penelope's car, a bright red Camaro pulled into the driveway. The engine rumbled as the car idled for a few seconds before it shut off. A man stepped out. He was a good head shorter than Zed, and to Penelope's eye, about twenty pounds heavier than he had been in college. When the newcomer spotted them, his eyebrows shot up in surprise, followed fleetingly by a sour expression that mirrored Penelope's own feelings pretty well.

"Bertram Brown," she said, "it's been a while."

He nodded, the tart lemon grimace replaced with a bland smile. "That it has, Penelope."

A second or two passed while they stared awkwardly at each other.

"So, what are you doing here?" Penelope eventually asked.

Bertram motioned toward the house. "Dad called me. He said there was some trouble last night."

"No, I mean *here*. What are you doing in Greenville? Last I heard you were in Atlanta being a general pain in the ass."

He shrugged. "I moved back a few months ago. Many more opportunities to be a pain in the ass right here. Now it's your turn. What are *you* doing here?"

"Your dad called me, too. He wants me to look into the 'trouble' as you called it."

Bertram's smile melted. "Seriously?"

"Seriously."

He drew his mouth into a sneer. "So you're still playing at being a private eye?"

She crossed her arms. "I'm not playing, Bertram."

"Maybe you leave this one alone, Penelope."

"That's up to your dad."

Bertram took in a deep breath and let it out slowly. "I'll talk to him." He gave a small salute and started to walk toward the house. "Good to see you again, Penelope."

"What's wrong, Bertram?" Penelope called after him. "Why don't you want me working for your father?"

Bertram stopped. "Don't get all bent out of shape. It's nothing personal. I just think maybe this is a job for someone else."

"Like who?"

"Someone with a little more experience."

She glared. "What are you trying to say?"

"I'm saying that this isn't a cheating husband. You don't want to get in over your head."

Penelope balled her hands into fists. "I'm really tired of having this conversation with people. I'll be fine."

His sneer returned. "You haven't changed a bit, have you, Dreadful Penny?"

Penelope stiffened at the name. "Excuse me?"

Bertram took a step toward her. "You heard me."

Zed moved to put himself between Penelope and Bertram, but she waved him off. "You know I wouldn't even be here if our fathers weren't fraternity brothers."

"And that's probably the only reason my dad called, but sometimes he puts too much stock in loyalty."

"Did it occur to you we might actually be good at what we do?" Zed asked.

For the first time since he stepped out of his car, Bertram acknowledged Zed. "And who are you? The bodyguard?"

"Zed works with me," Penelope said. "I don't need a bodyguard."

Bertram took another step forward. He was close enough for her to smell the beer on his breath. "Really now? Are you sure about that?"

She stamped her boot down on his foot and cut short his yelp by seizing his wrist and twisting his arm around behind his back. "Absolutely positive," she hissed in his ear. "Zed works with me for the simple reason that I can't be in two places at once. Now do you want me to remind you how I got the name you just called me?"

Penelope let him go. He staggered a few paces—out of her reach—before he straightened up and attempted to retrieve what was left of his dignity. He jabbed a finger in her direction. "You need to watch yourself, Penelope."

"Thanks, Bertram. I will." She put on her best fake smile. "You have a good day, now."

She turned on one heel and walked away with Zed close behind.

They climbed into Penelope's black Lincoln, another leftover from her father. As she started the car, Zed regarded her with a mixture of curiosity and amusement.

She rolled her eyes. "Go ahead, ask the question. I know you're dying to."

"How'd you get the name Dreadful Penny?"

"Sophomore year in college. I beat up a football player."

Zed laughed. "Really, now?"

"A kicker. Second string. Scrawny guy named Bobby. He reminded me of a weasel."

"What did he do?"

Penelope sighed. "It's honestly not much of a story. I was at a party. He put his hand where he shouldn't have. I dislocated his pinky finger and might have sprained his wrist, but I still maintain the fractured ankle and the concussion were his fault. I didn't make him trip over that coffee table trying to get away from me."

Zed's grin diminished. "I'm surprised they didn't do more than just give you a bad nickname."

Penelope was surprised, too. She didn't leave her dormitory for two days after the incident, afraid someone might try to physically put her in her place. "Come to find out, no one else really liked Bobby either, but the football team still did their best to make my life hell."

"I'm even more shocked a bunch of football players knew what a penny dreadful was."

"They didn't. One of my professors gave me the name when he heard the story."

Zed grunted. "I'm beginning to see why you don't talk about college that much."

She shrugged as she turned off Crescent Avenue onto Church Street. "I got through it. That's the important thing."

"By the way," said Zed, "Ephraim is hiding something. So is Bertram."

One of Zed's more useful skills was his knack for knowing when people were lying. Penelope didn't need to rely on his talent in this case, though. "They're both afraid I'm going to find something out, but Ephraim is more afraid of someone *else* finding out whatever it is."

"What do you plan to do?"

As the car crested the Church Street Bridge, Greenville's downtown spread out before them, brown and dreary under the dark clouds that had gathered. It looked like rain again.

"We'll do what we promised to do."

2.

SATURDAY, MAY 20, 1972

When Penelope came downstairs to her office the next morning, the stapler on her desk had been moved to the windowsill. She sighed as she picked it up and carried it back to its rightful place.

"You know, Dad, we worked out a system, remember? One knock for 'no,' two for 'yes'?"

Somewhere in the building, a door closed of its own accord.

She bit her lip to keep it from trembling. "I know your contact with the material world is spotty. Still, I can wish. I miss talking to you."

In the beginning, they had tried Morse code, but that had proven too exhausting for him.

Two muffled knocks.

Penelope had never been able to figure out exactly where the knocks came from. "In any event, I got to a really interesting case yesterday. It seems the Brown family had a break in."

One knock.

She looked at the wall incredulously. "But I haven't even told you everything."

One knock.

"Is it the Browns? You don't want me involved with them?"

Two knocks.

"But why?" Penelope asked. "I'll admit Bertram's a jerk, but I think I put him in his place. And Ephraim seems to think very highly of you."

One knock.

She shook her head. "I wish you could talk. Or at least write a note. What reason could you have for moving the stapler?"

Silence.

"Dad?"

No response. Her father had apparently gone wherever he went when he wasn't haunting her office.

She grabbed the Brown file off her desk. She had a visit to make.

———

The paint was chipping off the side of the old farmhouse. The yard was overgrown. The steps leading up to the porch leaned at a troubling angle. The neighbors probably would have complained, if there were any, but the house stood by itself on a desolate stretch of Piedmont Highway. Neglected for decades, the acres of surrounding farmland had returned to nature.

The front door wasn't locked. Penelope pushed it open and stepped into what would have been the front parlor in days gone by. A large room, it spanned the entire width of the house. Bookshelves lined every wall, floor to ceiling, and every shelf practically groaned under the weight of the books stacked up. There were no chairs or any other furniture.

Penelope's boots echoed on the hardwood floor. "Charles? Are you here?"

She didn't get any answer, though faint light shone underneath the door to the next room. Penelope hesitated with her hand on the old-fashioned cut glass doorknob. She'd stopped by unannounced. She'd be invading his privacy if she ventured any farther. He'd resent that, and she needed his help. But also, Penelope worried. She turned the doorknob.

Charles wasn't in the next room either. It was supposed to be the dining room, and in fact, a table stood in the center under a tarnished bronze chandelier, but like the parlor, bookshelves lined every wall. Books were piled on the table as well. Most were old, their bindings falling apart.

To Penelope's left, a doorway led to the kitchen, and a set of stairs led up to the second floor. To her right, there was another closed door. Again, light spilled from underneath, and something else as well—music. Penelope took a deep breath and pushed the door open. More bookshelves. More books. But also, a small black-and-white TV on a stand showing a rerun of *Bewitched*. The volume was turned all the way down. The music came from a record player. The voice of Mahalia Jackson singing "What a Friend We Have in Jesus" poured from the stereo speakers.

A black man holding an X-Acto knife sat in a folding chair in front of a card table. He wore a white undershirt and a pair of work pants. A book lay on the table with its cover removed. An awl rested next to it as well as a glue pot, a needle, and some thread—all things used for bookbinding.

"What are you doing here?" Charles asked without looking up.

"You didn't pick up your telephone," Penelope answered.

He shot her a sideways glance. "Maybe there's a reason for that."

She crossed her arms. "And maybe I'm not going to let you get away with cutting yourself off from everyone again, Charles."

Charles used the knife to continue cutting apart the book's old binding. "Last I checked, it's a free country. I'm not obligated to speak to anyone I don't want to speak to."

Penelope and Charles had danced this dance so many times she had the steps down cold. *He's doing this on purpose. He's trying to push you away. Don't let him.* "Why wouldn't you want to speak to me?"

The knife paused. He put it down and looked her squarely in the eye for the first time. "You tell me why you're here first."

She glanced away. "I need your help."

"And there's your answer." He shook his head. "I'm not in the business of helping anymore."

"I can pay you this time."

Charles picked up the knife again. "Doesn't matter."

Penelope took the Polaroid of the symbols on the Browns' back door from her purse and held it out to him. "All I need you to do is look at this picture Zed took and see if you can tell us what it is."

Charles didn't make any motion to take the photograph from her. "Zed couldn't help you with that?"

"You're the one who knows all about these things."

He gestured to the books on the shelves. "And yet what I know could barely fill a thimble."

She twisted her mouth into a wry grin. "That's still more than the rest of us."

The knife in his hand hovered over the yellowing pages of the book on the table. "I'm not dying for you, Penelope."

Penelope regarded him in silence as he calmly continued to deconstruct the book and struggled to keep her temper in check. *How could he think such a thing?* "I'd never ask you to do that."

"You do every time you ask me to help you." His knife skipped along the book's spine, cutting the threads that held the pages together.

She thrust the picture toward him. "How? It's just a Polaroid."

He glared. When he spoke, there was ice in his voice. "It's never just a Polaroid."

"I swear that's all it is this time."

He sighed. "If I look at it, will you go away and leave me alone?"

Penelope opened her mouth to protest, but then thought better of it. She nodded. "I promise."

He arched an eyebrow. "I mean it. For real."

"Charles, I promise."

He took the picture from her. After scrutinizing it for a few moments, he handed it back. "Hungarian runes."

Penelope glanced at the symbols again. "What do they mean?"

He shrugged. "Probably something in Hungarian."

"Dammit, Charles, you said you'd help."

"No, I didn't. I said I'd look at your picture."

Back to the dance. Penelope was at least familiar with this *pas de deux*. She pinched the bridge of her nose. "Charles."

He held up a hand. "Fine. It looks like some kind of charm, to me. What's the story?"

"My client's house was broken into. He found those symbols carved into the back door. The family is a little concerned, obviously."

Charles idly tapped the knife handle on the tabletop. "They could have been carved there for any number of reasons. To make the burglar blend into the shadows, to dampen the sound so no one heard them, even to make everyone in the house fall into a deep sleep. I'd have to do some research to know more, but you can tell your clients they're likely not under any sort of curse, if that's got them worried."

"Thank you, Charles." Penelope slipped the Polaroid back into her purse. "I'm going to go now, like I promised. But I want you to promise something for me."

"What's that?"

"If you need to talk about anything at all, you pick up the telephone and call me, okay?"

The corners of his mouth turned up in a faint smile. "I'm fine, Penelope, but I promise."

———

Zed wished Penelope had let him go talk to Charles, although things probably would have ended up the same—with him dodging punches. The man taking a swing at him was surprisingly agile given his size, but Zed was faster. He ducked, and the man's own momentum threw him off balance. Zed helped him along with a right hook to his jaw. He crumpled to the ground in a heap.

There were four of them total, all sporting Confederate flags, tattoos of crosses and skulls, and leather jackets with Bible verses taken out of context. They'd been leaning on an old Oldsmobile in the motel parking lot, smoking and laughing, passing around a bottle of some brown liquor so cheap it didn't even have a name. To anyone else, they would have looked like they were just loitering, but Zed knew better. They were staking out the motel, and chances were they were there for the same person he'd come to see. He just wanted information. They obviously were planning something different.

That Oldsmobile had a pretty large trunk.

Another one of them came at Zed with a knife. Zed kicked it out of his hand and jabbed him in the collarbone. Before the tough hit the asphalt, Zed spun around, and his fist connected with the nose of the third one, who had come up behind him wielding a knife of his own. Cartilage crunched, and he staggered backward, blood streaming down his face.

Zed flexed his fingers and turned to the fourth. "You want to give it a try, too?"

The last of the roughs shook his head and backed away. He was slightly chubby, and young, maybe not even eighteen. Zed sensed his fear, but underneath it, his anger, his resentment, his self-loathing. These were men convinced that life hadn't given them what they were owed, so they might as well just take it. Easy to manipulate. Easy to dupe into doing violence.

"Why don't you gentlemen go now, before the cops show up?"

The two still standing dragged their unconscious colleagues and threw them into the back of the Oldsmobile. The car peeled out of the parking lot, leaving a cloud of smoke behind.

Zed turned and walked toward the Off-ramp E-Z Lodge. He would have said the motel had seen better days, but he wasn't sure it had ever seen any good days. Rooms jutted outward from the central office in a single story, forming a wide V. Cracks ran up the stucco walls, bright turquoise at one point but now faded to a pale, sickly green. He passed an empty swimming pool with moss growing up the sides. Cars and trucks rumbled down Interstate 85, literally feet away, and Zed wouldn't have been surprised if the vibrations from a speeding eighteen-wheeler knocked the whole building flat.

In exchange for a five, the manager gave Zed the room number he wanted. He'd put it on his expense report, though Penelope got mad at him the last time for including a line labeled "Bribes." He'd just have to get more creative.

He banged on the door of room 17.

No response.

He banged again, louder.

Still no answer.

"Eddie," he called, "it's just me, Zed. I need to talk to you. I'm not here to collect a debt, at least not this time." The last part he added under his breath.

"Swear it!" came a voice from the other side.

"I swear," Zed said.

"On the grave of your mother."

"That may be difficult, seeing as how my mother is very much alive at the moment. Eddie, I promise you if you open this door, no one is going to hurt you. I just want to talk."

"You don't understand. If I open this door, I'm a dead man. Those guys hanging out in the parking lot, they're here for me."

"You don't need to worry about them. They're gone."

A moment of silence.

"Gone? How?"

"I asked them nicely to leave."

Eddie opened the door a crack and peered out. Zed smiled and waved. Eddie was short and thin, but wiry. Since the last time Zed saw him, he'd grown out his sideburns and cultivated a mustache. He frowned and opened the door a little wider. Sticking his head through, he looked past Zed toward the parking lot, first to the left and then to the right.

Apparently satisfied at last that Zed was telling the truth, he opened the door all the way and stepped back. "Okay, you can come in."

Zed stepped over the threshold but stopped short when he saw a woman sitting on the bed. She wore a short, sleeveless dress made of some shimmering gold material and gold boots with three-inch heels to match. The dress did a very good job of following her curves and showing off her tan skin. Tight auburn curls framed her face.

She wouldn't look Zed in the eye.

Eddie stooped over her and whispered something in her ear.

She shot Zed a quick glance. "Are you sure?"

"Yeah," Eddie said. "It's okay. You can go."

She stood and, with a nod to Zed, fled out the door, slamming it behind her.

"They … they showed up this morning early, banging on the door and causing a racket." Eddie stammered as he tried to flatten out his rumpled shirt. "She … she couldn't leave. She was starting to freak out."

Zed held up a hand. "Eddie, take it easy. I just came here because I need some information."

At the word *information*, Eddie's ears perked up. "Yeah? What can you give me for it?"

Zed barked a laugh. "Eddie, I just saved your ass. I'd say you owe me for that." He surveyed the surroundings. "And for forcing me to visit this fine establishment."

A television with a bent antenna huddled on a broken stand in the corner of the room. One of the two lamps was missing a shade. Cigarette burns dotted the rust-colored shag carpet and the blue-and-red-striped bedspread. A water stain started at the ceiling and ran down the wall behind the bed. The smell of mildew and stale cigarettes competed with the lingering smell of ammonia disinfectant.

Eddie let his shoulders fall. "Okay, fine." He gestured toward the suitcase at the foot of the bed. "Just as long as I don't miss the bus."

"Where are you going?" Zed moved to put himself between Eddie and the door, just in case.

"Does it matter?" Eddie slumped onto the bed. "Away from here."

"I'm just curious."

He stared up at the ceiling. "Los Angeles."

"What are you going to do there?"

Eddie shrugged. "Start over. Somehow. I have a place to stay for the first couple of nights. After that, I'll figure something out." He returned his gaze to Zed. "So, what do you want to know?"

"There was a break-in Thursday night or early yesterday morning over on Crescent Avenue. I thought you might have heard something about it."

Eddie whistled. "Crescent Avenue? Takes some balls to hit up a house there. Definitely out of my league, if I weren't anything but a law-abiding citizen, of course. Probably out of the league of anyone I know."

"So you can't tell me anything about it?"

"I didn't say that."

Zed glared. "Don't be cute, Eddie."

He shook his head. "I'm not. I swear. Look, it's a long shot. I don't know if this is your guy or not. I was out at a bar about a week ago—"

"Which bar?"

Eddie shook his head. "Right. Let the dick know where the snitch gets his information? Why would I ruin a perfectly good drinking spot like that? Oh, no. I'm not giving that up." A smile spread across his face. "Can't make things too easy for you and your girlfriend."

Zed frowned. "My girlfriend?"

"The lady private eye?"

"I work for her," Zed growled. "She is not my girlfriend."

Eddie smirked. "Sure, whatever."

"Back to your story, Eddie." Zed pushed as much menace into his voice as he could muster.

Eddie's smile faded. "There was a guy there. We're not friends or anything. He and I have had some … dealings in the past. I overheard him talking about a job. He didn't say what house he was going to hit, just said he'd found a way to break into any house. No need to worry about alarms or dogs or running into the homeowner in his pajamas on the way to the bathroom."

"You got a name for this guy?"

"Jeremiah Morrison."

"Any idea where I can find him?"

"You mean other than the bar? He lives somewhere over on Washington Avenue, I think. I don't know anything beyond that. Like I said, we're not friends."

"Thank you, Eddie. You've been a big help." Zed reached into his pocket and pulled out his wallet. He retrieved another five and held it out to Eddie. "Take it. For your trip."

Eddie stared at the bill for a moment before snatching it out of Zed's hand. "Thanks."

Zed nodded. "I hope you find whatever it is you're looking for."

He wouldn't include that five on his expense report.

———

Mrs. Louise Brown stared at the brooch on her dresser. She was certain she had never seen it before. A gift from Ephraim maybe? Though it wasn't his usual taste. The jewelry he gave her was typically showier, not that the large oval gemstone on the brooch was subtle by any means. She couldn't tell what the stone was. The color changed depending on how she looked at it, one minute deep purple, then red, and then green.

She picked it up.

Whispers filled the room. Louise turned around, expecting someone to be there, but she was alone. She returned her attention to the brooch. So pretty. Perhaps she might wear it to church the next day.

More whispers. Just behind her. And was that someone laughing?

The brooch was heavier than she expected. She examined the silver backing. No, not silver, never silver. Whatever the metal, it gleamed. The ornamentation around the stone reminded her of a vine with spiky leaves and thorns.

She looked in the mirror over the dresser and frowned. The brooch's reflection didn't quite match the brooch itself. The gemstone seemed to glow, pulsing almost like a heartbeat, her heartbeat.

"This would look really nice with my new lavender dress," she said to no one. "I could wear it tonight even."

The whispers grew louder. She could almost make out the words, but not quite. And there was another sound, too. Scratching. She'd have to get Ephraim to make sure there weren't mice in the walls again. Although this scratching didn't sound the same.

It sounded like something bigger than a mouse.

She put the brooch down. The whispers immediately grew quiet. She pulled her lavender dress out of the closet and hung it by the dresser while she got ready. Every now and then her eyes wandered to the brooch. After one last check of her hair and makeup, she picked it up and pinned it to the collar of her dress.

Laughter echoed through the room, or so it seemed. A figure appeared behind her in the mirror, a man with pale skin and empty black eyes. She closed her own eyes. When she opened them again, nothing was there.

"No more cocktails before dinner, Louise," she whispered to herself.

Louise found Ephraim downstairs, a deep frown on his face. For reasons she'd yet to uncover, he'd been wearing that frown a lot lately. The burglary only added a few more creases. He'd even suggested they stay in that evening, but she immediately shot that idea down, saying the night out with friends would be just the thing to take both their minds off the break-in.

"Sorry, dear," she said. "It took me a little while to figure out what to wear."

Ephraim's frown vanished, replaced by a broad smile. "You look lovely as always." Then his gaze came to rest on the brooch, and a tiny wrinkle reappeared in his brow. "We shouldn't keep the Kellys waiting too long, though."

On the car ride, Louise noticed strange things about houses they had passed by countless times before. There were either too many windows or not enough doors. Walls jutted out at odd angles. Trees grew where trees shouldn't be, and dark shadows danced everywhere. Every now and then, out of the corner of Louise's eye, a figure appeared standing on the side of the road, watching the car as it passed.

With every mile, Louise's distraction grew, to the point she didn't even notice they'd arrived until Ephraim opened the door for her and extended a hand. He said something to her.

"What was that, dear?" she asked.

He regarded her with a puzzled expression. "Nothing."

"Are you sure? I thought I heard you say something."

He let out a chuckle. "I'm pretty sure I would know if I said anything."

Someone had spoken to her, though.

Alice Kelly greeted them at the door wearing a bright lime green and peacock blue wrap dress. The Warrens and the Prichards were already there. Louise went around and greeted the other women while Ephraim shook hands with their husbands. The four couples had a years-long tradition of getting together once a month for a dinner party. They took turns hosting. Ephraim and Louise hardly ever missed.

Louise had known these women for decades and felt as close to them as sisters. She always looked forward to their get-togethers, but that evening she found herself wanting to leave even before dinner. Making conversation seemed an impossible challenge. She decided to blame her mood on the dreary weather. Perhaps all the rain was getting to her. She shot Ephraim a grateful look when he handed her a martini.

The shadows at the edges of her vision remained. Intangible figures stood in corners or in empty doorways, but every time she looked straight on, they vanished. When she went to take her seat at dinner, she jumped. A strange man loomed in the kitchen doorway directly behind Alice, his skin sickly gray, his eyes hollow black voids. She blinked, and he was gone. Everyone looked at her. She pretended she'd tripped in her heels.

The conversation went as it always did, but Louise only half-heartedly followed. The whispers returned, and this time she could even pick out a few words.

Your fault.

Won't let you leave.

These women had told Louise quite a few secrets over the years, things their husbands didn't know. Mostly these secrets were harmless, like just exactly how much a certain dress cost or everyone's true feelings for the game of golf.

But other secrets could do a lot of harm. The whispers were harsh when Louise looked at Marjorie Prichard.

Adulteress. Whore. Jezebel.

She almost said the words out loud. She was even afraid she had, but if she had, she would have been confronted with shocked silences or mouths agape, right?

The other women had secrets, too. Hidden bank accounts. Marriages of convenience. As the night progressed, the whispers became louder, threatening to drown out the conversation altogether. The shadows became darker too. She'd come to accept the black figures prowling at the edges of the room.

Eventually, the men retired to the porch to smoke cigars and drink Scotch while the women remained at the table. A slim cigarette perched in her fingers, Bonnie Warren launched into another rant against the game of golf. Now that the weather had warmed up, Harold was gone every weekend. He even skipped her mother's eightieth birthday party.

"He told me his boss asked him to fill out his foursome," she said. "It would have been 'career suicide' for him to refuse."

You did this.

"That's a load of bull if you ask me."

You don't deserve to be happy.

"I told everyone he wasn't feeling well, but they all know the truth. I'm sick of making excuses for him."

You don't care about me.

The others commiserated, providing their own unsolicited advice on exactly what she should do the next time he wanted to go play a round. Normally, Louise would have joined in, but she really couldn't pay close attention. The voices were just too loud.

"I tell you, I've had it." Bonnie took a long pull on her cigarette. "Next time I'm putting my foot down."

"It's your fault. You have to live with it. You did this."

They three other women looked at Louise with raised eyebrows.

"What did you say?" Marjorie asked.

Louise panicked, her face growing hotter by the second. "I'm sorry," she stammered as she stood. "I'll be back in a minute."

She raced toward the powder room to catch her breath, but the shadow figures followed her. They weren't shadows, though. She knew that now. They were beings from another place. The hands reaching out for her were real. They wanted her. They wanted to take her with them, but she knew if she went, she'd never come back.

When she reached the powder room, she slammed the door shut and locked it, but she was too late. The whispers were louder now, and there were so many of them, so many scratchy, hollow voices, saying so many vile things. She covered her ears, but she could still hear them. The scratching in the walls was louder too, like something trying to break through, into the small room with her.

Then everything went crooked, and she found herself lying on the floor. She rolled onto her back and looked up at the ceiling. Two hollow black eyes stared down at her.

Louise Brown screamed.

3.

SUNDAY, MAY 21, 1972

More than just trespasses and debts separated Baptists from Presbyterians, Penelope mused. Baptists were easier to catch having an affair. They liked to show off and got reckless. Presbyterians, on the other hand, took a more practical approach to marital infidelity. Penelope realized she ought to find a more appropriate line of thinking, though, as she studied the stern portrait of her great-grandfather, a Presbyterian minister.

Penelope stood in the front parlor of her grandmother's house. Her gaze wandered from the portrait to the floral wallpaper. A nick marred the pattern just above the floor a few feet to the right of the door. A result of the first and very last time she tried to roller-skate inside the house. Nothing had changed since her previous visit. Even the magazines on the side table next to her grandfather's old recliner were the same—a *Reader's Digest* from May of 1951 and a *Good Housekeeping* from October of 1953. She'd read them both so many times she knew all the recipes by heart. If only she had an occasion to make lobster Thermidor.

She glanced around the room at the old, worn furniture—the oval-backed chairs, the chaise lounge, the pie-crust tables, the converted kerosene lamps with flowers painted on their porcelain globes. Every flat surface held at least three ceramic knickknacks, dust catchers her father called them.

Penelope had been waiting on the porch for her grandmother to come home from church. She wore her best dress. She even put on stockings. Her grandmother pulled into the driveway in the same powder blue Chevrolet she'd been driving for twenty years. She refused to get another car. What was the point of getting rid of it if it still ran? Besides she had a nice "boy" who would look at it if it needed to be fixed. Never mind her mechanic was in his fifties.

When Mrs. Drake entered the room, she'd changed out her heels for flats and removed her gloves, but that was all. She still wore the rest of her church clothes, right down to the string of faux pearls around her neck, the one Penelope's grandfather had given her on their wedding day.

"I wished I'd known you were stopping by for a visit. I would've fixed us something for lunch. I'm afraid all I have are leftovers."

Penelope smiled. "Whatever you have is fine, I'm sure, Grandma."

The way her grandmother twisted up her mouth meant she was mentally going through the inventory of the refrigerator. "Well, I have a good bit of ham and some egg salad. I could make you a sandwich. There's also some chicken and some tuna casserole. Oh, and I have green beans and cream corn. I may also have a biscuit or two left over. And for dessert there's pie—apple or blackberry. Maybe some lemon meringue."

For someone who lived alone, her grandmother always had enough food on hand to feed an army, or at least the Junior League of Greenville.

"A ham sandwich with a slice of blackberry pie sounds pretty good," Penelope said. "But I can fix my own."

Her grandmother dismissed the idea with a wave of her hand. "Nonsense."

"Grandma, please—"

She wagged a finger at Penelope. "My house. My rules. Now go wash up and have a seat. It'll only take a few minutes."

They ate their feast of leftovers at the kitchen table where they had shared so many meals over the years. Every memory Penelope had of that house contained her grandmother. Other people were there, too, of course. Though she barely remembered her grandfather, she'd never forget his booming baritone, especially when he laughed. She also had memories of her father in the house, some good, some not so great. The one constant, however, was her grandmother.

They made small talk, though Penelope mostly listened as her grandmother offered opinions. She had a few—about all the rain, about the decision to tear down the old city hall building, about President Nixon's visit to Russia so soon after his trip to Red China. On all three counts, her grandmother disapproved.

Inevitably, though, the conversation found its way to a few well-tread topics.

"I haven't seen you in church, lately, sweetie. The Stricklands were asking about you. So were the Robertsons." Her grandmother took a sip of iced tea. "They wanted to know if they should be expecting a wedding invitation any time soon."

Penelope hadn't darkened the threshold of a church in months, actually. She took her time chewing and swallowing the last bit of her sandwich. "I'm sorry, Grandma. I've just been a little busy."

Her grandmother arched an eyebrow. "Too busy for Jesus?"

"No, of course not." Penelope was, in fact, praying silently for divine intervention at that very moment. "Just, there's a lot going on with Dad's old business."

Her grandmother pursed her lips. "You know my opinion on that."

"I do, Grandma."

"It's not proper."

"I'm helping people."

"Your father said the same thing." Her grandmother's expression darkened. "He was shot at, beaten, even stabbed once."

"I don't help people the same way."

"There are others—"

"Other *men*." Penelope immediately regretted interrupting, but she couldn't help it. "Some of the people I help, especially women, are afraid to go anywhere else."

Her grandmother shook her head. "That ought not be in a Christian society."

A lot of things ought not be.

Penelope used the silence that followed to change the subject. "By the way, I was going to tell you, I ran into Ephraim Brown the other day. You know his son Bertram and I went to the University of Georgia together."

Edith Drake knew everyone in Greenville, and that included everyone's extended family tree. She knew the difference between second cousins once removed and first cousins twice removed. She could tell you who you were related to going back to the Civil War. She kept every program from every wedding she'd ever attended and every funeral, too. She had a file for birth announcements. She kept score. She knew who should have married but didn't and who shouldn't have but did anyway. If anyone had any dirt on the Browns, she would.

For a fraction of a second, her grandmother failed to hide her scowl before managing to turn it around into a smile. "Really? I haven't spoken to the Browns in years. I hope everything is going well for them."

"It seems like it. He offered his condolences for Dad and apologized for not being able to come to the funeral."

The scowl made another brief appearance. "Well, I'm sure he had his reasons."

Penelope chose her next words carefully. "You know he and Dad had an odd friendship. Most of the time they were warm and cordial, but every once in a while, things would get really tense between them. When I was older, I asked Dad about it. He mumbled something I didn't understand and changed the topic."

Her grandmother took another long sip of her iced tea before she spoke. "Now, you know I don't like to speak ill of people, but I always had my doubts about Ephraim Brown. Something always seemed *off* about him."

"How so?"

"The first time I met him, he was extremely friendly and courteous. I could tell he had a proper upbringing, but everything he said and did seemed like he had practiced it in front of a mirror. He had a certain look in his eye, too. Not always, but sometimes you could catch him watching everyone in the room, like he was calculating odds at the racetrack."

Penelope shot her grandmother a sideways glance. "You don't gamble, Grandma. What do you know about horse racing?"

A sly grin crept across her grandmother's face. "Maybe I don't gamble, but did you ever wonder how your great uncle Josiah afforded his shiny Cadillac? Or why he had to 'move away' for five years after the sheriff paid him an unannounced visit? Every family has skeletons in the closet, dear."

Skeletons … and other things. What Penelope's grandmother didn't know wouldn't hurt her, hopefully.

"In any event," Mrs. Drake continued, "I knew I was right when Ephraim had your father almost expelled from the University of South Carolina."

Penelope, poised to take a bite of blackberry pie, lowered her fork. "He never told me anything about almost getting kicked out of college."

"More skeletons, sweetie. It wasn't something we liked to discuss."

"So, what happened?" Penelope asked, leaning closer.

Her grandmother scrunched up her nose in concentration. "It was spring semester of his sophomore year. One night very late, your grandfather and I received a phone call from the dean of students asking us to drive down to Columbia for a chat. The next day, we got to listen to how our kind, well-mannered Jonathan—along with Ephraim and several others—broke curfew, snuck out of their dormitory in the middle of the night, and had almost gotten someone killed."

Penelope lost interest in the blackberry pie as her stomach tied itself in knots. "Killed? How?"

"Well that's the question. No one would talk about it, including your father. All anyone knew was that Jonathan and Ephraim brought another of their friends to the hospital unconscious. I don't even remember that boy's name. They were all out in the woods doing God knows what. If they had left the boy, he would have died of exposure, but your father refused. That's why they didn't expel him or Ephraim, and for that reason alone."

Penelope struggled to make sense of the story her grandmother was telling. "So, Dad never said what they were doing?"

Her grandmother shook her head. "Never. And believe me, his father and I raked him over the coals. We had been so proud of him, getting a scholarship to go to college. We never could have afforded it otherwise. And then for him to almost throw it all away on some stupid prank."

"That doesn't sound like Dad," Penelope said quietly.

"No, it doesn't, not at all." Mrs. Drake sat in her chair, back rigid, hands folded in her lap, jaw clenched. "I would have thought it was just boys being boys. Some joke gone wrong ... except your father seemed afraid, specifically of Ephraim."

"You mean afraid of what Ephraim would do if he talked?"

Her grandmother hesitated. "More like afraid of what Ephraim did."

"But they stayed friends. At least until a few years ago." Penelope had always assumed the two men had just gotten too busy to keep in touch. Friends do drift apart after all, but faced with this new information, she wasn't so sure. "Do you think something else happened?"

Her grandmother sighed. "I wouldn't know about that, dear. Your father stopped confiding very much in me a long time ago."

In that moment, her grandmother seemed to shrink, to become a little frailer. Penelope's heart ached for her, for both of them. Ephraim Brown had been right. As much as it hurt to lose her father, she couldn't imagine the pain of losing a son, however old, so suddenly. The fact that her father wasn't always the easiest person to live with just made everything that much harder. "He's been gone over a year, and he's still finding ways to surprise me."

Her grandmother took Penelope's hand and squeezed almost until it hurt, the strength of her grip startling. She looked Penelope in the eye. "He loved you so much. He tried so hard to protect you. I worry about you, too, Penelope. You promise me you'll be careful out there, okay?"

Penelope nodded. "I promise."

She'd had to promise a lot of things lately.

Her grandmother held her hand for a few seconds longer, her gaze steady. The look in her eye made Penelope wonder if she knew more than she was letting on. Just when Penelope was about to say something, her grandmother stood and began collecting the dishes.

"I kept the paper from this morning if you want to read it," she said. "The spring bridal section came today."

Penelope smiled and took another sip of her tea.

———

Ephraim opened the front door before Penelope even managed to climb out of her car. She and Zed hurried up the walk to the house, and he ushered them both quickly inside.

"What happened?" Penelope asked, noting the dark circles under his eyes, his uncombed hair, his wrinkled clothes. "What's going on?"

Ephraim's lip trembled. He took in a deep breath before he answered. "It's Louise. Something's wrong."

Zed frowned. "Is she's sick? Shouldn't you call a doctor?"

Ephraim glared. "Believe me, if I thought a doctor would do

any good, I would have called one by now. Maybe you should go up and see for yourself. She's in our bedroom." He braced himself against the doorframe. The sleeve of his shirt shifted, revealing a bandage on his arm. "I can't go back in there."

Penelope and Zed climbed to the second floor. Except for the steps creaking underneath their feet, the house was silent. A cold, hard lump of dread sat in the pit of Penelope's stomach. When they reached the bedroom, she eased the door open. She and Zed peered inside. Louise Brown, hair wild and makeup smeared, sat on the edge of the bed staring at a point on the wall. She wore a lavender dress with a brooch pinned to the collar, a large, odd purplish red gem in the center.

Penelope slipped into the room. Zed followed, Polaroid camera dutifully hung around his neck. The temperature in the bedroom sat a good twenty degrees colder than the hallway, enough to make Penelope shiver. Louise didn't look at them. In fact, she didn't do anything at all to acknowledge them.

While Zed unobtrusively took pictures of the room, Penelope eased herself into Louise's line of sight. "Mrs. Brown?"

No response.

Penelope stepped closer. "Mrs. Brown, what's wrong? Do you need help?"

A quiver of a lip. A flicker of eye movement.

"Mrs. Brown," Penelope repeated, "do you need help?"

Louise moved her jaw, like she was trying to form words, but no sound came from her mouth.

Zed took a step forward. "It's the brooch," he whispered. "It's doing something to her."

Penelope glanced sideways at him. "How could you possibly know that?"

Zed didn't take his eyes off the piece of jewelry. He slowly raised the Polaroid camera and snapped a picture of the brooch. Even the flash failed to trigger a reaction from Louise, not even the smallest flinch. "I just do. Take it off of her."

Charles said some people were more sensitive to magic than

others. Penelope's father had been very aware of the world unseen, an ability she'd failed to inherit. She'd always suspected Zed might have the same awareness, though he never showed any interest in learning how to use magic, which was just as well. She didn't think Charles would be too eager to take on an apprentice.

Slowly, Penelope reached for the brooch. As her fingers brushed across the strange gem, Louise's hand clamped around her wrist. She tried to jerk away, but Louise's held on like a vise. Zed tensed as she pulled Penelope closer. For the first time, Louise's eyes focused on her, but Penelope had the sense it wasn't Louise looking at her.

"She shouldn't have left," Louise rasped. "She didn't have any right."

Her hot breath smelled like a smoldering cigar.

"Who?" Penelope asked. "Who shouldn't have left?"

Louise squeezed Penelope's wrist until she cried out in pain. The older woman's face contorted in rage. "It's her fault. She made me do it. She didn't give me a choice."

Penelope fought to break free. Zed lunged for Louise, but the older woman threw Penelope backward. She toppled into Zed, and they both tumbled to the floor. Louise's expression became impassive once again. Her gaze lost its focus. Her hands fell to her lap. Her lips still moved, though, forming silent words.

Penelope and Zed picked themselves up from the floor. They traded glances, but before either of them could do anything else, the sound of yelling reverberated through the closed bedroom door. Ephraim's deep bass clashed with another angry voice. Penelope recognized it immediately. Heavy footsteps on the stairs followed the shouting, and Bertram threw open the door to the bedroom.

"What the hell is going on here?"

Penelope tried to put herself between Bertram and his mother. "Bertram, we just—"

Bertram shoved her out of the way. "Get out," he snarled. "Get out, both of you." He knelt beside Louise. She didn't seem to notice him, just as she hadn't noticed Penelope and Zed at first. "Momma? Momma, what's wrong? Momma, talk to me."

Louise continued to mouth words only she could understand.

"The brooch—" Zed began.

"Shut the fuck up, pretty boy," Bertram growled. "I thought I told you to get out."

Ephraim appeared in the bedroom doorway, looking more haggard even than he had downstairs. "Bertram, please—"

Bertram silenced him with a glare. "No, not one more word. Have you all lost your goddamn minds?"

"You'll never leave me," Louise said.

Everyone's gaze fixed on her.

Bertram took one of her hands and cradled it in his. She didn't react. "Momma, it's me, Bertram. I'm not going anywhere. I promise."

The tenderness in his voice contrasted sharply with the anger Bertram had leveled at his father and at Penelope, but she could hardly fault him. She only wished she could save him from the heartbreak of what was to follow.

"You'll never leave me," his mother repeated.

Bertram tried to put on a pleasant smile, but the tears welled in his eyes. "Momma, what are you talking about?"

"I'll make you sorry for trying to leave. You'll see."

Bertram glanced over his shoulder at his father, his eyes pleading for an explanation, but Ephraim shook his head. He didn't have one to give. Bertram reached out and gently, lovingly grasped his mother's shoulder.

Louise Brown screamed.

A wail. A keen. A shriek so loud it rattled the windows. Bertram stumbled backward, letting go of Louise, but she continued to scream. She swiped a hand across his face leaving four angry, red parallel lines on his cheek. Bertram wiped the blood away with his hand and stared at his mother, stunned. Zed grabbed him by the arm and jerked him away just as Louise, eyes full of insanity and pain, clawed at him again.

Bertram let Zed drag him from the room. Penelope followed and slammed the door behind her. The screams continued for a few moments before dying down. Penelope glanced around at the others. None of them wanted to open that door again.

Bertram stared at the floor, rubbing the scratches on his cheek, his breathing heavy. "What's wrong with her, Dad? Why haven't you taken her to a hospital?"

Ephraim didn't respond.

Bertram balled his other hand into a fist and pounded it against the wall hard enough to make the pictures shake. "Dammit, Dad, why won't you tell me what's going on?"

Ephraim sighed and turned to Zed. "Mr. McKay, will you please take my son downstairs? Penelope and I have some things to discuss."

The color rose in Bertram's face. "You're not going to dismiss me—"

"I'm not dismissing you, Bertram. I promise you we will continue our 'conversation' after I've talked with Penelope. Now please, go downstairs. Get a drink. Take a moment to calm down. I know this is hard for you, but it's hard for me, too."

Bertram opened his mouth to protest again, but Zed clamped a hand on his shoulder. His fingers digging into the muscle and tendons at the base of Bertram's neck, he steered Bertram toward the stairs. "Come on, Bertram. Maybe you can show me where your dad keeps the good liquor."

Penelope waited until she heard someone, no doubt Zed, rummaging through the cabinets in the kitchen. "I'm sorry. I don't know what else to say. When did she start … acting this way?"

"Last night. We were at the home of some friends. Getting her home took an act of God."

Maybe not God.

"Did you notice the brooch Louise is wearing?"

Ephraim nodded.

"Have you ever seen it before?"

"Never."

Penelope glanced once more at the closed bedroom door. "Maybe whoever broke into your house wasn't trying to steal anything. Maybe they were leaving something here."

Ephraim narrowed his eyes. "Are you saying that brooch is doing something to her?"

"Zed thinks so." She bit her lip. Everything hinged on what she said next. "Would you believe I was crazy if I said I agreed with him?"

A faint smile appeared on Ephraim's face. "Penelope, your father and I had a long history. Even when he was on the police force, he had a reputation for dealing with, shall we say, unusual cases. An insanity-inducing piece of jewelry wouldn't be the strangest thing he ever told me about."

It wouldn't have been the strangest thing he'd ever told Penelope about, either. She let go a bit of the tension she'd been holding between her shoulder blades. As complicated as things were getting, at least she wouldn't have to tiptoe around the magical flying pink elephant in the room. "If someone did leave the brooch for her to find, the next question is why. Can you think of anyone who might want to hurt your family?"

Ephraim frowned. "Not that I know of. But …"

"But what?"

"I had a strange incident a few weeks ago. One of my long-time customers called me screaming and yelling. He was clearly drunk. He was slurring his words so badly I couldn't make out half of what he said. What I did understand was mostly cursing. He went on for a few minutes and then hung up. I asked Bertram if he knew anything that might have caused the tirade. He just told me there'd been a misunderstanding, but that he'd take care of it."

"And you trusted him?" Penelope winced. She did wish sometimes her mouth didn't outpace her brain.

Ephraim's faint smile returned. "Believe it or not, my son does have his good points. Bertram's been really helpful since he came back."

"You think your angry customer might have something to do with this?"

"Maybe?" He squeezed his eyes shut and rubbed his temples. "Honestly, Penelope, I don't know what to think anymore. That's all I can come up with right now. I'm sorry."

"Don't be. That's at least something to go on." She placed a hand on his arm. "We'll get to the bottom of this."

Downstairs, they ran into Zed as he was leaving the kitchen.

Ephraim gestured toward Bertram, seated at the kitchen table. "How is he?"

Zed shrugged. "He's calmed down a little. That's probably thanks to the bourbon."

"Thank you," Ephraim said.

"Do you need us to stay while you talk to him?" Penelope asked.

Ephraim shook his head. "No, this needs to be a conversation between just the two of us."

Penelope glanced over Zed's shoulder. Bertram sat and stared into an empty glass. "What are you going to tell him?"

Ephraim followed her gaze. "I'll come up with something."

———

Zed lowered himself into the passenger seat of the Lincoln and slammed the door shut. "Pretty boy? He couldn't come up with a better insult than that? You get to be Dreadful Penny."

Penelope scowled at him from behind the steering wheel. "Really? That's what you're concerned with right now?" She sighed. "Look, Bertram Brown isn't my favorite person either, but he doesn't deserve to be going through this. None of them do."

Zed brushed a stray lock of blond hair from in front of his eyes. His hand trembled. "Don't you think I know that?"

"Then why the jokes?"

Zed's voice took on a steely edge. "Because I would have checked myself out a long time ago if I didn't maintain some sense of humor."

Penelope studied his profile as she stared out the windshield. Zed was always so lackadaisical; she had to remind herself there was much more under the surface, more than he ever let anyone see.

"Mrs. Brown is going to die unless we do something," he continued.

She nodded. "You're right. She can't keep going in the state she's in for much longer. Dark magic aside, if she's not eating or drinking—"

"That's not what I mean." Zed handed her the Polaroid picture he took of the brooch. "You might want to take a look at this."

The purple-red gem seemed to throb, even in the picture, and there was something more. A face stared out from its facets, with sunken eyes and mouth open in a silent scream.

4.

MONDAY, MAY 22, 1972

As Zed strode along the cracked and trash-strewn walkways, he was sure whoever settled on the name Foxcroft Manor had nothing but good intentions. And yet the pretentious name hadn't been enough to save the housing project, a row of cinderblock buildings with faux French chateau-style roofs, all identical except for the letter displayed on the side of each one. Dilapidated and crumbling around the edges, Foxcroft Manor had gone right along the road paved with those good intentions.

Jeremiah Morrison, the alleged master thief Eddie told Zed about, lived in Unit 4 in Building E, the next-to-last one. Finding his address had required only a five-minute visit to the Division of Public Records. Mr. Morrison, apparently, was no stranger to the police.

Zed knocked on the door, flanked by two scraggly, half-dead bushes. There was no answer from inside. He knocked again. Still only silence. He tried the door and found it unlocked. The smell of rot hit him as soon as he stepped inside. A mismatched dinette set occupied the center of the small kitchen. A dozen or so empty beer cans were stacked on the table. In the corner, an old Frigidaire hummed and sputtered. A few dirty dishes lay in the sink, and a half-eaten sandwich rested on the counter. Flies swarmed around it in frenzied circles, but the sandwich wasn't the source of the stench.

The odor grew ten times worse when Zed opened the door into the next room. A dark-skinned man, probably in his mid-thirties, lay splayed in an armchair in the corner. A bullet hole, still angry and raw, marred his temple. One arm hung over the side of the chair. Nearby on the floor lay a Beretta. A fat maggot crawled out of the man's mouth, and the bile rose in Zed's throat when he realized the whole chair writhed with them.

A television next to the chair flickered, showing *The Newlywed Game*. Zed turned it off. He studied the room. Filthy orange carpet and grimy walls. More beer cans littering the floor. A few dirty magazines. Zed closed his eyes. Despair and sadness lingered in the air. Hope fled that place long ago. He knew if he visited any other apartment in Foxcroft Manor, he'd sense much the same, but in that room, there was also a trace of something darker, something bitter tasting, something wrong. He tried to focus on that feeling of darkness, but he might as well have been trying to grasp smoke with his hands.

Zed opened his eyes and glanced around the apartment again, his gaze resting once more on the corpse of Jeremiah Morrison rotting in the armchair. He didn't need to spend any more time there. As he left the apartment, though, he felt eyes on him. He made his way back along the broken walkway, making sure to keep his pace even and resisting the urge to look over his shoulder. Not until he reached his car, key poised to unlock the door, did he say anything.

"Who are you?" he asked the shadow that appeared behind him.

He turned to see a startled boy, probably no older than ten or eleven.

"My … my name's Alex," the boy said. "Who are you? I never seen you here before. Are you friends with Mr. Jeremiah?"

"I wouldn't say that." Zed cocked an eyebrow. "You creep around his apartment much?"

The boy's eyes grew even wider, if possible. "I wasn't creeping. Momma says we're not supposed to come here, but …"

"But what?"

Alex glanced toward the ground. "He gives us candy sometimes if we deliver packages for him. One time he gave me a whole dollar."

Zed narrowed his eyes. "Do you know what's in these packages he gives you?"

The boy shrugged. "Mr. Jeremiah tells us not to look." He peered over his shoulder, back toward Building E. "Is he home?"

Zed shook his head. "No, he's not."

Alex's shoulders slumped. "He hasn't been around for a few days."

Zed studied the boy for a moment. "Alex, have you seen anything weird happen?"

The boy froze. "Like what?"

"Anything strange. That's all."

Alex alternately chewed his lip and wrinkled his nose. Zed could practically see the debate happening inside his head until the boy finally made up his mind. "I saw a ghost," he said quietly.

Zed remembered the ephemeral darkness in the apartment. "When?"

"The night before last. I was coming by on my bike." Alex pointed to the rusted-out frame and worn wheels lying in the grass and puffed up, obviously proud of it.

Zed nodded. Saturday. The day after the break in. The day of the attack on Louise Brown. "What did it look like?"

Alex held out his arms wide. "It was a big black shape. It flew around the building before tearing down the street wailing and screaming."

"Did anyone else see it?" Zed asked.

He shook his head. "No. Just me. I told Momma, but she don't believe me. She told me she didn't have time to deal with my nonsense. No one at school believed me either. I bet you don't."

Zed knelt down. Sadness clung to Alex. Sadness and longing,

and the bile rose again as he realized Jeremiah Morrison had come to be some sort of twisted father figure. Never mind he had made Alex and probably a lot of other children into his drug couriers. Zed's anger nearly boiled over at the thought, but he forced it down. There would be a time for rage later.

He looked the boy in the eye. "Alex, I believe you when you say you saw a ghost."

Alex shot Zed a wary look, but he couldn't suppress his grin. "You do?"

"I do." Zed realized something else. Alex possessed a spark of magic in him. It had, like his hope, nearly been smothered, but all it needed was some kindling to catch fire. "And you know what else? I think maybe your momma's right. I think you shouldn't come around here anymore."

He looked back to the apartment building, clearly disappointed. "But ..."

"Alex, I know you're having a hard time at home. Your momma has to work a lot, and she doesn't have very much time for you."

Startled, Alex took a step back. "How do you know that?"

"I just do, but I want you to listen to me." Zed put a little power behind his next words. "Your momma works hard because she wants something more for you. Things might not be easy right now, but everything's going to turn out okay. You've got to believe me on that. Do you understand?"

Alex nodded.

Zed smiled and motioned toward Alex's bike. "Now go on home. I'm sure your momma's wondering where you are."

Alex hopped on the bike and rode away. Zed watched him, hoping his words had made some sort of difference. As he climbed inside his car, though, his thoughts turned dark again. Picturing the scene in Jeremiah Morrison's apartment and the look of horror on the corpse's hollow face, Zed couldn't honestly say he believed everything was going to turn out okay.

When Charles couldn't deal with the silence anymore, he put on a record. Mother Willie Mae Ford Smith belted out "Going on with the Spirit" while he sat down at his worktable and picked up a stack of loose signatures. He carefully lined the signatures up before threading a needle and beginning the process of sewing them back together. Once the book was sewn together again, he would glue on a new cover.

Normally, the steady back-and-forth of the needle and thread acted to calm his mind. When he was mending books, he could shut out the world. Only the books, his tools, and his hands existed. Today, though, he had trouble stilling all the voices in his head.

He pricked his finger with the needle and watched as the drop of blood beaded up. Charles swore under his breath and reached for a rag. A bloodstain on the pages of an ordinary antique book would have been a disaster, but on any of his books, the result could have been literally explosive.

Charles stood up and lifted the needle from the record, cutting off Mother Smith's deep alto in the middle of "Blessed Assurance." Silence descended upon the house again. Charles climbed the stairs to the second floor and followed a narrow hallway to the very end. Before he opened the door, he closed his eyes and recited a few words in a language dead for a thousand years. When he grasped the doorknob, a keen observer might have noticed the faint, blue glow around his hand.

Like the rooms below, floor-to-ceiling bookshelves lined the walls, and every shelf overflowed with books. A small, metal-framed bed was shoved to one side, almost as an afterthought. A reading lamp rested on a three-legged table next to the bed.

Charles knew the place of every one of the thousands of books, on both floors of the house. He crossed the bedroom to the far corner and knelt down so he was eye-level with one of the lower shelves. When he closed his eyes, he could see vividly the

Hungarian letters carved into the door in the picture Penelope showed him. He couldn't get his mind off them, despite his best efforts. He had looked up the word. *Hidden.* What or who was hiding? And whom were they hiding from?

Charles let his fingers travel over the spines of the books on the shelf. Most of these he had repaired himself. Still, when he found the one he wanted, he removed it as if it were made of glass. The book was four hundred years old at least, written by an Austrian monk in some forgotten monastery high in the Alps. Charles took care to only touch the corners as slightly as he could. Again, the same blue glow surrounded his hands, a bit of magic protecting the book.

That magic also protected him.

Charles spent the next hour leafing through the spells the unnamed monk had collected and transcribed, but he didn't find any spells that employed runes carved into a door. He replaced the book and pulled out another. The second book was older than the first, written not by a monk, but by a woman the Church would have burnt as a witch. The spells in the front were simple ones. Charms for good luck, wards for safety, remedies for various illnesses. The further back he went, the more complex—and more dangerous—the spells became. Weather spells, recipes for love potions, hexes. He was about to give up when he turned a page and found a drawing of runes written across a door. A single word. *Hidden.*

The runes carved into the door would conceal a person from everyone inside once the would-be intruder recited a certain phrase, but the ritual to set the spell was complicated. It required a preparation of herbs, including edelweiss, wolfsbane, and chicory, mixed with blood, as well as petitions to a minor Germanic god of darkness. Those petitions had to be made at the stroke of midnight under a new moon. The ritual also required more than one person.

Charles shut the book. Chicory was easy enough to find, but the other two herbs weren't, not in South Carolina. Whoever had broken into that home had gone to a lot of trouble for a simple burglary. There had to be more. He needed to call Penelope.

Her riddle wasn't the only thing that weighed on his mind, though.

Charles put the spell book back and walked to the bed. He reached underneath the mattress and pulled out a photograph in an old frame. The picture was more than a decade old. In it, he posed with an elderly black woman, their faces somber as they faced the photographer. The portrait held none of the warmth of their relationship, nothing of how he felt toward the woman he regarded as his mother, but that one photograph was his only reminder of her.

"Things are getting complicated, Margaret," he said to the photograph. "The dreams, they're getting worse. I thought I saw the Shrouded Man the other day, standing outside in the field. I wish you were here to tell me what to do."

Downstairs, the telephone rang.

———

Penelope hesitated in front of the antique store, the fifth on her list. This one occupied the space vacated by an old bank on Coffee Street, a block off Main Street. Faux Greek columns topped with a frieze still framed the door. A giant display window had been carved out of the blond brick façade. Gold lettering across the glass spelled out the name "Grayson & Sons Antiques & Collectibles" On the other side of the glass, a green brocade Federal-style couch stood on display.

After a day full of frustration, all Penelope wanted to do was go home and soak herself in a steaming hot bath, but she took a deep breath and made herself push the door open. The jingling of tiny bells announced her entrance. With only fifteen minutes to closing time, she found herself the only customer. Toward the back of the store, a man sat at a desk piled high with books. He glanced up at her briefly before returning to whatever he was doing.

She wound her way toward him through the maze of furniture and other knickknacks and hovered close to the desk while he continued to ignore her. She glanced at her watch. Ten minutes to closing. "Excuse me," she said, trying to keep the irritation from her voice.

He glanced up again over the top of his black-framed glasses. "Can I help you?" He, on the other hand, didn't try to hide his annoyance.

Penelope had gotten similar reactions all day long. The antique dealers in Greenville were apparently all snobs, with little patience for anyone but "serious collectors," whatever that meant. She continued with her script anyway. "I'm looking for something. I was hoping you could help."

He sat back in his chair and regarded her with icy blue eyes. "I'm afraid you'll have to be more specific than 'something.'"

He was only maybe a few years older than Penelope, with short, dark hair slicked back like Clarke Gable, but his flat Chicago accent was a far cry from Rhett Butler's Southern drawl.

Penelope produced the Polaroid Zed had taken of the brooch and held it toward him. "How about this?"

The antique dealer took the photograph from her.

"The brooch belonged to my grandmother," Penelope continued while he studied the picture, "but it was stolen. It means a lot to me, and I've been checking every place in town trying to find it. Have you seen it? Maybe someone came in trying to sell it?"

His mouth twisted into a smirk. "You're lying."

He may as well have punched Penelope in the stomach. "What?"

"You're lying." He waved the Polaroid at her. "This didn't belong to your grandmother. I bought it as part of an estate sale a month ago."

She kicked herself. "It … it was stolen a little while ago."

He shook his head. "Not working. Why are you interested in it? Because it's supposed to be haunted?"

Startled, Penelope backed up and nearly tripped over a porcelain Chinese Fu dog. She held her breath as it teetered several times before coming to rest again. She exhaled in relief. Whatever it cost, she was sure she'd never be able to pay for it. "Haunted? How is it haunted?"

He raised an eyebrow. "You mean you don't know?"

Penelope frowned. "Why would I?"

"I just assumed you were one of those ghost hunters. I get them in here whenever I buy something that's supposed to be paranormal. If you're not a ghost hunter, why are you interested in the brooch?"

"I'm a private investigator."

He cocked his head to the side. "Really?"

She eyed him. "Why is that so shocking?"

"I've just never met one who's—"

"A woman?"

"I was going to say so bad at lying."

Her cheeks grew warm. "I'm usually not, although my cases generally involve taking pictures of people from a car across the street or digging through county records. I've never had to make up a cover story for an antique dealer."

He chuckled. "In the future, you're going to have to do better than the dead grandmother thing. We can see right through that one. I'm Dan, by the way."

"Penelope," she replied, taking his offered hand. "You're one of the 'sons' I assume."

A puzzled look crossed his face. "What do you mean?"

Penelope pointed to the window. "The sign says Grayson & Sons."

He grinned as his confusion dissolved. "Oh, no. I bought the store from the last Grayson a few years ago, and he was ninety-eight at the time. I just kept the name. It's bad enough being a Yankee around here. I didn't think changing the store to Kowalczyk Antiques & Collectibles would've been the best idea." Then his smile faded. "Of course, that was before Downtown started going to hell. You know they're closing the hardware store next door? The dress shop on the other side went out a few months ago."

Penelope glanced around the store. She couldn't imagine it crammed any fuller. "You seem to be doing okay."

"For now. In any event, tell me why you're so interested in this brooch?"

"It was stolen. I'd like to return it to its rightful owner."

He grunted. "Another likely story."

Penelope glared. "Do you believe the brooch is haunted?"

Dan shrugged. "It depends on the customer. If someone wants it to be haunted, then of course it is. If they don't, well everyone knows there's no such thing as ghosts. But really? Who knows?"

"What's the story behind it?" Penelope asked.

He sighed. "Like I said, I bought the brooch from an estate. The family goes back to before the Civil War. The version of the story I got was that just before the war started, a daughter was engaged to a man from another prominent family around here. Everyone thought the match was perfect ... except for her. Apparently, her Prince Charming got a little violent with her from time to time, but of course, back then that sort of thing was just accepted."

A familiar story for Penelope. It seemed not much had changed after a hundred years. "So let me guess, they got married and he killed her."

"Not exactly. Not long before the planned wedding, she broke off the engagement. No one knows what exactly happened. Some say he had a dalliance with another woman. Some say he threatened her parents. He took the brooch, one he had given to her, and raked the pin across her face. The next day, they found him hanging by his neck from a tree outside his family home, still clutching the brooch in his stiff, cold hand. No one ever figured out of it was a suicide or if her family took care of him. Ever since, odd things have been associated with the brooch. Whispered voices. Strange shadows. The occasional scream. Slamming of doors. The usual stuff."

Penelope thought of Louise Brown's tortured face. "No accounts of possession?"

"Possession?" He narrowed his eyes. "Not that I'm aware."

Penelope wrinkled her nose. Something didn't seem right, but she'd have to talk to Charles again to know for sure. "Sounds like a residual haunting, but nothing really dangerous."

"Residual haunting." Dan crossed his arms. "So you do know something about ghost hunting."

"Let's just say this isn't the first time an investigation has involved something out of the ordinary." She leaned on his desk. "I really need to know who you sold the brooch to."

He shook his head. "I can't—"

Penelope sighed. "Look, this is going to come off as cliché, but it's a matter of life and death. Really."

"You don't understand. I haven't sold it." He jabbed a thumb over his shoulder at a chest of drawers behind him. "It's in one of these drawers."

For the second time, Penelope reeled as if Dan had hit her. "Then I was right about it being stolen."

"What do you mean?" Dan asked.

Penelope snatched the Polaroid back from him. "This picture was taken yesterday."

His face fell. Spinning around, he whipped a key ring out of his pocket, unlocked the top drawer, and slid it open. After a few moments of rummaging through the drawer, he pulled out a small, black, velvet-lined box. He opened it with trembling fingers. When he looked inside, his face went white. "It's empty. The brooch is gone."

"When was the last time you saw it?"

Dan scratched his chin. "Sometime last week, maybe? I was gone a few days, looking at some pieces in Atlanta. My assistant was in the shop."

"Can we talk to your assistant?"

"Sure. She was coming in tonight to help with some inventory. In fact, she should have already been here. It's not like her to be late."

A shaft of ice traveled down Penelope's spine. "Maybe you should call her."

"You don't think …"

"Call her."

"Okay, but she goes to Furman. She lives in one of the dorms. They have a phone in the lobby everyone has to share." He picked up the phone on his desk and dialed a number. After a moment, he slammed down the receiver. "It's busy."

"I think we should go check on her," Penelope said.

———

Twenty minutes later, they pulled up to McBee Hall on the campus of Furman University. Dan leapt out of the car and took the steps up to the door two at a time.

He grabbed a girl coming out of the dorm by the arm. "Have you seen Mary Wilson today?"

The startled girl shook her head and hurried away.

Dan and Penelope rushed into the lobby. In one corner, a girl perched on a stool, cradling the receiver of the dorm's only telephone between her ear and shoulder. Dan glared at her. An older woman in a prim skirt and blouse with her graying hair in a tight bun came trotting toward them. The dorm mother. She put herself directly in Dan's path. "Sir, this is a women's dormitory. You can't come in here."

Dan opened his mouth to protest, but Penelope stepped forward. "I'm sorry. We're here to see Mary Wilson. Which room is hers? I can go fetch her."

The woman regarded her with an appraising eye. "And you are?"

"I'm her cousin."

Behind Penelope, Dan groaned quietly, but the woman didn't seem to notice. She motioned for Penelope to come with her. "I haven't seen Mary today," the woman said as they climbed the stairs to the second floor. "I'm sure she's busy, what with the school year nearly being over. All the girls are."

She stopped in front of a door near the end of the hall and knocked lightly. "Mary? Mary, dear, you have visitors."

No answer.

The woman knocked a little louder, but there was still no answer.

She turned back to Penelope. "I guess she's not here right now."

Penelope put her hands on her hips. "Well that doesn't make any sense. We were supposed to meet today."

"I can relay a message to her if you'd like, Miss …"

"Drake. Penelope Drake."

Just then, Penelope glanced down to see something at the bottom of the door that made her heart sink, a red stain spreading across the carpet. She grabbed the door and threw it open.

The dorm mother reached toward her. "Miss Drake, what are you—"

When she saw Mary lying on the floor in a pool of blood, glazed-over eyes frozen in horror and staring at the ceiling, she screamed. Dan came running up the stairs, eliciting more screams from the other girls, unaware there was a horror worse than a man in the building.

He stopped in front of the door. "Oh, God."

The older woman, trembling and sobbing, slumped against the wall.

"Dan, could you take her downstairs and call the police, please?" Penelope asked.

Dan, who had gone pale himself, nodded and guided the dorm mother back down. Penelope didn't want to linger either, but she wouldn't have a chance to inspect things once the police got there.

By now, a ring of girls had surrounded her. Penelope tried to ignore them. She knelt down beside the body. A red, ragged red gash ran down Mary's side. By all appearances, she'd stabbed herself with the scissors she still clutched, but not for one second did Penelope believe Mary had committed suicide.

A hairbrush rested on the table near the door. Penelope picked it up and hid it in her purse. By the time she stood, Dan had returned. "The dorm mom is lying down in one of the girls' rooms. The police are on their way. I suppose there's not much to do but wait until they get here."

Penelope bit her lip. "Yeah, about that."

Dan frowned. "You're not planning on leaving, are you?"

"Trust me. If I could, I absolutely would."

"You're not on good terms with the police?"

"Oh, no that's not it at all." She held up her hands. "A lot of them were friends of my father when he was on the police force. If there's a problem, it's that they all treat me like I'm still a little girl in pigtails."

"Then what is it?" Dan asked.

"This isn't the first time I've gotten to a crime scene before them." She leaned in and whispered, so no one else could hear. "Besides, you want to try explaining how a haunted piece of jewelry got your assistant killed?"

Dan grimaced. "So more lying?"

Penelope nodded. "Fortunately, I have more experience lying to cops than to antique dealers."

When the police arrived, they corralled everyone downstairs while they examined the room, and someone from the coroner's office came for the body. Penelope was relieved to see they sent Jim Everett. She didn't mind him as much as the other police detectives. One by one, they questioned all the girls, saving Dan and Penelope for last and giving them time to concoct a plausible story.

"You came to see Mary because some things are missing from the store," Penelope told him. "You needed to ask her about them before tomorrow because you have a customer coming to look at them."

"And why are you here?" Dan asked.

"Because if the things were stolen, you need help recovering them discretely."

Dan grunted. "So what things are we talking about?"

Penelope shrugged. "I don't know. A diamond necklace?"

Just then, Jim came out of the room they were using for the interviews and pointed to Dan. "Your turn," he said cheerfully.

Penelope waited, thinking over everything that had happened. She needed to talk to Zed and Charles. She didn't have time for all this, but if she left, she knew she wouldn't make it far. She glanced around at the girls huddled nervously. Some were crying. Most were just hugging one another silently. Penelope stood by herself, trying not to fidget too much. She hated feeling helpless.

She thought back to the day her father died. She didn't remember much. The knock on the door at two o'clock in the morning. Jim standing there, looking somber. Shot during a botched hold-up, he said. The would-be robber got away. They never caught him. Penelope suspected it was the reason her father's ghost hung around. Unfinished business.

She hoped they never caught who killed him.

Penelope wondered if Mary's ghost would linger in the dormitory hallways, become a scary story they told to haze the freshmen.

The door opened, and Dan emerged. He made eye-contact with Penelope and deliberately tugged on his ear. She frowned at him but didn't get a chance to ask him what he was doing. Jim's imposing frame filled the doorway, and, smiling at Penelope, he motioned for her to join him.

Inside the makeshift interview room, a study room off the lobby, Jim gestured toward a chair. Instead of taking a seat opposite her, though, he picked up another chair and set it beside her. Jim was a big man, well over six feet tall with broad shoulders and a girth to match, but he had always been like an uncle to Penelope. He still went to the same church as her grandmother.

"How are you doing, Penny?" he asked as he patted her shoulder.

One of the very few who could get away with calling her that. "I'm doing okay, Jim. I've had better days."

He chuckled. "You and me both. Been a while. Wish we were meeting under better circumstances."

Penelope nodded. "I know. Me too. You know how time just gets away. Been busy."

"Mm-hmm. The family's having a barbecue this coming Saturday. You're welcome to join us. Margie would love to see you."

"Thanks, I'll think about it."

Jim sighed. "What are you doing mixed up in all this, Penny?"

"Pure chance, I promise." She held up a hand. "I was helping Mr. Kowalczyk. He thought someone stole some … jewelry from his shop."

"You know I had to ask him to spell his name five times before I got it right?" Jim shook his head, as if Dan's name was some sort of moral failing on the antique dealer's part. "What sort of jewelry?"

"A necklace."

Jim raised an eyebrow. "He said it was a pair of earrings."

She silently cursed Dan. "It was both, at least that's what he told me."

Jim just nodded.

"In any event," she continued, "he wanted me to help him recover it."

"Why didn't he just come to the police?"

"I got the impression it's a delicate situation."

Jim grunted. "How so?"

"He didn't say."

"And why were you looking for Mary Wilson?"

"She was Dan's assistant," Penelope replied. "He had a

customer coming in the morning to look at the necklace … and the earrings. He thought she might know something."

He glanced over his notepad. "Did he think she stole them?"

"I honestly don't know. You'll have to ask him that."

"You didn't know Mary at all, then?" Jim asked.

"Not at all."

"So you wouldn't know any reason she might have committed suicide?"

Penelope sat up a little straighter. "Is that what happened?"

"You didn't hear me say that," Jim said flatly.

"You're taking an awful lot of time here for a suicide."

He drew his mouth into a thin line. "Penny, please don't tangle yourself up in this. It's bad enough you do what you do."

She clenched her fists. "Bad?"

Jim placed a hand on top of hers. "I mean dangerous. Your father would never have wanted you to follow in his footsteps, especially after what happened to him."

"I know how to take care of myself," she said, gritting her teeth.

He met her gaze. "So did your father, Penny."

Penelope looked away. "Do you need to ask me anything else?"

"No, that's all I have."

She stood. "I really need to be going then."

"It was good to see you again, Penny. Hope you stop by on Saturday."

"It was good to see you again, too, Jim." But she was already halfway out the door.

Outside, Dan was waiting for her.

"Earrings?" she asked as they walked to her car in the dark. The sun had set hours earlier.

Dan shoved his hands into his pockets and stared at the ground. "I panicked."

She barked a laugh. "Sounds like someone else isn't very good at lying, either."

"I tried to let you know. Why did you think I was tugging on my ear when I walked out?"

"Because your ear itched?"

He shook his head. "Look, I know Mary. There's no way she would have … done what it looked like she did."

They had reached the car. Penelope glanced back at the dormitory, still surrounded by police cars and flashing blue lights. "I get the impression the police don't think it's a suicide either."

"What's going to happen now?"

She opened the door to the Lincoln. "The police are going to hunt down their leads, and I'm going to hunt down mine."

5.

TUESDAY, MAY 23, 1972

enelope pulled into the parking lot of a warehouse off Stone Avenue, the home of Brown Tractor & Farm Supply Co. since the 1920s. As she stepped out of her car, she tried to remember her last visit there, if in fact she'd ever visited. Maybe with her dad, when she was a kid. The original building had been expanded and added onto over the years as the business grew, until it was a patchwork of brick, corrugated metal, and glass. Patches of rust, peeling paint, crumbling bricks, and cracks in the asphalt made the place seem worn, dingy, not at all in keeping with the well-heeled image the Browns usually put forward. Then again, that well-heeled image probably wouldn't go over with the clientele, so maybe the shabbiness was just good marketing.

Two men on a smoke break stood near the corner of the building. They paused their conversation and stared at her as she approached. One of them opened his mouth to say something, but at Penelope's glare, he shut it again.

There was no receptionist. The entrance opened directly into the main office. Bertram Brown sat at a desk flanked by rows of filing cabinets. On the wood-paneled wall behind him hung a clock and a calendar with a picture of a half-dressed woman perched atop a tractor. The calendar didn't surprise her, given that

Ephraim Brown's family had sold farm equipment for more than a hundred years, but Penelope had to wonder at someone who would find a tractor that … exciting.

Bertram stared at a ledger lying on the desk in front of him, making marks with a pencil on occasion and typing things out on an adding machine. His fingers danced across the keys, which clicked as the paper spooled through, and the machine spit out numbers, making its own music.

Penelope had forgotten that for all his bluster and general bull-headedness and reputation as a party animal, Bertram was actually a pretty good student when they were in college. He'd even helped her through a semester of calculus, though he would probably have described it more as dragging her kicking and screaming.

He glanced up at her as she closed the door behind her. A lopsided grin spread across his face. "And what exactly did I do to deserve a visit from you today?"

"How's your mother doing, Bertram?" she asked.

Bertram brushed a hand over the scratches on his cheek. "Better. Dad wouldn't take her to the hospital, but at least he brought someone in. Gave her a sedative or something and some I-V fluids. She's sleeping now and not talking nonsense."

Penelope stiffened. Sedatives and fluids wouldn't have calmed the spirit plaguing Louise Brown. Only magic could have done that. "Your dad brought someone in? A doctor?"

"That's usually the course of action when someone's sick." He shook his head. "Honestly, I don't know what it is with you people."

"Do you know this doctor's name?"

"I never saw him. Sorry." Bertram paused, studying her for a moment. "Why is it important?"

It's important because your father didn't tell me he was going behind my back to have another magic user perform a spell on your mother. But she didn't say that. "Bertram, I came by today to ask you about something your father said to me. A few weeks ago, he got a call from an irate customer. You said it was some sort of misunderstanding, and you told him you'd take care of it."

Bertram rolled his eyes. "That again?"

"What do you mean?"

"That 'irate customer' was old Arthur Payton. I told the bastard to pay his bills or we'd repossess the tractor he bought from us. We haven't seen one penny from him in over a year. Dad didn't like me saying that."

We. Interesting choice of pronouns.

"Why didn't he like that? Sounds kind of reasonable to me."

"Something about being a good neighbor over being a good businessman. 'Old Arthur ran into some trouble and fell behind, that's all. He'll make it up.'" Bertram leaned across the desk. "Here's the truth. Arthur spent his tractor money at the liquor store. We're never going to see a dime from him. At least if we get the tractor back, we can resell it or use the parts. Hated to do it, but I had to." He pointed to the ledger. "We've got bills, too."

There it was again. "*We?* Does that mean you're part of the business now? You here permanently?"

Bertram gave a small nod. "For a little while at least."

"Is there a reason?"

"That's not exactly any of your business," he barked.

Penelope crossed her arms. "It is if it has to do with whatever's happening with your mother."

He slammed a hand down on the desk. "Look, Arthur may be a mouthy drunk, but at the end of the day, he's harmless. And I still don't understand what this has to do with my mom. She needs a doctor. A real one, not some voodoo witch doctor." His mouth twisted into a sneer. "Did you tell Charles what's going on with her?"

"Charles isn't a witch doctor," Penelope snapped, "and he doesn't do voodoo."

Bertram shrugged. "Close enough."

"I'm not asking you to understand, Bertram. I'm just asking you to help me figure out who might want to hurt your family."

"There's plenty of people who don't like us, but I can't think of anyone who would hate us enough to break into the house and do something to make my mom sick."

"Not even a competitor?"

He glanced at the ledger on the desk again. "Our competitors don't have to do anything that complicated."

His voice quavered, just slightly. The bluster was gone. The bravado had disappeared. For a moment, the façade came down, and Penelope saw a man at the end of his rope, shaken, confused, struggling to hold it all together. She could relate.

"Bertram, is everything okay?"

He looked away. "Everything's as fine as it can be with Mom the way she is."

"You sure there's not something else?"

He took in a deep breath and let it out slowly. When he met her gaze again, the mask was back in place. "Nothing you can help with, Penelope. You just stick to doing what you're doing, and I'll stick to doing what I'm doing."

"What exactly are you doing?" Penelope asked.

Bertram clenched his jaw. "Everything I can."

———

Penelope appreciated that Charles had at least gone to the effort of clearing away a space for her to sit. He was also wearing a shirt that looked like it had been pressed sometime within the past decade. He turned the chair at his worktable and sat down facing her. Hands tucked under his chin as if praying, expression on his face more somber than usual, he remained still except for his measured breaths.

"Charles, is something the matter?" Penelope finally asked.

He picked up a book from the table. When his fingers touched the cover, a blue spark of static electricity danced over the dark leather, or so Penelope thought. Charles opened the book to a page near the back and held it out toward her. An illustration was there, a door with the same inscription as the one carved into the Browns' back door.

Penelope's hand trembled as she reached toward the page, but Charles jerked the book away before she could touch it. She still felt it, though, the crackle of energy surrounding the volume.

"What are you showing me, Charles?"

"I found this spell yesterday right before you called me." Charles explained how it worked—the new moon ritual, inscribing *hidden* on the door, speaking the words of power. "Ever since we talked, I've been going over things in my head. Someone went to a lot of trouble to get that brooch into the house."

Penelope grimaced and massaged her temples. "Too many questions. Who would want to hurt the Browns that badly? Why? And what exactly did the brooch do to Louise? Please tell me you can help, Charles."

Charles placed the book back on the table and picked up another. Again, a faint blue light shimmered across the cover as he touched it. "I'm doing what I can. I have an idea of what's happening to Louise Brown, but you're not going to like where that path leads."

Penelope threw up her hands. "At least it's a path. That's more than we have now."

Charles opened the book to a page covered in cramped writing. Penelope recognized it as Hebrew. An illustration of a skeleton adorned the bottom corner, arms and legs akimbo, its mouth open in a silent scream.

"In some traditions, residual hauntings are caused when there's enough psychic trauma surrounding a person's death to tear open the Veil between this world and the next. Usually the tear heals itself immediately, but not always. A small hole remains, and just enough energy leaks back through to manifest as echoes, shadows of the death itself." Charles pointed to the skeleton. "There are ways, though, when you find one of these openings, to make the hole larger, to drag a portion of the spirit back into this world."

Penelope stared transfixed at the illustration. "I don't think I'd be very happy if someone did that to me."

"It's not a pleasant experience for the spirit involved. Performing this spell turns something frightening but otherwise harmless into something malevolent and dangerous. Spirits in this condition aren't really open to dialogue. You can't reason with them or convince them to pass over again. They usually have to be exorcized."

"Can you do it?" Penelope asked.

Charles pursed his lips. "Given enough preparation, yes. But, Penelope, you need to realize that there's something bigger going on here. This isn't everyday street magic we're dealing with. These are major, complicated spells that take multiple people to perform. As cutthroat as tractor sales may be, this is much more personal. Whatever this is, it might even go beyond the Browns."

The voice of Penelope's grandmother echoed in her head. Her father was afraid of Ephraim Brown because of something Ephraim did. Could something from his past have come back to haunt him, quite literally?

Penelope reached into her purse and pulled out the hairbrush she had stolen from Mary Wilson's dorm room. "I have something that might help sort this all out."

Charles stared at the hairbrush in her hand. "What am I supposed to do with that exactly?"

"This brush belonged to Mary Wilson. It still has her hairs on it." She drew a long brown hair from among the bristles. "I thought you might be able to use them to find out what happened to her. Maybe you can find out what happened to Jeremiah Morrison, too."

He eyed the strand of hair dubiously. "That's not a lot to go on. I wouldn't get my hopes up. Do you have anything from Mr. Morrison?"

"You'll have to talk to Zed about that."

Charles scowled. "Of course I will."

———

No one had come yet for Jeremiah Morrison's belongings. After Zed discovered the body, he made a call from a pay phone to report it. The police had come, and the coroner. They had taken the body, questioned the neighbors, collected evidence, but now they were gone, as were the police barriers. Only his belongings remained, and they would probably stay there until the landlord decided to rent the unit out again.

As far as Zed could tell, nothing had been disturbed, despite the door being wide open. None of his neighbors had tried to help themselves to any of his former possessions. The television was still there, the old radio, his chair, his mattress, his clothes. No one came for any of it. The thing hanging in the air, the greasy, black stain that eluded Zed's grasp, kept them away.

Zed watched as Charles surveyed the room where he found Jeremiah Morrison. "I assumed you'd be more comfortable here than at Furman. You'd be a little conspicuous there."

Charles cocked an eyebrow. "You assumed that, did you now?"

Zed sighed. "That's not what I meant. It's a women's dormitory. I don't think it would end too well for either of us if we tried to get in there."

Charles grunted. "It would be harder there to do what I'm doing. Too much conflicting energy. Everyone coming and going all the time and all the emotions. Not ideal conditions."

"And here?" Zed asked.

Charles glanced around the room again. "Near perfect. Only the dead are here. Still, it's not going to be easy. The spell might not work at all. At least in a way that's useful."

"What should I do?"

Charles motioned with his head to a corner of the room. "Stand over there and try not to breathe too much. Whatever happens, don't disturb the spell."

"What if it looks like you're in trouble?"

"Especially if it looks like I'm in trouble."

Charles opened his bag and removed a piece of chalk. He drew a circle on the floor around the chair. When he closed the circle, he etched letters around the entire perimeter, some Aramaic, some Latin, some Enochian. Interspersed with the words were the alchemical symbols for lead, antimony, and silver. Those were just the ones Zed recognized.

When Charles finished the inscriptions, he retrieved other items from his bag—old coins, feathers, what looked like bones from a human finger, a few lodestones. He scattered them about the circle, seemingly at random, but Zed knew better. Nothing was random when it came to magic.

Finally, Charles took out the hairbrush Penelope had stolen from Mary Wilson's room and placed it in the chair next to one of Jeremiah Morrison's shirts, one that had definitely not been washed.

His preparations complete, Charles stepped inside the circle and closed his eyes. Silence reigned inside the apartment. As Charles instructed, Zed tried not to breathe. Several minutes passed in which Charles stood perfectly still, eyes shut. Then he began to mumble—low at first, then growing louder—the words a jumble of languages just like the words written around the edge of the circle. The letters in chalk glowed as Charles spoke.

A knife appeared in his hand, conjured from nowhere as far as Zed could tell. Zed hadn't seen him pick it up, and his bag was outside the circle. Charles slid the blade across his left forearm, where there were already more than a few prominent scars. Deep scarlet blood welled up from the small cut, not much, but enough to trickle down his arm and drip from his hand. He guided one or two drops of blood each onto the brush and the shirt. Charles' murmuring grew quieter until he was barely speaking, merely mouthing the words.

When Charles' lips stopped moving altogether, Zed wondered for a moment if the spell had worked, but then Charles' body jerked, as if he were a marionette being pulled by invisible strings.

When he met the edge of the circle, he came to an abrupt stop. He hung there for a few moments, body bent at an impossible angle, arms out and taut. Zed crept forward but scrambled back again when Charles started shaking.

The dark thing that lingered in the apartment didn't like what Charles was doing. Jolts of anger and fear and hatred stabbed through Zed's brain, forcing him down to his knees. Wincing, he glanced back at Charles.

Charles moaned and began to chant again. His voice was hoarse, his breaths ragged, his cadence uneven. He struggled to form the words, as if someone were trying to keep him from saying them.

Then Charles screamed, and Zed's world went black.

———

Charles produced the knife from the sleeve of his jacket, where he always kept it. He drew the blade across his arm, just enough for a few drops of blood. It wouldn't do him any good to pass out. In fact, it would probably be fatal if he did. He let the blood fall on the brush and the shirt, closed his eyes again, and opened his mind. He chanted the words that would open the connection between him and the world on the other side of the Veil, where the others now resided.

Every time he made the trip it was different, but every time it was painful. His body seized and slammed against the protective circle he had made. He made it as much to keep things in as to keep things out. He became vaguely aware of tree branches around him and the crunch of leaves underneath his feet. He walked through a primeval forest. Birds called. Animals scurried in the underbrush.

This was only the transition, though, the liminal space. Charles' destination was someplace quite different. As he followed the path through the trees, he came to a clearing, and blinding white light obliterated the forest. When he could see again, he was back in the apartment of Jeremiah Morrison, but not everything was the same. The proportions were skewed. Some objects were bigger than they should have been, and others were smaller. Charles couldn't see anything at all outside the windows except black nothingness.

Morrison sat in the chair, holding the gun, staring at it, almost as if he didn't know what it was. Then a black, vaguely humanoid shape rose up behind the chair. Matted black fur covered the foul thing in some places, black scales in others. Some of its too many arms ended in giant hands with claws like razors. Other arms ended not in fingers but tentacles. The thing's eyes glowed a sickly yellow, and its mouth contained row on row of dagger-shaped teeth. Its stench permeated the air, the smell of rot and death and decay.

One of the tentacled arms brushed Morrison's forehead, and his face went blank, expressionless. The spark of awareness left his eyes. Other tentacles coiled around the hand holding the gun and lifted it to his head.

Then the thing spoke.

Its voice cut, like raking claws across Charles' brain. He didn't know the words, didn't even know if they could be translated into a human language, but the message was clear. The utter lack of hope. Nothing but bottomless despair.

The gun fired.

Everything disappeared again in another flash of white. When Charles could see again, he was in a different room. It had the same out-of-proportion quality to it, the same odd light, the same nothingness outside the sole window. This room was much smaller, with barely enough space for the bed, desk, and chest of drawers there. Standing by the bed, a woman in her early twenties appeared to be getting ready to go out. She looked in the mirror hanging on the wall over the chest of drawers, applied her lipstick, checked her hair, and smoothed the front of her blouse. Then she glanced at the desk, at the pair of scissors lying there.

Charles smelled the stench first, all of a half second before the dark creature appeared behind her. The thing wrapped its tentacles around her head, and just like Jeremiah Morrison, she went blank. Then another black tentacle grasped the girl's hand and made her pick up the scissors. Again, the thing spoke, making Charles want to claw off his own skin.

After the last of its diabolical words faded away, the woman jammed the blades of the scissors into her side, again and again until blood covered the wall, the desk, the bed. Then Mary Wilson collapsed to the floor.

The scene shifted again, this time to what appeared to be a motel room, a cheap one at that. Broken blinds let garish neon light in from outside. The bedspread was stained. Cigarette butts overflowed the ashtray on the nightstand. Jeremiah Morrison sat on the bed. Another man was in the room, too, a white man who looked to be in his late fifties or early sixties. Even in his badly cut suit, he looked out of place. Charles guessed he would have been more at home in an accountant's office.

The two were talking, but Charles couldn't make out the words. Their voices were distorted, as if they were underwater. The unknown man reached inside his wrinkled coat and pulled out a thick envelope. He tossed it to Morrison, who opened the flap to reveal a stack of bills. Morrison smiled and nodded. Then the man did something odd. He touched Morrison on his forehead. At the strange touch, Morrison froze. The man said a few words, words Charles recognized. They were the words the black creature used, though coming from the man in the suit, fortunately, they didn't make Charles feel like a railroad spike was being driven through his skull.

Out of the corner of his eye, Charles saw the creature lurking in the shadows of the motel room. He could almost feel the thing's anticipation.

One last time, the scene changed. This time Charles found himself in an antique shop. Mary Wilson stood behind a desk. At the jingling of bells, she looked up toward the front door and smiled. The same man entered the shop, wearing the same wrinkled suit. The two of them spoke for a moment, exchanging pleasantries no doubt. Then the man looked around the shop for a little while before stopping at a small jewelry case near the desk. He asked the woman a question. She reached into a pocket in her skirt, pulled out a key, and unlocked the case to retrieve a brooch.

The jewel in the center was an odd color, changing from green to red to purple depending on the light. Mary handed it to the man, who held it in his palm and smiled. He nodded, and then asked another question. When she answered, he pulled a checkbook and a pen from his coat pocket, but he didn't write a check.

As Mary leaned over the counter, the man reached up and touched her forehead. She froze. He said the same vile words again, and the thing appeared, its yellow eyes reflected in a mirror, its misshapen mouth drawn in an eager grin.

Then the man in the suit, wearing a wicked grin of his own, turned and looked directly at Charles.

Zed opened his eyes to find himself on the floor. He struggled to get to his feet, his legs unsteady underneath him. Charles lay half in and half out of the chalk circle, gasping for breath. Zed staggered across the room toward him.

When he reached the magician, Zed grabbed him by the shoulders and shook him. "Charles. Charles, are you okay?"

His eyes wild, Charles turned in the direction of Zed's voice. He grasped Zed's arm. Gradually, his breathing became even, and his eyes regained their focus.

"I'm fine," he said, sitting up. His voice was little more than a raspy whisper.

Zed grunted. "Really, because you don't look fine. You look like you've been through hell."

Charles smirked. "That wouldn't be far from the truth."

A headache was flaring up behind Zed's eyes. "Dude, what the fuck was that?"

"The aftereffects of my walk through the spirit world," Charles replied.

"Why didn't you warn me?"

Charles frowned. "Warn you about what? What happened?"

Zed massaged his temples. "Nothing except I feel like I've been hit in the head by a two-by-four. I was out most of the time you were having your little stroll through the spirit world."

The creases in Charles' forehead deepened. "That spell shouldn't have affected you at all."

"Well, it did." Zed winced as the throbbing increased.

"Did you ... see anything?"

"Only if pitch black darkness counts."

Charles looked away. "Sorry. Nothing in my research mentioned the spell affecting bystanders like that. Maybe there never were any bystanders."

The last thing Zed expected from Charles was an apology, but he'd gladly take it. "Did the spell at least work?"

"Unfortunately."

"What do you mean by that?"

"I saw what happened. It's dark magic, darker than I've ever seen."

"So ... what are we dealing with?"

Charles glanced at the armchair. "A literal nightmare."

———

It took all Zed had to keep from retching as he staggered up the stairs to his apartment. He all but fell through the door, lurched to his bedroom, and collapsed onto the bed. A minute passed, then five, then ten, then thirty. Still wide awake an hour later, Zed pushed himself off the bed and stumbled into his bathroom. He turned on the shower, stripped, and stepped underneath the scalding water. The fog in his head began to clear, enough for him to decide he really didn't want to be there anymore, and soon he was out the door again.

O'Shaughnessy's was his bar. Not rundown enough to pose a health hazard, but not upscale enough to overcharge for drinks. While other businesses fled downtown, leaving plywood boards in place of window displays, O'Shaughnessy's stubbornly stayed put. Zed admired the tenacity. He also appreciated the fact the owner didn't overdo the Irish theme, even if his name was Patrick.

"A Horse with No Name" was playing on the jukebox as Zed walked in. He counted only three other people apart from Russell, the bartender, not too surprising on a Tuesday night. Just like him, they all seemed to be there alone. He took a seat at the bar. Russell put a Bass ale in front of him without saying a word. He sat for a while, nursing the beer.

The more he tried to think about the spell Charles had done, the more his head hurt. The details got all fuzzy. All he could remember was the dark thing that lingered in the apartment. A literal nightmare, Charles had said. Being typical Charles, he wouldn't explain further until he could go back to his books for more research. That meant Zed was left to clean up the mess by himself. Again.

The song on the jukebox ended, and "Joy to the World" by Three Dog Night started playing. Annie loved that song. She had spent all of the last summer singing it. Zed caught himself smiling. He still thought about her a lot. He hadn't told Penelope the whole truth.

He missed Annie. Her bright blue eyes, her straight auburn hair that hung almost to her waist. He liked the way she crinkled her nose when she was trying to concentrate on something, her generously given smile, her soft skin, the fact that she was ticklish. It had been hard to let her go, but Zed didn't have any other choice. Her life was to take a different path from his. Prolonging the inevitable would've just made it all the more painful.

The door opened, letting in a swirl of damp air from outside. A man ambled over to the bar and sat two stools down from Zed. He waved to Russell and ordered a Guinness. Zed studied him out of the corner of his eye. Maybe a few years younger than Zed, his chestnut brown hair brushed his shoulders. He wore a pair of jeans and a short-sleeved shirt that showed off his biceps. Not exactly business attire, but not what you'd wear for a night on the town either.

He had a book tucked under his arm, which he set on the bar. Zed scanned the title. *Fear and Trembling* by Søren Kierkegaard.

Zed caught the man's eye briefly. When his beer came, he gave Zed a small salute. For several minutes, they sat side-by-side in silence, the man reading his book and Zed nursing his drink.

Though he hid it well, the man gave off a certain kind of melancholy. In fact, Zed had picked up the same sort of feeling from Annie when he first met her—a quiet acceptance that life would never be any different and that people would always disappoint.

As the man finished his beer and flagged down Russell for another, Zed finally took the opportunity to say something. "Interesting reading choice for a bar. You see more Kant or Sartre in a place like this. Maybe some Nietzsche."

The man drew his mouth into a brittle smile. "Look, I don't want to be rude, but I kind of came here just to unwind a little. I'm not really looking for conversation."

Zed shrugged. "I can respect that."

Russell brought the man's second beer. A few more minutes of silence passed while Zed stared into his now empty glass. His mind wandered back to the incident at Jeremiah Morrison's apartment. Thinking about Charles' spell threatened to instantly revive his headache, so Zed, instead, tried to focus on what he had felt. Charles knew magic, but Zed knew people, specifically their emotions. For most, *anguish, despair, sadness,* and *sorrow* were words next to each other in a thesaurus. To Zed, they were as distinct as different shades of the color blue, and he could sense them in others. He knew who felt guilty, who felt ashamed or afraid, despite whatever plastered-on smile they presented to the world. He always knew when someone was lying. Although that didn't help much when everyone was lying.

"I don't like Nietzsche."

The statement jolted Zed out of his reverie. "Excuse me?"

"I don't like Nietzsche," the man repeated. "He gets a little bleak. Listen, I'm sorry I was so gruff. I've just had a day. I needed a few minutes without someone trying to talk to me."

Zed held up a hand. "No offense taken. I totally get that."

"My name is Jake."

"Zed." He lifted his glass in salute.

"Unusual name. Is that short for something?"

Zed ran a finger over the amethyst ring on his right hand. "Yes."

Jake grunted. "Guess I deserve that answer."

"What drove you to drink today, if you don't mind my asking?"

Jake started to answer, but then shook his head and waved a hand. "Nah, it's not even worth getting into. Let's just say I was hoping I'd get a break, and that didn't happen."

"I can relate to that," Zed said with a chuckle.

"Why are you here?" Jake asked.

Zed shrugged. "Same as you. Bad day. Just needed to clear my head."

"Rough day on the job?"

"You might say that."

"What do you do for a living?"

"Lots of odd jobs, actually," Zed replied. "I spent today helping out a private detective on one of her cases."

Jake raised an eyebrow. "Her?"

Zed lifted a finger as a warning. "Don't. She's damn good at what she does."

Jake, his book forgotten, swiveled his stool to face Zed. "Never said I didn't believe she was. What's helping a detective like?"

"You watch *Mannix*?"

Jake nodded. "Every now and then."

"It's nothing like that. Pretty boring most of the time. Lots of sitting and waiting. My other jobs are usually more exciting."

"Those must be some amazing other jobs."

"Well, the bookstore I work at can get pretty wild sometimes. I also deejay on the radio a couple of nights a week."

Jake eyed him, his mouth twisted in an incredulous grin. "You deejay? Really? What station? Would I have heard your show?"

"Are you normally up at three in the morning? If you are, I'm on WQRX."

"What do you play?"

"That early in the morning? Anything I damn well please."

Jake laughed. Zed liked the sound of it. "When's your next show?"

"Thursday. Well, technically Friday morning."

"Maybe I'll give you a listen."

"Great. One listener at least."

Jake pointed to Zed's empty glass. "Let me buy you another beer?"

Zed stood and slapped some bills down on the bar. "Thanks, but I should get going."

"Maybe I'll see you around, then."

Zed smiled. "Maybe."

6.

WEDNESDAY, MAY 24, 1972

enelope shivered as she stepped into her office. The temperature dropped ten degrees at least from the foyer. That only happened when her father really wanted to get her attention.

"Dad? Are you here?"

Two knocks.

So yes, obviously.

"Do you have something to tell me?"

Two knocks.

She scanned the top of her desk, looking for anything out of place. The stapler was where it was supposed to be. So was the painted river rock she had given her father when she was eight, the one he used as a paperweight. Her penholder hadn't moved either.

In fact, nothing at all seemed out of place. It wasn't until she walked around the desk that she discovered one of the desk drawers halfway out. She pulled it the rest of the way. As she peered inside, the room became deathly still. The temperature dropped even more, to the point her breath came out in white puffs.

The only thing in the drawer was an envelope. Penelope scooped it out and opened it. Inside was an old picture of her mother—with a man who wasn't her father. They were at the beach, sitting together on a blanket on the sand. He had his arm around her.

Penelope's stomach twisted in knots. "Where did this come from?"

No answer.

In the months after her father died, she went through every room of the house. Every closet, every drawer, every cabinet, every box, every file. She'd never seen that picture before. Where could her father have hidden it? And why was it hidden in the first place?

She sighed. "Okay, fine. Yes or no questions only. Is this picture from before you and Mom met?"

Two knocks.

"Who's the man?"

Silence.

"Does this have something to do with the Brown case?"

Two knocks.

"So this man. Was he seeing my mother?"

Two knocks.

Progress finally. "Was it serious?"

Two knocks again.

"So obviously it ended. And since we're talking about it in the context of the Browns, I'm guessing it didn't end well. He left her? He cheated on her?"

One knock.

Penelope was silent for a moment, hesitant to ask the next question. "He hit her?"

One knock. A pause. Then two knocks.

"Well, which was it?"

Silence.

Penelope struggled to work through what her father was trying to say. "She left him?"

Two knocks.

"Let me guess, he didn't take it well." She sighed. "I wish you could just tell me what happened."

The series of knocks that followed startled Penelope. After a moment's pause, the pattern started again. Her heart pounded. Her father was actually trying to spell out something in Morse code, even knowing what the cost would be. She grabbed a pencil and a scrap of paper. When the pattern started over again, she wrote down the letters as her father tapped them out, while trying to keep her hands from shaking too much:

B-E-N-J-A-M-I-N-F-R-A-Z-I-E-R

Penelope studied the smiling faces in the photograph. They looked so happy. Penelope never remembered her mother being happy. "Is Benjamin Frazier the name of the man in the picture?"

Silence.

"Dad? Dad, are you there?"

He didn't answer. The temperature began to rise. He was gone.

Paper in hand, Penelope picked up the phone and dialed a number.

"Division of Public Records," a woman's voice said on the other end of the line in a clipped, professional tone.

"Carolyn, it's Penelope," she replied. "I'm so glad you're the one who picked up. I need you to look up a name for me."

———

A few hours later, a knock echoed through the house. For a fraction of a second, Penelope thought her father had returned, but when another knock rapidly followed, she realized someone was at the door.

Penelope answered to find Carolyn Cole waiting on the other side. "Hi, Penelope, I got that info you wanted." She was smiling, but something about her expression seemed forced. "Can I come in?"

Penelope stepped aside to let Carolyn into the foyer. "Sure, but you didn't have to make a special trip. You could have just called."

Carolyn's smile faded. She bit her lip. "Not this time, Penelope." She held up the file in her hand. "This is a talk I'd prefer to have face-to-face."

Carolyn's words instantly tied Penelope's stomach in knots. "Okay, now you're worrying me. Why?"

Carolyn gestured toward Penelope's office. "Can we sit?"

Carolyn took one of the chairs in front of Penelope's desk while Penelope took the other. Carolyn sat back straight, legs crossed, and hands folded on top of the folder that rested in her lap. With her cat-eye glasses perched on the end of her nose, she looked every bit like a schoolteacher. As far as Penelope was concerned, though, the file clerk at the Department of Public Records was just as much a magician as Charles. Carolyn had the uncanny ability to dig up the most obscure bits of information. Penelope was sure she could blackmail half the City Council if she wanted.

"What's going on, Carolyn?" Penelope asked.

"Benjamin Frazier." Carolyn peered at Penelope over the rim of her glasses. "Are you telling me you've never heard that name before?"

Penelope shook her head. "Not before this morning."

"Where did you come across it?"

"On the back of an old picture of my mother I found stuck in the middle of a book." Penelope hated to lie to Carolyn, but she wasn't about to tell the truth.

"So this has nothing to do with a case you're working on?"

"I didn't tell you where I found the book."

"You know a few days ago Zed had me find the address of someone involved in some ... questionable things." Carolyn frowned. "Are you sure you're not getting yourself into something dangerous?"

Penelope huffed. "You, too, Carolyn?"

Carolyn's expression softened, a little. "Friends can't worry?"

"I'm as careful as I can possibly be. I promise."

Carolyn nodded, though the quick glance she threw Penelope indicated she didn't quite believe her. "Your mother never told you anything about this man?"

"Never. Should she have?"

Carolyn opened the folder and passed it to Penelope. Inside were police reports, newspaper clippings, and old photographs. "Penelope, he tried to kill her. It was apparently a big deal at the time. He came to the secretarial service where your mother worked and attacked her with a knife. Fortunately for her, he was three sheets to the wind. He tripped trying to get to her and ended up stabbing himself in the stomach."

Penelope pawed through the stack of documents, trying to take in the details of what Carolyn was telling her. In one article, there was a picture of her mother taken around the time of the incident. Penelope forgot how much she favored her. Suddenly light-headed, she gripped the arm of her chair. "Oh, God. She never said a thing."

"Maybe it was just too traumatic for her," Carolyn suggested. "To have someone so bent on revenge because you ended a relationship. I can't imagine what that would be like."

It would be like the angry ghost haunting the brooch Louise Brown is wearing. That's what her father had been trying to tell her. All this time she'd been focused on who might want to hurt Ephraim Brown. But what if Louise Brown was the target all along?

"Thank you, Carolyn. You're amazing."

"I am?" Carolyn narrowed her eyes. "Wait, you're not upset?"

Penelope shrugged. "What's the point? My mother left almost twenty years ago. I don't even know where she is. This is just something else I didn't have a clue about. I'll add it to the list of conversations we're going to have if I ever see her again."

Carolyn managed an awkward grin. "Well, I'm glad I could help."

———

Penelope's grandmother handed her a cup of coffee and sat down across the kitchen table. Penelope wished her coffee had bourbon in it.

"Grandma, why didn't you ever say anything?"

Mrs. Drake paused, her own cup of coffee poised in her hand. "Because it wasn't my place. Your mother asked me not to. Besides, that was all in the past by the time she met your father. No doubt she wanted to forget it ever happened."

Penelope couldn't hide her smirk. "Seems like she wanted to forget a lot of things."

For once her grandmother stayed silent. The years had taught them both that no good could come of a discussion about the reasons why Penelope's mother left her and her father.

"You remember our last conversation?" Penelope dropped a spoonful of sugar into her coffee as casually as she could. "I've been thinking a lot about the Browns these few days."

"I heard about poor Louise. Suffered a nervous breakdown it seems. The story going around town is that they sent her to some spa up in Virginia, but I don't believe it for a minute." Her grandmother dropped her voice, despite the fact they were the only two there. "She's still in that house."

Penelope shifted uncomfortably. Sometimes her grandmother's intuition bordered on supernatural. "Why do you say that?"

"Well, again, these are just rumors, but I've heard the business is having trouble paying bills. Longtime clients are going to other places or going under themselves. Times change, you know. Not as many family farms around these days. So, given all that, I really don't see how they could afford to send Louise to a fancy sanitarium right now."

"Do you know much about Louise Brown, her family?"

"The McClellans? Why, yes, of course. I know all about Louise's people. They do go back a while. The family had a small textile mill out toward Piedmont."

"Was there anything in Mrs. Brown's past similar to what happened to my mother?"

Mrs. Drake eyed her. "That's a peculiar question."

Penelope stared into her coffee cup. As a little girl, she'd always wanted to have a tea party with the fine china set all covered in pink and white camellias. Of course, her grandmother never let her, until one day she'd asked what the point of having nice dishes was if no one ever used them. Her grandmother looked at her sternly, but after a moment she smiled, and she opened the china cabinet. They had a fine tea party that day where they shared all their secrets, and ever since, they'd always used the good china whenever they had a talk like this one. It was their special thing, which is what made the current conversation so hard.

"It's a peculiar situation."

Her grandmother gazed out the window, where the wind rustled the leaves in the big maple tree. "You know, Penelope, I never told your father how to run his own life. Maybe I should have. Maybe things would have turned out differently." She put her hand up when Penelope opened her mouth to try to say something. "But maybe they wouldn't have. What I'm trying to say is that I'm not going to tell you how to run your life either. Just be sure that whatever you do, you go into it with your eyes wide open."

"I will, Grandma."

"Now getting back to your question. There was some talk of some … unpleasantness when she was younger. A man her parents didn't approve of. She had to go away for a little while, as they put it back then."

"They still call it that," Penelope muttered.

"In any event, when she came back, she ended things with this boy. He apparently didn't take it well, though I don't remember anything about him hurting her."

"Do you know his name?"

"No, I'm sorry. I can't remember that either."

Penelope reached across the table and placed a hand on top of her grandmother's "Thank you, Grandma."

Her grandmother met her gaze. "The Browns. They're not like other families. A lot of misfortune there." A hint of warning entered her voice.

"A lot of misfortune in every family." Penelope squeezed her grandmother's hand. "We ought to know."

"That's not what I meant. There have been some other strange doings over the years. You're not involved in anything over your head, are you, Penelope?"

Penelope barked a laugh. "Well, everyone certainly seems to think so, even Da—"

"Even who?" Mrs. Drake asked, tilting her head to the side.

"No one," Penelope replied, cursing herself.

Her grandmother patted her hand. "Do be careful, dear. You know I worry. Every night I pray for God to watch over you."

———

The light of the near-full moon illuminated the overgrown fields surrounding Charles' farmhouse. The first fireflies of the season drew meandering paths through the air while the crickets sang a disquieting song. Penelope found it easy to imagine dark shapes standing in those fields every time she glanced out the window. After a while, she tried to avoid looking outside altogether, instead concentrating on the array of books on the table she, Charles, and Zed sat huddled around.

Thick and thin, leather-bound, cloth-bound, gold leaf, blackletter, typeset, handwritten. English, Latin, Hebrew, and languages long forgotten. Charles' library amazed her. She'd love to spend an afternoon just browsing the titles, but Charles would never let that happen.

He picked up a particularly ancient-looking volume bound in a flaking leather and flipped to a page full of symbols and signs. "I think I've found a spell that will exorcise the ghost from the brooch. It took me a few days to gather up all the ingredients, but I think I have everything now."

Again, a faint, blue glow appeared when Charles touched the leather-bound cover. Penelope glanced at Zed, but he didn't seem to notice. "I'm not sure how much time Louise has left. Can you be ready to do this tomorrow morning?"

"I can." Charles placed the book back on the table and leaned forward. "But I asked the two of you to come here because I need you to understand. The exorcism is going to be the easy part. That only solves half the problem. The person who did this, he's too dangerous to roam free. We have to find him."

Zed sat back and crossed his arms. "How do we do that? We don't know his name, and you're the only one who knows what he looks like."

Anger flashed in Charles' eyes, there one second and gone the next. "I'll think of something. All I know is that if we don't stop him, more people are going to die."

"Why do you say that?" Penelope asked.

"He's too powerful. The concealment spell was worrying enough, then we find out he pulled a spirit through a tear in the Veil." Charles picked up another book, one of the thinner volumes. Penelope's German was rusty, but the spine said something about a field guide to demons. Charles opened it to a page with only an illustration, a woman lying prone on a bed with a dark figure sitting on her chest. Its features were vague except for its teeth and claws and eyes filled with malice. "But what I saw in that apartment froze my blood. He summoned and collared a nightmare."

Penelope couldn't take her eyes away from the picture. "A nightmare?"

"The demon the bad dreams are named after," Charles explained. "The demon that whispers in your ear while you sleep, plays on your fears, steals your breath, makes you give up hope."

Zed frowned. "I didn't know they could kill."

"They can't. Usually."

Penelope glanced back at Charles. "Usually?"

"They can only manifest in our world as a shadow of their true selves," Charles said. "That's why they attack people sleeping. It's when they have the most influence, when our consciousness is gone, our souls most vulnerable. Our friend somehow brought one into our world and put it under his control. Don't think for a minute he's done using it."

Zed continued to scrutinize the picture. "Too bad we can't just look at the Yellow Pages under evil wizards."

Charles shot Zed a look that could have melted lead. "There's one more thing. When I cast the spell in Jeremiah Morrison's apartment, he saw me. He knew I was there and what I was doing."

The bile rose in Penelope's throat. "How is that even possible?"

"I'm not sure." Charles closed the book with the nightmare illustration and placed it with the others. "All I know is that everything is tied together. Energy weaves back and forth through the Veil in patterns we can't even begin to discern."

"Charles, I'm sorry." She had promised not to involve him this time. And here he was, neck deep. "I never meant for you to get—"

He held up a hand. "Don't be. It happened. If the time comes to deal with it, I'll deal with it."

Zed leaned back in his chair and crossed his arms. "Do you think he's more powerful than you?"

It wasn't a challenge. It was a simple, straightforward question, and a legitimate one at that. Still, Penelope tensed, waiting to see how Charles would reply.

Charles placed his hand on the stack of books on the table.

This time the blue light emanating from the books was unmistakable. "Power comes from knowledge. I'll be ready."

Penelope allowed herself a tentative smile. "So will we, then."

Charles' expression didn't change. "Penelope, you understand there's no turning him over to the police. He's just too dangerous. We have to end him."

Penelope nodded. "We'll do what we need to do. First, though, we need to make plans for sending the ghost possessing Louise Brown back where it came from."

Charles arched an eyebrow. "Who said anything about sending the ghost back? We're going to pull it the rest of the way through."

7.

THURSDAY, MAY 25, 1972

ertram threw open the door to the bedroom just as Charles finished the chalk circle around Louise Brown's bed. "What the hell do you think you're doing?" he bellowed.

Zed intercepted him before he could set foot in the room. "We're trying to save your mother."

Bertram peered over Zed's shoulder at the chalk sigils adorning the bedroom walls. "How? You're crazier than I thought if you really believe this supernatural bullshit. I can't believe you convinced my father to go along with this."

Zed tried to push him out of the room. "Please, Bertram."

Bertram pushed back. "Don't you 'Please, Bertram' me. You let me into this room right now. She needs a doctor."

"Bertram, there's nothing a doctor can do."

"Like hell. Now step aside."

Penelope sighed. "Zed, let him in."

Zed craned his neck and shot her a suspicious look. "What?"

"Let him in, Zed," she repeated. "He's not going to go away. He might as well see what's going on for himself."

"You sure?"

She nodded.

Zed stepped aside. Bertram rushed into the room, only to stop short at the edge of the chalk circle. Ignoring him, Charles continued to work, writing out the symbols and words needed for the spell. Louise Brown lay in bed, wearing the same clothes she'd had on Sunday when Penelope saw her last—with one addition. A thin chain encircled her neck, and from it hung a metal disc with a sigil stamped into it. She was perfectly still, save for the slight rising and falling of her chest. Too still. Unnaturally still.

The work of the mystery magician. Penelope planned to confront Ephraim about it after everything was done. When they had arrived, Ephraim asked if he needed to be there for the exorcism. Charles told him he didn't, and Penelope hadn't seen him since.

"What are you doing?" Bertram asked with a tremor in his voice.

Penelope took a deep breath and exhaled it slowly. "Charles is preparing the room to exorcise the spirit that has possessed your mother through the brooch she's wearing."

Bertram stared at her, incredulous. "You're serious, aren't you?"

"Afraid so."

He shook his head. "You're nuts."

"Bertram, growing up, were there ever times when you saw or heard something you just couldn't explain? Maybe involving your dad? Something you've written off as a dream, but you know, deep down, it wasn't?"

Bertram hesitated.

Zed closed the door. "Can't you feel the energy in the room? That crackle of electricity making your hairs stand on end? That slightly unsettling feeling? That little impulse you had to stop before you smudged the chalk line Charles drew?"

Bertram glanced down at his shoes, a hair's breadth from the chalk line. He then glanced around the room, his eyes darting from his mother, to the sigils on the wall, to Penelope, to Zed. The panicked expression on his face told Penelope he was mere seconds from completely losing it.

Penelope held out her hand toward him. "Bertram, why don't you stand next to me where you'll be out of the way? You can watch, but if you do anything to interfere with what Charles is about to do, Zed will not hesitate to throw you out the window. Am I clear?"

Bertram eased away from the bed. "Absolutely."

"Good," Penelope said. "How are we coming, Charles?"

Charles added the final stroke to the last symbol along the inner edge of the chalk circle. "Almost there. Zed, get the jar ready."

Zed picked up a Mason jar from the dresser. The unsealed jar contained a sprig of sage, a piece of brimstone, an aniseed, and a shard of a broken mirror.

Charles closed his eyes and began to chant quietly. Even though his voice was barely above a whisper, it filled the room, blocking out all other sounds. The bracelet around Penelope's right wrist grew warm. Charles had given her and Zed each identical bracelets with charms woven into the leather strands to protect them from unforeseen side effects of the spell. It occurred to her Bertram didn't have one, but it was too late to do anything about that.

As the arcane words tumbled out of Charles' mouth, he produced a knife seemingly out of thin air. Next to Penelope, Bertram tensed. As graceful as a dancer, Charles drew the knife blade across his arm. Drops of blood fell on Louise's forehead. The knife went back to wherever it had been, and Charles grasped the pendant around Louise's neck. With one solid jerk, he yanked it free.

Louise's eyes flew open as she sucked in a huge gasp of air. "No," she screamed. "You won't get away with this. I won't let you win. You'll be sorry. You'll never get rid of me." The voice was no longer even remotely hers.

Charles raised his voice to be heard over her. Louise's screaming rose in volume to match. She thrashed on the bed, head jerking from side to side.

"What's he doing to her?" Bertram asked.

"Helping her," Penelope replied.

"She's in pain."

"She's been in pain this whole time."

Bertram took a step toward the bed. "No, he's hurting her."

Penelope grabbed his arm. "Bertram, let him finish."

For a moment, Bertram watched, the pain on his face mirroring that on his mother's. He broke free of Penelope's grip. "No. I'm sorry. I can't do this."

Zed moved to intercept Bertram but didn't reach him in time. Bertram crossed the barrier of the chalk circle and seized his mother by the shoulders, trying to hold her down, to stop her from thrashing. Charles, eyes closed and seemingly oblivious to the commotion, never stopped chanting. Louise screamed and clawed at Bertram, raking her fingernails down his arms. Blood fell from a deep scratch on Bertram's forearm onto the gem in the brooch, sizzling on contact. An invisible force threw Bertram across the room into the wall. Dazed, he slid to the floor.

Penelope called out to him. He groaned and tried to stand, but as he worked to get his feet back underneath him, an inhuman screech filled the room. A shadow arose from the brooch like dark smoke, taking the loose form of a man's upper body.

"Zed, the jar," Charles said, his tone eerily calm.

Zed opened the lid on the jar, and Charles resumed his quiet chant. The whole room smelled of an unholy combination of sage, licorice, sulfur, and coppery blood. But the shadow-smoke-person didn't go into the jar like it was supposed to. It rushed toward Bertram. His eyes grew wide as it entered through his mouth and nose. He tried to scream, but the thing choked him. He thrashed from side to side, kicking his legs, pulling at his clothes, clawing at the floor, but the thing just pushed farther inside him until it disappeared.

Then he changed.

The fear left his eyes. A raspy laugh escaped his lips. His

predatory gaze settled on Penelope, even as Charles's voice droned on.

"I'll make you pay for trying to get rid of me," Bertram said in a voice too low to be his own. "I'm never leaving."

"Wanna bet?" Zed handed Penelope the jar.

He charged at Bertram, who threw up his arms to block a punch. Zed, however, ducked and barreled into Bertram's midsection, slamming him into the wall right on top of the sigil Charles had drawn there. The thing inside Bertram shrieked while Zed held him there.

"You didn't think they were just pretty pictures, did you?" Zed snarled. "We came prepared."

The shadow-smoke-person poured out of Bertram the same way it had entered. Charles' voice rose to a shout again, his words becoming commands. A wind billowed the curtains and lifted the sheets on the bed. The spirit, caught up in the whirlwind, was pulled into the open jar Penelope held out. Once it was inside, she twisted on the lid. A shadowy face reflected in the shard of mirror before fading away.

8.

Penelope spent part of the morning filing some paperwork for a case out of Asheville—finding a deadbeat dad who'd skipped out on child support. He didn't do a great job of covering his tracks. In fact, he did such an awful job he might as well have painted a giant red arrow on the street pointing to his house.

The criminal masterminds were rare.

A little before noon, a knock came at the door. When Penelope answered, she found Bertram on the porch. He stepped inside without waiting for her to invite him in. His gaze darted around the foyer of the old house. "You know, I'm not sure I've ever been here before."

Penelope pushed down the retort that nearly flew out of her mouth. "What can I do for you, Bertram? How's your mother?"

"Mom? The doctor who came to see her today—the real doctor —says she'll be okay. She … has questions, but for now she's resting."

"I'm glad to hear that."

Bertram locked eyes with her. "Penelope, I have questions, too."

Upstairs a door slammed shut, startling them both.

"What was that?" Bertram asked.

Penelope smiled and let out a sort of half chuckle. "Oh, you know how these old houses are. Nothing's plumb. All it takes to slam a door like that is a good draft."

Bertram eyed the staircase, then glanced outside. "There isn't any breeze today." His gaze returned to her. "Penelope, what exactly happened yesterday?"

"What do you remember?"

"I remember Charles chanting and then my mom screaming. I didn't want to see her that way. She was in pain. I just wanted to help her. Then I remember someone—something—forcing its way inside me, making me think its thoughts, feel its anger, its jealousy, its hatred." His words came out faster and faster. The muscles in his shoulders tensed. He balled his hands into fists.

"Bertram—"

"I couldn't stop the thoughts. That ghost or demon or whatever it was, it was making me think horrible things, and then it occurred to me, what if these are my thoughts? What if I'm thinking these things on my own? Does that make me the monster?" He was sweating now, his face flush, his breathing pained.

She placed a hand on his arm. "Bertram, we can talk about this later."

He shrugged her off. "Why don't you want to talk about it now?"

"Because you're not ready. It's clearly too much for you to handle right now. You need a little more time. Wait until the nightmares go away."

His voice dropped to a whisper. "But what if they never go away?"

A crash came from Penelope's office. She and Bertram ran inside to find her painted rock lying in the middle of the floor.

Penelope stooped and picked up the paperweight. "It must have fallen off my desk." Part of her was thrilled her father was back after he had used so much energy to communicate with her the last time. Part of her wondered what he was doing. Was he trying to warn her about something? About Bertram? But Bertram wasn't dangerous, was he?

"How?" he asked. "It's a good three feet from your desk. Someone would have had to throw it. What's going on, Penelope?"

She didn't answer, suddenly aware Bertram was between her and the door, and reminded of how close he was to her by his still heavy breath on her neck. He'd also taken a huge psychic hit and wasn't completely rational at the moment.

He grasped her shoulder. "Penelope, answer me."

She was about to protest when a searing pain encircled her wrist. To her horror, the bracelet Charles had given her burst into flame, scorching the skin on her arm. She screamed and tried to pull the bracelet off, but as suddenly as the fire appeared, it vanished, leaving everything as it was. No burns. Nothing.

Seconds later, her telephone rang. She didn't take five rings to pick it up this time.

"Drake Detective Agency," she said, keeping a wary eye on Bertram, who frowned in confusion.

"Penelope," Zed said on the other end, a note of panic in his voice, "did you just now ... Did Charles' bracelet—"

"Just burst into flame?"

"Yeah, that."

Penelope turned away from Bertram and lowered her voice. "Something's wrong, Zed. Meet you at Charles' place in fifteen minutes?"

"Make it ten."

She hung up the phone. "Bertram, I have to go."

"What's the matter?" Bertram asked. "Is Charles in trouble? I should come with you."

"Bertram, no."

He grabbed Penelope's arm again. "Charles saved my mother, and me. I know that, even if I don't understand how."

She glared. "I don't have time to argue with you right now."

"Which is why you're going to let me come with you."

They stared at one another for a moment, until finally Penelope relented. "Fine then, but it's your funeral."

———

Penelope didn't recognize the rust-colored, beat-up Oldsmobile parked in the front yard of Charles' house. Zed's car was nowhere to be seen. Penelope and Bertram rushed up the steps to the porch to discover the front door wide open. Bertram's eyebrows shot up at the shelves full of books. As they crossed the front room, he muttered something about a "goddamn library." From farther in the house, Mahalia Jackson's voice came through again, this time singing "Just a Closer Walk with Thee." At the smell of burning paper, Penelope quickened her pace.

When they entered Charles' workshop, Penelope's stomach lurched. A fiftyish-year-old man with shaggy, graying hair and an ill-fitting suit loomed over Charles, who lay on the floor. The man clutched a book in his hand. He shifted his gaze toward them, and smile spread across his face so wicked the devil himself would have turned and run.

Charles, curled up on his side, was bleeding from a cut on his cheek. His left eye was swollen shut, and more bruises covered his neck and arms. He lifted his head weakly when Penelope and Bertram came in, struggling to focus his one good eye, but then he slumped to the floor again.

I'm not dying for you, Penelope.

Penelope aimed her .22 caliber at the man. "Step away from him."

He chuckled. "I don't think so."

Penelope held her gun level, just like her father showed her. "Maybe you're misunderstanding. I'm the one holding the gun. Get away from him, and if you so much as twitch a finger or utter a syllable in a language that isn't English, I will put a bullet between your eyes. Do you understand now?"

The man glared. "You don't have the fortitude to shoot me."

"Why do you say that?"

"Because you would have done it already. The truth of the matter is that you don't like to get your hands dirty, do you? You let everyone else do all the work, like this colored magician or that movie star you got on your payroll. But they've got secrets of their own. You might not like them so much if you knew what they were really like."

"Neither of them has murdered innocent people."

He sneered. "Maybe you should ask them about that. As for innocent? Do you honestly believe anyone is innocent? That Negro I hired to break into the Browns' house. How many times do you think he was in and out of jail? It was only a matter of time before he murdered someone himself. And that co-ed in the antique store in her tight little skirt and sweater. Just asking for it. She certainly wasn't innocent."

"What about Louise Brown?"

His face creased in lines of pure hatred. "She's the most guilty of all. Her family didn't think I was good enough. She should have chosen me over them. But in the end, she was just like all the rest. She ruined my life. Poisoned everyone against me. I should be living in that house on Crescent Avenue. Me. I would be running this goddamn town, if it weren't for her lies. Do you have any idea what that's like? To spend your life being dismissed as a nobody?"

Penelope smirked. "I may have some inkling of that."

"I doubt it." He took a step forward.

Penelope held up the gun. "Don't. I'm not letting you inflict your nightmare on me."

He laughed again. "See, I knew you were weak. I knew you wouldn't shoot." His upper lip curled in a way that made Penelope's skin crawl. "Maybe it's because you want to know more about me. Maybe you're intrigued by me, by what I can do. I already know your name, Penelope Drake. Why don't you ask me mine?"

Penelope fought the urge to back away. She said the one thing she knew would break his smug façade. "Because your name doesn't matter."

He flinched.

"It's going to matter to you very soon," he growled through clenched teeth as he held up the book in his hand. Without a word from him, the book burst into flames. What was left drifted to the floor as white ashes. When he spoke again, his voice took on a different timbre, like a car on a gravel driveway. "My name is Roy Arnold, and I am the nightmare."

Penelope pulled the trigger on the .22. Two shots rang out. Both bullets struck him point blank in the forehead.

Nothing happened.

The bullets fell to the floor without even leaving a mark. Arnold lunged toward Penelope, but before he could reach her, the door burst open, and Zed flew into the room, tackling him to the floor.

Bertram took Penelope by the arm and pulled her toward the door. "We should go get help."

She jerked away. "I'm not going anywhere."

With an inhuman roar, Arnold threw Zed off, sending him halfway across the room. Zed hit the floor hard enough to shake the bookshelves. Arnold scrambled to his feet, hatred in his eyes.

"Penelope, don't be stupid," Bertram said.

"Who do you think is going to help here?" Penelope snapped. "The police? The fire department? I'm staying, Bertram. You can run if you want, but I won't leave Charles and Zed."

Zed raised his arms to block Arnold's attack. He repelled the older man, but it was clear Arnold's age wasn't going to work in Zed's favor. Arnold came at Zed again and again, every new blow sending Zed staggering backward.

"Just what do you think you're going to do?" asked Bertram.

Penelope scanned the room. "I'll think of something."

Zed and Arnold collided with Charles' worktable, scattering his tools everywhere. Zed rolled away from the table just before

Arnold's fist came down, smashing the piece of furniture to pieces.

Charles groaned. Penelope dashed toward him, leaving Bertram's protests behind.

"My books," Charles said as Penelope knelt beside him. "He burned up my books."

Penelope tentatively placed a hand on top of his. "I'm so sorry, Charles. I didn't know what I was asking you to do."

Charles' gaze followed Arnold and Zed as the older man shoved Zed into a bookcase. Books rained down over both of them. "He's possessed. He invited the nightmare inside him."

Penelope's face grew hot with anger. She wasn't about to let Charles or Zed die. For her, there was only one question. "How do we get it out?"

Charles shook his head weakly. "You don't."

Arnold's features didn't even look human anymore. His eyes were sunken and hollow. He twisted his mouth—lined with sharp teeth—into an inhuman grin. He backhanded Zed across the face and sent him to the floor again. Zed struggled to stand, fatigue etched in his features. Arnold, on the other hand, showed no sign of slowing down. He grabbed Zed by the collar of his shirt and hurled him across the room, narrowly missing Bertram, who scuttled around the room's periphery toward Penelope and Charles.

Arnold made his way to where Zed lay trying to push himself up from the floor. He put a knee on Zed's chest and wrapped his hands around Zed's neck. Zed gasped and trashed his hands and feet, attempting to throw Arnold off, but there wasn't any point. Arnold, after all, had the strength of a demon. Zed's struggles became weaker as Arnold's grip tightened.

Bertram stared wide-eyed, his hands shaking. Briefly, his gaze met Penelope's. Then he swallowed, squared his jaw, and with a look of determination, he charged at Arnold. What he lacked in Zed's grace, he made up for in brute force. His foot connected with Arnold's jaw and sent him sprawling into the wall.

Unfortunately, within seconds Arnold was back on his feet.

Zed all but forgotten, he appraised Bertram with a crazed and hungry look. Taut muscles strained the seams of his clothes. His eyes glowed yellow from the bottom of deep, black sockets. Claws grew from the tips of his fingers. At some point during the fight with Zed, his shirt had been ripped open, revealing a pendant on a chain around his neck. A blood-red stone in the center glowed, casting ominous shadows across Arnold's face.

It reminded Penelope of Louise's brooch.

Bertram stepped back and stumbled over a large book lying face down on the floor. His ankle turned, and he went down. He tried to stand, but when he put weight on the ankle, his face contorting in pain. He resorted to dragging himself backward along the floor as Arnold advanced on him, mouth drawn into a wide lizard grin.

"I can't feed off the colored magician or this movie star here," he said as he slunk closer, "but you and the girl, you're a different matter entirely."

Penelope picked up a book from the floor and flung it at Arnold. The heavy volume hit him square in the head. He stood stunned for a moment before he turned his attention to her, his face contorted in rage. Penelope did the only thing she could think to do. She threw another book at him, and then another.

"Fine," he growled after batting both books away, "since you insist, I'll take you first."

Charles' X-Acto knife lay near Arnold's foot. She dove for it and scooped it up from the floor. Fingers wrapped white-knuckle tight around the handle, she pointed toward the night-mare-man.

Arnold sneered and licked his lips with a forked tongue. "You saw what good two bullets did. What makes you think a tiny knife is going to work any better?"

In the instant he leapt at her, she drew the blade of the X-Acto knife across her palm. A line of bright red blood immediately welled up. As one of Arnold's clawed hands closed around her neck, she grabbed his ruby pendant with her bleeding hand.

At the same time, Charles muttered a single, unintelligible word.

Arnold shrieked and drew back. Shadows leapt out from the pendant and surrounded him, obscuring his form. His screams echoed through the room, becoming wilder, more desperate, until eventually they faded away. When the shadows dissipated, Arnold was gone.

"Where did he go?" Bertram asked.

"The nightmare claimed him," Charles said as he pushed himself up to a sitting position. He gritted his teeth in obvious pain. His voice was hoarse and dry. "All of him. Wherever he is, death would have been a better fate."

Penelope pressed down on the cut in her palm. "What about the nightmare? Is it gone, too?"

"Without him tethering the demon here? Probably," Charles said.

Bertram's eyes grew wide in panic. "Probably?"

"Someone, somewhere will make the same mistake he did and bring the nightmare to this side of the Veil again." Charles surveyed the ruins of his makeshift workshop. "Why do we even try when it's so obvious we'll never learn?"

Penelope had the impression his question didn't entirely have to do with Roy Arnold. Bertram followed Charles' gaze and seemed on the verge of asking his own—likely inappropriate— question when Zed groaned and sat up.

"Is it over?" he asked, looking around the room.

Penelope nodded. "It is. That thing ate him from the inside out."

"Well, better him than me."

Bertram looked sidelong at Zed. "You didn't learn to fight like that in the army."

Zed shook his head. "Nope, never was in the army."

Bertram frowned. "How'd you manage that?"

"Bum knee," Zed replied, patting his leg.

"Your knee doesn't look so bum to me."

Zed shrugged. "It got better." Then he winced and grabbed his side.

"You might have a few broken ribs right now, though," Penelope said. "You need to get to a hospital." Her gaze went to Charles' cuts and bruises, Bertram's swollen ankle, and her own cut hand. "I guess we all need to get to a hospital."

9.

ertram and Penelope stared at one another across the table in a booth at the Carolina Drive-In. Neither of them had said much of anything since sitting down. When the waitress brought out their burgers, she eyed Penelope's bandaged hand and Bertram's crutch. She continued staring at them even after she went back to the counter.

"How's the hand?" Bertram asked, handing Penelope his tomato slice.

Penelope handed him her pickle wedge. "Better. I cut myself a little deep, but luckily I didn't need stitches."

Bertram nodded. "Glad to hear it."

"How's the foot?"

"Feels like it's about to fall off, but the doctor says that's normal for a bad sprain. The swelling should go down in a few days."

Penelope attempted a weak smile. "At least it's not broken."

Bertram grimaced. "Thank goodness for small blessings, I guess."

"It looks like Zed and Charles are going to be okay, too, by the way. They each had a few broken ribs, but that was the worst of it."

Bertram grunted. "Good for them."

Awkward silence remained the rule as they ate. Penelope could tell Bertram was working up to something by the way he kept picking up his hamburger, hesitating halfway to his mouth, and putting it down on the plate again.

Penelope pointed to his burger with a French fry. "Something the matter?"

Bertram frowned. "What? No. I mean yes, but not with the burger. Look, I just … I just need to know everything I saw was real." He bent forward over the table. "This is really the world you live in?"

Penelope sighed. "More or less."

"And here I thought you just spied on cheating husbands." He leaned back and stuffed a handful of fries in his mouth.

"I do that, too. Mostly that. But sometimes a person's secrets aren't so straightforward."

Bertram glanced over his shoulder at the waitress, who still stared. "Speaking of secrets, Roy Arnold seemed to think Zed and Charles are keeping a few of their own. He also said he—or I guess that nightmare thing—couldn't feed on them. What did he mean by that?"

Penelope took a gulp of her milkshake. "I don't have a clue." Arnold's statement bothered her, too, more than she'd like to admit.

"You going to ask them about it?" He dragged his burger through the ketchup on his plate before he took a bite. He was the only one Penelope had ever seen eat a burger that way. He'd done it since they were kids.

Penelope shrugged. "If they have things they want to talk about with me, they will. Otherwise I figure it's none of my business."

Bertram held her gaze. "So, you trust them."

"Of course. With my life."

"You even buy Zed's story about the bum knee? You think that's the reason he never went to Vietnam?"

"If that's what he says, then I believe him."

Bertram shook his head. "I'm not so sure."

Penelope could have brought up the "tennis elbow" that kept Bertram out of the army, but she didn't like where the conversation was going and took it upon herself to change course. "How's your mother?"

"Better." His mouth twisted in a crooked smile. "She was more worried about what the ladies in the bridge club would say than anything, but it seems like the nervous breakdown is a trendy thing right now. All her friends are falling over themselves to pay her visits and run errands for her. I'd almost say she was enjoying it." The smile faded. "Except …"

"I know."

Bertram looked past her, focusing on a point on the wall. "The bad dreams. It's a wonder she sleeps at all."

Penelope reached across the table and tentatively placed her hand on Bertram's. "She's stronger than you give her credit for. After all, she has to put up with having you as a son."

He glared, but the crooked smile returned. "Watch it now, Dreadful Penny."

Penelope returned the grin. "I'm feeling generous today, so I won't break your arm over that. Can we call a truce at least, seeing as you're going to be back home for a while?" She held out her open hand.

He grasped it. "You have yourself a deal there, Penelope."

———

Roy Arnold had lived in a small mill house in the Dunean community. From the outside, it looked just like all the other houses on the street, small but charming. The siding was painted a cheerful yellow, and it even had a white picket fence surrounding the front yard, the tiny patch of land dominated by an old oak tree.

Charles picked the lock on the back door and slipped inside. It was dark, and the air was cool. He found himself in the small kitchen, all spotless chrome and white Formica. He opened a cabinet to find it full of cans of soup. Another cabinet held nothing but tins of Vienna sausage. The refrigerator was empty.

Charles walked into the living room. Again, nothing was out of place. A sofa rested against one wall. A leather recliner sat in the corner. A bookshelf stood beside the front door. It held mostly paperbacks. A scan of the spines confirmed the books Charles was looking for weren't there.

The house had two bedrooms, neither of which looked like anyone had ever slept in them. After inspecting both, Charles still hadn't found what he'd come for. The books had to be there some-where, though.

As Charles stood in the middle of the larger bedroom, he closed his eyes for a moment and massaged his temples. Before Penelope arrived at his house, Roy Arnold had tortured him with visions of the Shrouded Man, sickly arms reaching for him, grave stench rising from tattered robes, face hidden in darkness. But the voice had nearly driven him insane, the whispers of every wrong thing he had ever done. Charles had no idea how Arnold knew about the Shrouded Man, but he aimed to find out.

When Charles opened his eyes, a figure stood in the doorway, a black woman, her hair short in the style of the 1920s. The flapper dress she wore, too, was from that decade. She looked at him over the top of a pair of tortoiseshell glasses.

Most importantly, though, Charles could see through her.

Sometimes ghosts appeared to him. They normally just stared at him, as if they expected him to do something. Maybe they did. Maybe the Shrouded Man was after them as well, or maybe he had already claimed them.

The ghost pointed up toward the ceiling. Charles glanced up to see a trap door. An attic. When he looked back at the doorway, the ghost was gone.

Charles pulled the string hanging down from the door. The door opened downward, and a ladder slid to the floor. Charles climbed up into the attic. He found them there, stacks and stacks of old books, many of them in dire need of repair. He reached for the nearest one, but pulled his hand back at the last second. His books were protected. Arnold would have been an idiot not to do the same. Still, he didn't sense any magic except what was written on the pages.

He picked up the book.

Nothing happened. Any spells of protection must have dissipated with Arnold's death. Like a child on Christmas morning, Charles happily spent the afternoon digging through the books. There were more than enough to replace the ones Arnold had destroyed.

10.

At eleven-thirty-two in the morning, Zed's phone rang. He rolled over in bed and knocked the receiver to the floor before fishing it up by the cord and groggily speaking in its direction. "Hello?"

"Hi, Zed," said a woman on the other end of the line.

He sat up. "Annie? Hi, it's been a few months."

"Yeah, I know. I just wanted to give you a call."

"It's good to hear your voice."

"Yours, too." She paused. "I've got some news. You know how you were always trying to get me to go back to school? I finally took up your advice. I applied to nursing school, and I got in."

"That's great, Annie! I'm happy for you." And he really was.

"Yeah, I'm excited about it. I start in August." Another pause. "The thing is, it's in Cleveland. I'm moving up there in a few weeks."

"I see." He managed to keep his voice even.

"I just wanted to say thanks, Zed, for everything. And maybe if you find yourself up that way, look me up. We can have a drink."

"I'd like that."

Zed could tell she wanted to say more but wasn't quite sure

what to say. "Well, I'd better be going. Got a lot of loose ends to tie up down here, you know."

Zed wanted to say more, too. To tell her he missed her. To ask her if she remembered the weekend trip they took to Myrtle Beach on the back of a borrowed Harley, or the night they saw the shooting star on top of Paris Mountain. To tell her part of him thought breaking up was a mistake. To tell her he really did love her, but he knew there wasn't anything more to say. "It was nice talking to you."

"Goodbye, Zed."

"Bye, Annie."

He hung up knowing, too, that they'd never have that drink.

11.

Dan was with another customer when Penelope walked into the shop. While she waited for him to finish, she wandered the maze-like path past the old dressers and tables, pictures and mirrors. It was an interesting life, she gathered, picking through the lives of so many others and selling them piecemeal. So much didn't survive. The conversations over the tables. The moment after the scribble in the old grammar primer. The reflections in the mirrors.

She was so lost in thought, she didn't realize the other customer had left until Dan was standing directly next to her. "See anything you're interested in?"

Penelope jumped. "Don't sneak up on me like that. You're likely to get an elbow in the stomach."

Dan chuckled nervously and took a step backward. "Noted for next time." He pointed to the table Penelope had been looking at. "That's a Shaker table. A hundred years old. Probably will last another hundred."

"Flattering that you think I can afford it, but I'm not here to buy anything today." She held up the brooch. "I actually came to give you something back."

His eyes grew wide. "How did you get that?"

"Long story. You don't want to hear it."

"I'll trust you on that one." He tentatively took the brooch from her hand. "How much do I owe you?"

She shook her head. "Nothing. You were never my client."

"Thank you." He grinned, a little less uneasily this time. "So next time I have trouble with a haunted piece of jewelry?"

"You know how to get in touch."

———

Ephraim slid Penelope a check across her desk for an amount larger than she had ever been paid. "Thank you, Penelope, for everything you did for my family."

Penelope picked the check up and stared at it. "Well, I would say it's my job, but honestly, I wasn't expecting any of what happened. Zed and Charles deserve a lot of the credit."

"Then please let them know I thank them as well."

She bit her lip. "Ephraim, I could take this check and say thank you, have a nice life, but it would be wrong of me to do that."

He shot her a look of supreme skepticism. "You don't want it?"

She folded the check in half and slipped it into the drawer of her desk. "Oh, no, I'm taking the check, but I have to warn you. Roy Arnold didn't come into that much magical power overnight. Someone had to teach him to do the things he did, to stoke his anger. This is bigger than someone just trying to get revenge on Mrs. Brown."

Ephraim nodded and smiled the way someone might smile at a misguided puppy. "Your concern is appreciated, Penelope, but it isn't warranted. This Roy Arnold person was obviously deranged. He likely spent years planning his revenge. Plenty of time to learn to do the things he did."

Penelope didn't know what reaction she was expecting, but certainly not that one. She took a long moment to reply. "Still, I think it would be a good idea for you to be careful, Ephraim."

He pulled up the sleeve of his shirt to reveal a charm bracelet similar to the one Charles had made for her. "I promise you, we're all being careful."

She tried to get a better look at the bracelet, but he covered it up again too quickly. "That charm bracelet was made by the same person who used a pendant to put Mrs. Brown into a magical coma. Who is it?"

Ephraim drew his mouth into a thin line. "Someone I employ from time to time."

Penelope's nose twitched. That was the wrong answer. "Someone who knows magic. Someone *else* who knows magic."

That condescending smile again. "Penelope, I didn't get to where I am today by betting all my money on a single hand. Let's just leave it at that. I know how to take care of my business." He put an edge into that last sentence, one Penelope had never heard from him before. She was beginning to understand what might have frightened her father. "Now that this bit of nastiness is over," he continued, "we'd love to have you over for dinner sometime. It's been too long since we've all gotten together."

Penelope wanted to argue the point some more, but she pushed down the urge. "Thanks for the invitation. I'll think about it."

He stood to leave. "Seriously, Penelope. Any time."

"We haven't seen the end of this, have we?" she asked the seemingly empty room once Ephraim was gone.

One knock.

UNSETTLED SPIRITS

A DREADFUL PENNY NOVELLA

1.

MONDAY, JULY 10, 1972

Rumors are the lifeblood of society. They are the ties that bind.

Steve and Cheryl are getting married.

Awfully fast, isn't it?

Well, you didn't hear this from me, but …

If you ever meet someone who says they don't gossip, they're either lying or they've lived in a hole in the ground their whole lives. Who can resist the siren call of *you'll never guess what I heard*?

Boyd and Pam are getting a divorce.

I heard he fell off the wagon again.

I heard she caught him stepping out on her.

Everyone talks, and if you think they don't talk about you, then you're wrong. Rumors don't discriminate. Rumors don't care about class or sex or color.

Hey, did you hear about Dave?

Yeah, saw him leaving his office with all his stuff in a box.

You know why he got fired, don't you?

But you know what's worse than everyone talking about you?

No one talking about you.

———

There's no such thing as ghosts, Bobby told himself. They were just joking about the warehouse being haunted, something to scare the new guy. Still, as he counted off the rows until he came to the one he wanted, he couldn't help but notice how deserted this part of the warehouse was. He caught himself glancing over his shoulder more than once.

He needed to find a part, a crankshaft that would fit a 1963 John Deere 1D10T. Everyone else was grabbing their stuff out of their lockers, getting ready to clock out and go home, but not the new guy. Apparently, this part had to go out via special delivery that evening to a customer in Greensboro, and being the low man on the totem pole, the job fell to Bobby.

But after about twenty minutes of wandering back and forth along the row, searching the giant shelves in vain, it occurred to him maybe they were playing another joke on him, sending him after a fake part. Come to think of it, Lloyd was looking awfully smug while Gerald, the floor supervisor, told Bobby what he needed to do. Up until then, he had never heard Gerald put more than two words together.

If he didn't need the money so badly, he probably would have quit right then. Working the warehouse at the Brown Tractor & Farm Supply Co. wasn't his first choice. It wasn't even in the top ten, but given his spotty employment records of late—not his fault at all—they were they only ones who would hire him.

After another few minutes of scanning the shelves without any luck, he was ready to throw in the towel. He'd just have to go back and tell Gerald he couldn't find the part for the 1D10T. If Lloyd was still there, he might wipe the stupid grin from his face, too. Bobby—who prided himself on being a good judge of character despite what happened at his last job—definitely didn't like Lloyd. He talked too much. It didn't matter if anyone else participated in the conversation, Lloyd would carry the whole damn thing himself. It didn't help either that Lloyd smelled like a giant reefer most of the time. He didn't even have the common decency to share.

As Bobby turned to walk back to the front of the warehouse, only the quiet whir of the air conditioning and his own footsteps on the concrete floor broke the silence. *Strange*, he thought, because he should have heard the other guys talking.

He never expected the child's laughter.

Startled, he glanced around, but nothing seemed out of the ordinary. He shook his head and swore at himself under his breath. That was when the lights went out.

"Hey, y'all!" he called out. "Not funny anymore. Turn the lights back on."

No one answered. Thanks to the long days of summer, the sun hadn't yet set. Shafts of sunlight punched through windows high above. He could still make his way back, though plenty of deep shadows escaped the light's reach.

The child's laughter echoed through the warehouse again. Bobby spun around. Half disassembled tractors and machine parts loomed from the darkened corners of the building and sent his mind off in directions he'd rather it didn't go. Out of the corner of his eye, he thought he saw a shadow move. He froze, one leg extended mid-stride, ready to run like hell if he had to. His heart pounded as he fought to control his breathing.

Another shadow stirred, followed by more high-pitched giggles. A small voice in the back of his head told Bobby something wasn't right, but his curiosity overcame his fear. He followed the shadow and the laughter, until he saw a little boy running between the shelves in a patch of failing sunlight.

"Hey," he called out. "What are you doing back here?"

The boy didn't pay attention. Instead, he climbed on one of the defunct tractors, all the while squealing and laughing.

"Hey, stop that." Bobby stepped toward the tractor. "You'll get hurt."

The boy turned toward him. He couldn't have been any older than three. He was dressed in shorts and a tee shirt, with knee socks and a pair of black and white saddle oxfords. His dirty blond hair was cut into bangs across his forehead. Bobby took a step forward. Laughing, the boy hopped down and ran off again.

Bobby hurried after him. He caught sight of the boy in the next row and sprinted to the end to try to catch up with him. When he did, he found the boy climbing on top of another half-stripped tractor.

"Be careful, you could fall off," Bobby yelled.

The boy looked up, apparently startled. He lost his footing and tumbled off the hood of the tractor, hitting the concrete floor. There was no crying, only silence. Bobby stood for a moment, stunned, before he remembered to breathe. He rushed over to see if the boy was okay, but the toddler wasn't there. He scanned the floor all around the tractor. There was no sign of the boy anywhere.

Another sound echoed in Bobby's ears, a low moan. At the edge of his vision, he glimpsed a different shadow moving beside a nearby shelf.

"Hey, little boy, are you there? Is that you?"

No answer, no laughter, just another low moan that sent chills up his spine. He eased his way toward the shelf. The boy couldn't have crawled there without him seeing, even in the dim light. He wished he had a flashlight.

As he neared the shelf, he called out again. "Little boy, are you okay? Did you get hurt?"

The moaning grew into a full-blown shriek. Bobby stumbled backward and nearly lost his balance. When he turned toward the shelf again, something gazed back at him with glowing green eyes.

The shadow-thing flowed from the shelf like water and rematerialized in front of him. Bobby couldn't run, couldn't scream.

Vaguely human-shaped, the shadow-thing stood at least ten feet tall. The two glowing green dots where its eyes should have been bore into him. He squeezed his eyes shut, but it didn't do any good. The thing ripped through his brain, through his soul.

An arm reached out and clamped down a massive clawed

hand around his shoulder. Its grip was ice cold. The temperature in the room dropped. Bobby's breath came out in white puffs. The shadow sucked the heat out of him as it pulled Bobby closer.

He struggled against the shadow-thing, but he might as well have been fighting gravity. He came inches from being engulfed when the thing mercifully stopped.

Seconds later, though, he wished he'd just been pulled inside.

It spoke. He couldn't understand any of the words, but he knew what the thing said nonetheless. Its words were cruel and sharp and harsh. Cutting words. Tearing words. Biting words. It spoke of pain and despair and death.

The shadow released him, dissipating like smoke, leaving Bobby alone among the shelves. As soon as he could use his legs again, he ran. Unfortunately for him, what light remained was rapidly fading, and he didn't see, of all things, a crankshaft lying in his path. He tripped over it and went sprawling, smacking his head on the cold, hard floor. He struggled to get back on his feet, but his head swam. He couldn't push himself up. Blackness crept in from the edges of his vision, and he collapsed back to the floor.

His last thought before the darkness took him was of the little boy's playful laughter.

2.

Penelope pulled her black Lincoln into the parking lot of the Brown Tractor & Farm Supply Co. It was only ten o'clock in the morning, but the heat was already making the air above the asphalt parking lot wavy. She let the car idle for a moment before turning it off.

"Everything okay?" asked Zed from the passenger seat.

The building, a hodgepodge of brick, glass, and corrugated metal, loomed in front of them. Penelope thought back to the last time she'd been there, a few months earlier. It felt like years. "Does something seem … off to you?"

Zed squinted and peered through the windshield at the front of the building. "Now that you mention it, things seem a little quiet for a Tuesday."

She nodded. "They do, don't they?"

"Any idea why Bertram wants to talk to you? Think someone's stealing from the till? Maybe someone trying to pass off counterfeit tractor parts? Do you think you could tell counterfeit tractor parts from real ones?"

Penelope rolled her eyes. "If it was anything like that, he wouldn't have called me."

Zed nodded. "You're right. There's probably some sort of

federal agency that regulates tractors and ploughs and scythes and the like. I'm sure they have agents fighting twenty-four hours a day against the international cartels trafficking counterfeit tractor parts. Sounds like an idea for a TV show."

Not for the first time, Penelope wondered about Zed's mental state. "I just meant he'd hire a normal private investigator for something like that."

Zed smirked. "Where is he going to find one of those?"

Penelope punched him in the arm. "There are a few around. Greenville's not *that* small a place. After what happened back in May, though, I'm expecting Bertram wants to talk about something a little less … mundane."

"So how are we playing this? I didn't think you and Bertram were on the best of terms."

She shrugged. "We've come to an understanding. And the way we're 'playing this' is that you are letting me talk and keeping your mouth shut."

Zed grinned. "I make no promises."

She raised an eyebrow. "I mean it, Zed."

The grin diminished. "I though you enjoyed my rapier wit."

"Is that what that is?"

Zed clutched his heart. "I'm hurt, honestly."

"You're supposed to be my assistant, Zed."

"I am. Part-time."

"I can make that no-time if you want," Penelope teased. "Look, I know I said Bertram and I had an understanding, but things are still a little touchy. Not everyone appreciates your clever banter like I do." She opened her door. "Now come on and assist. Quietly."

Bertram Brown was seated at his desk when Penelope and Zed walked into the main office. He pored over a ledger, pencil tucked behind his ear and an adding machine at the ready by his side. Without glancing up, he waved them over to the two chairs set up in front of his desk. Another minute passed while he scanned the columns and rows of the ledger, frowning and occasionally making marks with his pencil.

Wood paneling. Overstuffed filing cabinets. Dead potted plants. At least in here nothing had changed, except a different half-dressed woman perched on top of a tractor smiled out of the calendar hanging on the wall over Bertram's head.

Penciling in one final mark, Bertram put the ledger down and raised his head. "Thanks for taking the time to come over, Penelope. I really appreciate it."

Zed cleared his throat.

Bertram eyed him. "You too, Zed."

Zed nodded. "Any time, Bertram."

"How's your mom doing?" Penelope asked.

Bertram shrugged. "Better. Most days, she's able to convince herself everything that happened was a bad nightmare, but there are still some days when I find her sitting in the living room just staring out the window."

In May of that year, a vengeful ex had used a cursed brooch to get back at Louise Brown for supposedly ruining his life. The ghost bound to the brooch assaulted her mind and her soul for days until Penelope, Zed, and their magically adept friend Charles were able to exorcise the malicious spirit. She'd be dealing with the scars from that experience for a long time to come, if not for the rest of her life. Not exactly what Bertram needed to hear at the moment, though.

"Hopefully there won't be too many more days like that," Penelope said. "At least he can't hurt her anymore."

They'd dealt with the vengeful ex, too, though it cost them all their own emotional trauma before it was over, along with some cuts and bruises and broken bones.

The corner of Bertram's mouth twitched. The lines around his eyes were deeper than Penelope remembered. He'd also lost a few pounds. "Yeah, that's the good thing, I guess."

"What did you want to talk about, Bertram?"

Penelope's question seemed to bring him back from wherever his thoughts had taken him. "We had an accident last night. New guy named Bobby Parker. He's only been working here a week. They found him lying on the floor. Looks like he smacked his head pretty hard. We got him to the hospital, but we can't figure out what happened."

"What was he doing right before he got hurt?" Penelope asked.

"Truthfully? The other guys were playing a trick on him, told him it was an emergency and he needed to go get a part for a John Deere One-D-Ten-T right away."

Zed frowned. "What's the joke there?"

Bertram rolled his eyes. He grabbed a scrap piece of paper and scrawled on it with his pencil. Then he held up the piece of paper for Penelope and Zed to see.

1D10T.

IDIOT.

"Get it now?"

Penelope crinkled her nose. "Kind of a cruel joke, don't you think?"

Bertram waved away her concern. "It's just guys ribbing each other. It's harmless."

"Except this time, it wasn't," Zed added.

Bertram glared. "Like I said, we don't know how he got hurt."

"Do you think someone attacked him?"

Bertram pressed his hands together in front of his face. He wore a leather bracelet on his right wrist. Penelope had seen one exactly like it, on the wrist of his father, Ephraim. She assumed bracelet was charmed to ward off dark magic, one of the precautions the family had taken since the incident.

He took a deep breath. "I think *something* attacked him."

Penelope had an inkling of why the warehouse didn't seem to be as busy as it should have been. "What makes you think that?"

"When Bobby came to, he started babbling nonsense, talking

so fast all his words ran together. He was flailing his arms around, screaming and yelling about divine retribution, fire and blood raining from the sky, judgement for everyone. Then he started speaking in fucking Latin. They had to sedate him."

"You sure he's not Catholic?" Zed asked.

Bertram barked a laugh. "Bobby Parker has more of a chance of knowing an alien from Mars than a member of the Holy Roman Catholic Church. Trust me on that."

Penelope's sense of dread was growing. "What is it you want us to do?"

"Help me figure out what's going on." Bertram jabbed a finger in the direction of the warehouse. "I can't even get half my guys to show up for work now."

He let his shoulders slump and leaned back in his chair, covering his face with his hands again.

Penelope had known Bertram pretty much her whole life. She'd seen him stressed before, but never so haggard. "Where's your dad, Bertram?"

He sat up again, picked up his pencil, and twirled it between his fingers absentmindedly. "He's ... taken a step back from the business. He started handing things over to me after what happened to Mom. He said he needed to take some time for himself."

"So, you're running the day-to-day by yourself?"

"Pretty much. I was already running most of it before, to be honest."

Penelope wondered if taking over the family business was what Bertram wanted to do, or if anyone had even asked him. "Anything else we need to know about?"

Bertram stood. "Yeah, but this is something you have to see for yourself."

He ushered them through a door in the back of the office. On the other side, fluorescent lights illuminated row after row of shelves laden with tractor parts and other pieces of farm machinery.

Bertram led them into the heart of the warehouse. The looming shelves made for strange shadows. Penelope began to imagine the warehouse as a sort of tractor mausoleum, holding the deceased remains of the departed farm machinery, at peace in eternal slumber. She blamed Zed for inspiring that ridiculous train of thought. She glanced over at him, but he had the best poker face of anyone she knew—when he wanted to anyway. She couldn't get any sort of read on his opinion of the situation.

Finally, Bertram came to a halt. When he stepped aside, Penelope and Zed exchanged looks. This time she knew without a doubt what her assistant was thinking.

Someone had drawn a pentagram inscribed in a circle on the floor. Symbols and words clustered where the lines intersected. In the center lay what looked like a splatter of blood. Zed raised his Polaroid camera and snapped a few pictures.

"This," Bertram said, "is the real reason I called you."

———

"Does Bertram know you're here?"

Ephraim Brown didn't look up as he slowly peeled the label off his bottle of beer. He had offered one to Penelope, but she opted instead for a bourbon and Coke. They sat together at the kitchen table in his Crescent Avenue house. Ephraim had aged in the last two months. He seemed smaller, lesser. The charmed bracelet even hung looser on his wrist.

"Not exactly," she answered.

"I won't tell, then."

"It's not a secret, really. I can handle Bertram. I just didn't want to deal with the argument that would've resulted if I told him I was coming to see you."

Ephraim chuckled. "He is pretty hard-headed, isn't he?"

"You said it, not me."

Ephraim was there alone. Louise had gone out with a few of her girlfriends. The house, overshadowed by the giant maple trees outside, was dark and quiet. Penelope had played countless games of hide-and-seek among those trees with Bertram and the other neighborhood kids during her summer vacations, run through sprinklers, swum in the kidney-shaped pool in the back yard. Growing up, she'd always been a little bit jealous of Bertram, his house, and his complete family, but on that day, all the big empty rooms struck her as oppressive and lonely.

Penelope's father and Ephraim had been close friends since college, but sometime before her father's death, they'd had a falling out. Her father never talked about it. Ephraim didn't seem terribly eager to discuss what happened, either.

"Ephraim, I asked you before if there was anyone who might want to hurt you or your family. I need to ask you the same question again."

He shook his head. "The answer hasn't changed, Penelope. I can't think of anyone who might hate me or my family enough to want to go to so much trouble just to hurt us. God, I thought this was over when we took care of that Roy Arnold bastard."

Penelope took a sip of her drink, mustering all her strength not to remind Ephraim she'd warned him someone had to be working with Roy Arnold. She also refrained from pointing out that Ephraim didn't have anything to do with "taking care of" the bastard. "We'll do everything we can to find who's responsible for this, I promise."

"Thanks, Penelope. If anyone can get to the bottom of this, I'm sure you can."

"Anything you can tell me about Bobby Parker?"

"Never met him. Bertram hired him." His mouth twisted into a grin. "I didn't think they were playing that dumb prank anymore. I wonder if they told him about the ghosts first. That usually gets them good and keyed up before they get sent into the dark warehouse on a snipe hunt."

Penelope nearly spat out her drink. "Ghosts? For real? You're just now bringing this up?"

Ephraim held up a hand. "A building that old, you're going to have your share of stories about strange noises and weird shadows, but that's all they are. Just stories."

Penelope blurted out the next question before she could talk herself out of asking it. "Are you going to have your own magician go out and look at things?"

Her friend Charles, whom she'd know almost as long as she'd know Bertram, was the one who freed Louise Brown from the influence of the spirit in the brooch. Charles owned a library's worth of magical books, and he'd spent his life studying them, prying the secrets out of them. He was good, too. No one could negotiate the world beyond the Veil like Charles could.

Ephraim was all about hedging his bets, though, and had brought in another magic user to at least calm the spirit, even if he —or she—couldn't exorcize the angry ghost. The same magician had also made the bracelets Ephraim and Bertram wore. When Penelope demanded their identity, Ephraim refused to tell her.

He finished peeling the label off his beer and discarded it on the table. "Bertram wouldn't be happy if I … consulted."

"But it's still your company."

"It is, but Bertram's been running the day-to-day for a while now. He's good at it. He doesn't need me looking over his shoulder."

Penelope didn't need Zed's special talent for spotting bullshit to know he was lying. "Why the step back from the business?"

"Because the Brown Tractor & Farm Supply Co. has been a part of my life literally since I was born. I've never had another job, never had another purpose. And I'm tired. After what happened with Louise, I realized I needed to take a step back and reassess some things."

Penelope nodded, thinking of the day she'd come home and told her father she wanted to be a cop just like him. He did not react the way she expected. "Fair enough."

"One other thing, though, Penelope."

"What's that?"

Ephraim's gaze met hers. He straightened up in his chair and cleared his throat. "You may find yourself in the course of your investigation wanting to go down certain paths of inquiry. Just remember what you were hired to do, and don't stray from the path you're on." For a moment the old Ephraim returned, the Ephraim that scared her, just a little.

3.

After spending the morning having doors slammed in his face, Zed was beginning to regret convincing Penelope to let him talk to the warehouse workers.

———

"I'm going to need to interview your employees," Penelope said to Bertram after they returned to his office from viewing the pentagram.

Bertram raised an eyebrow. "All of them?"

"At least the ones working in the warehouse yesterday. They all had access to that area. Any of them could have drawn that pentagram."

"Really? Do you think so?" Bertram scratched his chin. "Penelope, most of them didn't even finish high school. Do you honestly think any of them could write out spells in Latin or whatever language those other symbols were from?"

"Enochian," Zed muttered under his breath.

Penelope crossed her arms. "Someone did."

"Maybe you should leave talking to the workers to me," said Zed.

She whipped her head around. "Why should I do that?"

"They might be a little more open to talking to me." Zed just hoped he'd cut the right wire to disarm that landmine.

"Because you're a man."

Zed winced. "I wasn't going to put it that way."

"He's right." Bertram slumped in his office chair. "They're not going to talk to you."

"They will if you make them." Penelope balled her hands into fists. "Come on, Bertram, I thought we were past this. You called me. Let me do my job."

"Penelope, I know these men. For the most part they are decent, hardworking people, but when you knock on their doors, they're just going to think you're selling Avon or handing out church flyers." Bertram held up a finger, preempting Penelope's protest. "I'm not saying they're right. I'm just telling you the way it is. You go in guns blazing and you're not getting any useful information out of any of them."

She glared. "Fine, then. Could you give Zed a list of who was working yesterday? I'm going to go talk to Charles after I make a stop first."

She never did tell Zed where she was going.

———

Zed pulled into the parking lot of the Brown warehouse. About half a dozen men were taking a smoke break near the loading dock. He pulled a cigarette out of the pack of Winstons in his glove box and strolled over to join them.

"Any of y'all got a light?" he asked, holding the cigarette up.

They immediately stopped their conversation, and Zed was faced with six hostile glares.

"Who are you?" one of the men asked, an older guy with a salt-and-pepper beard and a gut hanging over his belt.

Zed let his hand drop. "So, is that a 'no' on the light?"

"I recognize you. I saw you going into Mr. Brown's office yesterday," said another one of the workers. He was maybe in his thirties, with glasses and dark eyes that were just slightly too close together. "That girl was with you."

"Did Mr. Brown send you down here to talk to us?" asked a third. He had a baby face, with pale blue eyes and curly blond hair. "Because if he did, we got nothing to say."

The first one poked Zed in the chest with a meaty index finger. "You tell him if he wants to fire us, he needs to do it himself. Let him look us in the eye. I tell you what, things weren't like this when his dad was in charge. All that boy cares about is numbers."

"Fire you?" The reason Zed kept getting doors slammed in his face suddenly made a whole lot more sense. "I'm not here to fire you. Bertram—Mr. Brown—brought us in to try to find out what happened to Bobby Parker."

The older one took his finger away. "You telling the truth?"

"Absolutely. Why would I be here to fire everyone?"

"We heard rumors the company is in trouble," the baby face explained. "And then last month our paychecks were a day late. Some of the other guys were saying you were accountants or something, and you were telling Mr. Brown which of us to get rid of to save money."

Zed held his hands up. "I promise you I'm not here to do that at all."

"You say you're trying to figure out what happened to Bobby?" the one with the glasses asked. He pulled a lighter out of his shirt pocket and tossed it to Zed.

Zed lit his cigarette and tossed the lighter back. "Yeah. The name's Zed McKay." He held out his hand.

They all went around and introduced themselves. The older one's name was Lester. He'd been with the company the longest, almost twenty years. The one with the glasses was Martin, and the baby face was George. They'd both worked there for a little over five years.

"Anybody know anything about Bobby?" Zed asked. "Anybody see or hear anything weird or strange?"

They all shook their heads.

Zed took a long drag on his cigarette. "What about this 1D10T joke? Were any of y'all in on that?"

"I think we all helped a little with that," Martin said.

"Gerald was the one who sent him back into the warehouse though," George added quickly.

"Who's Gerald?" He wasn't on the list Bertram had given Zed.

"One of the managers," replied Lester.

"Is he here today?"

Lester frowned. "Come to think of it, I haven't seen him since Monday." He turned to the rest of the guys. "Have any of y'all?"

His question was met with shaking heads and a chorus of "no's."

"So, how did the rest of you help with the joke on Bobby?" Zed would tackle Gerald later.

Martin glanced around at the others, as if he were asking their permission to share. "We ... we told him about the ghosts."

Zed pulled on his cigarette too hard and choked. "There are ghosts?"

Lester chuckled. "Not really. But it's more fun that way." He turned to the others again. "Hey, you remember what happened with that Childress boy last year? Accidentally got his shirt caught on an axle sticking out from a shelf. Screamed like a girl and ran out of the warehouse. Ripped his shirt clean off."

He doubled over in laughter, and the rest joined in.

Zed flicked the ash off his cigarette. "So, the pentagram on the floor, that part of the joke, too?"

The laughter stopped.

"Probably some teenagers up to no good," said Lester, "breaking in and wanting to do mischief."

"You get teenagers breaking in a lot?"

"Not a whole lot," admitted Lester, "but it has happened."

The others nodded, but one of them wasn't agreeing as enthusiastically as the rest. A skinny guy with a wispy mustache, he'd introduced himself as Lloyd. Zed, ever since he could remember, had possessed the ability to sense the emotions of others.

Everyone else, when thinking about the pentagram, felt a combination of fear and guilt over what had happened to Bobby. Lloyd, though, wasn't just afraid. He was terrified.

"Well, thank you all for your time. You've been very helpful. I'll let you get back to your day. If any of you think of anything else, all you've got to do is tell Mr. Brown. He knows how to get in touch with me." He looked at Lloyd the entire time he was talking.

Zed turned to walk back toward Bertram's office. When he was about twenty paces off from the group, a voice called out behind him. "Mr. McKay." Zed grinned slyly. He turned, expecting to find Lloyd, but was surprised to see George running after him. "Mr. McKay, I need to talk to you for a second."

"Sure," he said, "but please call me Zed."

George glanced over his shoulder at the rest of the group. Lester and Martin were absorbed in their own conversation. The others were all busy getting one last drag before going back to work. "What Lester said back there, about there not being any ghosts, that's not totally true."

Zed raised an eyebrow. "Oh, really?"

"Yeah," George replied. "There's this story. I never really paid much attention to it. Just thought it was made up, but now I'm not so sure. I guess one day a worker brought his son to work with him. He was young, maybe four. There was an accident, and the boy was killed. People have said they've seen him playing in the warehouse or heard him laughing."

Zed leaned forward. "Are you saying *you've* seen him?"

"I think. I don't know. Maybe?" George's face turned pink. He paused and took a deep breath. "It was last week, near the end of my shift. I was in the back of the warehouse when I heard something that sounded like a little kid laughing. I looked around, and I thought I saw a little boy peering around the corner at the end of the aisle, but it was kind of dark, and I couldn't really tell. Anyway, I looked away for a second, and whatever it was disappeared. I didn't really think any more about it. I was busy and tired and just wanted to finish up what I was doing so I could go home. I figured my mind was playing tricks, but now I'm not sure."

Zed nodded. "Thanks for letting me know."

The heat of the day had crept up on them. George wiped off the sweat beading up on his forehead with his sleeve. "So, what do you think happened to Bobby?"

"Not sure yet."

"He didn't just bump his head, though. There's something else going on, isn't there?"

Zed didn't see any reason to lie. "No, you're right. There is something else going on."

George glanced over his shoulder again. "Should we be worried?"

A thousand replies ran through Zed's head, none of which sounded very assuring. "Just don't go chasing after any ghosts," he said finally.

———

Back at the door to Bertram's office, Zed paused. Bertram was speaking with a man Zed didn't recognize. Arguing, more like it.

The man was older, with a full head of unnaturally black hair shellacked against his scalp. His three-piece suit barely contained his girth, and in the July heat, it had developed a few damp places. In the man's right hand, he held a Bible.

Zed paused to listen.

"Mr. Brown, this is not something to be taken lightly," the man said.

Bertram looked like he was about to burst a blood vessel. "Reverend, out of respect for your position, I have avoided the use of profanity, but for the third time, I'm asking you to leave. I assure you the matter is being handled."

The man gestured toward the warehouse. "But you are not equipped to deal with something like this."

Bertram twisted his mouth into a sneer. "And you are?"

He held the Bible over his head. "The Lord guides me. And He guided me here today. His Word will be my sword and shield."

"A sword and shield are pretty useless if you don't know how to use them," Zed said, stepping through the door.

Bertram and the man both turned their heads to look at him.

The man's plastered-on smile never wavered. "I'm sorry, sir, but this is a private conversation between me and the owner of this business."

Zed narrowed his eyes. "Sounds like the owner of this business doesn't want you here."

The man appraised him. "You know, I'm afraid I didn't catch your name."

"Zed McKay." He crossed his arms. "I'm afraid I didn't catch yours either."

"Reverend Lowell Purdue. Little Rock Southern Baptist Church. Several of Mr. Brown's employees are members of my flock."

Zed wrinkled his nose. He hated that term. "Well maybe you should do what Mr. Brown told you and tend to your sheep instead of trying to push your way into somewhere you don't belong."

The smile slipped, just a little. "Mr. McKay, I belong wherever the enemies of God are. I am prepared to battle this evil."

"And reap the publicity."

"I am here for His glory only."

Zed glanced out the window. A van had pulled into the parking lot. The doors opened, and two men climbed out, one with a camera and the other with a microphone. "Then why did you bring the television crew?"

"What?" Bertram stepped out from behind his desk. "Oh, hell no." He intercepted the newcomers at the door. "Get out of here now."

"Sir," the man with the mic said, "we just want your thoughts on the Satanic activity that's taken place here."

He was young, maybe just out of college, and clean-cut like a good Christian boy should be. *Probably went to Bob Jones University*, Zed thought. The cameraman wasn't so well-groomed, with messy hair and at least a day's worth of stubble. He'd have a hard time fitting in on the campus of the Christian university, but he'd be right at home at a Pentecostal commune somewhere.

"There is no Satanic activity," Bertram barked.

The Bob Joneser thrust the microphone in Bertram's face. "Then how do you explain the pentagram drawn on the floor of your warehouse?"

Bertram swatted the mic away and shoved the cameraman. "Out, before I call the police."

The cameraman stumbled backward. He glared at Bertram. "Hey, man, do you know how expensive this camera is?"

Bertram, already a dark shade of red, balled his hands into fists. Zed decided to step in before any blows could be traded.

"Okay you two, you heard him." Zed seized the two men by the arm and dragged them back out into the parking lot. They both tried to struggle, but neither could break Zed's grip.

"You can't handle members of the press like this," the man with the mic growled.

Zed rolled his eyes. "I don't see a news logo on the side of the camera, or the van for that matter. You're not press."

"We're independent journalists," he replied, jutting out his chin. "We're producing a documentary on the inroads Satanism has made into our society."

"Is that so, huh?"

"Aren't you concerned about the soul of our great nation?"

Zed squeezed the man's arm until he winced. "Am I concerned? Yeah, every day. Every time I see a story about children in this country going hungry, every time I see a story about a white man killing a black man just because of the color of his skin, every time I see a story about rich men sending poor kids off to fight in a war to make them richer, I am concerned. You want to make a documentary about Satan's inroads into our society, go make a documentary about those things. Or you know what, the Miss South Carolina pageant is this weekend. If you want to play journalist, you can always go cover that."

"But—"

"But nothing. Let me be very clear. You are not welcome here. The next time you show up, the police will be called. If you're stupid enough to come around after that, Mr. Brown will call me, and I will make you wish he had called the police."

Scowling, the two men skulked back to their van.

Just before he climbed inside, the Bob Jones boy turned and shouted at Zed, "God will prevail."

He slammed his door, and the van drove off.

Zed stalked back into the office. "Now as for you," he said to Reverend Purdue, "I will not lay hands on a man of the cloth, but I will again request on behalf of Mr. Brown that you leave, or he will have you arrested for trespassing."

The pastor's ever-present smile twisted into a haughty smirk. "Ephesians 6:12. 'For our struggle is not against flesh and blood, but against the rulers, against the authorities, against the powers of this dark world and against the spiritual forces of evil in the heavenly realms.'"

Zed was hoping he'd do that. "Luke 20:46 and 47 'Beware of the teachers of the law. They like to walk around in flowing robes and love to be greeted with respect in the marketplaces and have the most important seats in the synagogues and the places of honor at the banquets. They devour widows' houses and for a show make lengthy prayers. These men will be punished most severely.' You're not the only one who can quote scripture, Reverend. Do not play that game with me. You won't like the outcome."

Reverend Purdue's smile dissolved. He turned toward Bertram. "I'm warning you. You're taking the side of the Devil if you listen to this man."

"I'll take my chances," Bertram replied. "Now get the hell out."

With one last glare, Reverend Purdue stormed from the office.

"Thanks," Bertram said once the Reverend had left.

Zed watched out the window as the pastor peeled out of the parking lot in his powder blue Cadillac. "No problem. People like that always get my hackles up. I do enjoy putting them in their place."

"You think they'll give us any more trouble?" Bertram asked.

"If the Reverend Purdue's ego is any indication, he's not going to take too well to being embarrassed. He'll be back. Just let me and Penelope know when that happens, okay?"

———

The cicadas sang in the trees as Penelope climbed out of her car. The old farmhouse stood by itself in the middle of a field choked with weeds and tall grass. The air was hot and damp. Penelope's blouse stuck to her back as she made her way down the narrow path to the front door. Charles' house wasn't easy to find, even if you knew the way. A blind driveway off Piedmont Highway almost to the Anderson County line wound through the woods for what seemed like forever, until the trees suddenly fell away, opening up to farmland left neglected since at least the Great Depression and a white clapboard house, paint chipped and windows darkened. Charles had inherited the house from the woman who raised him, but that was all Penelope knew. Whether it belonged to her family or she bought it at some point remained a mystery for another day.

The shade on the porch provided only the slightest relief from the heat, but for even that Penelope was grateful. She hesitated before pushing open the door. Charles could be difficult. Sometimes he went for months without speaking to any of them, and the recent events with Roy Arnold would have given him every reason to retreat into himself again.

Still, though, Penelope had made a promise to herself that she wouldn't let him slip away from them and get lost in whatever dark place he went to sometimes. Besides, if Charles was in the back of the house where he normally spent most of his time, he wouldn't hear her knock anyway.

A fan blew in the front room. Bookshelves loomed all around her, lining every wall. In their confrontation with Arnold, he had destroyed more than a few of Charles' books, but to Penelope, the shelves appeared as full as ever, fuller even.

Penelope crossed the room and passed into the dining room, where she paused. Books were stacked five or six deep on the dining room table. Most of them were damaged in some way and in need of repair. Still, they were all remarkable, whether bound in leather or cloth, many with gold leaf on their spines. A few were open to elaborate illustrations that would make a Dutch master jealous. Penelope paused for another reason, though. Someone in the next room was singing, the room where Charles did all his book repairs. A deep, rich baritone resonated with the lyrics of "Swing Low, Sweet Chariot." Penelope couldn't help but stop and listen for a few moments.

When she finally pushed the door open to go into the room, she was shocked to discover that the singing wasn't coming from the record player Charles kept in the corner, but from Charles himself. He sat hunched over his work table. In front of him lay a piece of leather, its finished side down, and two pieces of cardboard.

He stopped singing when she came in but didn't act like he was embarrassed. "I was wondering when you'd stop by," he said.

"How did you know I was going to be paying you a visit?"

He motioned toward the newspaper on the floor by his feet. "Saw it in the paper this morning. Guy admitted to the hospital after an accident at the Browns' place of business. I figured it was just a matter of time."

"Do you think this is related to the Roy Arnold case?"

"How could it not be?"

Penelope watched as Charles brushed glue onto the pieces of

cardboard and fixed them on the leather to make a new book cover. Once he had the front and back panels set, he turned the cover over and began smoothing out the leather. "But you don't think he's … He can't be … He hasn't come back, has he?"

Charles shook his head. "No, Roy Arnold is gone for good. You don't trade with the demonic forces he did and come back. So, tell me what happened."

Penelope told Charles Bertram's story, beginning with the practical joke gone pear-shaped and ending with the pentagram drawn on the floor.

"Did you get a picture?" Charles asked.

Penelope fished the Polaroid from her purse and handed it to Charles. "Zed snapped one."

Charles studied the photo for a moment and then reacted by doing something she hadn't heard him do in a while. He laughed. She found herself happy to hear the sound, despite her confusion.

"That's not a summoning circle," Charles said, handing the photo back.

"What do you mean?"

"This pentagram wouldn't summon a pizza. It isn't real. This is from a movie or something. I'm not even sure that's real Latin. Someone's going to a lot of trouble to play a hoax. That's just not how things are done."

Penelope crossed her arms. "Well, Bobby Parker is in the hospital. That part isn't made up. There's obviously something going on."

"Oh, I'm not saying it's all a joke. Obviously, there's something sinister afoot, but there's no satanic cult calling up higher demons among the tractors."

"Do you think you could help out on this one?"

Charles went back to smoothing out the leather on the cover. "Is Bertram Brown paying?"

"He sure is."

"Then I'm in."

Penelope cocked her head to the side. "Really? That's it?"

Charles paused and looked at her. "Was there supposed to be more?"

"I didn't have to cajole you or bargain with you. Usually you make things a lot more difficult."

He shrugged. "I'm feeling generous."

Penelope still worried about Charles, but since the Roy Arnold incident, their friendship seemed to be on a surer footing. If only she could get Charles and Zed to bury the hatchet.

———

Penelope picked up the rock on her desk. She had painted it when she was eight to give to her father. The paint was a little chipped and faded, but the pictures were still mostly there. On one side was a sun, with a smiley face in red and wavy yellow and orange rays. On the other side was a tree with big green leaves. She tried to paint a squirrel in the tree, but it had come out as a brown smudge.

"Dad? Are you here?" she asked the seemingly empty room.

Silence.

It had been over a year since her dad was killed in a botched robbery and Penelope took over the family business. Some days she felt like she was doing pretty well at the reins. Other days, she wasn't so sure.

"Dad, I could use some advice right now. If you're here, I really need to talk to you."

The days after he died were fuzzy in her memory. She didn't remember when exactly her father's ghost first made himself known, but he had done it by moving the rock. The house, built around the turn of the century, was divided into two parts. Downstairs was the office for the detective agency. Upstairs was an apartment she and her father had once shared. Her father preferred the office.

He didn't respond to her question.

She let her shoulders slump. It looked like she wasn't going to get the pep talk she wanted. She sighed and put the rock back down on her desk. "Ephraim is in trouble again. Something attacked one of his employees. The guy's in the hospital in a coma. And if that weren't enough, someone drew a fake pentagram on the floor of the warehouse apparently trying to convince everyone Satanists are using it for demonic rites."

Silence.

"Ephraim's not being really helpful. Seems Bertram has pretty much taken over the business." She stood up and walked over to the window. "I've half a mind to ask him what when on that night all those years ago when you were in college."

One knock.

One knock meant "no" in the system they'd worked out. Penelope had never been able to figure out where the noise came from. This knock was so forceful, though, it shook the things on Penelope's desk. She turned back to face the room.

"Why not, Dad?" she asked quietly. "You're gone—"

One knock.

Even harder. The rock jumped. He was using up a lot of what limited energy he had.

"Okay, okay. I won't say anything to him if it's that important. But it makes it hard to help when you know he's hiding something. Who are you trying to protect anyway?"

She knew the answer. He was trying to protect her. Even from beyond the Veil, or wherever he was, he was still trying to keep her out of danger. The only problem was, the more she thought about it, the more she was convinced there was a connection between what was going on now and what happened all those years ago.

When they were in college, Ephraim and her dad and several of their friends had broken curfew by sneaking out of their dorm in the middle of the night. They'd wound up in the woods some ways out of town, and one of the other boys ended up getting hurt. Ephraim and her dad brought him to the hospital. Everyone else was expelled, but they were only put on probation because they hadn't abandoned their friend.

"Dad, one more question. Do you know who this magician is Ephraim has been hiring to do things for him? Did he ever mention anything to you?"

A pause. *One knock.*

It seemed almost hesitant. If she didn't know better, she would have thought her dad just lied to her. She was still contemplating that unsettling idea when she heard a different knock, this one at the front door. She found Zed on the porch.

"Get in here." She grabbed his arm and pulled him inside. "We need to talk."

"Why? What did I do?" Zed asked as he stepped over the threshold.

"I'm hoping you found out something important that cracks this case wide open because I tell you, my conversation with Charles this morning didn't go the way I was expecting."

"Really? Did he do that thing with his left eye when he's really annoyed, like it twitches really fast. Did he actually talk to you, or just glare at you until you're pretty sure you're going to die some horrible death?"

"No, that's not it. We had a very pleasant conversation, actually."

Zed stopped and looked at her sidelong. "You did?"

"We did." She walked past him into her office.

"This is Charles we're talking about."

Penelope sighed. "Yes, Zed. Honestly, I know he's difficult, but he's been through a lot, too. You could cut him some slack."

Zed frowned. "I will when he cuts me some."

Penelope knew better than to press her luck on that subject. "Well, what exactly *did* you find out today?"

Zed took his place lounging across one of the chairs in front of Penelope's desk. "One, rumor has it the company's in trouble. Everyone's afraid they're getting laid off. And two, there's a ghost, and I have reason to believe it's legitimate."

She let out a chuckle as she leaned against her desk. "Funny, because the pentagram's not."

Zed sat up straight in his chair. "What do you mean?"

Penelope shook her head. "You go first."

Zed huffed, making a grand showing of his disappointment before he told her about his conversation with the workmen on their smoke break, as well as George's possible encounter with the child ghost. He also told her about Reverend Purdue and the two "journalists." "I'm not sure where that gets us, but it gets us somewhere, right?"

Penelope sighed. "If out to sea counts as somewhere."

Zed twisted his mouth into a crooked grin. "Touché. What's this about the pentagram being fake?"

"That's what Charles said. Apparently, none of the inscriptions or symbols are real."

"Well, if this is all a hoax, then maybe it *is* one of the warehouse workers trying to get back at the Browns for something. None of them seem too happy with Bertram's management style."

"That doesn't explain Bobby Parker."

"Maybe he caught whoever drew the pentagram in the act."

"And the shouting in Latin?"

Zed wrinkled his nose. "Oh, that."

Penelope picked up her rock and held it in her hands. "I've asked Charles to help."

"Is he going to?"

"He said he would."

Zed took a deep breath and ran his fingers through his shaggy hair.

"Something the matter?" Penelope asked.

"Just thinking about Reverend Purdue and the camera crew." His expression darkened. "A bunch of goddamn hypocrites. They're just going to make getting to the bottom of this harder."

"We'll deal with them if we have to."

"I know. I just wish for once something would break our way."

"Now, you know as well as I do that's never going to happen because God has a warped sense of humor."

Zed's twisted grin returned. "He sure does, doesn't He?"

Something else was bothering him. Zed hadn't quite been himself since their run-in with Roy Arnold, but Penelope had been hesitant to bring up the subject. She was about to ask what was wrong when he headed her off, almost as if he knew what her question was going to be.

"There is one person I didn't get to talk to today. Gerald, the guy who was the manager the night Bobby Parker had his run-in with whatever it was. He didn't come in today. No one seems to be able to get hold of him."

"Guilty conscience?" Penelope asked.

"If we're lucky."

He stood. "I was going to pay him a visit at his house. Hopefully I'm not walking into a crime scene. I just wanted to let you know where I was in case you see me on the news tonight."

"Zed," Penelope called as he was leaving. "Be careful."

———

Zed surveyed the house as he pulled up. It was small, but the front yard was neat and appeared as if someone cared for it. Rose bushes full of big pink and red blooms lined the walkway to the front door. A swing hung from a branch of the oak tree shading the yard.

Nothing at all seemed out of the ordinary as Zed pushed the doorbell.

It bothered him.

Inside, footsteps approached the door. It opened to reveal a woman, short and pleasant-looking. Behind her a little girl peered out, probably around four or five years old.

"Can I help you?" she asked.

"Yeah, I'm looking for Gerald," Zed replied. "Is he here? He called in to work sick today."

She tried to maintain her smile, but her expression wavered. "You know, he's not really up for any visitors right now."

She was lying. Zed always knew when someone was lying. He could sense her guilt, too, and a little bit of sadness. "I'm sorry to hear that," he said. "I hope it isn't serious."

"Oh, no, it's only a head cold."

Just then, a pickup truck pulled into the driveway alongside Zed's ancient Pacer. A man stepped out wearing his Sunday suit. He was younger than Zed expected, mid-thirties at best. He was big, too, without being stocky. Zed suspected he'd be good to have on your side in a bar fight.

When he saw Zed, he froze. The fear, guilt, and shame practically radiated off of him. No doubt this was Gerald, miraculously recovered. Zed glanced back at his wife. She wouldn't look him in the eye.

Gerald walked fast toward Zed. He tensed up, in case Gerald decided to do something rash like throw a punch, but Zed didn't really sense any anger.

"You're the one Mr. Brown sent, aren't you?" he asked Zed. "You're going around asking everyone questions."

"That's me." Zed held out his hand. "Name's Zed McKay."

Gerald hesitated before shaking the offered hand. "Gerald Holloway."

"Mr. Brown sent me to talk with everyone who was working on Monday," Zed continued. "That's the last time anyone seems to have seen you."

Gerald bit his lip. "I ... I've been sick."

Zed glanced down at Gerald's suit. "Looks like it."

Panic flashed in the warehouse manager's eyes. "Please don't tell Mr. Brown, either one of them."

Zed cocked his head to one side. "Tell him what?"

Gerald's entire body slumped, as if someone let the air out. "I was interviewing for another job."

"Why?" Zed asked.

He glanced back up at Zed. "Are you going to say anything?"

Zed raised his right hand. "Scout's honor I'm not."

"I heard through the grapevine that there were going to be a lot of people laid off. Mr. Brown—Ephraim, I mean—hasn't been around lately, and a lot of people are saying the company is in trouble."

"So, you're looking to jump ship."

He shook his head. "I don't want to be disloyal, but I've got a family. I can't afford to go without a job."

"Your secret is safe with me, Gerald."

"Thank you."

"Provided you answer the questions I have."

"Whatever they are, I promise."

"I just want to know what happened on Monday. Were you the one behind the prank on Bobby Parker?"

Gerald scowled. "Not at all. It was Lloyd Baker who brought up the idea. The rest of them just went along with it. It's not like I could really stop them."

"Do they do that with all the new hires?"

"No, not really. Just the ones they see as easy pickings."

"So, Bobby Parker was easy pickings?"

Gerald scratched his head. "Come to think of it, not really, not like some of the others." A smile spread across his face. "There was one guy last year—"

"Got his shirt ripped off. Yeah, I heard about him."

"Bobby really wasn't like that, though," Gerald continued. "I mean he wasn't the brightest bulb, but he wasn't a pushover, either. I gather he'd gotten himself into some scrapes."

"Have you ever heard or seen anything in the warehouse that you couldn't explain?"

He tensed. "What do you mean?"

"Weird sounds? Strange shadows?"

"There are always weird sounds or strange shadows. It's a warehouse full of half-built tractors." Gerald shook his head. "I don't put much stock in all that weird séance, Ouija board stuff."

He was lying.

"What about that one time, Gerald?" his wife asked.

Gerald glared at her.

"Yeah, Gerald." Zed locked gazes with the man. "What about that one time?"

Gerald lowered his eyes to his newly polished loafers. "It's nothing."

"It was apparently enough to scare you pretty bad."

He looked back up at Zed. "How do you know that?"

"It's kind of obvious." To Zed, anyway. "So, tell me what happened."

Gerald sighed. "One night a few month ago, I had just gotten off my shift, but I forgot my car keys in my desk. I went back to get them, and I noticed the door to the front office was open. Mr. Brown was in there."

"Which one?"

"Ephraim Brown. I thought it was weird because all the lights were off. He was talking to someone. I couldn't see who, but he didn't seem happy. I couldn't really hear what he was saying, and being that it was none of my business, I turned around to leave, but just then, a strange wind blew through the warehouse and slammed his door shut. You know the feeling you get when someone scrapes their fingernails across a chalkboard? It felt like that in my head. I don't know how, but I knew that if I didn't leave right away something really bad would happen to me. So I ran out."

Zed nodded. "Thank you, Gerald. I promise I won't say anything to anyone about your interview." He offered his hand again. "I hope you get where you want to be."

Gerald smiled as he shook Zed's hand. "Thank you."

His smile was genuine, but he was relieved to see Zed go.

———

Charles had not dreamt of the Shrouded Man in over a month. It was the longest time in his adult memory the pale, emaciated man in death clothes had not come to him in his nightmares to taunt him with the promise of claiming him one day.

Charles used to believe the worst part of the curse was being claimed. Now he understood better. Not knowing was worse, not knowing when the Shrouded Man would come. Some days he wished for everything to be over, especially recently, with his visions of the Shrouded Man spilling over into his waking moments, seeing him in the fields around his house, in the shade of the trees. He hadn't yet seen him inside his home, but it was just a matter of time.

That summer, though, the Shrouded Man had not come when the sun set. Some small voice in the back of his head told Charles to be worried. But honestly, after living for so long with the nightly dream visits, the relief allowed him to easily ignore that voice.

Not that he ever let his guard down. Somehow Roy Arnold had known about the Shrouded Man and had taunted him with visions of the skeletal spirit. Charles paid a visit to the magician's house not long after their run-in and discovered his secret cache of magic books. He took them to replace the ones Arnold destroyed, and now he scoured them for any scrap of information about the Shrouded Man. For Charles, any bit of knowledge helped.

He sat cross-legged on the floor of his work room, a half-eaten sandwich and a forgotten glass of milk near one foot. Shirley Caesar sang "My Testimony" in the background. A fan pivoted from side to side, blowing air that wasn't exactly cool, but at least a little more bearable than the thick soup it would have been otherwise. He read through one of the books he had taken from Roy Arnold's house, written by a Frenchman traveling through southeast Asia in the nineteenth century.

The traveler encountered a village with the burned-out ruins of a small Catholic church at its edge, and adjacent to it, a tiny graveyard. French missionaries had come through and converted a handful of the villagers some thirty years or so earlier, he discovered, but when the church burned to the ground, all the new Christians scattered to other villages.

Walking through the village at dusk, the traveler noticed a man setting up a chair near the entrance of the abandoned graveyard. The Frenchman asked the man what he was doing. The man explained that someone had to guard the entrance to the graveyard every night, and that night, it was his turn. When the Frenchman asked why, the guard shrugged, as he had been just a small boy when the church burned, and no one ever told him why, only that someone needed to guard the graveyard. He showed the Frenchman the small silver cross they passed around for each of them to wear during their vigil.

Puzzled, the traveler asked others about the guard's stories. Most didn't know any more than the guard, and a lot of the older villagers simply wouldn't talk at all, but one older woman told him that shortly after the church burned, a man in a shroud began to attack those who walked by the churchyard at night. After several months of these attacks, someone found a silver cross in the dirt among the church ruins and used it to drive the thing back. They had put a guard up at the entrance to the graveyard every night since. The name of the village was Đien Tinh, a name that struck Charles as familiar somehow.

A noise from the next room distracted him. He shut the book quickly and put it back in its place. Charles expected another visit from Penelope, maybe Zed even, although judging from the thermometer, hell was far from freezing over.

He climbed to his feet and walked into the dining room. His visitor was not Penelope or Zed. A woman stood next to the dining room table, the same woman he had seen in Roy Arnold's house, or rather her ghost. She wore the same dress, too, a short, black flapper-style dress from the twenties. She was holding one of his books, actually holding it. As he stepped toward her, she looked up. A smile spread across her face, a very attractive smile. She put the book down and faded from view.

Charles ran over to the spot where the woman had stood. The

air was cool. It felt good after the heat of the day. Charles glanced down at the book the woman had been holding, a text in Latin by a seventeenth-century Dutch alchemist, part of Roy Arnold's collection. Charles had put it on the dining room table because it needed repairing. Its cover was flaking and crumbling in places, but the binding was good, so he hadn't made it a priority.

Maybe he should have. The apparition left it open on a page about communicating with the dead, something having to do with vibrations in metal. Electronic Voice Phenomenon three hundred years before the invention of the phonograph. An intriguing idea, but the woman intrigued him more. She had actually picked the book up.

4.

THURSDAY, JULY 13, 1972

The globe made one revolution every three and a half minutes. At least that's what the little plaque said. Penelope watched as it silently turned. Well, almost silently. The motor that made it rotate hummed quietly, practically the only sound in the entire library. The giant globe, six feet across, stood in the central atrium of the public library, flanked by two winding staircases that led up in sweeping arcs to the second floor.

Greenville was marked by a giant red square, bigger than the black markers for New York or Los Angeles or London or Tokyo. Funny thing, there were a lot of people who really did think that little city in the foothills of the Appalachian Mountains was the center of the universe. Nothing more important than Sunday dinners at Grandma's after church, Friday night football games, school bake sales. A picture-perfect Norman Rockwell scene. Why would anyone want to live anywhere else?

But as Penelope knew, scratch the surface, and the gilding comes off. You see what's real. Most everyone has something they want to hide from the world, even without taking into account the bona fide ghosts and demons.

Penelope had stopped by the library on her way from the Department of Public Records. Bertram Brown wasn't her only client, and tracking down people who—for various reasons—didn't want to be found still paid most of her bills. That morning she'd found yet another deadbeat dad, hiding in plain sight not five miles from where his children lived. She'd also found his boat, his lake house, and his Corvette. A pretty good day, normally, but she couldn't shake the idea that storm clouds were gathering.

The visit to the library wasn't helping like it usually did either. The quiet typically silenced all the voices in her head, but not on that day. They were all louder than ever, telling her she had no business doing what she was doing, that she was just playing at being a cop because they wouldn't let her be a real one. Her father's voice was in there, too, telling her there was more than one way to help people. He said that a lot after he left the police force himself.

The globe had almost made one complete turn, and Penelope was finding no answers in watching its quiet rotation, so she headed for the door, but before she reached it, she spotted a familiar face. Coming through the door was Dan Kowalczyk, the antique dealer who had unwittingly provided Roy Arnold with the haunted brooch he used to attack Louise Brown. His assistant Mary was the one who paid the price, though. Penelope wanted to think they had vindicated her. Still, she knew her death weighed on Dan.

She had meant to pay him a visit in the months since then, but something always seemed to get in the way. He hadn't noticed her yet. She was debating whether to talk to him or slip out another way when the decision was made for her.

The charm bracelet around her wrist grew warm, not painful, but enough that it startled her. She looked around. At first, she didn't see anything unusual, but then out of the corner of her eye, she noticed a figure lurking behind one of the staircases. The bracelet was supposed to ward against magic. It wouldn't have grown warm unless someone was directing magic at her.

She spotted Dan again walking toward the stacks and hurried

over to him. "There you are," she said in a stage whisper as she hooked her arm around his. "I've been looking all over for you."

"Penelope? It's been a couple of months." He glanced at her arm intertwined with his, but he didn't do anything to remove it. "How have you been?"

She laughed. "Oh, you're funny. I was only gone a moment." She lowered her voice even more. "Please play along. There's someone following me."

Dan's eyes grew wide. He started to look around, but Penelope jerked on his arm. "Well, you know, it's easy to get lost in here," he said a little too loud as he forced a smile.

Penelope pulled him back toward the globe.

"Where are we going?" he asked.

She didn't answer until they reached the spot where she saw the figure. "He was standing right here."

She wasn't even sure about the "he" part, though.

"How do you know he was following you?"

Penelope's gaze went to her charm bracelet. "He was … staring at me, acting suspicious."

Dan wasn't completely clued in on the reality of magic, and she didn't really feel like educating him.

"What did he look like?" Dan asked.

Penelope concentrated for a second. "Dark pants, dark shirt, baseball cap pulled over his eyes."

"Kind of like that guy?" Dan pointed to a man standing among the stacks.

Penelope followed Dan's gaze, and her heart skipped a beat. It was him. She still couldn't get a good look at his face, but as soon as she spotted him, he ran. Penelope went after him.

"Penelope," Dan called before remembering where he was.

She didn't answer, instead following the man farther into the stacks. It didn't occur to her until she was deep among the rows of shelves that she could very well corner herself. She managed to catch glimpses of the stranger in the spaces between the books, always a row or two away from her. She thought she had him when she rounded a corner and saw him standing at the other end of the long shelf, his back to her.

She expected him to double back on the next row, but instead, he stepped into the shelf itself, between the books, as if he pulled back a curtain and walked through a hidden door. Only his shadow lingered for a second or two before it also vanished.

A hand fell on her shoulder. She jerked away and jabbed an elbow into the person's stomach.

"Penelope." Her name came out as a sort of half gasp, half grunt.

Her heart sank. She looked to see Dan doubled over, clutching his middle. "Oh, God, Dan, are you all right? I'm so sorry."

"Guess I should have taken you seriously about that elbow to the stomach thing, huh?" he said as he slowly straightened up.

"I thought you were the man following me."

He grinned. "It looked more to me like you were chasing *him*."

"I lost him." She was still cursing herself.

"I'm almost afraid to ask, but the curiosity is killing me. Why do you think he was following you?"

She fingered her charm bracelet. "I'm not exactly sure."

"But you have an idea."

She nodded. "You know your haunted brooch?"

The wry grin disappeared. "How could I forget about it?"

"It's another problem like that."

Dan's expression darkened, little wrinkles of concern appearing across the bridge of his nose. He glanced around and then leaned in toward her. "Are you … in any sort of danger?"

"No more than I usually am."

He looked at her sidelong. "You should let me walk you to your car."

"Thanks, but I'll be fine."

"No, I insist." He offered his arm.

Penelope didn't move. "What did you come to the library for?"

He shook his head. "It can wait. Some research on a family I just bought a bunch of junk from."

She laughed. "Junk?"

The lopsided grin returned. "I mean priceless antiques. A fine addition to any home."

She didn't need him to protect her. He *couldn't* protect her. But she'd enjoy his company. "All right, fine. You can walk me to my car."

He offered his arm again, and this time she slipped her hand around the crook of his elbow. Together they walked toward the exit. Penelope couldn't help glancing back over her shoulder, though, toward the shadows cast among the stacks.

5.

Reverend Lowell Purdue showed up again two days later, and this time, he brought more than just the camera crew with him. He and about a dozen protesters marched on the sidewalk across the street from the Brown Tractor & Farm Supply Co. The protesters all held signs either heavily implying or directly stating that Bertram, Ephraim, and all the rest of those affiliated with their business were going to Hell for harboring Satanists. The Reverend, for his part, opted to wield his Bible and a megaphone, which he used it to hurl Scripture in the general direction of the warehouse.

Penelope and Zed had come to update Bertram on the current state of their investigation, such as it was. Now they were holed up with Bertram in his office, listening through the window to the muffled sound of the Reverend's yelling.

Bertram peered out the window between a gap in the closed blinds. "I called the police. They said there isn't anything they can do as long as the protesters stay where they are. They're not technically on the property."

"I could go give a few of them a shove in the right direction." Zed sprawled in one of the chairs in front of Bertram's desk, fiddling with a glass paperweight.

"And then they get to claim you assaulted them." Penelope

leaned against the edge of the desk, her arms crossed. "That's what they want, the attention. The best thing to do is ignore them."

The megaphone screeched as Reverend Purdue continued his tirade.

Zed grunted. "Good luck with that."

Bertram kept staring out the window. "Jesus, is he going to recite the entire Bible?"

"I'm pretty sure Jesus doesn't want you to bring him into this," Zed muttered.

"This is a nightmare." Bertram let the blinds fall back down and stalked to his desk. "My dad is going to kill me."

"Does he know about all this?" Penelope asked.

Bertram pointed at the window. "Did you see the circus out there? Purdue's got that goddamn camera crew with him again. The entire Upstate knows all about this by now. I'm sure Dad's already gotten a hundred phone calls."

Given what she knew of their mental states, Penelope wouldn't have been surprised to learn Ephraim and Louise were both sitting in the dark as their phone rang, neither of them picking up. "Still, don't you think it's weird he hasn't called you about it yet?"

"Don't think that hasn't occurred to me." Bertram's desk chair squeaked in protest as he fell into it.

Penelope placed a hand on his shoulder, which came off a lot more awkward than she intended. She ended up tucking both hands under her arms. "I think something's wrong with your dad, Bertram. It's more than just needing to take a step back from the business."

His gaze fell to the papers strewn across his desk. "I've lately come to that conclusion myself."

"What do you think it could be?"

Bertram shrugged. "You'd have to ask him."

Penelope sighed. She wanted to ask Ephraim about what happened at the University of South Carolina all those years ago, but she didn't want to go against her dad's wishes. "Had you ever heard the ghost story about the little boy?"

Bertram scrunched up his brow. "I don't know. Maybe? It sounds vaguely familiar. I must have heard it at some point."

The megaphone screeched again, and more shouts erupted from the protesters.

Bertram glanced toward the window. "What the hell's going on now?"

Penelope walked over and pushed back the blinds. Another white van had pulled up to the protest, this one with a network logo on the side. "Looks like you got another news crew. A real one. Channel 4."

Bertram groaned and buried his face in his hands.

"What if you just went out there and told them the pentagram was a fake?" Zed asked as he continued to play with the glass paperweight, using it as a prism to throw tiny rainbows onto the carpet.

Bertram fixed him with a glare. "Based on what? The opinion of a black occult magician?"

Zed lowered the paperweight and met Bertram's gaze. "Charles is very good at what he does."

Bertram shook his head. "They'd crucify me, literally."

Penelope watched the protesters holding out their signs to passing cars. Reverend Purdue had, thankfully, lowered his megaphone, but he was talking to one of the reporters for Channel 4. "Until we can get to the bottom of what happened, I'm afraid the only thing you can do is put up with it."

Bertram closed his eyes and pinched the bridge of his nose. "If the business lasts that long."

———

Zed thanked God he was away from the Reverend Purdue's protesters and Bertram Brown's fretting. As he drove along Highway 276 out of the city toward Laurens, he was finally able to take a deep breath and clear his head. Lately he'd even found himself getting wound up around Penelope, and she had always been the one person who could talk him off a ledge, not that she ever actually realized it.

Rolling green fields dotted by the occasional farmhouse passed by outside. Somewhere beyond Fountain Inn, he turned off the main highway onto a road that barely qualified for the name. On one side, an old split-rail fence marked the perimeter of a pasture where cows grazed. On the other side, trees loomed close.

After about ten minutes, he grew paranoid he'd missed his turn. He'd left the pasture behind, and now trees lined both sides of the road. Occasionally, he caught a glimpse of some building set back in the woods or came upon a gravel driveway with a lonely mailbox. The driveways all had names here—Reid Lane, Jackson Drive, Miller Road. Whether the Reids, the Jacksons, or the Millers still actually lived there was anybody's guess.

After ten more minutes, he was debating whether to turn around when he spotted what he was looking for. A crooked street sign marked Parker Drive. Zed made the sharp left onto the gravel road, the rocks crunching under his tires. He eased his car past the burned-out remains of a house, reduced to nothing more than the outlines of the foundation. Vines grew over the bricks, and other plants sprouted through the cracks. An elm tree stood proudly in the center of the ruins, taking full advantage of the sunlight pouring through the break in the canopy. Whatever had happened, it happened a long time ago.

Beyond the house, the condition of the road worsened. Zed had to dodge a few holes, and at one point, he hit a bump so hard he was sure he'd left his muffler behind. The road bent to the right, and a single-wide trailer came into sight. A pick-up truck sat by the door, but Zed was fairly confident no one was home. Bobby Parker was lying unconscious in a hospital bed.

Zed pulled his Pacer up next to the truck and climbed out. The breeze moved through the tree branches. It was cooler here than in the city and would have been almost pleasant if it weren't for the humidity. Birds chattered, and the ever-present cicadas sang their summer song.

As Zed climbed the wooden steps to the trailer's makeshift porch, he touched his amethyst ring and said a prayer the ramshackle construction would hold his weight. At the top, he realized the mobile home sat on a low ridge and afforded a view of a small valley through the trees. At the bottom, the darker, thicker greenery gave away the location of a creek meandering its way toward the Reedy River. It wouldn't be a bad way to end the day, watching the sunset over the distant hills.

Zed needed less than ten seconds to pick the flimsy lock on the door. Inside the trailer, all the curtains were drawn, making it dark and cool. He fumbled around looking for a light switch and nearly stumbled over a table stacked high with newspapers and magazines. They slid off and toppled to the floor. Swearing at himself, Zed stooped to pick them up. That's when he noticed the faint smell of smoke, of burning wood, of charcoal and ash. He brought the paper in his hand close to his face. It definitely smelled like it had been through a fire. The edges of the paper, too were flakey and brown and partly disintegrated in Zed's hand. He quickly stacked everything back up and resumed his blind search for a light switch.

When he found the switch and flipped it, he was not expecting what he saw. The entire room was crammed with furniture— chairs, tables, cabinets. Most of it looked antique, and as Zed stepped farther inside, the smell of smoke and fire grew stronger. To his left, a narrow path led back to the bedroom. A small television was crammed in between a bookshelf and a curio cabinet, opposite an orange and green plaid couch, the only modern-looking piece of furniture there.

Zed turned to his right and scrutinized the kitchen. A dining room table way too big for the space dominated the center, surrounded by high-backed chairs. The counters were all full of crystal glasses and vases and stacks of plates and saucers with gilded edges. Someone had apparently saved whatever they could from the burned-out house and stuffed it all into that tiny trailer. He went back over to the stack of papers on the table by the door. The paper on top was the *Greenville News* from Sunday, November 3, 1961. A quick scan of the rest of the stack turned up a date no later than December of that same year.

Eleven years. Why did everything still smell of smoke and fire after eleven years?

Zed turned back to the living room. The bookcase next to the television caught his eye. To his surprise again, it contained actual books. Most of them were trashy romance paperbacks, stacked two deep, covers adorned with bare-chested men and women spilling out of their corsets. He flipped through a few before continuing his scan of the shelves.

The books on the lowest shelf were different. Many of them tattered, they had wordless spines of dark brown, red, or black, and Zed detected a musty note underneath the ever-present smell of smoke. He reached for one of the thicker volumes, one with a rust-red cover. It vibrated under his touch. Just as he expected, the yellowed pages contained magic spells.

Written in a small, cramped hand, most of the spells were simple, for good luck, for a happy marriage, a healthy birth, good weather, or a good harvest. As he leafed through the pages, the book struck Zed as more a collection of family recipes than a book of spells.

He never heard the door open. Only the sound of the gun cocking let him know someone else was in the room. Curiouser and curiouser.

He always knew when someone else was in the room.

"Put the book down and turn around as slow as you can," said a woman, "or I swear to God, I will blow your balls off."

"Yes, ma'am." Zed closed the book and placed it back on the bookshelf. He turned around slowly, as he was told, keeping his hands up in the air.

The woman behind the revolver was young, probably in her early thirties. She had long, straight auburn hair and was wearing a tee shirt and jeans with work boots. Zed, though, was more focused on the barrel of the gun in his face.

"You have ten seconds to tell me who you are and why you're here."

No sense in lying. "This is where Bobby Parker lives, right? My name's Zed McKay. I work with a private investigator his employer hired to try to figure out what happened to him."

She raised an eyebrow. "So that just gives you the right to break in?"

"Not exactly the right, but you know sometimes we use unorthodox methods. Besides, Bobby's not really in a position to object right now."

"Except he's not the only one who lives here."

Zed glanced at the couch again and noticed for the first time the blanket folded up on one arm, a pillow resting on top. "You mean you live here, too?"

"I do."

"And you are?"

"Bobby's sister. Amy."

She shifted slightly, and the necklace around her neck caught the light. A pendant hung from a silver chain, a black onyx set among the silver petals of a lily. Both onyxes and lilies were used in protection spells. That explained why he didn't sense her enter.

"That's a pretty necklace," he said.

Her face flushed as her anger rose. "Are you trying to hit on me?"

He ignored her question. "Where did you get it?"

"It belonged to my grandmother." Her eyes narrowed. "Why do you care?"

"Those books on the bottom shelf. Did they belong to your grandmother, too?"

She nodded. "They did."

"Do you know what they are?"

"They're her books is what they are. What were you doing pawing through them?"

She was putting on a good show, but Zed sensed the sadness emanating in waves from her whenever she thought about her grandmother. Sadness and regret. The smoky odor in the room had become stronger, too.

"Look, I'm sorry for coming in here uninvited, but I really do want to help your brother. I don't mean either of you any harm."

The hand with the gun trembled.

"Why don't you put the gun down so we can have an actual conversation, okay?"

A few seconds passed in which Zed worried she'd make good on her threat, but she eventually lowered the gun. She didn't take her finger off the trigger, though. "Talk fast. I just came home to change. I've got to be at my second job in thirty minutes."

"When you were growing up, did you notice anything usual at all when your grandmother was around?"

She chuckled. "You clearly didn't know Grandma Mabel. Everything about her was unusual."

"Do you know what those books were for?"

"Family recipes."

"Not exactly." Keeping his hands where she could see them, Zed slowly reached for the book he had been looking through.

"If you're going to show me all the weird drawings and crazy symbols, don't bother. I already know about them. And yes, I know they're magic spells. Doesn't change the fact that they're still family recipes."

"The fire that burned down the house I passed on the way here. Your grandmother died in that fire, didn't she?"

Amy nodded. "So did Mom. Me and Bobby would have died too if it weren't for the angels."

"Angels?"

"Jesus, I can't even believe I'm telling you this, but yeah, that's the only word I can use to describe them. Me and Bobby woke up, and there were these … figures in our room. They picked us up and carried us through the fire itself and laid us on the ground outside. The fire burned up all the second floor. We saved what we could from the first floor before it collapsed. Strange enough, all Grandma Mabel's books weren't even singed."

They hadn't been real angels. They couldn't have been. Still, Zed wasn't about to tell her that. "Back to Bobby. Anything strange or unusual happen recently that you recall? Anything at all? Did his new job with the Brown Tractor Co. have him worried in some way?"

"I can't really think of anything strange. Bobby was ... well, I wouldn't say he was *excited* about his new job, but he was looking forward to getting out of this trailer, and maybe having a little cash left over at the end of the month for a change."

"Thank you. I know you need to go to work, so I won't keep you any longer." Zed reached into his pocket. The hand with the gun tensed. He checked himself and then eased out a business card. "I'll leave this with you. If you think of anything, just give me a call."

Amy took the card from him. "Thanks. I will."

"I'll do what I can to figure out what happened to Bobby. I promise."

"I'm going to hold you to that." She waved his business card in his face.

With a quick salute, Zed took his leave. Walking back to his car, he thought over what Amy had said about her grandmother. She had told the truth, at least as she knew it. Amy wasn't a magic user herself.

But someone was.

Zed hadn't picked out the book he was perusing when Amy cocked her revolver at random. A thick layer of dust covered Grandma Mabel's magic "recipe" books, all of them except for that one.

6.

At ten minutes past midnight, Penelope and Zed found themselves in Penelope's black Lincoln on their way, once again, to the Brown Tractor & Farm Supply Co.

"Did Bertram tell you what's so important that we had to venture out when most decent folk are asleep?" Zed asked.

Penelope glanced sideways at him. "What are you talking about? You're never asleep this early."

Zed grinned. "I said 'most decent folk.'"

Penelope rolled her eyes. "No, Bertram didn't say. He just told me to meet him at the warehouse, and he wanted me to bring you along."

Zed chuckled. "That's a surprise."

"What do you mean?"

"He's jealous of me."

"What?" Penelope swerved out of her lane for a split second. "Why do you say that?"

"Because it's true. Or more specifically, he's jealous of our friendship."

Penelope shook her head. "You're crazy."

"Maybe, but I'm right about this."

"Why would he be jealous?"

"It's pretty obvious to me. You've known each other your whole lives. You were close friends once, right?"

"Yes."

"So, what happened?"

Penelope shrugged. "Nothing really. We just ran in different crowds in college. He had his fraternity brothers. I had my carrel on the fourth floor of the library."

It was Zed's turn to roll his eyes. "Oh, come on. You had friends. Tell me you had friends."

"I had a few. But I was never into the party scene. Especially after the 'Dreadful Penny' incident."

She had earned the nickname after a run-in with a football player—who had also been named Bobby. At a party he had made the mistake of putting his hand where it shouldn't have gone. She dislocated his pinky finger. He fractured his ankle tripping over a coffee table while trying to get away from her.

"So there never was a single thing that did it?"

"Not really. At least not anything I know about. I do know something changed between our sophomore and junior years. We were already drifting apart, but that's when he really stopped talking to me. I never understood why. I guess the resentment just grew from there."

"Do you think it has to do with what happened between Ephraim Brown and your father?"

Penelope was almost certain the two were related. "It's possible."

"It's been a few years now. Maybe you could just ask Bertram what happened, or Ephraim even."

Her father's emphatic *no* echoed in her head. "I don't think that would be a good idea."

Zed frowned. "That was quick. Why not?"

"I just don't."

At that point, Penelope pulled the car into the warehouse parking lot, thankful Zed didn't have an opportunity to continue the discussion. Bertram's Camaro wasn't the only car there.

"Do you think Reverend Purdue is back?" Penelope asked.

"I don't see his Cadillac," Zed said, "or a camera crew."

Once out of the car, they noticed a group of people huddled around Bertram, who was blocking the door. When Bertram spotted Penelope and Zed, a look of relief spread across his face. "Thank, God. Please help me try to talk some sense into these people."

Penelope surveyed the group. She counted six men, all of them dressed in black, carrying flashlights and heavy backpacks. With only the streetlights illuminating the small area where they stood, Penelope had trouble seeing all their faces, but none of them looked like burglars. Most of them were a little too well-fed and well-groomed, not to mention they could have beaten Bertram into the pavement if they had really wanted to.

"Who exactly are these people?" she asked.

One of the men, sporting a bushy walrus mustache, stepped forward. "My name is Clay MacDonald. We're ghost hunters, and we're trying to convince Mr. Brown here to let us into the warehouse to look for evidence of paranormal activity."

"You mean I caught you trying to sneak in," Bertram corrected. "I was working late in the office when I saw their cars pull up. They unloaded all this stuff and started the loading dock." He jabbed a thumb in the direction of one of them, a lanky man with glasses close to the same age as Bertram and Penelope. "The only reason I didn't call the police is because I know Abe Johnson over there, and I don't think his momma would appreciate having to bail his ass out of jail in the middle of the night."

Abe Johnson suddenly found the tops of his shoes very interesting.

"We apologized." Clay threw up his hands. "And we did try to reach you this evening. You just weren't answering your phone."

"So that gives you the right to trespass?" Bertram crossed his arms. "I'm not letting anyone in. Do you even understand the liability?"

"We would take full responsibility, sign a waiver even. We'd really like to investigate here. We're trying to establish Greenville as a hot spot for paranormal activity, like Charleston."

"This is a working business, not a tourist attraction." Bertram looked to Penelope and Zed. "Guys, help me out here. Tell them all the ways this is a very bad idea."

Zed smiled. "I think it's a great idea, actually."

A vein on Bertram's forehead popped out, and for a moment, Penelope thought he might tackle Zed to the ground. "You what?"

Penelope studied Zed's expression, but as usual, she had no idea what was going on inside his head. "I'm with Bertram on this one."

"I think it's a great idea." Zed pointed to the warehouse. "We'll lock you up in there all night with all your little recording devices and cameras and voltage meters to see what you can find."

Clay obviously had expected a little more resistance. "Well, that is what we're here for."

"What do you do when you find evidence of ... paranormal activity?" Penelope asked.

"We document it," Clay replied. "We share it with other groups like ours. Some of them might come try to verify what we've found."

Bertram heaved a sigh. "Well this just sounds better and better."

Penelope discretely waved for him to back off. "So, it's in your best interest to find something?"

Clay pointed toward the backpack of one of the other ghost hunters. "We're pretty scientific in our methods. We gather a lot of evidence, and it has to be pretty solid for us to conclude something paranormal is going on."

"But even so," Penelope continued, noting with some satisfaction the mild annoyance in his voice, "isn't there a tendency to give anything you find the benefit of the doubt? If you catch an unusual shadow or hear a weird noise, aren't you more likely than not to attribute it to something supernatural?"

"That doesn't happen," Clay insisted.

Penelope fought to keep herself from smiling. He was getting flustered. She wanted to see how twisted up in his own logic she could get him. "Seems to me like it could. What if there really is no ghost?"

"If there's no ghost, we won't find any evidence of one," he snapped. He turned back toward Bertram. "So, are you going to let us in or not?"

Before Bertram could answer, Zed spoke up. "He will on one condition."

Bertram opened his mouth to protest but was apparently too stunned to make any words come out. All he could manage was a sort of half grunt.

"And what condition is that?" asked Clay.

"You have to let us review whatever recorded footage you have after you're done."

Clay shook his head. "Absolutely not. I'm sorry, but we don't let others review our footage. How do we know you won't alter or erase something?"

Zed shrugged. "I guess you'll just have to trust us. Just like Bertram here will have to trust you don't steal or break anything. That's the condition. Take it or leave it."

Clay glared at Zed, a pretty close match to the hate stare he was getting from Bertram. "You'll have to give us a minute."

Zed nodded. "Take your time."

They all huddled together, exchanging hurried whispers.

Bertram stepped up beside Zed. "What the hell do you think you're doing?"

"I'm curious about that myself," Penelope added.

Zed held up a finger. "Just wait. You'll see."

After a few minutes, the cluster of ghost hunters broke up, and they all approached Zed again.

"Fine, we agree," Clay said. "After we're done you can have our recorded footage for twenty-four hours. Then we get it back."

Zed grinned. "You've got yourself a deal."

He and Clay shook hands.

"I sincerely hope you know what you're doing," Bertram growled to Zed as the ghost hunters entered the darkened warehouse.

Zed slapped Bertram on the back. "Of course I do. Just wait until it's time to review their footage. It'll be hilarious."

———

When Penelope and Zed arrived at the warehouse that afternoon, three police cars were already there, blue lights flashing. Reverend Purdue and his protesters had returned as well, though their chanting and sign waving were a bit subdued as most of them craned their necks from across the street, trying to get a better look at what was going on.

A uniformed officer, who looked like he might have been fifteen years old, intercepted Penelope before she even had a chance to get out of the car.

"Miss, you can't—"

Bertram burst through the office door and stepped between the officer and Penelope. "Wait, she's with me. I called her."

The officer stopped short. "Mr. Brown, this is a crime scene—you can't just invite people to come look at it."

"Why not?" He squinted at the officer's name on his uniform. "Officer Barnes, last I checked, this was still my property."

"Mr. Brown, that's not how this works," Officer Barnes said icily. "Given … what took place, the detective on the scene is in charge until he says otherwise. He decides who can come and go, not you."

"Well, we'll just have to see what he has to say, then," Zed said as he climbed out of the passenger's side of the car. Bertram frowned, and to be honest Penelope wasn't too happy with him right then either. She didn't really want to deal with the police any more than she had to, much less talk to the detective in charge at the scene.

Zed smiled and winked at her. "In fact, here he comes now."

She spun around to see Jim Everett lumbering over toward the car, a huge scowl on his face.

"What's the commotion?" he asked before he caught sight of Penelope. The scowl softened, but it didn't entirely vanish. "Penny? Why are you here?"

Jim had been a good friend of her father both before and after he left the police force and had known Penelope since she was a little girl. Jim had been the one to break the news about her father's murder.

"I called her," Bertram said.

Judging by the way Jim looked at him, Bertram might as well have announced he was a unicorn. "Why? You can't just invite people to a crime scene, son."

"That's what I tried to explain," said Officer Barnes.

Bertram pressed his palms together. "Look, I know this is all irregular, but I need her help with some things. I hired her to investigate some … irregularities in the books and the inventory that turned up recently. She won't interfere, I promise."

Jim eyed them each in turn. "Well, as long as you don't let her back into the warehouse, at least not until the coroner's finished."

Penelope traded glances with Zed.

Coroner?

Bertram led Penelope and Zed into the office and shut the door firmly behind them. "Well, that didn't go as I'd planned."

Zed fell into what was increasingly becoming "his" chair. "Probably should have given us a heads-up about the police. Just tell me something didn't happen to the ghost hunters."

Bertram glowered. "You don't think I would've gotten hold of you if I thought I could? I'm not an idiot. And no, all the ghost hunters were alive when they left this morning. The thing is, I needed you both to come today. I feel like time's running out, and I don't think the police are up to handling what's going on."

Penelope glanced outside to see Jim still talking with Officer Barnes. "What happened, Bertram?"

Bertram took a deep breath and let it out slowly. "Bobby was killed in the warehouse last night."

Zed bolted up straight. "Isn't he in a coma in the hospital?"

"He was." Bertram fell into his own chair. "They reported him missing this morning."

Zed traced the route from the hospital to the warehouse in the air. "How did he get out of the hospital and all the way here without anyone seeing?"

"That's the $64,000 question, isn't it?" Bertram grabbed a coffee mug on his desk and threw back whatever was left. The dark circles under his eyes spoke to how the rest of his night had gone.

"When was he found?" Penelope asked.

"About eight."

"Who found him?"

No matter how complicated the case, gather the easy facts first. That's what her father always told her.

"We keep a skeleton crew on the weekends, just in case an urgent order comes in. One of them found Bobby."

"Do you know what time Clay MacDonald and his ghost hunters left?"

Bertram scratched his chin. "A little before five, I think. I locked up after them and headed home to try to get a couple of hours of sleep. So much for that."

Penelope thought for a moment. "That's a tight window. And no one saw *anything*?"

"Not a thing." Bertram stood up again and ambled to the coffee maker in the back of the office. He poured the dregs from the pot into his mug and took a sip.

Penelope waited until he sat back down to ask her next question. "How did he die?"

"Would you believe he got run over by a tractor?"

"I would," said Zed.

"The police are telling me it looks like an accident. At first, they suggested Bobby was fiddling with the tractor and somehow started it, and then it rolled on top of him. They're not entirely sure, though, because … there's not really a lot to go on. He got mangled up pretty bad."

"Why in the world would he be fiddling with the tractor?" Penelope asked.

Bertram let out a humorless chuckle. "I asked that, too, and still in a hospital gown no less. They didn't have an answer, but they didn't seem too concerned about it. That's when I explained to them how their theory was shit."

Zed glanced over at Penelope. "I hope you used those exact words."

He had even less of an opinion of the police than she did.

Bertram nodded. "That and more. The tractor is a Case Model 500. It's a good twenty years old and missing half its parts. Not to mention it doesn't have any fuel in it. Do you know what they had the audacity to say? Maybe it just rolled over on him."

"But you don't think that's what happened." Penelope didn't believe it either.

"You didn't see Bobby." Bertram stared into his coffee mug, which was empty again. "To do what that tractor did, it would've had to hit him with some velocity. It didn't just roll over him, and no one could have pushed it hard enough. He was … It was … There was a lot of blood."

Penelope shook her head. "Jim's too good a detective to go for the convenient answer like that. That's not his style at all."

But Penelope remembered the last time she'd seen Jim, at the scene of the murder of a college co-ed who had just been in the wrong place at the wrong time. The police ruled it a suicide, even though no one ever did uncover a reason for her to take her own life.

Maybe Jim really was listening to Bertram. He just didn't like what he was hearing.

Bertram ran his fingers through his uncombed hair. "There's more. It's just a feeling, but this morning it seemed like there was something else there in the warehouse. A presence, I guess. The police can sense it, too. I can see it in their faces. None of them want to stay in there for very long. If you can wait until they leave, you can see for yourselves."

The police wrapped up their investigation a little over an hour later. Jim stopped by the office to let Bertram know they were leaving. He met Penelope's gaze and lingered there a little longer than seemed necessary. His eyes held a warning, but the corners of his mouth turned up in a slight smile, as if he knew just how much good warning her away would do.

After the last patrol car pulled out of the parking lot, Bertram led Penelope and Zed through the warehouse along a familiar path. She didn't need magic to figure out where they were going. The pentagram had been cleaned up, but in its place, a red stain covered the concrete floor. The old tractor stood to the side, covered in patches of rust where the yellow paint had flaked off. A ring of police tape surrounded it, as if it were some penned beast. Penelope half expected the tractor to burst through the tape and come crashing toward them, but it, thankfully, stayed put.

"That stain's never coming up," Zed said. "You'll have to paint over it."

Bertram glared. "Thanks. That never would have occurred to me."

Zed saluted. "Any time."

Penelope hugged herself. "You're right. It's colder in here than it should be."

"There's definitely a presence here, too," Zed added.

"Can you tell what kind?" Penelope wished again she'd inherited her father's awareness of the paranormal. That talent had saved his life more than once, according to him. Not that she didn't trust Zed, but Zed wouldn't always be around.

"A human one." Zed pointed. "Over there, behind that engine block."

A blurry figure dashed from its hiding place, running deeper into the warehouse. Bertram swore. Zed sprinted after the intruder, and Bertram followed. Penelope stripped off her shoes and ran after them both, though she soon lost track of the others as the chase weaved through the rows of farm machinery Footfalls echoed through the warehouse, but every time she chose a direction to go, the footsteps shifted. After a minute or so, she came upon Bertram, doubled over and wheezing for breath.

"I'm not cut out for this anymore," he said.

"You know Zed's a few years older than we are, right?"

Bertram scowled.

Shouts and the sounds of a scuffle bounced off the metal walls. Penelope took off again, with Bertram behind her. They rounded a corner to find Zed had tackled a man to the floor. Zed pulled him up by the collar and held him with an arm pinned behind his back. He was a small man, in his forties, with thinning hair and a wispy mustache.

"Lloyd? What are you doing here?" Bertram asked.

"I didn't mean no harm, Mr. Brown, I swear," the man said.

"You know him?" Penelope asked.

Bertram nodded. "He's one of my workers."

"You were in the group I talked to the other day," Zed said. "You didn't have very much to say then. Care to have a chat now?"

"Lloyd, you shouldn't be here," said Bertram. "What were you doing hiding back there?

Lloyd never lifted his gaze from the floor. "I just wanted to see for myself, to see if it was true what they were saying about Bobby."

Bertram rolled his eyes. "Do you honestly expect me to believe that bullshit?"

Lloyd struggled against Zed, but Zed held him firm. "It's the truth. I … I feel bad for playing that joke on Bobby. We didn't mean any harm by it. You know that. None of us ever thought something like this would happen."

Bertram shook his head. "Just get out of here, Lloyd, and don't come back until I say you can. Then we'll talk about whether you still have a job. Do you understand?"

Lloyd nodded.

"Let him go, Zed." Bertram waved his hand in dismissal.

Penelope stepped forward before Zed could comply, though. "Wait. I want to know more about what you saw."

Lloyd looked Penelope up and down. She'd seen the look in his eye before, somewhere between open leering and contempt. "Who are you?"

"My name is Penelope Drake."

"Why should I talk to you?"

"Because I say so," Bertram barked. "Just answer her question, Lloyd."

Lloyd twisted his mouth up in a sullen smirk. "What I saw was Bobby's body all mangled underneath that tractor."

"Do you have any idea how he got there?" Penelope asked.

"Not one clue." Lloyd chewed his lip, struggling to choose his next words, if Penelope had to guess. "It's the damnedest thing. That old Case doesn't work. Hasn't worked since it came here. As far as I know, we don't even have all the parts for it. But to see Bobby lying underneath it, you would have thought it hit him going forty miles an hour."

"What do you think of that?" Penelope pressed.

"I think Bobby had some pretty bad luck." He stared at her.

Penelope decided he was sharper than he looked. "Did you see anything else unusual?"

Lloyd shook his head. "Not really. I watched them lift the tractor and remove the … the body. That's it."

"Were you in here the whole time the police were?" Bertram asked.

"Almost."

Bertram frowned. "How did you get in without them seeing?"

"The side door near the front office." Lloyd jerked his head to one side. "You gave us all keys, remember?"

Bertram huffed. "Greenville's finest there. Didn't even notice someone watching them not ten feet away."

"I was real quiet." Lloyd grinned, obviously proud of himself.

Bertram didn't seem too impressed. "I'm going to need that key back."

Before Lloyd could reply, an inhuman wail that set Penelope's teeth on edge echoed through the warehouse. Zed let go of Lloyd. The worker took off again. Zed moved to chase after him, but Penelope put a hand on his arm.

"No, just let him go. We can find him later if we need to ask him more questions."

Another scream, back in the direction of the tractor.

"You're going to make us go toward that, aren't you?" Bertram asked.

Penelope nodded. "Absolutely."

She turned around and headed back toward the scene of Bobby's death. Zed followed, and, reluctantly, so did Bertram. The unnatural chill remained in the air, and as the sun moved lower in the sky, the shadows grew up from the floor, dark tendrils wrapping around the loaded shelves and scattered machine parts like ravening vines.

All three of them stopped short upon reaching the scene of Bobby's death. On the blood-soaked floor deep, charcoal-black markings showed through the rust-red stain. The pentagram had returned.

But that wasn't all.

"It's not the same," Zed whispered.

The symbols and words were different. Penelope still couldn't read any of it, but all she had to do was glance at the tractor standing off to the side, shrouded in shadow, to know this pentagram was the real deal.

7.

Zed knew he wasn't alone in his apartment as soon as he opened his eyes. As the fog of sleep cleared from his brain and his vision adjusted to the semi-darkness of his bedroom, he lay still, listening. Outside birds sang. A car door slammed. The car's engine revved, and it rumbled away. One of his neighbors called down from their balcony to someone in the parking lot below.

Then a muffled thump came from somewhere on the other side of the door.

As quietly as he could, Zed reached under his bed for the baseball bat he kept there. With his fingers wrapped around the smooth wooden handle, he climbed out of bed, his bare feet silent on the thick carpet. He reached the door in a few steps and paused with his hand on the doorknob. Although he didn't hear anything more, his certainty someone else was in his apartment grew. He turned the doorknob slowly so the bolt wouldn't click and cracked the door open just enough for him to peer out. A shaft of light spilled from underneath the closed door directly opposite.

His kitchen light was on.

Zed crept out into the tiny space separating his bedroom and bathroom from the living room and kitchen. To call it a hallway would have been generous. On the count of three, he pushed the door open and leapt into the kitchen with a loud cry, baseball bat at the ready.

Amy Parker sat at his kitchen table smoking a cigarette and drinking a cup of coffee. She regarded him with an appraising eye. Zed glanced down and realized he was wearing only a loose pair of sweatpants. He lowered the bat and cinched up the waist.

"This coffee is terrible," Amy said.

Zed picked up the jar of instant coffee on the counter and scanned the label. "Well, there's a good chance it's a little past its expiration date."

He opened a nearby cabinet and retrieved a mug. There was still hot water in the pot on the stove. Zed scooped a couple of spoonfuls of the coffee into the mug and poured some hot water over. His coffee made, he took a seat opposite Amy at the table.

"So, are you going to tell me how you found me—and how you got in?"

"I did a little detective work myself. It really wasn't that hard. There's only one Z. McKay in the phone book. As for getting in, you're not the only one who knows how to pick locks."

Zed took a sip of the coffee and grimaced. She was right. "What are you doing here?"

Her expression darkened. Sadness. Regret. But first and foremost, anger. "You promised you were going to figure out what was wrong with Bobby."

Zed reached across the table and placed a hand on her arm. "Amy, I'm sorry."

She jerked her arm away and glared. For a moment Zed expected another gun in his face. Instead she spoke with ice in her voice. "You promise me you're going to find the bastard who did this, and when you do, you're going to nail his ass to the wall."

Zed met her gaze. "I promise."

They stared at one another for a few moments longer until Amy glanced away, toward the brightening sky through the window above the sink.

She put out her cigarette in the ash tray on the table in front of her. "Thanks for the coffee."

After she left, Zed sat and finished his own coffee. Then he stood and headed back to his bedroom. He was awake. Might as well get dressed.

———

Clay MacDonald was in a less talkative mood when he showed up at Penelope's office with the footage from the investigation of the warehouse, and Penelope didn't need Zed's perception to tell he was more than a little anxious. He insisted they borrow his group's equipment to review the footage and practically fell all over himself to show them how to spool the tape reels and adjust the audio playback. After the last cord was plugged in, Penelope stood back to survey the makeshift studio she, Zed, and Bertram would be using to listen in on the ghost hunters' investigation.

She hoped her dad would behave.

"Maybe you'll stumble onto something we missed," Clay said as he was leaving. "It was a pretty quiet night, which is kind of surprising given … what happened."

Zed glanced up from fiddling with the dials on one of the tape decks. "Well, we're not going to be listening for ghosts."

Clay frowned. "What are you going to be listening for then? There wasn't anyone else in that warehouse but us."

Zed shook his head. "Bobby Parker was there. Who knows for how long? And what if he didn't come alone?"

Clay grew a few shades paler. "I'll … I'll be back to pick up everything later tonight. Around nine?"

Penelope nodded. "That'll work."

Once Clay had left, Zed rubbed his hands together and popped on a set of headphones. "I can't wait. This should be pretty entertaining."

Penelope tucked her hair behind her ears and slipped on her

own headphones. "Why do you say that? You heard what Clay said. They didn't find anything."

"He said it was quiet. That's not the same thing." Zed went back to toying with the audio dials in front of him. "Now are we going to get to it or not?"

Penelope pushed *play* on her tape deck. "I don't see anyone stopping you."

She had Clay's tape from his time in the warehouse. The recording started out with a walkie-talkie check after the team fanned out across the warehouse floor. Clay's voice was first.

"Check MacDonald."

"Check Avery."

"Check Johnson."

"Check Jones."

"Check Campbell."

That out of the way, Clay continued speaking directly into the recorder. "This is Clay Johnson at the Brown Tractor & Farm Supply Co. in Greenville, South Carolina. The date is July 15, 1972. The time is 12:37 a.m." A pause, and he spoke again, his voice pitched up a little. "Whatever spirits are inhabiting this place, we invite you to come forward, to make yourselves known. We mean you no harm. We only wish to communicate."

Judging by Zed's fit of laughter, she guessed each ghost hunter made a similar appeal wherever they were located. What followed for Penelope were several tedious hours mostly of shuffling, shifting, grunting, and fumbling around in the dark. Sometimes Clay's voice broke the monotony, usually to tag a sound.

"Unidentified noise from above. Thirty degrees south."

"Faint metallic clang. Sixty degrees east."

"Potential footsteps, due north." At the last one, he got on his walkie-talkie. "Hey, are any of you guys on the move?"

A chorus of "no's" followed, and then more silence. Another hour passed. Penelope caught herself nodding off more than once, only to be jolted awake by Zed's muted chuckles. Just when she thought she couldn't take it anymore, Bertram tapped Zed on the shoulder. Zed paused his tape deck and lowered his headphones. Eager for any relief from the crushing boredom, Penelope removed her headphones, too.

"Hey, could you listen to this sound?" Bertram asked. "The guy says he can't identify it. It's weird."

Zed put on Bertram's headphones. After listening for a few seconds, he removed them solemnly and handed them back. "Rats."

"Rats?" Bertram echoed, his eyes growing wide.

"You should probably get that taken care of."

Bertram frowned. "What's so hilarious about all this anyway? I'm on my third cup of coffee, and I can barely stay awake."

Zed chuckled. "Oh, come on, If you were a ghost would you get within a mile of these idiots? They take themselves so seriously with their 'scientific' approach to the spirit world, but the truth is they don't have any fucking idea what they're doing. I'm just enjoying listening to them make fools of themselves."

Bertram shook his head and put his headphones back on. "You have a really warped sense of humor, you know."

They all went back to listening for bumps in the night. Penelope sighed. At least there was a lot more tape on the take-up reel than the feed reel.

Not ten minutes later, though, Zed shook her shoulder hard enough that she nearly fell out of her chair. He did the same to Bertram. "Hey, you both need to listen to this," he said, ripping his headphones off.

Penelope and Bertram each took an earpiece. Zed played the tape back.

"There, do you hear it?" Zed was so excited he practically shook.

Silence.

"What am I supposed to be hearing?" Penelope asked.

Zed's face fell. "What do you mean?"

"I don't hear anything either," Bertram said.

"You're serious?" Zed broke into an incredulous grin. "Really? You don't hear it?"

Penelope was almost touching foreheads with Bertram. She removed her ear from the headset and sat up. "Zed, what are you talking about?"

"The little boy. You can't hear the little boy laughing?"

8.

Zed put on Don MacLean's "American Pie," the LP version. There, that was eight minutes and thirty-three seconds he didn't have to entertain anyone. He sat back in his chair and took off his headphones. The darkened radio station was quiet and still. He was alone. Even the janitor had gone home. For the tenth time in as many minutes, he checked the clock. Another hour until the morning deejay came in and took over for him.

Zed wondered how many were listening that night. How many of them would notice there was something different in his voice, something a little melancholier about his playlist.

He kept going back to that night in May at Charles' house, when they had all confronted Roy Arnold. Though he supposed it would have been more accurate to say he had confronted Roy Arnold's fist. Over and over again.

Arnold had almost killed him. Penelope had been the one to save *him*. That wasn't supposed to happen. *He* did the saving. And he didn't get hurt. True, he had bounced back a lot sooner than others would have, but Arnold shouldn't have been able to hurt him like that, even with a nightmare demon inside him, and he should have been able to hurt Arnold a lot more. Zed thought he knew all about himself.

Seems like he had a little more to discover.

He put his headphones back on as the song played itself out, turned the mic off mute, and leaned forward in his chair. "That was 'American Pie' by Don MacLean. I have a feeling we're going to be debating what those lyrics mean for a long time to come. Next up is 'Nights in White Satin' by the Moody Blues, but before I spin that one, I just want to throw a few thoughts out there in the universe.

"Lately I've been thinking a lot about faith. Someone I met a little while ago reminded me of a certain philosopher's take on the subject, and I'm just pondering some questions. How far are you willing to go for what you believe in? What would you give up to keep your faith? What if you found out your faith wasn't enough to see you through? Heavy stuff for a rock and roll deejay, I know, but hey, if you're up listening to me, you're probably not going to sleep anyway, right?"

He sat back in his chair again as Justin Heyward's deep baritone wailed the lyrics to "Nights in White Satin." An image of Annie's smiling face came to him when he closed his eyes, freckles and dimples and shining blue eyes. She was in Cleveland now, getting ready to go to nursing school, something she had always dreamt of doing. She was where she was supposed to be, but Zed still missed her.

Her features shifted, morphing into the square jaw and tousled brown hair of Jake, the man he met at O'Shaughnessy's who read Kierkegaard, whose infectious laugh Zed could still hear. Then, to his surprise, the face changed one more time, to Amy Parker's, so full of anger but whose eyes betrayed a deep sensitivity. Zed didn't know the path his own faith was taking him down.

He just hoped for once someone didn't get hurt.

———

Jake Dempsey lay wide awake staring at the ceiling and listening to the night noises. The windows were open, and moonlight spilled into his bedroom. The curtains fluttered in the breeze, and the scent of honeysuckle wafted in.

What if you found out your faith wasn't enough to see you through?

He'd searched for the answer to that question in the stack of books on his nightstand, only no one seemed to know. Not the philosophers, not the poets, not the politicians or the preachers. He didn't know what possessed him to turn on the radio at three o'clock in the morning, but when he did, there it was. Not exactly the answer he'd been looking for, but an indication at least he wasn't alone.

Jake sat on the edge of his bed and listened to Zed McKay's voice as he rambled on about faith. He listened to the radio until Zed signed off and the morning deejay took over. Predawn light crept into the room. Songbirds replaced the crickets. Jake reached to turn the radio off, stretched, and ran his fingers through his hair. He had a long day ahead of him. But maybe he'd pay a visit to O'Shaughnessy's after work.

Penelope meant to pay Charles a visit. She'd been trying to get in touch with him ever since Bobby Parker's mangled body was found, but he wasn't answering his phone again, and every time she set out to make the trip to his farmhouse, something derailed her plans. That morning, "something" was a call from Jim Everett.

He was waiting for her in the lobby of Greenville Memorial Hospital when she arrived. They greeted each other with a hug, and then Penelope stood back, looking at the police detective expectantly, wondering why he had wanted to meet her here of all places.

He regarded her with a wistful grin and sighed. "I shouldn't be doing this, but there's something here I think you'd be interested in seeing."

"Here?" Penelope glanced around the hospital lobby. Orange and yellow chairs were arranged in small groups. A few people sat, speaking to one another in low voices or clasping hands and gazing silently at the floor. Others milled about, obviously too anxious to sit down. Penelope realized that the last time she'd been there with Jim was the night her father died.

Jim raised a hand and beckoned her. "Just follow me."

As he passed the reception desk, he flashed his badge at the woman sitting there. With a nod and a bland smile, she let them pass. They rode the elevator to the fourth floor, where they stepped out next to the nurse's station. The lights in the hallway were dim. Only faint beeps and whirrs disturbed the silence.

When a young nurse in a white uniform looked up from behind her desk, Jim flashed his badge again, as well as a 10,000-watt smile. "Good afternoon, miss. We're here to see Earl Boggs."

The nurse frowned at the name and glanced down the door-lined hallway. "Mr. Boggs didn't have a very good night last night. Now might not be the best time."

"We'll only take a few minutes. I promise."

The nurse chewed her lip for a moment. "I'd have to talk with the shift manager, and she's on a break right now."

Jim leaned forward. "Please, miss. I assure you we wouldn't be asking to talk to him if it weren't important." His smile broadened, and he winked at her. "You rest assured we'll clear up things with your shift manager if we need to."

The nurse took in a deep breath and let it out slowly. Finally, she nodded. "Okay, but only for a few minutes."

"Thank you." Jim gave her a small salute and waved for Penelope to follow him again.

"Am I supposed to know who Earl Boggs is?" Penelope asked as they walked.

Jim shook his head. "No, but you do know who was in the room next to his. Bobby Parker."

"Really? That's what this is about?"

Jim glanced sidelong at her. "What else would it be about?"

Penelope studied Jim's profile. Solid, dependable, trustworthy, normal Jim. Her dad never let on how much Jim knew about his more … unusual cases. Penelope had always assumed he remained blissfully in the dark. Maybe he was aware of more than he'd been letting on.

About midway down the hall, Jim stopped. "I may be old, but I'm not blind, Penelope. I know Bertram has you investigating more than just funny business with his books."

"Jim, you know I'd never interfere with the police—"

Jim waved off her protest. "Look, you and I both know Bobby Parker's death wasn't an accident, but we're at a dead end." He pointed at the door. "At least we were before we got a call this morning about something Mr. Boggs here said."

Penelope glanced into the empty room next to Mr. Boggs'. "Did he see something?"

Jim shrugged. "He says he did."

Penelope returned her attention to the closed door in front of them. "I still don't understand why you brought me here."

"I brought you here because my hands are tied. I can't pursue this lead without getting laughed off the police force. You, on the other hand, can follow it to Hell if that's where it goes."

Let's hope it doesn't come to that.

Jim gently pushed the door open, and he and Penelope stepped into the room. In the sole hospital bed an elderly man rested, thin and pale, like a living skeleton. Blue veins stood out against the almost translucent skin of his arms and legs. Wisps of white hair still clung to his head in places. His chest rose and fell in time to the beeping and buzzing of the machine next to his bed, connected to him by wires that snaked underneath his hospital gown.

His eyes were open. They were the lightest blue Penelope had ever seen. His gaze fixed on them as they came into the room, and despite the failings of his body, Penelope had no doubt he retained every scrap of his reason.

"Mr. Boggs?" Jim said.

"Who the hell are you?" the elderly man rasped.

Jim inched forward. "Please, pardon the intrusion. My name is

Detective Jim Everett, and this is Penelope Drake. We'll just take a minute of your time."

He grunted. "Well, at my age, I don't have that many minutes left. I need them all."

Jim chuckled a little nervously. "We'll get to the point, then. I don't know if you've heard, but your next-door neighbor, Mr. Parker, got himself into a little bit of trouble the other night. This morning you told one of the nurses you saw something."

"Sure did. I saw a black demon take him."

Jim glanced at Penelope. "Are you sure that's what you saw? It was dark, in the middle of the night. You could have been sleeping—"

"I said what I meant." He glared and tried to lift himself up, but only managed to make his heart monitor bleat frantically. Penelope expected an alarm to go off that sent all the nurses running to the room.

"Mr. Boggs, I didn't mean—"

The old man hushed Jim with a raised finger. He lay back down, and after a moment, his heart rate settled. "I saw him plain as day," he continued. "Black skin, yellow eyes, big bat wings, knees and elbows that bent the wrong way. Once when I was a boy, I came across the corpse of a horse dead for a week. The demon brought with him a smell just like that. He went into that man's room, and he led him out again."

"No one else saw Mr. Parker leave," Jim said.

"No one else could. The demon hid himself pretty good from those who don't know how to see."

Penelope stepped forward, to the edge of his bed. Up close he seemed even smaller, thinner, as if merely touching him would cause his bones to break. "Do you know how to see, Mr. Boggs?"

Something approaching a smile spread across his face as he focused on her. "I do, miss. I've had the gift ever since I was small. I'm not sure why God chose me. The gift hasn't done much to help me in life, but maybe it will help you." He reached out and squeezed her hand. His grip was surprisingly strong. "I'm tired now. If y'all don't mind, I'd like to take a little nap."

He let go and closed his eyes. His head lolled forward. The only remaining sound was the steady beeping of his heart monitor. Without a word, Jim and Penelope retreated from the room.

"Was it worth your time to meet me down here?" Jim asked after he shut the door to Earl Boggs' room.

Penelope nodded. "Thank you."

His eyes narrowed. "You be careful, Penelope."

"I always am."

"I know." Jim glanced up and down the empty, darkened hallway. "Let me walk you to your car anyway."

She didn't try to argue. As they left Earl Boggs behind, Penelope thought about how much she really needed to talk to Charles.

———

Zed should've been sleeping. By the time he got off his shift at the radio station at five o'clock that morning, he'd been awake for the better part of the last twenty-four hours. But when he stumbled into his apartment and toppled into his bed, the black nothingness he'd been looking forward to didn't come. Instead, he tossed and turned, getting more annoyed with each minute. Finally, he gave up and threw the sheets off.

Might as well do something productive with his time.

Since catching Lloyd in the warehouse, Zed felt like there was unfinished business. He still had the addresses of all the warehouse employees he'd gotten from Bertram. Surely Penelope wouldn't mind if he took some initiative and did some reconnoitering on his own.

About twenty minutes later, Zed pulled his Pacer over across the street from Lloyd's house, a dingy little brick shoebox in a dingy little neighborhood on the backside of the former Donaldson Air Force Base. He waited. No signs of life—inside or outside the house. Zed had hoped to catch Lloyd at home. After all, the warehouse was closed until further notice. What else would he be doing?

Zed was about to give up when Lloyd opened the front door and stepped outside. Locking the door behind him, he scurried around to the garage that stood behind the house. Moments later, an old Chevy pick-up truck rumbled out onto the street. Zed slumped down as Lloyd passed by.

Zed followed him to a bar on White Horse Road in a strip of businesses that included an insurance agent, a barber shop, and a drug store—just the kind of bar you'd expect to be open at ten o'clock on a Monday morning.

Lloyd was perched on a stool at the bar when Zed entered. He took a seat in a corner booth where he could watch Lloyd without being noticed. The air inside was stifling. The whole place smelled like stale cigarettes and cheap beer. Blinds drawn over the windows kept the daylight at bay. What little light there was came from dim wall lamps as well as a dozen or so neon beer ads. A few other patrons were scattered about, slouched over their drinks. A radio played behind the bar—not Zed's station. A couple of guys arguing over the Atlanta Braves' prospects for the rest of the season, from what he could hear.

Lloyd caught the bartender's attention and ordered a beer. When the bartender returned, bottle in hand, Lloyd asked him to turn the radio up. He collected a staggering number of empty Miller High Life bottles while he sat there and listened. Although, for such a slight guy, the beers didn't seem to affect him as much as Zed expected.

When Lloyd looked like he was about to get up and leave, Zed abandoned his lookout spot. He took the seat next to Lloyd at the bar, putting a firm hand on Lloyd's shoulder to hold him down on his stool.

"What's the rush, Lloyd?" He flagged down the bartender. "One more here for my good friend."

Lloyd tried to swat Zed's hand away. "Now just who—" His

gaze met Zed's, and his eyes grew wide in horror. The bartender put another High Life down in front of him. He reached for it and took a giant swig. "What do you want?"

Zed shrugged. "I was in the neighborhood. I guess it's just dumb luck I ran into you. I've actually got a question I bet you could answer."

Lloyd narrowed his eyes. "What question is that?"

"Why did you lie back at the warehouse?"

The corner of Lloyd's mouth twitched. "I was telling the truth."

Zed stroked his chin. "That's possible, I suppose, but it's still awfully suspicious. The police would definitely be interested to know why you were there, spying on them. They'd certainly have a question or two about that."

Lloyd glared. "That's blackmail."

Zed grinned. "Whatever you want to call it."

Lloyd continued shooting eye daggers. "Fine. You want to know the truth. I left some things in my locker. I was afraid the police would find them if they searched it."

"What things?"

"These." He leaned toward Zed to show him three blunts in his shirt pocket. "I guess you're going to tell Mr. Brown I've been toking on the job."

"Not necessarily."

Lloyd frowned. A bead of sweat ran down his forehead. "What do you mean by that?"

"You're still lying," said Zed. "There's something else you're not telling me."

Fear. Guilt. The strength of Lloyd's emotions nearly knocked Zed off his stool. "I don't know what you're talking about."

"I think you do." Zed worked to keep his voice even. "Come on, now, Lloyd. They say confession is good for the soul."

"You can't tell Mr. Brown."

"That depends on you."

Lloyd finished the rest of his beer in one gulp. "Someone paid me to leave the warehouse's side door open a few days before Bobby's accident, the one that put him in the hospital, not the other one."

Zed just barely managed not to jerk Lloyd clean off his seat and shake him senseless. "Does this someone have a name?"

"He never told me."

"What did he look like?"

Lloyd opened his mouth to answer, but then a puzzled look came over his face. "I … I don't know."

"You met with him, didn't you?" By now Zed's patience was paper thin.

"Yeah, but I … I guess I can't remember."

Zed's blood froze. Lloyd was telling the truth. He really didn't remember. There was a hole in his recollection, one that could have only been made by magic.

He settled Lloyd's tab and had the bartender called a cab. Outside, Lloyd went for his truck, but Zed grabbed him by the arm.

"Hey, let go," Lloyd said, struggling to break free. "I've got to get home."

"Take it easy." Zed tightened his grip. "I'm not letting you get behind the wheel in the state you're in. Your truck's still going to be here when you sober up."

When the cab arrived, he put Lloyd in the back and paid the fare. Zed was putting together a theory about what happened to Bobby.

He hoped to God he was wrong.

———

Penelope returned to her office from her visit to the hospital bed of Earl Boggs still haunted by the thought of a giant leather-skinned demon snatching Bobby Parker away. It took her a few moments to realize the telephone was ringing. She rushed across to her desk and snatched up the receiver just in time to choke off the fourth ring.

"Drake Detective Agency."

"Penelope, great, you're there." The voice on the other end of the line belonged to Carolyn Cole, file clerk at the Department of Public Records. "I have that information you asked me to look up."

Penelope glanced at the top of her desk and frowned. Her painted rock was missing. "I'm sorry, Carolyn, what?"

"I have the information you wanted me to look up," Carolyn repeated. "About the ghost at the Brown warehouse?"

Penelope scanned the room, searching for where her father could have put the rock. "Right. Sorry, it's been a long week."

"It's only Monday."

Penelope stooped to look under her desk for the missing paperweight. "Yeah, well, the statement stands. What did you find out?"

If a document existed, Carolyn could find it. She could tell you blindfolded where every single scrap of paper in the Department of Public Records was. Penelope had the utmost faith Carolyn would be able to tell her all about the ghost boy and where he came from.

There was a pause on the other end of the line. "Actually, nothing."

"Nothing?" Penelope tried to stand but only succeeded in smacking her head on the edge of her desk. "Are you sure?"

"I'm positive. There's no record of a small child dying at the Brown Tractor & Farm Supply Company, ever, going back to the purchase of the building in 1923."

"Then where did the story of the little boy ghost come from?" Still rubbing her head, Penelope dropped into her chair. The rock was nowhere to be found. Her father was playing games, it seemed.

"Power of suggestion maybe? If enough other people say they

saw or heard something, it's easy to convince yourself that you did, too."

Maybe Zed had imagined the child's laughter on the recording. After all, she and Bertram hadn't heard anything, and none of the ghost hunters reacted to the little boy's giggles either. "You could be onto something, there. Thanks for trying, Carolyn."

"Any time. And Penelope, you should stop by the Department more. I miss our chats. Not that I don't enjoy Zed's visits."

Penelope chuckled. "You just like how he flirts with you."

Carolyn's eye roll was evident even through the phone. "Don't be silly. He flirts with everyone. He does do wonders for the scenery, though."

"I'll be sure to let him know you said that."

Carolyn laughed. "Let's not inflate his ego any more. Seriously, though, we need to have lunch. No shop talk allowed."

"That sounds great. I'll make it a point to stop by soon."

"Soon, Penelope. You promise?"

"I promise."

After she hung up, Penelope glanced down at that morning's unread *Greenville News* folded on her desk. She opened it up and scanned the headlines. A picture of the new Miss South Carolina dominated the front page, right next to a story about B52 bombers attacking bases in North Vietnam. Two companion stories on the third page interested her the most, though. The first one reported on Bobby's death, calling it an accident. The second story was an interview with Reverend Purdue and included a picture of the preacher and his "flock" outside the Brown warehouse.

When she glanced at the picture again, her heart skipped a beat. She recognized one of the protesters. She'd met him just recently. Before she had a chance to do anything with her new information, though, her telephone rang again.

This time she picked it up after the second ring. "Drake Detective Agency."

"Penelope, it's Ephraim."

The last person she expected. "How are you doing, Ephraim?"

"Could you stop by the house this afternoon, Penelope? I need to talk to you."

Penelope grimaced inwardly. So much for seeing Charles. "Of course. I can be there in half an hour."

"As soon as you can." He hung up without saying goodbye.

When Penelope knocked on the door, Ephraim answered. Louise was still nowhere to be seen. Ephraim led her through the quiet house back to the kitchen. He reached into the refrigerator and pulled out two beers. He popped the top on one and offered it to her. This time she accepted. They sat at the kitchen table.

Ephraim lit a cigarette and took a long pull. "I owe you an apology, Penelope."

"What for?"

"I haven't been entirely truthful with you."

She knew that, but she'd reasoned she'd get more out of him if she played along. "What do you mean?"

He took another long drag. "Your father and I had our ups and downs as friends, and it was mainly because of me."

"My father could be difficult, too."

Ephraim held up a hand. "No, really, it was me. I saw Jonathan's relationship with you, and I knew that was never something I could have with my own son. I watched Bertram grow up like I was watching a movie."

"You could've made a choice to be different."

He chuckled, but there was no humor in it. "Easy for your generation to say. I didn't know how to do anything different. It's a failing of our family. The business has always come first. My father was the same way. I never knew any better. I always resented how close you and Jonathan were."

She had to ask herself if Bertram also harbored some of that resentment. "You can't dwell on regrets. We all have to move on."

He shook his head. "Some of us don't get to move on, Penelope. I left some things out about the ghost in the warehouse, mainly the fact that it's not a ghost."

"I know."

He regarded her with a puzzled look. "How?"

"I had someone do some digging. There isn't any record of an accident where a little boy died. But you said before they were just stories. What else did you leave out?"

"The fact that I saw it."

"But you just said there isn't any—"

"I said it's not a ghost. Whatever it is. Apparition. Phantasm. I saw it. It's Bertram when he was little. Laughing. Happy. Asking me to come play with him. That's why I haven't been back there. I can't take seeing him again."

Penelope's anger rose. "Someone's playing a cruel joke."

"No, it's no joke. I should have listened to you before when you tried to warn me. Now I'm afraid it's too late."

She reached across the table and placed her hand on his. "It's not too late. Not as long as we have some fight left in us."

"I'm not sure I do."

Penelope studied his face. The creases were deeper. The circles under his eyes darker. "Bertram does. You should believe in him. Whatever mistakes you think you made, you raised a good man, even if he's a pain in the ass."

Ephraim smiled. "Jonathan raised a good woman, too."

When Penelope left, he was still sitting at the kitchen table, gazing at something she couldn't see. That house was full of ghosts, she realized, a lifetime of memories impossible to escape.

———

Zed pulled up to Charles' farmhouse as the sun was setting. As he followed the overgrown path to the front door, a breeze kicked up and rustled the leaves in the trees. Dark clouds gathered in the distance. A flash of light followed several seconds later by a low, distant rumble confirmed a storm was coming. Just as well. He didn't intend to stay long.

Zed told Penelope he'd pay Charles a visit to discuss the death of Bobby Parker, not because he had any burning desire to talk to

Charles, but because Penelope asked him to. They needed to know about the new symbols around the resurgent pentagram on the warehouse floor, killer tractors, bat-winged demons walking hospital corridors, and ghost boys, and the only person who could tell them anything about any of those things was Charles. For whatever reason, though, Penelope hadn't been able talk to him. She'd hung up the phone muttering about some picture in the paper.

So, there he was.

About halfway up the steps to the porch, Zed hesitated. Some invisible force pushed back against him. Odd thoughts entered his head. He didn't really need to talk to Charles, did he? It wasn't important. He could come back later. He really ought to get home before the storm hit and the sky opened up.

A spell, one that might have worked on other people. Zed, though, closed his eyes and focused on putting one foot in front of the other. Step by step, he willed himself onto the porch, and as he neared the front door, the unbidden thoughts receded.

Zed shook his head. Charles was getting paranoid again, setting up extra wards. *Idiot*. Still, this magic felt different. It was subtle, insidious. It reminded Zed of the silky strands of a spider's web. Then he remembered Penelope's words. She'd been trying to talk to Charles but just hadn't been able to. But the idea was absurd. Charles couldn't cast a spell with that kind of range. No one could.

As Zed reached for the doorknob, the wind whipped up again, bringing with it the crisp scent of rain mixed with the ozone tang of lightning. Zed both loved and hated storms. So much wild magic abounded in them it was hard not to get intoxicated on the rush of the wind, the roar of the thunder, the brilliance of the lightning, and the wet, earthy smell. On the other hand, magic, wild or otherwise, was dangerous, and storms could cause spells to spiral out of control if you didn't know what you were doing.

The door opened before Zed could touch the doorknob. He

jerked his hand back. Charles stood in the doorway, looking at him expectantly.

Zed waved. "Hi, Charles. Can I come in?"

Charles nodded and stepped aside. "Watch your step. I've been doing a little rearranging."

The floor of the front room, normally clear of everything, was littered with books stacked haphazardly, some of the piles defying gravity. Several of the shelves, which had literally groaned under the weight of the books on them, were empty.

Zed gingerly stepped around the volumes, knowing a shoe on the wrong book would be the equivalent of stepping on a land mine. "What brought all this on?"

Charles glided across the floor and around the books like a dancer. "Just needed to make room for some new acquisitions. It seemed like as good a time as any to take inventory."

He led Zed through the dining room, where he kept all the books that needed repairing. Nothing out of the ordinary there. The dining room table was covered in old tomes. Beyond the dining room, they entered the back parlor Charles converted into his workshop.

He pulled out one of the two folding chairs and sat down, gesturing for Zed to sit in the other one. "So, you want to talk about this Bobby Parker business."

As Zed took a seat, he watched Charles. He was being alarmingly pleasant. "That's why I came."

Charles leaned forward. "I need to know everything then."

Zed told him about all of it, the new pentagram, the demon in the hospital, the not-exactly-a-ghost boy. He pulled a Polaroid of the symbols drawn on the warehouse floor out of his shirt pocket and handed it to Charles. "So, I have a theory."

"About what?" Charles held the picture about an inch from his nose, tilting it at an angle and frowning.

Zed bit down on the sarcastic remark that nearly escaped his lips. "Someone decided to call a demon, a powerful one at that, and needed to sacrifice a person with magical aptitude to do it. I think whoever did this used the apparition of the little boy as a lure. I could hear him laugh on the tapes we got from the ghost hunters, but Penelope and Bertram couldn't. Bobby Parker's grandmother was a fairly competent magic user, and he might have dabbled as well. And there's at least one other worker who saw the illusion. I'm willing to bet he has some talent for magic, too. He just didn't take the bait. That was Bobby's misfortune."

Outside flashes of lightning illuminated the fields surrounding Charles' house every few seconds, followed by rumbles of thunder Zed felt as much as he heard. The storm was almost on them.

Still clutching the Polaroid, Charles stood up and left the room. He came back a few moments later with a book in his hand, a thin volume with a threadbare cloth binding that had been a brilliant blue at some point. "So, you think this 'someone' was successful in calling the demon?"

"I was hoping you'd be able to tell me that."

Charles opened the book and began flipping through the pages. "It's possible, but I can't say for sure only going on a picture. I'd need to examine the site in person."

"I'm sure we can set something up with Bertram."

"Good, just let me know when."

Several minutes of awkward silence passed while Charles continued to leaf through the book, never bothering to explain why he had gone to get it or what he was looking for.

Finally, Zed pushed himself to his feet. "I should be going before this storm gets any worse. I'll be back in touch after I talk to Bertram."

Charles didn't respond.

"Goodbye, Charles," said Zed, a little louder.

Charles glanced up for a split second before returning his attention to the book. "See you later, Zed."

"And Charles?"

Charles sighed and looked up again, leaving the book splayed open in his lap.

Maybe it was the lack of sleep, or the fact that Charles wasn't being a complete ass, but Zed decided to offer an olive branch, at least a small one. "If you ever want to talk about what happened last year in the Christ Church graveyard, you just let me know."

Charles' expression hardened. "I wouldn't hold my breath while you wait on that, Zed."

9.

TUESDAY, JULY 18, 1972

By day, ghost hunter Clay Johnson was an accountant with an office near downtown, and according to his secretary, he just happened to have an opening in his schedule that morning. So, a little after eleven-thirty, Penelope walked into his office to find him staring pensively at a pile of spreadsheets, a pair of glasses perched on the end of his nose. He wore a short-sleeved white dress shirt with a navy tie, a stark contrast to his all-black ghost hunting attire. He glanced up, his smile already prepared to greet his new potential client.

The smile wavered when he saw her. "You're not Mrs. Bradley."

Penelope took a seat in the chair facing his desk. "I am, actually, for the next half hour at least."

The smile disappeared. "I don't understand."

Penelope threw the newspaper from the day before onto the desk, folded open to the story about the protesters at the Brown warehouse. "Who is this?" She'd circled the mystery ghost hunter in red marker.

Clay studied the picture. "That's Patrick Wheeler."

"I saw him with you the night you all visited the Brown warehouse. What's he doing in a picture of the protesters from that Southern Baptist church?"

Clay continued to stare at the photograph, his brow furrowed. "I have no idea, but I'll certainly ask him."

"I was thinking about it, and I also don't recall Mr. Wheeler participating in your walkie-talkie check that night."

"He didn't?" Clay's frown deepened. "I could have sworn he did."

"How long has he been involved with your group?" Penelope asked.

"For about a year now. He's been really enthusiastic about our investigations. In fact, he's become kind of our expert on occult things related to hauntings."

The hairs on the back of Penelope's neck stood on end. "What do you mean by 'occult things'?"

Clay's eyes narrowed. "I think you have a good idea of what I'm talking about. I'll give you an example, though. We had reports a few months ago of a haunting out in Anderson. Patrick was the one who found out about the occult activity on the property and was able to prepare us all."

"Prepare you for what?"

"Before we started our investigation, he went in and did something to keep any non-human entities from harming us."

"Non-human entities. You mean demons."

Clay wrinkled his nose. "We don't like to use that word. It has too much baggage. What we mean is an entity that has never been a human, so anything that's not a ghost, basically."

Call them whatever you wanted, they were still demons.

"Do you know what he did?"

Clay shook his head. "Not really."

"You just trusted him?"

If Charles had been there, he would have been spitting profanities.

Clay shrugged. "Look, all I know is that nothing harassed us during our investigation that night. And there have been other times Patrick helped out like that."

"Whatever he did, it certainly didn't help at the warehouse."

"What do you mean by that?"

She ignored his question. "I need to get in touch with him. I could find him on my own, but that would take time I'm not sure we have. It would make things easier if you just told me how to contact him."

Clay let out a nervous chuckle. "You make it sound like he's in some kind of trouble."

Penelope pointed to the photo of Patrick Wheeler standing next to the megaphone-wielding Lowell Purdue. "If he's not now, I'd say it's a good bet he's going to be."

———

Patrick Wheeler's apartment was empty.

"He paid through the end of the month," said the landlord, a squat, balding man who reminded Penelope of the picture of Humpty Dumpty in one of her storybooks from when she was a little girl, "but he moved everything out a few days ago, not that he'd had that much to begin with. Didn't leave any kind of forwarding address."

That left Penelope with only one place to go.

Sitting in the sanctuary of the Little Rock Southern Baptist Church, Penelope felt a small pang of guilt for not attending more herself. Her father had rebelled early, but he never objected to her going with her grandmother. Penelope had happy memories of church—candlelight services at Christmastime, her grandmother slipping her peppermint candies wrapped in cellophane that would crackle when she opened them during the worship service, Vacation Bible School with cookies and fruit punch and macaroni necklaces, hymns played on the booming pipe organ.

But there were bad memories, too. Penelope would never forget what happened the time a deacon resigned for cheating on his wife. She was the one who eventually left the church. Everyone behaved as if the affair were her fault, as if she's somehow made her husband sleep with another woman. A few years later. they asked the man to serve as a deacon again. He'd remarried by then and everyone loved his second wife.

The hypocrisy left a bad taste in Penelope's mouth, one she'd never quite been able to get out.

The sanctuary at the Little Rock Southern Baptist Church could have fit into the First Presbyterian Church's sanctuary four times over. A board hanging at the front posted the previous Sunday's attendance—fifty-two. Stained glass windows with abstract patterns threw red, yellow, and purple light over the rows of wooden pews. There was no pipe organ, only an upright piano to the left of the small platform where the pulpit stood.

"Can I help you?"

Penelope turned around to see an older woman standing in the aisle, graying hair pinned up on her head. "I'm not sure," she said. "Maybe? I was hoping to speak with Reverend Purdue."

"Oh, well, I'm not sure he's here right now." The woman extended her hand. "I'm Edna Green, chair of the sanctuary committee. I just came in to replace the flowers on the offering table."

Penelope took her hand. "Penelope Drake. I … I didn't really know where else to go. I'm a friend of a member of your congregation. Patrick Wheeler. I'm worried about him."

Edna took a seat on the pew next to her. "How so?"

"I stopped by his apartment this morning, but the landlord said he moved out without leaving a forwarding address. I saw his picture in the paper yesterday with the protesters at that warehouse off Stone Avenue. I thought maybe someone here might know where he was."

Penelope suppressed a smile. Dan would be proud of her for coming up with that lie on the spot. Then she heard her grandmother's voice in her head telling her she should be ashamed for lying in a church.

Edna scrunched up her nose at the word *protesters*. Maybe that meant at least some of the people in the church were reasonable.

"He's had a tough life, you know with his father committing suicide when he was in high school."

Penelope nodded, trying to hide her surprise. "How long has Patrick been attending your church?"

"About a year."

The same amount of time he'd been a part of Clay's team of ghost hunters.

"He's very quiet," Edna continued. "He doesn't talk to many people, but he's always been courteous, at least to me. There were some who were surprised when he took up the cause Pastor Purdue has been pushing."

That face again.

"But you weren't."

Edna leaned forward and lowered her voice. "Well, you didn't hear this from me, but he makes certain people nervous, the way he stares, and some of the comments he's made."

"What sort of comments?"

"In Bible studies, he seemed to be more interested in certain passages."

Penelope nodded. "Ones that talk about demons."

Edna's eyes grew wide, her drawn-on eyebrows arching upward. "How did you know?"

"That's part of why I'm worried."

"Do you think something's happened to him?"

"I don't know. I wanted to talk to Pastor Purdue, maybe."

Another face.

"How long has Pastor Purdue been here?" Penelope asked.

"Almost three years now."

"How is that going?"

She pursed her lips. "Well, his style takes some getting used to, but there are those here who like it. And he does have attendance up."

Fifty-two. Penelope wondered what it was like before. She stood up. "Thank you for your time. I don't want to keep you from your business."

As she slid out of the row, the side door by the piano burst open, and Reverend Purdue entered the sanctuary, holding a Bible as if it were attached to his hand. Upon seeing her, he immediately made a bee line for her, a smile plastered on his face much like his hair plastered on his head.

It wasn't that Penelope disliked preachers. Her own great-grandfather had been a Presbyterian minister. She just approached them with a great deal of cynicism.

"How do you do, Miss ..."

"Drake. Penelope Drake."

"Miss Drake. A pleasure to make your acquaintance. I'm Reverend Lowell Purdue, head pastor here at Little Rock Southern Baptist Church. Can I help you with something?"

Edna made a discrete retreat but remained within earshot while she tended to the flower arrangement on the offering table.

"I came here because I needed to talk to you about someone who attends your church," Penelope said. "Patrick Wheeler."

His smile showed signs of strain. "How do you know Patrick?"

Penelope repeated her lie.

"Well, just because he's moved doesn't mean he's left the area. If I were a betting man, I'd wager he'll be here on Sunday. Why don't you come to our Sunday morning service? Are you looking for a church home?"

"My family goes to the First Presbyterian Church."

The smile nearly faltered again. "We're always welcoming to our Presbyterian brothers and sisters."

"Truth be told, I wouldn't be so worried if I hadn't seen his picture in the paper among the protesters you brought to the Brown warehouse. He looked so angry and hateful. That's not like him at all."

She was poking the bear.

Reverend Purdue drew himself up to his full height. Finally, the smile cracked. "That's where you're mistaken, Miss Drake. What we're doing, we do out of love, love of God and our fellow man. Patrick Wheeler, in my experience, is a fine young man of faith, and I don't think you should be concerned."

"But it just seems like he's becoming obsessed."

"It's no easy task, standing up to the wicked, and often we can ill afford to let down our guard. We just have to pray to God to give us strength. You've seen what Satan is capable of already. A man is dead. Now is not the time to rest."

"Why does there have to be something Satanic going on? Why can't it all just be a big coincidence? Kids playing pranks and a freak accident."

Another poke with a bigger stick.

The Reverend's smile returned, just several times more patronizing. "How old are you, Miss Drake?"

"Twenty-eight."

"I have been a pastor longer than you have been alive, young lady. There are evil forces in this world you don't understand. We are called to fight them."

"How does yelling slogans from across the street do that?"

He held up his Bible. "We bring the presence of God. That's all that's necessary. He will take care of it however He sees fit."

"You make it sound like a threat."

"You remember the story of Sodom and Gomorrah."

Penelope nodded. "One of the many seared into my memory during Sunday school."

The Reverend arched an eyebrow. "Sometimes cleansing fire is necessary."

10.

WEDNESDAY, JULY 19, 1972

harles checked the time on the grandfather clock in the hallway. He was supposed to meet with Penelope and Zed at the Brown warehouse at noon, but as he came downstairs to leave tinny notes from his record player wafted through the first floor of the house.

Clara Ward was singing "There is a Fountain Filled with Blood." When he entered the workroom, he found the ghost woman sitting in a chair and reading another one of his books, and his record player on. The woman wore the same short black dress as the other times she'd appeared.

Something about her intrigued him, enticed him even, but he didn't relish the thought of sharing his house, even with a spirit refusing to pass beyond the Veil.

She looked at him and smiled, like she had done before.

"Hello?" he said this time.

She put the book down, and he expected her to fade away, but instead, she stood and walked toward him. When he backed away, she hesitated.

"Who are you?" he asked.

She smiled and took another step forward, prompting Charles to take another step back.

"What do you want? Why are you here now?"

The look on her face was like the one a mother gave a child who didn't understand the rules. She remained where she was, but she reached out a hand.

Charles stared at it. "You want me to take your hand."

She nodded.

"I'm not so sure that's a good idea."

She cocked her head to the side.

"This is some kind of magic I don't know about. I don't know how to protect myself."

That smile again.

Charles shook his head. "No. I can't do it. Besides, I have somewhere to be right now. I'm sorry. I'll research this later."

He turned his back on the ghost, but at that moment, the door flew open. The smell assaulted him first, the stench of rot and decay. And then the apparition appeared. A mass of filthy graveclothes, bones, and viscera leaving a trail of maggots behind it.

The Shrouded Man.

In his house.

The wretched spirit reached a bony hand toward Charles. Charles tried to get away, but he stumbled and tripped and fell into the arms of the ghost woman. Her skin was soft, her body warm and comforting. But then he kept falling, passing through her. The warmth fled, replaced by bitter cold. As his vision darkened, the panic set in. He struggled to breathe. He tried to claw his way up, but a wave of numbness washed over his limbs, and then the nothingness took him.

Zed and Bertram stood in the middle of the warehouse. Zed looked down at the pentagram, trying not to actually read the symbols drawn around it. Bertram paced, fingering the charm bracelet around his wrist and stealing glances at the old tractor still corralled by police tape.

"You don't need to be here," said Zed. "Penelope, Charles, and I can do this by ourselves."

Bertram stopped pacing for a moment. "But I do. This is my business, or at least I'm responsible for it. What are you going to do anyway?"

Zed shrugged. "Not sure exactly. Charles is going to examine the circle, figure out the nature of the magic that created it, and see if he can't come up with a way to neutralize it. Penelope and I will help any way we can."

"I don't understand why erasing the circle wouldn't do the job."

Zed shook his head. "It doesn't work that way. If something nasty came through into our world, that circle might be the only way to put it back. Also, erasing the circle wouldn't get rid of the magical imprint it's made. This part of the warehouse, or maybe even the whole building, would likely always be cursed. There would always be accidents or other bad things happening."

"How do we know if something nasty came through?"

"We don't."

"What are we doing here, then? Is it even safe to be here?"

"Relatively. There were a dozen policemen swarming all over a few days ago. All that energy muddies up the water, so to speak. Demons get distracted easily. Also, it's daylight. Much harder for a demon to be active in the daylight." Zed pointed to his own charm bracelet. "Besides, these should give us enough warning in case anything mean and ugly tries to attack."

Bertram sighed. "I'd still be happier if Charles hurried the hell up."

———

Charles came to with a start. He wasn't in his house anymore. He wasn't sure exactly where he was. He sat at a table in a corner of a large noisy room full of people. On a stage at the front of the room, a five-piece jazz band played—a piano, a bass, two trumpets, and a trombone. Everyone in the room was black, and they were all dressed to the nines, even if their clothes were old-fashioned—a lot like the ghost woman's dress, in fact. Several men wore army uniforms.

Gas lamps on the walls and candles on the tables provided the only light. The windows were small and high up near the ceiling, leaving the room stiflingly hot. An iron set of stairs against the far wall led upward. Two couples came down, still knocking snow off their shoes, and took one of the few remaining open tables.

Charles shook droplets of water off his hand from the condensation on the glass of the ice-cold drink he held. He loosened the collar of the army uniform he inexplicably wore and reached down to pick up a flyer on the floor near his table. He smoothed out the paper.

February 23, 1919
At the Boiler Room
158 W 133rd Street
Millie Priest
With the
Paul Malcolm Quintet

He was in Harlem. That had to be it. And that explained the uniform. A good many of the black soldiers who fought in World War I made their way to Harlem when they came home. But that was impossible. How could he be seeing images from twenty-five years before he was born in a place he'd never been? It must have been the ghost. She must be doing this to him. He had to get out. He stood to leave, but the band stopped, and she came on stage. The ghost. Except she was a real, flesh-and-blood woman.

She wore a long sleeveless dress covered in black and gold sequins that hugged the curves of her body and black gloves that extended to her elbows. She began to sing, her voice low and smoky like cut glass. She sang a song about lost love and regret and loneliness, and she sang directly to him. Their gazes met, and a charge of electricity ran through his body. Unable to look away, he hung on every note. He watched every move of her hands and every sway of her hips as her sequined dress sparkled in the dim light. He wasn't the only one either. The crowd fell silent under the spell of her voice.

When the last note of the song faded away into the dark corners of the room, Charles was the first on his feet to clap. Everyone else followed, but soon their applause gave way to shouts of alarm. Heavy footsteps thudded on the stairs, and several men, all white, descended into the music club, raising crowbars and baseball bats they used to smash tables and chairs and anyone unlucky enough to come into range.

Charles held his breath. This strain of violence happened a lot in the years after the Great War, whites in major cities attacking newly relocated blacks for fear they would take their jobs. It was one thing to read about it in a history book, but nothing could prepare Charles for the reality. Seeing the equal parts hatred and glee on the faces of the men as they destroyed the club made him physically ill.

As panic spread through the room, the danger came not only from the men brandishing their weapons but from stampeding club patrons. On stage, Millie and the rest of the musicians huddled behind the piano. All Charles could think about was getting her to safety. He pushed his way through the crowd, only to spot one of the white men headed toward the stage with a bat. Charles watched helplessly as the man reached the stage first and hefted himself up. He went straight for Millie, but the trombone player interposed himself. For his trouble, the poor musician had the trombone bashed out of his hands. He went down wailing, clutching his broken fingers. The man kicked him in the head, and he didn't cry anymore.

Millie tried to get away, but the man's beefy hand closed around her small wrist. Before he could do anything else, though, Charles seized him by the shoulder and spun him around. He punched the man in the face. Cartilage snapped, and blood spurted from the mess that used to be the man's nose. He toppled back and fell off the stage.

Charles turned his attention toward Millie. "We need to get you and your friends out of here. Is there another door?"

"Backstage," she said, her voice trembling.

Charles reached out a hand. "I'll get you there."

Millie didn't move, her eyes growing wide. She opened her mouth to say something but never got the chance. A sharp pain radiated from the back of Charles' skull. His legs gave way, and everything went dark again.

———

Zed watched as Bertram traced a perfect circle in the floor while pacing around the perimeter of the pentagram. "Be careful, there, or you'll summon another demon."

Bertram stopped and looked at him, a horrified expression on his face. "You're joking, right?"

Zed shrugged. "Better safe than sorry."

Bertram stared down at the arcane marks on the floor and took a giant step back. "Where are Charles and Penelope? Shouldn't they be here by now?"

"I'm sure they're on their way. Your fretting isn't going to get them here faster."

Bertram sighed and pinched the bridge of his nose. "If you told me six months ago I'd be dealing with all this, I don't know if I would've moved back to Greenville."

"Why did you?"

"Dad asked me to. Come to find out, he kept me in the dark about a lot of things."

"Magic is a hard pill for a lot of people to swallow."

"Yeah, there's that, but it's not the only thing. Every day I find out about some off-the-books deal he's done or some 'special arrangement' he has with a client. Things he should have told me."

"That sounds like it might be frustrating."

"I guess I shouldn't be surprised. My dad and I have never really been great at communicating. We've never had what you'd call deep conversations."

"So, I'm guessing he never talked to you about Penelope's dad, or Penelope."

Bertram laughed. "Are you kidding? Ask him anything about the Drakes and he'd clam up faster than a bank of oysters."

"So, he never said anything to you about why he stopped talking to Penelope's dad, or anything that caused you to break off your friendship with Penelope?"

Bertram frowned. "Is that what she told you, that I broke off our friendship?"

"Not exactly. Just that something happened and you two didn't talk to each other anymore. It's not a topic she likes to discuss either."

Bertram crossed his arms. "Nothing really happened. She just … I mean, we … Look, people change. That's all."

"If you say so."

Bertram shot him a dirty look. "I'm telling the truth."

Zed shoved his hands into is pockets and leaned against a shelf. "Fine. I believe you."

Bertram continued to glare. "At any rate, we were talking about my dad. He was all about the business. He was never 'off,' ever. Everything was a show for potential clients, even my birthday parties. He like to brag to everyone about how I'd run the company someday. Never mind whether I wanted to." He put on a pained smile. "Everyone has issues with their old man every now and then, though, right?"

Zed had been afraid the conversation would steer in that direction. "Sorry, I wouldn't know. I've never met my dad."

Bertram cocked an eyebrow. "Your mom raised you by herself? Any brothers or sisters?"

Zed shook his head. "No, just me."

"You don't know where he is or anything?"

"My mom has told me a few stories, but I really don't know that much about him. Funny thing is that she doesn't seem to resent him, even though he left her high and dry with a kid. I'm not sure I'd be so forgiving. So, I guess you should count yourself lucky you actually know your dad."

Bertram looked like he wanted to disagree, but instead he yelped and grabbed his wrist, the one encircled by the charm bracelet. A second later, Zed's own charm bracelet bit into the skin around his wrist. A scream tore through the warehouse, just like the one they'd heard the day Bobby Parker was killed. The symbols around the pentagram glowed faintly. The tractor that had run over Bobby roared to life and lurched forward, breaking through the police tape.

It turned toward them.

———

Penelope found her office in shambles. Papers covered the floor strewn from open drawers in her filing cabinet as well as her desk. Her chair lay on its side. In the center of her desk, the newspaper from Monday lay in shreds, the photo of Patrick Wheeler on top.

"Dad? What's going on?"

No answer.

Penelope stooped to pick up some of the papers scattered on the floor. It would take her hours to put everything back in order. "Dad, why did you do this? I have to go meet Zed and Bertram now. I don't have time for this."

One knock.

Frowning, she looked around. "No? No to what? Meeting Zed and Bertram?"

Two knocks.

"Why? Dad, it's important. Why did you go to all this trouble to get my attention? You've never done something like this before."

One knock.

Penelope sighed. "Dad, I need to go. Maybe we can figure out a way to discuss what this is about later."

She turned around just in time to see the bolt on the front door turn. Penelope tried to unlock the door again, but the bolt wouldn't budge. Her father had locked her in.

She banged on the door. "Not funny, Dad. Let me out."

One knock.

She made a run for the back door but found it wouldn't open either.

One knock.

"I get it, Dad. You don't want me to go. Why?"

Silence.

"Is it because of Patrick Wheeler?"

Two knocks.

"Who is he? Are Bertram and Zed in danger?"

No answer.

"Dad?"

Penelope rushed back to her office and scooped up the phone. She dialed Bertram's number at the warehouse and waited for Bertram to pick up, her heart pounding.

He never did.

———

"Holy shit!" Bertram screamed.

The old tractor, moving with a speed no normal tractor possessed, barreled toward them.

"Run!" Zed yelled.

They raced through the warehouse, trying to reach Bertram's office, but the tractor gained on them with every step.

Zed grabbed Bertram by the shirt. "Turn up here. We'll try to lose it in one of these rows."

But as soon as they took a left into the row Zed had pointed out, the tractor's tires screeched as it changed course, too. It raced parallel with them, overtaking them and pivoting when it reached the end of its row to come at them headlong. The roar of its engine sounded like hellish growls. Zed and Bertram spun around and ran back the way they came.

"Any other ideas?" Bertram asked.

"Lucky break. It can't be that smart."

But no matter how many zig-zag turns they made, the tractor stayed with them, gaining ground with every second.

"We're not going to make it back to your office," Zed said. "Where is this side door Lloyd was talking about?"

"Coming up on it," Bertram replied.

He ducked into another row, Zed on his heels. The tractor sped past, but the squeal of tires on the concrete floor told Zed it was quickly correcting course again. Ahead of them, the door loomed. Bertram slammed into it and rebounded.

He swore again. "Someone must have relocked it."

He pulled a keychain out of his pocket and fumbled with the keys. Behind them the rumble of the tractor's half-assembled engine grew louder. Zed glanced over his shoulder to see the tractor bearing down on them again.

He picked up the nearest thing he could get his hands on, a gear shift rod, and threw it at the tractor. It lodged in one of the back wheels, jamming the axle. The tractor skidded into a shelf while the rod scraped along the floor, throwing off sparks. The corner of the shelf buckled, even as the tractor continued with its single-minded pursuit.

At last Bertram found the right key. He unlocked the door and pushed it open. He and Zed leapt through. Behind them the sound of tearing metal echoed through the warehouse until Bertram slammed the door shut again. He bent over, resting his hands on his knees while he tried to catch his breath.

Zed gripped his arm. "Don't stop. Keep running."

Bertram, still breathing heavy, looked up at him. "Why?"

"Just do it."

A muffled bang reverberated through the warehouse.

"Now," Zed commanded.

The shelf the tractor hit held containers of diesel fuel. He didn't want to be anywhere nearby when the diesel met the sparks from the dragging gear shift rod. Zed and Bertram were maybe a hundred yards away when the explosion blew out the side of the warehouse and threw them both to the ground. Glass and other debris rained down around them. When it finally stopped, Zed, his ears ringing, scrambled back up and helped Bertram to his feet.

"You okay?" Zed asked.

Bertram nodded. He had cuts on his arms and face, some deep. He glanced over his shoulder at the results of the conflagration. They still weren't safe. They needed to get farther away, but Zed couldn't help but steal a glance himself. Tongues of flame leapt out of the opening made by the explosion and engulfed what was left of the warehouse, while in the distance, sirens wailed.

11.

Charles opened the door to find Zed standing on his porch. He didn't wait for Charles to invite him in, instead pushing past into the front room and knocking over a stack of books by the front door.

"Where the fuck were you, Charles?" His eyes blazed, and his mouth was pulled back in an angry snarl.

Charles glanced up from the overturned books by Zed's feet. "When?"

"You know when. At the Brown warehouse on Wednesday. The one that burned down? God, Charles, do you have any idea what I'm talking about?"

"Not really." Charles stooped to stack up the books again. They glowed faintly blue as he touched them. "What day is it?"

Zed narrowed his eyes. "It's Friday."

Charles grunted. "Wonder where Thursday went?" Having set the books straight, he stood and pointed to the bandage on Zed's forehead. "What happened to your face?"

"A demon-possessed tractor."

Zed's answer seemed to trigger something in the back of Charles' mind. "You mean the one that killed that guy? It came to life again? Interesting."

Some of the anger fled Zed's face. "Are you okay, Charles?"

"Yeah, I'm fine."

"No, something's wrong."

Charles had pieces of memories—a dark club in Harlem full of smoke and jazz music, a fight, the singer named Millie Priest. At that moment, her ghost appeared over Zed's shoulder as if summoned, wearing the same gold and black sequined dress she wore in the club. She put a finger to her lips.

Charles shook his head. "Nothing's wrong."

"Charles—"

"I said nothing's wrong."

Zed stepped forward. "Charles, if you're having another episode you need help."

"I don't need help. Look. I'm exhausted. I'm sorry, we can talk later." He turned to leave. He needed to get back to his workshop. He had two books he was trying to re-stitch.

Zed caught him by the arm. "We were depending on you, Charles."

"Maybe depending on me isn't your best idea." Charles shrugged him off and flexed his left hand. Energy crackled through the room. Zed massaged the wrist where he wore his charm bracelet. "Now, please go. And try to be careful of the books. Some of them can be dangerous, you know."

———

After Penelope's father had let her out of the house, she rushed to the Brown warehouse, only to find it in flames, surrounded by fire trucks. A panicked twenty minutes later, she found Bertram and Zed sitting in the back of an ambulance, being bandaged up for cuts and bruises.

They told her their story, and she told them hers.

No one knew where Charles was.

Two days later, they were still trying to sort through what happened.

Penelope walked into her office and found a surprise on her

desk, her painted rock on top of one of her father's old college sweaters. Her father had been so proud he could still fit in it. She hadn't been able to part with it after he died.

"Dad, are you here?"

Two knocks.

"What's this about? Does it have something to do with what happened at the Brown warehouse?"

Two knocks.

"You know who Patrick Wheeler is, don't you?"

Two knocks.

She picked up the sweater and ran the fabric through her fingers. "And whatever is going on with the Browns has something to do with what happened to you in college, doesn't it?"

Two knocks.

Penelope sighed. "Look, Dad. I know this is hard, but you have to trust me. I can take care of myself, and I have others looking out for me. I'll be careful. I promise. I love you."

Silence.

———

Penelope's grandmother smiled when she answered the door. "Penelope, what an unexpected surprise! So nice to see you. Come in. It's a little early for lunch. Do you want anything to drink?"

Penelope stepped inside, out of the late morning heat. "No, that's okay."

"I'll pour you a glass of tea."

She hurried into the kitchen and came out a minute later with two tall glasses of golden-amber iced tea. She handed one to Penelope. "Let's go sit on the porch and talk."

Penelope sipped her tea and listened to her grandmother's opinion of the new Miss South Carolina who was pretty "even if she's from Columbia." She also learned all about the latest church controversy in which the music minister—bless his heart—wanted to introduce "modern" music to the worship service.

"What's so wrong with hymns?" she asked. "By the way, everyone at church is asking when they can expect to see you again, but I just told them all you were very busy."

"Soon, Grandma. I promise."

Her grandmother's expression darkened, just slightly. "Speaking of being busy, I saw what happened to the Brown's company. It's an awful shame. I don't know how they'll recover from that."

Bertram swore insurance would cover the loss of the warehouse. Penelope doubted any insurance policy in the world had a clause addressing demon tractor attacks, but if he needed a project to keep himself occupied, she wasn't going to argue with him.

They talked about a good many other mundane things—the weather, the dress her grandmother had bought on clearance at Ivey's, why olive was not a good color for the music minister's wife. Penelope wished she could stretch out the lazy summer afternoon forever. When she was younger, she'd sit on the porch with her grandmother, or sometimes her father, and just watch the cars go by. Only then she preferred a popsicle to a glass of iced tea. Her grandmother kept a supply in her freezer. Probably still did. Penelope always ate the purple ones first.

But she was there for more than just a social visit.

"Grandma, do you know a Patrick Wheeler?"

Her grandmother tilted her head to the side. "Well, there are Wheelers over by Taylors. One of your great aunts married Joe Wheeler. And there are some more Wheelers down toward Simpsonville, but I don't think any of them are named Patrick. He must not be from around these parts."

The greatest condemnation Edith Drake could give was to declare you were "not from around these parts." If you were the recipient of that dreaded mark, you weren't to be trusted and you weren't worth her time. That path was a dead end.

Penelope tried something different. "Do you happen to have Dad's old yearbooks from college?"

Her grandmother frowned. "Why?"

"I'm just curious. I'd like to see them."

"Well, I have a few of his things, still, but most of it I had moved to the attic. They'd be there if they're anywhere. But you be careful. I don't think anyone has been up there in years."

Back inside, Penelope pulled down the trap door in the hallway ceiling and climbed up in the attic. The heat nearly suffocated her. After climbing over several boxes of her grandfather's old clothes, a few pieces of broken furniture, some pictures, and stacks of old magazines, she finally found a small box labeled with her father's name.

Upon opening the box, she discovered a few paperback books, some of her father's clothes, and finally, his copies of the *Garnet and Black*, the yearbook for the University of South Carolina. Penelope picked the one from 1936, his freshman year, the year before the incident that nearly got him expelled. She scanned his class pictures. It didn't take long to find what she was looking for.

Geoffrey Wheeler.

The resemblance was unmistakable. Same eyes, same nose, same chin. He had to be Patrick's father.

She tucked the yearbook under her arm and was about to climb down again when she noticed something else in the box, a notebook, the pages yellowed. As she leafed through, she recognized her father's handwriting, but the notebook wasn't like any journal she'd ever seen. In fact, it looked more like the inside of one of Charles' books, with diagrams and notes scrawled in different languages, some she recognized, some she didn't. She stopped cold though, when she reached the last page. There in faded pencil, her father had drawn a pentagram surrounded by the same symbols as the pentagram on the floor of the Brown warehouse.

"Well, Dad, looks like we have some more to talk about."

LOCAL HAUNTS

A DREADFUL PENNY NOVELLA

1.

SATURDAY, JULY 29, 1972

The Devil is the Father of Lies.

All lies.

Not just the big ones, the ones that destroy lives—secret affairs, hidden addictions, past indiscretions. He's the father of the little white lies, too, the ones you tell because you think you're sparing someone's feelings. How many unintended consequences do you think those little lies have? What's the price? How long before the lies get bigger? How long before the trust erodes?

The Devil's greatest handiwork, though, might be the lies you tell yourself, the ones you use to justify the things you do.

You're not a bad person.

You deserve to be happy.

It's not your fault.

But what if you *are* a bad person? What if you *don't* deserve to be happy? What if it *is* your fault?

———

Lloyd opened his eyes, suddenly awake. Maybe the air conditioner kicked on. Or he needed to take a piss. He lay still in the bed for a few seconds, letting his eyes adjust to the darkness, and also trying to figure out where he was. The last thing he remembered clearly was walking up to the bar at the White Horse Saloon and ordering a beer for himself and another for … someone else. As the events of the evening came back to him a piece at a time, he grinned.

Lloyd rolled over. No one occupied the other side of the bed, but the pillow was still warm. He propped himself up on his elbows and glanced around the room. Someone was standing at the foot of the bed.

"Tammy? Tammy, that you?" He patted the mattress. "Come back over here with me."

He thought her name was Tammy anyway. When he'd met her, his attention was focused on the lacy little red halter top and the pair of denim hot pants she was wearing. They just begged for him to try to get them off her. A few hours and a whole lot of drinks later, the two of them staggered through the door of the motel room and those hot pants came off.

But now she wasn't answering him.

"Tammy," he purred, "come back to bed. I'm up for a second round if you are."

The figure at the foot of the bed still didn't move.

Lloyd shook his head and let out a chuckle. "Oh, come on, now. You can't say I didn't show you a good time."

Finally, the figure shifted, and even in the dim light, Lloyd could tell it wasn't Tammy. Too tall. Too broad-shouldered. As his heart pounded, Lloyd fought through the alcohol-induced fog in his head, trying to figure out what to do.

"You're not Tammy. Who … who are you?"

Still no response.

Lloyd reached across the bed and switched on the lamp on the nightstand. He immediately wished he hadn't. A man stood by the bed dressed all in black. Despite the summer heat, he wore a coat with a hood that hid his face. Behind him, Tammy, her head lolled to one side, lay across a chair. A giant red gash cut across her throat. Blood trickled from the wound down her naked body and pooled on the floor.

Lloyd screamed.

The black figure lifted a knife. "Sure, Lloyd, I'm up for a second round."

The man's gravelly voice compelled Lloyd to reduce his screams to quiet whimpers. The man pulled back the hood to reveal his face. Lloyd's eyes grew wide with recognition.

The man laughed. "Come on now, show me a good time."

He leaned over and turned off the lamp.

———

As soon as Penelope knocked on the door to Zed's apartment, she knew she should have called first. From inside came the sound of footsteps, then stumbling and cursing and a loud bang followed by more cursing before Zed, at last, groggily opened the door.

When he saw her, he raised an eyebrow. "Penelope? To what do I owe the pleasure this morning?"

"I need to talk with you." She surveyed his old sweatpants and tee shirt, his messy hair, his slumped shoulders, and heavy eyelids. "Sorry to bother you so early."

"Don't worry about it. What time is it anyway?" He leaned on the door, apparently for support.

"It was about eight o'clock when I left the house."

He shrugged. "Well, I guess two hours of sleep is better than none."

Of course. How could she be such an idiot? "You were deejaying last night, weren't you?"

"This morning, technically, but yes." He stifled a yawn.

Three nights a week, Zed worked as the night deejay at a local station. Penelope often wondered how he'd landed that gig, but Zed always played coy whenever someone asked him that question.

She shook her head. "I'm sorry. I wasn't thinking. I can come back later."

Zed waved her inside. "No, that's okay. I'm already awake.

Wasn't doing much today anyway. So, what do you need to talk about?"

Penelope stepped into the apartment. Zed had once told her he found all his furniture and artwork at flea markets and yard sales. She had no reason to disbelieve him. In the living area, a brown leather couch and an orange recliner lined one wall. Above the couch hung an oil painting of a desert landscape he'd bought because he "liked the colors."

On the opposite wall, a television rested inside a dark wood console next to a bright green bookcase. Old movie posters for *Dracula* with Bela Lugosi and *The Wolfman* with Lon Chaney Jr. hung in frames on the wall over the television. In the corner sat a thriving giant potted fern. Penelope had never managed to keep a houseplant alive.

"I'd offer you coffee or something," Zed continued, "but I don't really have anything."

"That's okay. I'll make it quick."

Penelope went to the bookcase and reached behind the row of books on the second shelf. As with many parts of Zed's life, she'd learned not to try to make sense of the hodgepodge of philosophy books, histories, and pulp paperbacks. She retrieved a yellowed notebook hidden there. She'd found the old journal in her grandmother's attic. Her father's journal. The entries in it dated back to his college years, but they weren't the typical thoughts of a college student, and the drawings in the margins weren't just random doodles. The notebook was full of magic. Penelope had asked Zed if she could keep it at his apartment because she didn't want her father finding it at her place.

Her father's ghost generally respected Penelope's privacy. He preferred to stay in the office of the detective agency that had once been his, rather than in the upstairs apartment where she lived alone now. But he could go anywhere in the old converted house, and in the past, he had found things even she didn't know were there.

She didn't like keeping things from him, and she knew she

couldn't put off confronting her father about the notebook forever, but she didn't want him to find it, not until she was ready. Every scenario she ran through her head just ended in a fight. They'd never fought, even when her father was alive. Only once had they ever come close—the time she told him she wanted to be a police detective, just like him.

He told her no.

She was crushed. She thought he'd be happy, proud of his little girl for wanting to follow in his footsteps, for wanting to help people.

She'd never get the chance to help people, he said, because she'd never be anything but a meter maid. There was no way they'd ever let a woman be a detective. She responded that she'd be the first. He crossed his arms and told her that she was being naïve. At that point, she left the room before any words escaped her mouth she couldn't stuff back in.

Of course, he was right. He wasn't trying to be mean. He knew she'd be the Chief of Police someday if anyone ever gave her half a chance, but he also knew the world didn't work that way. Out of a total of one hundred fifty, the Greenville Police Department had exactly five female police officers, all meter maids. The most any of them got to do was pat down a woman who happened to be arrested.

She never bothered applying for the job.

The discussion about her father's college journal, though, was going to be even more difficult than that, which is why Penelope found herself at Zed's apartment early on a Saturday morning.

"Any closer to figuring out how a pentagram your dad drew in a notebook thirty-five years ago made it onto the floor of the warehouse at the Brown Tractor & Farm Supply Co.?" Zed asked.

He tactfully avoided the part about the same pentagram being associated with the death of a warehouse worker named Bobby Parker, a demon-possessed tractor, and ultimately, the explosion that destroyed the warehouse.

"Not exactly." Penelope opened the notebook to the sketch of the pentagram. An intricate array of symbols and words wove around the five points of the star. "I think maybe I made a mistake translating some of this. My high school Latin is a little rusty. I guess we're lucky it's a real language, though, not like these other symbols here."

Zed stiffened. "That's Enochian. It's a real language."

"I meant one spoken by people."

"It's spoken by people. A few anyway."

She shot him a sideways glance. "Where?"

"Other planes," he said. "Beyond the Veil."

"How do you know that?"

"Charles told me."

She returned her attention to the notebook. "Well, until you can find me an Enochian-to-English dictionary, I'll be sticking to what I remember of Mrs. Farr's conjugation drills."

"Did you try Charles again?" Zed asked.

She shook her head. "Still not answering my calls."

"Have you been out there lately?"

"Not in a few weeks. Do you think we need to have another talk with him? Together?"

Zed barked a laugh. "Because that went so well the last time."

"But it did. We almost had him back."

"Almost."

She sighed. She didn't understand the hostility between Charles and Zed, and she just wished Zed would try to be more understanding of Charles' ... unique problems. "We still don't know what happened to him while he was in Vietnam."

"My guess? They used to call it being shell-shocked, but from what I hear, now they're calling it post-traumatic stress disorder. Lots of soldiers coming back from over there have it. They're so traumatized by the stuff they see, they can't get over it."

Penelope considered for a moment what Zed was saying. It made sense, but she didn't buy it, not completely. "This is different, though. I can't put my finger on it, but something just seems off about the way he's been behaving since the incident with Roy Arnold."

Roy Arnold instigated everything, in a way. By attacking the Brown family, the rogue magician brought out revelations about her own father's past, culminating in the discovery of his notebook. Charles, unfortunately, had borne the brunt of Roy Arnold's frustrations when she, Charles, and Zed thwarted his planned revenge on the Brown family for all the ways, real and imagined, they had slighted him.

Zed shrugged. "Maybe you're right, but there's no telling with Charles."

"I just wish you and Charles could get along, put whatever happened behind you."

"I have tried."

"Have you tried hard enough?"

He clenched his jaw. "I've done everything I can. He has to meet me halfway."

Zed was just being stubborn, but Penelope couldn't say she didn't share some of his frustration. "I want to help him. I just don't know how."

She took a pen and a pad of paper out of her purse. Then she sat down on the couch and started copying the words and symbols coiled around one point of the pentagram. She could only copy part of it at a time, or else she ran the risk of her father figuring out what she was doing.

She wrinkled her nose as she studied her notes. "This doesn't make a whole lot of sense. I can't tell if 'blood and bones' are ingredients or the outcome of a successful spell. I could really use Charles' library."

"What about your antique dealer friend?" Zed asked. "Dan is his name? Doesn't he have antique books?"

Penelope shook her head. "What are the chances of him coming across a book that would help me with this? Besides, he doesn't actually get that many books. Seems the old families of Greenville didn't make reading a priority."

Zed grinned. "Given what I know, that doesn't surprise me. He's friends with other antique dealers, though, right? Maybe he could put feelers out or something."

"I guess it's worth a shot." Also, it would be nice to talk to Dan again. She closed the notebook and placed it back in its hiding place. "Thanks, Zed. Try to get some sleep."

He gave her a salute as she left. "Will do."

———

Zed shut the door behind Penelope and let out a deep breath. He considered trying to go back to bed but knew the quest for more sleep would be futile. Instead, he turned on the television and found the Saturday morning cartoons. As the Roadrunner outran Wile E. Coyote for the thousandth time, he went to the kitchen and poured himself a bowl of cereal. Breakfast in hand, he came back and threw himself into the recliner.

Just as Coyote ran off a cliff and plummeted to the earth below, the show was interrupted by a breaking news announcement, though Zed couldn't imagine what was so important to interrupt the Coyote and the Roadrunner.

The picture switched to a reporter standing in front of a motel somewhere. "We're interrupting this program to report on a grisly murder overnight here in south Greenville county. Police are telling us that two people were stabbed to death in a room in the motel you see behind me on Highway 25 just north of Sandy Springs Road. They haven't revealed any more details than that, although we do have the names of the victims. They are twenty-two-year-old Tammy Ryan, and forty-one-year-old Lloyd Baker. As soon as we have more information, we'll be sure to let you know."

The show switched back just in time for Coyote to be hit by a train coming out of a tunnel he had painted on the side of a mountain. Zed let the cereal on his spoon fall back into the bowl. Without a doubt, he knew who the killer was.

Patrick Wheeler.

Yet another rogue magician who seemed to have it out for the Browns, Patrick Wheeler had bribed Lloyd Baker—who used to work at the Brown warehouse—to leave a side door unlocked. He was responsible for all the demonic activity in the warehouse, including the pentagram on the warehouse floor, the death of Bobby Parker, and the homicidal tractor.

And now he was apparently back for more.

Zed leapt out of the recliner and grabbed his phone to call Penelope, but she didn't pick up. There was only one other person he could think to call.

———

Rather than go home after leaving Zed's place, Penelope pointed her car toward the Greenville County Public Library. The small occult collection—not generally accessible to the public—wasn't nearly the size of Charles' library, but until he decided to be more agreeable, it would have to do. She was about halfway there when she noticed the car behind her.

The gold Ford sedan always remained a few car-lengths back, slowing down when she slowed down and turning when she turned. Could just be a coincidence, of course, but she knew better. She drove down Buncombe Street past the library, just to see if her follower would stay with her. He did.

She glanced at her wrist. The charm bracelet Charles had made for her hadn't so much as twitched. The last time someone followed her, in the library itself, the bracelet turned warm to warn her about the dark magic directed her way. That in and of itself didn't mean much. The same person might still be behind the wheel of the car. He could just be waiting for the right moment.

Penelope thought fast. She could double back and pull into the library parking lot, where there would hopefully be other people around, but the lot was small and cramped, and she ran the risk of being boxed in. She could instead go back to Zed's. That might be safer, but even there she'd make herself a pretty easy target getting out of her car.

But before she could do either, her decision was made for her.

The Ford revved its engine and accelerated until mere inches separated the two cars. The glare off the tinted windshield kept Penelope from getting a clear look at the driver's face. The Ford swerved from side to side as the driver honked the horn. Penelope hit the gas and shifted up, trying to put some space between the cars, but the driver of the Ford had other plans. With another burst of speed, the car rammed into her back bumper. She lost control of the wheel, and her Lincoln swerved up onto the side-walk. She slammed on the brakes and screeched to a halt inches from a telephone pole. The Ford sped past her. She sat frozen in fear, expecting the driver to turn around, but the car receded into the distance.

Penelope waited for her heart to stop pounding before she eased the Lincoln back onto the street. The car didn't seem too damaged. At least it moved. She'd have to take a look at the back bumper later. At the next intersection, she turned right. She didn't have it in her to go to the library anymore, but she really didn't want to go home. She needed to talk to someone, someone who didn't have anything to do with ghosts or demons or dark magic.

———

Charles lay in bed, staring at the ceiling of the tiny room. The air was hot and sticky. The sounds of the city at night drifted in through the open window. He had to admit those sounds carried a certain melody, a song the city sang. He was sure if he stayed there long enough, he could learn to sing it, too.

But the bed wasn't his bed, and the room wasn't his room. He wasn't even himself. In this dream world, this facsimile of New York City in 1919, he was Isaiah Jenkins. At least that's what the letters he found from Isaiah's sister in Charleston said. He even had some of Isaiah's memories, nothing truly tangible, just flashes. People he'd never met. Places he'd never been. But at the same time all so familiar.

The face that appeared when he closed his eyes, though, belonged to Millie Priest. In Charles' own time, she was a ghost who had taken up residence in his house. In 1919 she was a jazz singer with a voice like smoky glass. The last time he visited this dream version of New York, he'd heard her perform at The Boiler Room, a jazz club in Harlem. That same night, a group of white men burst in, destroying everything in the club and attacking the patrons with baseball bats and crowbars. One of them hit Charles on the back of his head while he was trying to protect Millie. That was the last he'd seen of the living version of her.

As he drifted off to sleep, he wondered if he'd run into her again.

Charles woke up on the floor where he had fallen. Very slowly he sat up. His head pounded, and his shoulder hurt where he had hit the hard wood. He was back in the front room of his own home, an old farmhouse out in the middle of nowhere, far from the city, where he generally preferred to be. The book he had been holding when he went out lay open next to him, pages down. He scooped it up and tried to smooth out the bent paper. A section of the spine disintegrated in his hand, and he swore under his breath. He pushed himself to his feet and spent a few wobbly moments regaining his balance.

He glanced out the front window. Judging by the way the light hit the porch, he figured it was mid-morning. When he passed out it, had been close to midnight. Cradling the damaged book in his arms like a child, he went into the next room, the dining room, though he never used it for that. He kept all the books that needed repairing on the giant dining room table in the middle of the floor. Charles put the book on the top of the pile, but not before he leafed through it one more time. He shook his head. The spell he had been looking at wouldn't work either. He'd never be able to gather all the ingredients.

He sighed and continued on to the next room, his workroom, the place where he spent most of his time repairing all the old magic books. At some point, that space had been the house's back parlor, a gathering place for the family, when the house was a proper home to a proper family, but a proper family hadn't lived there for a long time.

If Charles didn't find a spell that worked soon, he wasn't exactly sure what he would do. The Shrouded Man, the Grave Walker, He Who Speaks to Death, whatever you called the entity, he had a claim on Charles' soul, and one day he would collect on it. That day was apparently closer than he expected. The night Millie took him away the first time, Charles saw the Shrouded Man inside his house—a place he'd never appeared before and a place Charles didn't even think he could enter. For all he knew, Millie had saved him then, but Millie wouldn't be able to save him every time. Charles needed to figure out a way to escape the Shrouded Man's icy grip, or else he'd never hear her sing again.

———

The bell jingled when Penelope opened the door to the Grayson & Sons antique shop downtown on Coffee Street. Going inside, she noticed the boarded-up windows of the shop next door. They hadn't been boarded up the last time she visited. She didn't even remember what was there before—a dress shop maybe?

Fortunately, nothing seemed to have changed inside the antique shop. The store was still crammed floor to ceiling with every kind of antique imaginable, from furniture to china to light fixtures and artwork, even some old farm equipment. Penelope followed the path laid out, feeling a little like Dorothy following the Yellow Brick Road.

When she came to the desk normally occupied by Dan Kowalczyk, the shop's owner, she found an unfamiliar face, a young woman in a summer dress covered in giant yellow flowers. She wore her dark hair in a bob held away from her face by a bright yellow headband. She was probably a college coed like Dan's last assistant.

"Can I help you?" the woman asked.

"I was looking for Dan," Penelope answered, a little taken aback. "Is he here?"

The woman tilted her head to the side, her eyebrows scrunched together. "Oh? Was he expecting you?"

She didn't seem like she fit in there, among all the antiques. Penelope didn't exactly know what she should have looked like. Perhaps a tweed skirt with a blouse and a cardigan. Maybe a pair of glasses on a beaded chain around her neck.

Penelope shook her head. "No, I was just in the neighborhood and thought I'd pop my head in to say hello. I'm Penelope Drake."

The woman smiled. "I'm Barbara, Dan's assistant."

"Oh, I didn't know he had hired someone else." She winced. That probably wasn't the best thing to say, given that his last assistant had been murdered by a demon.

"Yeah, I've been here since the beginning of June."

Since the beginning of June. There was no reason she should have known, no reason Dan should have told her, but still, for some reason, the idea she didn't know Dan had a new assistant bothered her.

Penelope backed up. "Well, can you just tell him I stopped by?"

Barbara nodded. "Sure. No problem."

"Thanks."

She turned to following the path back to the door when the bell over the front door jingled again, and Dan stepped into the shop. A smile spread across his face when he saw her. "Penelope? What are you doing here?"

"I just stopped by to say hello, like I promised to do."

Dan narrowed his eyes. "Is everything okay?"

Penelope shook her head subtly, hoping to avoid Barbara's notice.

Dan held up his watch and pointed to it. "Hey, Barbara, can you fly solo for another hour or so? I'm going to grab lunch with Penelope."

Barbara nodded primly. "Of course, Dan."

He turned his attention back to Penelope and gestured toward the door. "After you."

They found a diner with a serviceable burger a few blocks away. Penelope requested a booth where she could watch the door.

"What's going on?" Dan asked once the waitress left them with their food. "You glanced over your shoulder every thirty seconds on the walk here."

Penelope took a deep breath and launched into her story about the gold Ford hitting her and forcing her off the road.

When she finished, Dan leaned forward, his eyes wide with concern. "Oh, my God, are you okay?"

She nodded. "Yeah, I'm fine. Physically at least. I'm a little shaken up, though."

"Do you think it's the same person that followed you in the library?"

Penelope fingered her charm bracelet. "I don't know, but it makes sense. As my father had a habit of saying, the simplest solution is usually the right one."

"Sounds like a good motto."

"It served him well … usually."

She didn't mention that sometimes the simplest solution involved ghosts or demons or other things that go bump in the night.

"What are you going to do? Are you going to go to the police?"

"I'm not sure they'd be able to help in this case."

Dan frowned. "Why not?"

"Where do you think half my cases come from? Women too scared to go to the police or who don't think the police will take them seriously about their problem. The police don't bother with things like what just happened to me. Usually it takes someone getting killed before they pay attention."

"That's awful."

"Doesn't make it any less true." She glanced down at her uneaten pickle wedge. When she got burgers with Bertram, she usually traded her pickle for his tomato slice, but Dan had already eaten most of his tomato, along with the rest of his burger.

He wiped a dribble of mustard from his chin. "Does this have something to do with whatever's going on with the Browns, the ones who own the warehouse that blew up over on Stone Avenue?"

Startled, Penelope nearly choked on her Coke. "How much do you know about that?"

He lowered his voice. "I don't pretend to understand everything that's going on, and quite frankly, I don't think I want to. I believed you when you told me the person who ... was responsible for Mary's death was brought to justice, but I did just recently find out the brooch that was stolen from my shop somehow wound up in the possession of Louise Brown."

It would have been more accurate to say the brooch wound up possessing Louise Brown. Again, Penelope kept that part to herself.

"How did you find that out?" she asked.

"One of her friends, woman named Anne Prichard, saw it when she came into the shop. She told me it looked just like the one her friend Louise wore to a party. It was such a unique piece, I knew she had to be talking about the same one."

"You didn't sell it, did you?"

"No, of course not. Not to her, anyway." He popped a couple of French fries in his mouth.

A lump formed in Penelope's stomach, and not because of the burger. "Wait, you sold it to someone else?"

Dan stopped mid-chew and swallowed, a puzzled look on his face. "Why wouldn't I sell it? It's just a piece of jewelry. Are you upset because it's supposed to be haunted?"

The brooch *was* haunted. Charles, with the help of Zed and Penelope, exorcized the ghost attached to it, but then again, Dan didn't know that either.

"I just meant … Given its history, I thought you might …"

"Look, if you're worried about Louise Brown finding out somehow, I doubt that's going to happen. Rumor has it she suffered a nervous breakdown, and with the accident at the warehouse and the whole company shut down, she's gone to stay with relatives up in Virginia."

Penelope studied his profile as he innocently gulped his milkshake. Clearly, she had underestimated him. "Since when is a Yankee like you plugged into Greenville's rumor mill?"

His mouth twisted into a lopsided grin. "Since forever. How do you think half my acquisitions are made?"

She wanted to tell Dan the truth, but she stopped herself, not that she didn't think he could handle it, but because it wouldn't be fair to him. Of course, he resold the brooch. Why wouldn't he? He was a businessman, after all. Suddenly she wished she hadn't gone to his store. She should have just driven home.

"I hope you're being careful," he said, his tone more serious.

She nodded. "Always."

"Anything I can do?"

"No, not right now. I just needed someplace to go to get my head straight again. Thanks for letting me talk it all out. I think I'll be fine. I'm just going to go home."

"Let me walk you to your car, at least."

Penelope's car was parked only a few blocks away, but they strolled slowly. Penelope still couldn't help but look over her shoulder every few steps, a fact Dan didn't fail to notice.

"So, Barbara seems nice," she said.

"Barbara's been great. I was worried about business slowing down when the dress shop next door went out, but we're busier than ever. I couldn't manage right now without her. She's good with clients. She's good with customers. And she completely reorganized all my files in a way that actually makes sense. I can almost say I'm on top of everything."

"I'm glad things are going well."

He stopped beside Penelope's Lincoln. "And I'm glad you stopped by. It was good to see you again. Just promise me next time it'll be for something happier."

She managed a weak smile. "That I think I can do. Thank you for lunch."

He leaned forward with a grin. "Thank *you*."

As Penelope drove off, she watched his figure recede in the rearview mirror and wondered again why she'd gone to him.

———

Bertram Brown glanced around Zed's apartment as he stepped over the threshold. "So, this is where you live?"

"Well, it's really where I sleep, mostly." Zed had just barely managed to shower and put on clean clothes before Bertram got there. "Something wrong?"

"No. I just thought it would be a little more …"

Zed raised an eyebrow. "More what?"

Bertram wrinkled his nose. "I don't know. More of a bachelor pad."

"Says the grown man who lives with his parents." He smacked Bertram on the shoulder. "Sorry to disappoint. I don't do much entertaining."

Bertram rubbed his shoulder as he ventured farther into the apartment. "So, what was so urgent I needed to come over here right away?"

"You mean you haven't heard?"

Bertram shook his head. "Heard what?"

"It was all over the news."

"Don't watch much TV anymore. Been a little busy, if you haven't noticed." He fell into Zed's recliner.

"Still trying to get the warehouse rebuilt? How's that going?"

Bertram pantomimed a right hook. "I swear there are some people from that goddamn insurance company who are going to get a punch in the face if I ever meet them in person."

Zed let out a chuckle. "That good, huh? What does your dad say about the whole thing?"

"Not much. He seemed almost relieved after it happened, but the business is all we've got. I have to do whatever I can to rebuild it." For just a second, the mask slipped. Guilt, fear, regret. Zed could sense it all. Then the façade went back up. "So, what was on the news?"

"Lloyd Baker was murdered last night."

Bertram's eyes grew wide. "Where? How?"

"Stabbed to death at some seedy motel down Highway 25."

Bertram idly scratched his chin. "Well, can't say that I'm shocked. He wasn't my star employee. I had the feeling he was involved in some shady business."

Zed sat on the arm of the recliner. "Bertram, let me remind you that Lloyd was the one who got paid to leave the warehouse door open by the person who drew the pentagram on the floor and summoned the demon that possessed the tractor."

"That Patrick Wheeler guy Penelope mentioned?"

"Yeah, him. My fear is that he's cleaning house."

Bertram's hand went to the charm bracelet around his wrist. Charles made the ones Zed and Penelope wore. Bertram's was made by some unknown magician his father employed. "That would put all of us in danger."

Zed pointed at him. "Exactly."

"Does Penelope know?"

Zed shook his head. "I tried to call her, but she hasn't been picking up."

Bertram frowned. "Should we be worried about that?"

"Could just be that she's not home. Might not be a bad idea to check up on her, though." Zed grabbed his housekey from the hook next to the door. "Can you drive? My car's in the shop."

———

Penelope walked into her office to find her painted rock paperweight, the one she had made for her father in the second grade, sitting on the floor again.

She glanced around the room. "Dad? You here?"

Two knocks.

Yes, he was. That was quick. "Is there something you want to talk to me about?"

Two knocks.

"Does it have to do with the Browns again?" *Is it bigger than a breadbox?* Penelope really wished there were a better way to communicate with her dad. Sometimes being limited to yes/no questions was frustrating.

Two knocks.

Fine then. Penelope sat down in her chair, holding the paperweight in her hands. "What is it about the Browns this time? Why are our lives so tied up in theirs? What happened between you and Ephraim Brown that you stopped talking to one another? Why did Bertram Brown start being such a jerk to me? Is that enough to get started? Can you even answer those questions? Because it seems like the only person who can is Ephraim Brown."

One knock.

Penelope sighed. "Why, Dad? I know you want to protect me, but—"

One knock.

She balled her hands up into fists. She wanted to throw the rock across the room. This was getting really old. "Dad, I got it."

One knock.

She dropped the rock on the desk and pushed herself out of her chair. At the door to the office, she paused. "I wish we could have real conversations again."

One knock.

Penelope turned back toward the empty office. "What was that supposed to mean? Dad?" Then she thought through the things she had said and her dad's responses. "Wait, it's not about protecting me, is it? There's some other reason you don't want me to talk to Ephraim. Is it about protecting him?"

Two knocks.

"But protecting him from what? Dad, you've got to give me something else to go on."

A loud crash sounded from overhead. Penelope ran upstairs to the apartment over the office. On the floor of her bedroom, she found two issues of her father's *Garnet and Black* yearbooks from his time at the University of South Carolina. She had taken them from her grandmother's attic along with the notebook she left with Zed.

It was in that attic that she discovered Patrick Wheeler was the son of Geoffrey Wheeler, a classmate of Penelope's father and Ephraim Brown, at least for a year. During their sophomore year, the three of them, along with several others, broke curfew by sneaking out of their dorm in the middle of the night. Their adventure ended with one of their friends unconscious in the woods. Geoffrey and the others had been expelled. Penelope's father and Ephraim were not, because they took their friend to the hospital. When Patrick was sixteen years old, Geoffrey Wheeler committed suicide.

The yearbooks on Penelope's bedroom floor were from 1936 and 1937, her dad's freshman and sophomore years. As she picked them up, it occurred to her she hadn't dug far enough into them. She'd found Geoffrey Wheeler only because she was looking for a connection to Patrick, but if she compared the yearbooks she might be able to find the rest of her dad's accomplices. Since they were all expelled, they'd be in the 1936 yearbook but missing from 1937.

She sat down on her bed and began to comb through the two yearbooks, but she didn't get very far before more knocks sounded from downstairs. This time it wasn't her dad, though. Carrying the yearbooks, she headed back down. When she opened the front door, she found the last two people she ever would have expected to visit her together.

"Oh, good. You're here," Zed said, obviously relieved. "You don't know how glad we are to see you."

Penelope's gaze went from him to Bertram. "What's this about?"

"Where have you been?" Zed asked as he and Bertram stepped into the foyer. "I've been trying to call."

"I went to the library. Or, rather, I was headed for library. I got sidetracked on the way there."

Zed narrowed his eyes. "Sidetracked?"

"I had a minor accident." She told them the story of the stalker rear-ending her car and watched as the color drained from both their faces.

"Are you okay?" Zed reached out a hand.

She waved him off. "I'm fine."

Something was definitely up. Neither he nor Bertram could keep still. Bertram crossed and uncrossed his arms while Zed kept shifting his weight from one foot to the other, as if he expected a band of assassins to burst into the room and he needed to be ready.

Funny thing. That wasn't entirely outside the realm of possibility.

"What's going on?" she asked.

"Lloyd Baker was murdered last night."

"That's who we caught sneaking around the warehouse, right?"

Zed nodded. "That's him. He's also the one Patrick Wheeler paid to unlock the side door. Sounds like someone might be tying up loose ends."

Penelope glanced around her office. Her father didn't want her to say anything to Ephraim about the incident in college, but that didn't mean she couldn't talk to Bertram about it. "Bertram, did your father ever tell you about something that happened when he was at USC, about breaking curfew, sneaking out to the woods in the middle of the night, and nearly getting expelled?"

She listened, but her father didn't make any protest.

Bertram shook his head. "No, never. What happened exactly?"

"Like I said, your dad snuck out of the dorm one night along with my dad and a bunch of their buddies. I don't know all the details, but there was some kind of accident. Someone got hurt. The only reason our fathers weren't expelled was because they took their friend to the hospital."

"This is all news to me." Bertram ran his fingers through his hair. "Dad usually has to be muzzled before he'll stop telling old college stories. Wonder why that one never came up."

"Yeah, well don't tell him I told you." Penelope paused to listen again. Still not a peep from her father.

Bertram barked a laugh. "I can't imagine any reason I would. What does that have to do with Lloyd Baker getting murdered anyway?"

Penelope opened the 1936 yearbook to the photos of the freshman class. "One of their friends was a man named Geoffrey Wheeler. He was Patrick Wheeler's father. He committed suicide when Patrick was a teenager."

Bertram twisted his mouth into an angry sneer. "So, this is some kind of sick revenge thing? His dad got expelled and mine didn't?"

"What about the others?" Zed asked. "Do we know who they are?"

Penelope grinned. "Interesting you should ask that. I was just about to go through these yearbooks to see if I could find the rest of them. Care to join me?"

Jim Everett's feet hurt. He had been standing for going on four hours, and all he wanted to do was sit. He'd be having words with his boss later. He was all in favor of collaboration with the sheriff's department, but taking the lead on any cases that were "out of the ordinary" wasn't what he had in mind.

Especially not this.

He couldn't sit because every available surface was covered in blood. In his years as a police detective, he'd never seen anything like it—on the bed, the chairs, the walls of the motel room, even the ceiling. The blood was everywhere.

Some officers had left the room retching. The poor night guard who spotted the bloody handprint on the window and found the bodies had to be taken to the hospital with chest pains. And that was not even considering what the killer actually did with the blood. Lloyd Baker and Tammy Ryan had both been stabbed several dozen times each. The murderer took their blood and used it to draw weird symbols on the walls. Looking at them, Jim got the same feeling he used to get all the time around his old friend Jonathan Drake. Weird cold drafts and odd smells and strange shadows seemed to always follow him.

To make matters even worse, the killer carved symbols into the body of the man on the bed, smaller ones on his arms and legs and a bigger one on his chest. Some kind of ritual killing. Jim hoped this case wasn't going to be like what that Charles Manson lunatic did out in California. They didn't need that kind of thing in Greenville.

The deputy coroner sent to examine the bodies called him over. "We found this in his mouth," he said, delicately holding a piece of paper between his gloved fingers.

Jim took the scrap of paper in his own gloved hands. "Someone put it there on purpose?"

The deputy coroner nodded. "It was crammed down in there after he died. Otherwise, he would have gagged on it."

Jim unfolded the paper. The only thing written on it was a reference to a Bible verse.

Hosea 9:16.

Jim frowned. "I'm afraid I'm not familiar with that one."

He walked over to the nightstand and opened the drawer. Reaching inside, he pulled out the Gideon Bible resting on top of the phone book and looked up the verse.

Ephraim is smitten, their root is dried up, they shall bear no fruit; yea though they bring forth, yet will I slay even the beloved fruit of their womb.

Jim read through the rest of the chapter. The verse was related to the punishment of the Tribe of Ephraim, one of the twelve Tribes of Israel, for turning away from God to worship false idols, but Jim had a feeling the verse was directed at someone personally.

He called over an officer who was taking pictures of the bloody symbols on the wall.

"Where did you say Lloyd Baker worked?" he asked.

"I believe I said he was unemployed, sir," the officer replied.

"No. before that."

The officer picked up a notebook by the door and leafed through it. "The Brown Tractor & Farm Supply Co."

"Ephraim Brown."

Jim shook his head. What was that preacher's name, the one who protested at the Brown warehouse because of "Satanic activity"? Lowell Purdue. He'd have a field day if he saw all this. Of course, none of the details of what happened in that motel room would ever be made public, at least not by him. The citizens of Greenville who paid his salary entrusted him with their peace of mind, and he wasn't going to do anything to betray that trust.

Still, the weird feeling he always got around Jonathan Drake persisted, and he only got that same feeling around one other person.

2.

SUNDAY, JULY 30, 1972

Reviewing the old *Garnet and Black* yearbooks, Penelope, Zed, and Bertram came up with three more names: Bradley James, Edward McDowell, and Jude Hall. After Zed and Bertram left, Penelope asked her dad to confirm, which he did with two knocks for each name.

Any more information about them would require a trip to the Division of Public Records, but she'd have to wait until Monday to do that.

Penelope hated waiting. By Sunday morning, she was climbing the walls and desperate for a diversion, which is how she found herself walking through the doors of the First Presbyterian Church for the first time since at least Christmas.

Immediately, an older woman in a dark blue dress printed with white lilies gravitated toward her. Penelope held her smile as Mary Jo Manning took her hand. She insisted on hearing all the details of Penelope's life for the last year, throwing in surprised gasps every so often as Penelope talked about her job—though, of course, she left out the more unconventional parts—and making sympathetic murmurs when Penelope replied that no, there were no gentleman friends currently.

She scanned the gathering crowd and felt a rush of relief when her grandmother entered the vestibule. Edith Drake wore her favorite lavender and green dress. She's seen pictures of the Queen Mother in England in a similar dress and wore it whenever she wanted to feel a little bit like a queen. Penelope waved to her.

Her grandmother's mouth spread into a wide smile. She came straight over. "Penelope, dear, I'm so happy to see you. What brought you here today?"

Penelope gave her grandmother a hug. "Well, it *is* Sunday, and I promised you I'd come to church soon, remember?"

She took Penelope by the arm. "I'm sorry to interrupt, Mary Jo, but there are some people just dying to say hello to Penelope. How's Harold doing, by the way?"

Mary Jo drew her mouth into a tight smile. "Much better these days, but he still isn't up to going out much."

"Well, give him my regards." She gave Mary Jo a small wave. "Harold wouldn't have fallen and broken his ankle if he could keep is head out of the liquor cabinet," she whispered to Penelope as they made their way to a group having a conversation in one corner.

"I don't want to intrude on anyone," Penelope said.

"Oh, nonsense. You're not intruding."

She eased Penelope up to the group, two older couples. When they noticed her, they stopped their conversation. One of the women threw open her arms and hugged Penelope.

"It's good to see you, Mrs. Robertson," Penelope said. "How have you been?"

"Well, I don't know if you heard, but our Peggy just had her first baby." Mrs. Robertson beamed. "We love being Grandma and Grandpa."

Penelope nodded blandly. "Congratulations."

If she recalled, Peggy was a year younger than she was.

"Are you here by yourself?" Mrs. Robertson asked.

Penelope glanced at her grandmother, whom she was clearly with, but that wasn't what Mrs. Robertson meant. She shook her head. "No, I just came to spend some time with my grandmother."

"Well, that's nice, too." Mrs. Robertson patted Penelope's hand. "I know she appreciates having the company."

Inside the sanctuary, the organist started to play, the signal for everyone to find their seats. Of course, everyone always sat in the same spot, and no one would ever dare sit in someone else's place. The fourth pew back on the right belonged to the Drakes, even if there was usually only one of them now. The thought of her grandmother on the pew all alone sent a pang of guilt through Penelope. Maybe she could endure all the veiled remarks about her spinsterdom for her grandmother's sake.

The service progressed the same as it always did until the music minister, in his effort to drag the congregation into the second half of the twentieth century, attempted something he called "contemporary worship music." The incident only led to her grandmother muttering under her breath that a church was no place for a guitar, and Penelope had to admit the whole affair was pretty embarrassing.

It was later, during the second verse of "Power in the Blood," that Penelope spotted the man staring at her—glaring was more like it. She didn't recognize him, but he seemed vaguely familiar. He was older, maybe in his late forties. His dark hair had receded quite a bit up his scalp, but he had only a little bit of gray at his temples. Even after the hymn was over, she could feel his eyes boring into her.

The pastor's sermon was about forgiveness. He used the story of the Prodigal Son to illustrate his point, that no matter how far we stray, God will forgive us if we come back to Him. Penelope wondered if the son in the story ever forgave himself for what he put his father through.

After the service was over, Penelope risked another glance in the man's direction. She accidentally locked eyes with him, and for a few awkward seconds, they stared at one another. His angry expression never changed. Penelope took her grandmother's hand and made a motion to leave, despite her grandmother's protests, but before they could go anywhere, someone blocked her. Jim Everett wrapped his arms around Penelope in a giant hug that nearly lifted her off the ground. The other man was gone when she looked again.

"I was wondering when we'd see you here again, Penny. So good to have your pretty face here this morning."

Penelope was about to remind Jim that she'd seem him only a couple of weeks earlier, but then she remembered their meeting was supposed to be a secret. They had visited the hospital bed of an old man who said he'd seen a demon abduct Bobby Parker the night before he was found dead at the Brown warehouse.

"It's good to see you, too, Jim," she said. "How are Margie and the rest of the family?"

"Oh, just about the same. You know, Penny, that dinner invitation is still open. Any time."

"I might just take you up on that soon."

"Don't wait too long, now."

He took her hand and slipped something into it before turning his attention to her grandmother. "And Mrs. Drake, how are you doing today?"

Penelope's grandmother smiled and offered her hand. "I'm doing the same as usual myself, Jim."

"Now you be careful. You get any lovelier and I don't know if the hearts of some of these men around here could take it."

She laughed and blushed. "Oh, Jim, you stop with that, now."

While Jim flirted with her grandmother, Penelope took the opportunity to inspect what he had handed her—a folded piece of paper, torn from a copy of the church bulletin. On it he had scrawled a note:

Be at home at 3:30 today.

She looked at Jim, who glanced her way briefly and nodded. "Now you two ladies have a good day. And Penelope, I do hope to see more of you."

She smiled. "I have a feeling you will."

———

Things were slow at the bookstore. Zed was supposed to be restocking the history section, but he was really leafing through one of the new books. It was about the African slave trade as told through the lives of several generations on both sides of that business, based on documents found in an old plantation house just south of Charleston. The cruelty boggled Zed. He doubted he'd even have been able to survive back then. His special talent, the one he'd never told anyone about, not even Penelope, was being able to read the emotions of others. He didn't know if he could have taken so much pain on himself.

A bell jingled when the front door opened, snapping Zed out of his musings. He stood and found the book's place on the shelf. Even before he saw the new customer, he sensed something—anticipation, apprehension, but also excitement. The feelings put a smile on his face. He made his way to the front to see Jake, the man he'd met at O'Shaughnessy's Tavern a few months back, the one who had brought Kierkegaard to read. He wore another snug-fitting polo shirt, this time with the addition of a "McGovern for President" button.

"Well, hello again," Zed said.

A broad smile spread across Jake's face. "Hi, there. What are the odds, huh?"

Zed flashed a lopsided grin of his own, the one he used to make himself roguishly charming. "Pretty good, I'd say. I did tell you I worked the odd hour at a bookstore."

Jake held up a finger. "But you never said which one."

"Probably not that hard to figure out though."

"Not really, no," Jake admitted. "I just looked for the weirdest one."

"I wouldn't use the word *weird*," Zed said with mock indignation. "The owner, Mr. Keller, doesn't like it. He prefers the term *quirky*. *Off-beat* if he's in a good mood."

"Whatever floats your boat, I guess." Jake glanced around the shop. "But it *is* weird."

He was right, of course. The bookstore occupied a narrow building downtown seemingly built solely to fill the gap between the two buildings on either side. It had once been a bakery with an upstairs apartment. None of the walls were square. The bookshelves didn't follow any particular plan. They were simply placed anywhere they would fit. In the back, a wrought iron spiral staircase led up to the second floor where yet another maze of shelves awaited patrons. The actual classification of books was even more stupefying, and only made sense to Mr. Keller. Zed didn't even try. He just memorized where all the books were supposed to go.

To add to matters, signs with bold block letters written in black and red magic markers covered every available square inch of wall space. These were Mr. Keller's rules. The one that said *No food or drinks allowed* was to be expected. *Cash only* and *No smoking* were understandable, too. But the other signs left a lot of people scratching their heads. *No loud talking. No excessive reading. No political discussions. No religious discussions. No swearing. No existentialism.*

Jake pointed to the last one. "No existentialism?"

Zed leaned in and lowered his voice and said in as serious a tone as he could muster, "If I explained it, I'd be breaking the rule."

Jake laughed. "Fair enough."

"Hey, as long as you're here, can I interest you in a book? I think we might have a copy of *Kierkegaard's Journals* if I can remember where we decided to shelve it."

"Sure, why not?"

Zed motioned toward the labyrinth of bookshelves. "Follow me, then."

He led Jake toward the back of the store, to where Mr. Keller relegated the philosophy books.

As they were walking, Jake cleared his throat. "I … I've listened to your radio show a couple of times."

"I'm sorry," said Zed.

"No, I'm serious. Sometimes I have trouble sleeping—"

"And it puts you right out?"

"No. It makes me think at least I'm not alone."

Zed slowed his pace for a moment. Here was that feeling that he had picked up on the first time he met Jake. A sort of quiet melancholy. "So, I noticed the button. A McGovern supporter, huh?"

Jake pointed to one of the *No political discussions* signs. "I didn't think we were allowed to talk about that."

Zed continued past the foreign language books and the biographies. "But Mr. Keller isn't here right now."

"How would you even know?" Jake asked as they turned a corner and made their way through the gardening section.

"You'd know," Zed replied.

Jake regarded him with a skeptical eye. "I'll just have to take your word for that, I guess. I'm a volunteer for the McGovern campaign, actually."

Zed glanced back at him. "Really? So, handing out flyers and knocking on doors?"

Jake nodded. "Among other things."

"What do you do when you're not doing that?"

"That's pretty much all I do right now." He smiled sheepishly.

"What happens if he loses?" Zed regretted the question as soon as he asked it.

Jake shrugged. "Guess I'll have to start looking for a job."

Fortunately, they arrived at a set of shelves in the very back of the store, where the walls came together to make a small alcove, and Zed was saved from digging an even deeper hole.

Zed scanned the shelves. "Okay, Mr. Kierkegaard should be around here somewhere."

When he found the book he was looking for, he pulled it down and handed it to Jake. As he was passing off the book, he took a chance and let his hand graze Jake's. Images suddenly flooded his mind. Gravestones all lined up in a row. Old, worn ones, like the ones at the cemetery at Christ Church, the oldest church in Greenville, but these markers weren't in the Christ Church cemetery. Trees stood beyond the markers, a forest, but Zed couldn't see very much because it was dark. Night then. The air was crisp. Definitely not summer. Zed tried to look around some more, but he couldn't move. He tried to walk but only managed to stagger a few feet before he fell. His face came within inches of one of the gravestones, and when he looked up at it, he saw blood splattered across its face.

Everything happened in a few seconds, and then Zed was in the bookstore again. The book fell from Jake's hand and hit the floor with a loud bang. Jake staggered backward into the bookshelf and sagged to the floor.

Zed went to help him up. "Jake? Are you okay?"

Never mind Zed wasn't.

Jake put up a hand to stop him. "I'm fine."

He used the bookshelf to pull himself back onto his feet.

Zed took a step toward him. "Are you sure?"

Jake moved back. "Don't … I mean, yeah, I'm sure. I'll be okay. I … I just need to go."

He turned around and ran out of the store. Zed made to follow him but gave up after a few strides. What exactly was he going to do? Grab him by the shoulder? Zed had only ever sensed the feelings of others. He'd never had visions before, let alone ones accompanied by such fear and pain.

Unsure what else to do, he picked up the dropped book and put it back on the shelf. He wondered if Jake had seen the same things he did, if the terror he felt was Jake's or his own.

———

Jim was right on time for his three-thirty visit with Penelope.

As she led him toward her office, he glanced around the old

house. "I haven't been here in a while, not since ..." He checked himself and looked at her apologetically.

Since the days right after her father died, when he and everyone else her father had ever known came by to express their condolences. Everyone except Ephraim Brown anyway.

"It's okay, really." She tried to give him a reassuring smile.

"You haven't really made a lot of changes."

"People expect a private detective's office to look a certain way," she explained. "It puts them more at ease."

He nodded. Jim didn't approve of her career choice, that much he and just about everyone else had made clear a while ago, but when he realized she wasn't going to change her mind, his objections died down, replaced by disapproving looks and concerned murmurs.

"At any rate," Penelope continued, "I did a lot more to the upstairs apartment. That's where my taste differed from Dad's."

"He had a taste?" Jim chuckled.

One knock.

Jim looked around. "What was that?"

Penelope gritted her teeth. What was her father doing? "Nothing. House settling, probably."

Jim eyed her. "Awfully loud for the house settling."

"It's an old house. It happens."

He grunted. She could tell by the set of jaw he didn't quite believe her. "It was good to see you this morning at church, Penny. Hope to see you there more."

"We'll see. You of all people can understand how erratic my schedule can be."

"Mhmm, I certainly do."

An uneasy silence settled between them. Jim clutched a large manila envelope between his fingers so hard he made creases in it.

"Jim, what did you want to talk to me about? You went to an awful lot of trouble to make sure I was home this afternoon."

He shook his head. "Now I'm not so sure. I really shouldn't be here."

"You said that when we went to see Earl Boggs in the hospital."

She could still envision the eyes of the elderly man who said he'd seen a demon take Bobby Parker from the hospital the night he was killed.

He glanced down at the envelope in his hands and took a deep breath. "I brought some pictures. I thought I might get your opinion on them."

"Pictures? From the Lloyd Baker murder?"

His frown deepened. "How'd you know?"

Penelope pointed to the side of her head. "Detective. Remember? Let me guess. There's something strange you can't quite explain, but maybe I can, given my reputation for taking on … unusual cases."

"Like I said, I don't know about this, Penny."

"You can just let me see the pictures, Jim."

"They're a little … graphic."

"I can handle it. I promise."

Jim sighed. He opened the envelope and spread out the photographs on her desk. Once she saw the mutilated bodies of Lloyd Baker and Tiffany Ryan, the blood everywhere, the symbols carved into Lloyd's skin and smeared on the walls, she almost went back on her statement. Even finding the body of Mary Wilson, Dan's assistant, didn't affect her the same way, but this, so much carnage, was difficult to take.

She picked up one of the photos, a close-up of the symbol on Lloyd's chest. "It looks like some kind of ritual."

"That's what I thought, too. Any ideas what might be going on? Any clues you see we might have missed?"

Penelope forced herself to study the pictures. "You know Lloyd Baker worked for the Browns, right?"

Jim nodded. "I do."

"So, it's safe to assume Ephraim Brown is the primary target in all this." Penelope pointed to a picture of the woman, Tammy Ryan. "I think she was just in the wrong place at the wrong time, especially since there were no symbols carved into her skin."

"I thought that as well."

Penelope had seen the look in Jim's eyes before. He knew she wasn't being completely above-board with him. She didn't really want to put all her cards on the table, for a few very good reasons. She didn't think Jim was quite ready for a tale of tractor-possessing demons, but she needed help, too, and more manpower couldn't hurt. She wouldn't lay out her entire hand, but maybe she'd let Jim see a card or two.

"Patrick Wheeler," she said.

"Who's that?" Jim asked.

"Someone you should be looking for," Penelope replied. "He had an interest in the Brown warehouse and access to it. He may have some sort of grudge against the Browns, and he probably knew Lloyd Baker."

Jim cocked his head to the side. "How do you know all this?"

She grinned. "I have my sources."

He looked at her dubiously again. "Well, whatever your sources, thank them, and if you have anything else, let me know. It really is good to talk to you again, Penny. I wish the circumstances were different. You used to come over to our house all the time with your dad. We didn't just enjoy his company."

He turned to leave. Penelope glanced down at the pictures. She didn't want anything to do with them. She wished he would pick them up and put them in the envelope and take them with him. But, instead, she closed her eyes and gritted her teeth.

"The photos, can I—"

"Keep them?" he finished.

"I want to do a little research."

Jim nodded. "Thought you might. I had the lab make extra copies."

After he left, Penelope gathered up all the pictures and slid them back inside the envelope as quickly as she could. Then she sat down in her chair and covered her face with her hands. All she ever wanted to do was make her dad proud. It was the reason she wanted to be a police officer. It was the reason she became a private detective. Some days, though, she didn't feel very much like someone he could be proud of.

"Dad, I just did the right thing, didn't I? Asking for help?"

Silence.

3.

MONDAY, JULY 31, 1972

The sun rose on the body of Lester Hayes hanging from a tree in Cleveland Park, his outstretched arms tied to the branches with thick rope. His shirt was torn open. Angry red lines crisscrossed his chest and arms, strange symbols carved into his skin with a knife. Above his head, another symbol was carved into the bark of the tree.

"So much for keeping quiet about these things," Jim mumbled to himself.

No footprints in the grass. No fingerprints on the body. No witnesses. Lester was not a small man. It would have taken some time and effort to hang him from the tree, which stood not twenty feet from the road.

All he knew was that Lester Hayes worked for the Brown Tractor & Farm Supply Co., just like Lloyd Baker. Jim saw a discussion in his future with Bertram Brown, or better yet, Bertram's father Ephraim.

He didn't know what he was doing involved in another case like this. When Jonathan Drake was alive, he would always take on the strange cases, the ones where unexplained shadows appeared in the crime scene photos, or where the witnesses refused to talk, their eyes wide in irrational fear. He took the ones that no one else wanted, the ones that made the other detectives uneasy or sometimes just plain scared shitless.

In fact, Jim seemed to remember a similar case from years before, a murdered woman. They had taken a few weeks to identify her. She wasn't local. What was done to her wasn't as gruesome as this, but she did have a weird symbol carved into her arm. Jim couldn't remember if Jonathan ever solved the case. Still, he thought, it might be worth stopping by storage to look over the file.

Jim shook his head. This wasn't the Greenville he grew up in, but maybe the city he grew up in never existed. Maybe he just never saw it for how it really was.

———

Standing on a street corner, wringing the sweat out of his shirt, Charles cursed the bright sun. He was used to hot summers, having grown up the South, and that was before three years in the jungles of Vietnam taught him a new definition of the word *hot*. But this heat was different. He wasn't prepared for summer 1919 New York, a city of brick and concrete and steel.

The last thing Charles remembered before blacking out was picking up his X-Acto knife, ready to cut the damaged binding off a book. When he came to, he found himself standing on a dock, the salty smell of the ocean competing with dozens of other aromas, both sweet and sour, carried in the muggy air. A crate coming off a boat down a ramp nearly flattened him. A man twice his size picked him up by his shirt and yanked him out of the way.

"Uh, thanks," he said.

"Don't fucking thank me," the man replied, his accent hinting of somewhere in Eastern Europe. "What do you think you're doing? The boss sees you with your head in the clouds like that, you're off the docks, that's assuming that melon of yours is still attached to your neck. You got that?"

Charles mumbled a reply and turned his attention back to the crate. A few other men were already prying the crate open with crowbars. When the sacks of potatoes tumbled out, Charles fell in with the other dock workers loading the potatoes onto waiting trucks, likely going to restaurants and markets all through the city. Several hours passed like that, unloading crates and putting the cargo onto trucks and carts. When Charles was done, he was dirty and exhausted. All he thought about on the long bus ride up to Harlem was collapsing onto his bed.

He had just gotten off the bus when he saw her across the street. Millie Priest. She strolled down the sidewalk, going in the opposite direction from his apartment. A wide-brimmed hat shaded her face, and the plain, olive dress she wore looked nothing like the gold and black sequined gown she wore on stage the last time he saw her, but her eyes betrayed her. They were the same soul-filled eyes that haunted his dreams in both this world and the real one.

Staying on his side of the street, he followed her, pushing past people in an effort to keep from losing her. He wanted to catch up to her, to say something to her, but when he tried finally to cross the street, a speeding Model-T nearly ran him over. After scrambling back to the safety of the sidewalk, he looked down at his dirty, sweaty clothes. He couldn't let her see him like this. What would she think? Why would she bother with a dock worker?

He glanced across the street again just in time to see Millie to enter a building. A sign above the door proclaimed the name of the establishment in sleek, streamlined letters—The Blue Club. Charles smiled as he formulated a plan. He turned and headed back toward his boarding house. He needed to get cleaned up if he was going out that evening. He even found himself hoping he could stay in the dream long enough to see Millie sing again.

Knowing there was no chance of getting a hot shower at the boarding house, he opted to go to the communal shower a couple of blocks over and pay fifteen cents of his hard-earned salary for a tepid trickle of almost clear water. Still, it felt good to wash off the sweat of his workday.

It didn't occur to him until he was walking back to the boarding house that he shouldn't have known about the shower, or for that matter, how to do his job at the port, or how to ride the bus from work all the way up to Harlem. Isaiah Jenkins' memories were filling in more and more, to the point he had trouble distinguishing them from his own. He didn't like the idea.

His mood brightened, though, as he climbed the stairs to his room. He put on his army uniform again, partly because it was the nicest set of clothes he had, and partly because he thought it might be easier for Millie to recognize him.

The long summer days meant the sun was just setting when he headed out for The Blue Club. The big man at the door just nodded as he walked by, probably because of the uniform. Once inside, Charles learned why The Blue Club was called that. Everything was blue, from the carpet and drapes the color of the sky to the deep indigo tablecloths. Even the waiters wore blue tuxedos.

Charles claimed a table and signaled for a waiter and ordered a gin and tonic. He normally didn't drink at all, but he figured it wasn't really his body, so it didn't matter. When the drink came, he nursed it while he watched the club slowly fill with people. Like the clientele of The Boiler Room, they were dressed to the nines. Most were black, but there were some Hispanics and even a few whites mixed in the crowd.

The trio on stage played some low-key jazz, barely audible over the din of people talking. He caught snippets of conversations here and there. A lot of people were complaining about the unbearable heat. Others were talking about Babe Ruth's string of home runs, but Charles also overheard conversations in hushed tones about the recent riots in Chicago that started after a white man threw a rock at a group of black teenagers.

Finally, after an hour or so of waiting, the band stopped playing, and the lights in the club dimmed. A spotlight illuminated a small circle on the stage. Millie emerged into the circle of light, wearing a blue sequined dress that dazzled like a million-faceted sapphire. She parted her lips, and from the very first note, Charles was lost. Her low, smoky voice filled the room. Everything else fell away, just as it had before.

Some of her songs Charles had heard before, some he hadn't. He recognized "Some of These Days" and the "St. Louis Blues." But regardless of the song—happy, wistful, defiant—Millie's voice captured him completely. Their eyes met while she was singing "After You've Gone." She didn't miss a beat, though. If anything, she became even more mesmerizing. From then on, she wasn't singing to anyone else but Charles.

When Millie finished her set, Charles jumped to his feet and clapped so hard the palms of his hands stung. No racist hooligans burst into the club this time, and Millie retreated backstage amid the applause. The lights came back up on the original jazz trio. They started playing an upbeat rag, and some of the club patrons stood up to dance. Charles sat, his empty drink in front of him. He flagged a waiter for another. He didn't know what he'd eat later in the week, but hopefully that wouldn't be his problem.

When the waiter came back with his drink, he also handed Charles a note. Charles unfolded it and squinted to read the flowery handwriting in the dim light.

Meet me backstage. Third door on the left. Millie.

He scanned the area around the stage until he spotted a small door, painted blue like the rest of the club. Charles stood and stuffed the note into his pocket. About halfway to the door a man even larger than the one at the front of the house intercepted him.

The big bouncer very firmly placed a giant hand on Charles' chest. "Hold on, there. Where do you think you're going?"

Charles dug the note out of his pocket and showed it to the bouncer. With a crooked grin on his face, he stepped aside to let Charles pass. The door opened to a short hallway. As soon as he stepped through and shut the door behind him, the sounds from the club died away. The hallway also got dark, almost too dark to see. He felt his way back, counting off the doors as he went. When he got to the third one from the left, he knocked and waited.

A few seconds passed before the door opened. Light from a lamp spilled out into the hallway. Millie was still wearing her blue dress. Without saying a word, she stood aside and motioned for him to come in. After she shut the door, she went to her make-up table and sat down. Charles scanned the room for another chair, but he didn't see one, so he stood awkwardly by the door.

She smiled, the same demure smile her ghost gave him in his own house, like she knew a secret. "I'm glad we ran into each other again. Funny how fate works, you being here tonight."

He could have lied, but that didn't seem right. "Truth be told, I saw you this afternoon out on the street. You were walking into the club, so I made plans to come here tonight, hoping to hear you sing again."

She laughed, a sound just as musical as any song. "Still sounds like fate to me." Her smile faded just a bit. "I never had a chance to thank you for what you did at The Boiler Room."

Charles tried to remember what happened after he was struck in the back of the head with a baseball bat, but Isaiah Jenkins' memories failed him. He shook his head. "I'm sorry. After I got smacked in the back of the head, things got a little mixed up. What exactly happened?"

"The boys fought off the guy who hit you, and we all carried you backstage. You came to a few minutes later. With those … men still tearing up everything, we got you to your feet in a hurry, and we all went out the back door. It connects to the basement of the next building over. You really don't remember any of this?"

Charles shook his head. "Not really. That must have been a really bad blow to the head."

"When we heard the police sirens, you said you had to go."

"Well, like I said, a bad blow. Under any other circumstances, I'd never leave a lovely lady in such a lurch like that."

She laughed again. "You rest assured I was in good hands with the boys. You have a very charming accent, by the way. Where are you from?"

"South Carolina."

"Long way from home."

He glanced down at his shoes. "Not sure it's home anymore."

He almost believed what he said.

She took off her earrings and placed them on her dressing table. The small blue gemstones sparkled in the lamplight. "I'm sure you can make your home anywhere you want."

"How's the trombone player?" Charles asked. "It didn't look too good for him there."

Millie's lip trembled. "It'll be a long time before Jimmy is playing the trombone again."

"Sorry to hear that."

"We all are, but he's got people to look after him at least." The smile returned, but Charles noticed the set of her jaw. "We've got to take care of one another, you know. We're all we have. Can't count on anyone else. You learn that pretty fast here. How long you been in New York, anyway?"

"Not long."

"Did you see much fighting?"

Charles frowned. "What?"

She waved at his army uniform. "Over in Europe. Did you see much fighting?"

He shook his head. "Not exactly. I was stuck in England for most of the time I was over there."

He started out intending to tell a little white lie, but about halfway through, he realized he was telling the truth. Isaiah Jenkins did spend most of his time in England before the war ended.

"Just as well," she said. "I've known too many people who went over there and came back different. They saw things no one should ever have to see."

"I know a few people like that, too." Charles was thinking of a different war on a different continent, though, of the things he has seen and wished he hadn't, and of the things he'd done, too.

"What do you do for work?" she asked.

"I work on the docks."

"Do you like it?"

He shrugged. "It pays the rent."

"If you want, I can arrange to get you a job here at The Blue Club. I know the owner. Lewis is a good guy."

Warmth flooded into Charles' cheeks. To be able to hear Millie sing more was all he wanted, but he didn't want to seem too eager. "No, I couldn't possibly ask you to do that."

She stood. "No, really. It's okay. He owes me a favor."

"Why would you use your favor on me?"

She tilted her head to one side, exposing her long, graceful neck. "Why not? You did save my life."

"I was just doing what anyone would have done."

"But no one else did." She came closer. His instinct still was to back away, but there was nowhere to go. "You'd have to start as a waiter, but you could move up from there. And the pay would be twice what you're making at the docks. And on top of that, you wouldn't have to go all the way downtown every day. Promise me you'll think about it at least."

Her perfume smelled like roses, the antique ones that grew next to the back door of his house. She leaned in for a kiss, but before their lips could touch, there was a knock at the door.

———

Charles opened his eyes to a room bathed in bright sunlight. Gradually, the ceiling of his workroom came into focus. The theme song to *The Price is Right* blared from the television.

Back in his own house, in his own time, then.

He sat up slowly and glanced around. His X-Acto knife lay on the floor by one of the table legs, but thankfully none of his books had toppled off when he blacked out. His stomach growled. He'd made the mistake of skipping dinner again the night before, and apparently dream-world food didn't count.

There was another knock at his front door. That's what had brought him back. Charles took a few moments to gather his resolve and then pushed himself up from the floor. He stumbled through the house toward the front room. Opening the door, he nearly lost his balance.

Penelope waited on his front porch. "Hi, Charles. Can I come in?" She was holding a large envelope.

He hesitated for a moment. "Yeah, of course."

But he didn't move out of the way. Instead, he leaned against the door jamb, breathing in the scent of Millie's perfume as it lingered in the humid air.

You couldn't pick a different time to drop by, Penelope?

"Charles?" She looked at him expectantly.

Finally, he stepped to one side. "Sorry."

"Everything okay?" she asked as she came in.

"Everything's perfect." He shut the door behind her. "How do you need my help today?"

Her expression darkened. "That's not the only reason I come to visit you."

"Seems like it."

"Charles, please, let's not fight again. I'm sorry, okay? We've been through this. Would you come to a backyard barbecue if I invited you? Or to a church picnic? Or bridge night?" She gestured to the bookshelves lining the walls. "You'd rather be alone here with your books."

"Books don't betray you."

Her face flushed red. "I didn't—"

"I wasn't talking about you."

Penelope crossed her arms. "I miss the old Charles. I want him back."

He met her gaze. "So do I."

She held up the envelope. "I wouldn't have bothered you if I didn't really need your help."

Charles sighed, struggling to keep the lid on his anger. "Come on back and show me what you've got."

As irritating as she was, Penelope told the truth. Given the choice, Charles would have rather spent time mending his books and listening to his gospel music records than talking to another person. He was used to being alone. Growing up, it had been just him and Margaret in the house. And then just him. He remembered a time when he could enjoy a backyard barbecue, even a church picnic, but ever since he came back from Vietnam, other people were just too much to deal with.

Penelope was persistent, though. Penelope would not leave him alone, no matter what he did to push her away, so he managed to tolerate her. He even felt some begrudging gratitude because she refused to give up on him.

But not today.

Back in his workroom, Charles turned off the television and scooped the stack of books out of the extra folding chair before offering it to Penelope. Then he took his own seat at his worktable.

She handed him the envelope. "I don't know if you heard, but one of Ephraim Brown's employees and the woman he was with were murdered in a motel room a few days ago. These are the police pictures."

Charles opened the envelope and flipped through the photos. He had seen some gruesome things in his life, but the scene in that motel room actually managed to unsettle him. Someone savaged those two people.

"You see the marks all over his body?" Penelope continued. "I need your help figuring out what they mean. It looks like part of a ritual, but this is brutal. Someone must be planning something apocalyptic."

Charles took a deep breath and put the pictures down. Blood magic. A lot of spells used it. Even the most benign spells could call for a drop of the practitioner's blood, but this was not benign. This was dark. This was dangerous. "I agree. This looks like part of a ritual spell, but it's one that makes what Roy Arnold did look like parlor tricks."

"What do you think the purpose of the spell is? Summoning another demon? What kind of demon would require … all that blood?"

"Not any that can be controlled, that's for sure. You'd have to be a lunatic to try."

A grimace spread across Penelope's face. "That's a possibility here."

Charles shook his head. "No, whoever is behind this has been very methodical so far. What he's doing may seem like madness, but it's not. He hasn't been reckless at all."

"Maybe he's getting desperate. After all, he can't be too happy his demon tractor got destroyed."

"You're assuming the demon tractor was his goal."

She narrowed her eyes. "What do you mean?"

Ideas swirled in Charles' head. He was already putting together a list of books to consult. "Pentagrams and blood rituals are used for other things besides summoning demons."

"Like what?"

"A curse."

"That's one hell of a curse."

"Literally. I'll have to do some research, but that seems to be—"

A scream. When Charles looked up, Millie was standing behind Penelope. She clutched her heart. When she pulled her hand away, sticky blood covered her fingers. A giant red stain ruined her beautiful blue dress. She pointed to the pictures in Charles' hand.

"Charles, is everything okay?" Penelope asked.

As quickly as he could, Charles stuffed all the pictures back into the envelope and plunked it on the table. "Yes, I'm fine, but I've got a ton of work to do, so you should probably get going."

"Charles." Her voice had an edge to it.

"I don't need another lecture right now, Penelope. Things are fine. I'll call you when I find something, okay?"

She stood. "Okay, but if I haven't heard anything in a couple of days, I'm coming back here to check on you. Do you understand?"

"You do what you have to do, Penelope."

———

Zed sat waiting on the steps when Penelope got back to her office, a newspaper in his hands. As she stepped out of her car, he put on one of his easy smiles and threw her a casual salute. The sun danced off his shaggy blond hair, and no matter how many times she told herself it was a trick of the light, Penelope could swear his eyes shone bright violet. The top two buttons on his shirt were undone, which drew attention to the lines of his collarbones and his chest. She shook her head. Maybe in some parallel universe, if they had met under different circumstances, he'd be more to her than just an annoying older brother.

"What are you doing up at the crack of noon?" she asked as they walked up to the porch.

He didn't smile at the joke. "Kinda hard to sleep when people keep waking me up."

She slapped him on the arm. "That was two days ago."

"Didn't say it was you this morning."

"Who woke you up this morning?" she asked as she fiddled with her housekey.

"Bertram."

She stopped and looked at him. "Bertram? Why?"

He held up the newspaper. "Did you see the news today?"

Penelope shook her head. "No. What happened?"

Zed gestured toward the door. "Inside."

Penelope led the way to her office, where Zed handed her that morning's edition of the *Greenville News*. "Another murder. This one a little showier."

Penelope read the front-page article. They didn't include a picture, of course, but the article did contain a fairly graphic description of how the body was found tied to a tree in Cleveland Park, covered in strange markings. It also gave the name of the victim.

"Lester Hayes," Penelope said. "Should I know that name?"

Zed nodded. "Another former employee of the Brown Tractor & Farm Supply Co. I spoke with him about Bobby Parker's accident. He was there that day, too, but I don't think he ever had any contact with Patrick Wheeler."

Cold dread overtook Penelope. "This isn't about tying up loose ends, then. Lester Hayes was targeted because he was at the warehouse that day."

"Sure seems like it. That means anyone who was there could be next. And we have no way of knowing who that might be, or when the next murder will happen."

"That's not entirely true." Penelope pointed to the newspaper article. "These murders are obviously part of some ritual, and as Charles says, rituals have to follow rules. The timing of each murder, the murder weapon, the age of the victim, the order of the victims—it all has to be just so. If we can find the pattern, maybe we can get ahead of the killer."

"Hard to find a pattern with just two murders," Zed muttered.

"Three murders," Penelope corrected. "Two connected with the ritual, but three dead. They all deserve some justice."

"Sorry," Zed said. "Three murders. Have you asked Charles to help?"

"I actually just came from Charles' place."

"What did he say?"

"He said he had to research it."

Zed grunted. "We might not have time for that."

"I know."

"How was he?" Zed asked.

Penelope sighed. "I thought he was getting better, but he seemed pretty brittle today. He's gone back into his old habits."

"Yeah, that's my thinking too."

"What do we do about it?"

Zed threw up his hands. "We can't do anything if he won't let us."

"We have to do something. We can't just throw in the towel."

"Why not, Penelope?" Zed huffed. "I'm tired of spending the energy to reach out to him, only to get my hand chopped off. I've done everything I possibly can, and all I've gotten is grief. At some point, you need to recognize that you can't help him if he doesn't want you to."

Penelope was about to reply when a loud bang near the window demanded her attention.

Dad? What are you doing?

Zed's eyes grew wide. "Get down," he yelled as he pulled Penelope to the floor.

Seconds later, a large, dark object shattered the window. Glass and splinters of the wood frame fell all around. Whatever the thing was landed on her desk with a thud.

Zed and Penelope jumped up and ran to the broken window, just in time to see the back of a car, a gold Ford, speeding away.

"Was that the same car that hit you the other day?" Zed asked.

Penelope's heart raced. She hated to think what might have happened if her dad hadn't warned them. "It has to be."

She stepped back and turned her attention to the object on her desk. It was a brick. Part of her hoped to find some note attached to it, some cryptic warning like in the movies. At least that would give them something to go on, but this was just a brick.

Zed joined her. "You think it's Patrick Wheeler trying to stop you from investigating these murders? You said you thought he might have been the guy stalking you in the library."

"But when I was in the library, my charm bracelet tipped me off to him." She pointed to the brick. "There doesn't seem to be anything magical about this, and my bracelet didn't warn me when the car started following me the other day either." Then there was the man at the church who glared at her. Penelope still didn't remember where she had seen him before, but he was just so familiar. "I think maybe it's two different people."

Zed let out an exasperated sigh. "Well, that's really helpful right now. I'll go to the hardware store and get some plywood to put over the window until you can get it fixed."

Penelope glanced at the gaping hole where the window used to be. Suddenly she didn't want to be alone in the house, even with her father's ghost. "Mind if I tag along?"

———

When Zed and Penelope came back from the hardware store, a black car was parked in front of the office. Despite being unmarked, Jim Everett's police cruiser was unmistakable. As Zed pulled his Firebird up behind the car, Jim climbed out. Reluctantly, Penelope did as well.

"What happened here?" Jim asked, pointing to the shattered window.

Penelope really didn't want to answer, but she did anyway. "Flying brick."

Jim took a deep breath and stood up to his full height. His face turned red, and she could tell he was holding in what he really wanted to say. "Did you see who did it?"

"We saw the car but couldn't get the license plate number. It was a gold Ford."

"Maybe you should find a different place to stay tonight." The strain in his voice was obvious.

"I'll be fine, Jim."

"This is serious, Penny. We can even put you up. Margie would love to see you. She'd be delighted for the company."

Penelope gestured toward Zed, who was wrestling with the pieces of plywood shoved in his back seat. "No, really, it's okay. Zed's going to board up the window. I'll have someone here first thing in the morning to look at it."

"Are you sure you're not being reckless?"

"I'm not going to let someone scare me out of my own home."

Zed dragged the plywood through the shrubbery to the window.

"Do you at least have someone who can stay with you?"

She had her dad, of course, but she wasn't about to tell Jim that. She blushed when she realized what he meant. "No, Jim. It's okay. I'll be fine. I have precautions. If all else fails, the Louisville Slugger next to my bed should do the trick."

Zed ran around the back of the house. There was a utility shed where she still kept all her dad's old tools.

Jim put his hands on his hips and studied the broken window. "Well, I'm filling out a police report for you anyway. A gold Ford, you say? I'll have one of the boys look into it."

The boys. Penelope managed a thin smile. She glanced at the envelope he was holding.

"I came to give you these, too," he continued, holding the envelope toward her. "I presume you've heard."

She took the envelope from him. "More pictures?"

"Figured they might help."

She opened the envelope flap and slipped the photos out. Wincing, she glanced through them. In every single photo, Lester Hayes' eyes were open, his face contorted in pain.

"It looks like he was alive when he was hung from the tree and left to bleed out," Jim said. "We were hoping not to panic people about this, but I think the cat is out of the bag now."

Penelope dropped the pictures back inside the envelope, but the expression on Lester's face stayed in her head, like the burning afterimage that comes from accidentally looking at the sun. "I'll see what I can do."

"We're still looking for this Patrick Wheeler person, by the way. Nothing so far. He's done a pretty good job covering his tracks."

Penelope frowned. "Yeah, I was afraid of that."

"That's not to say we're done looking, though."

"I'm not done, either."

He held up a finger. "Penny, you know what I'm about to say."

She nodded. "Be careful."

Jim pointed toward Zed, who had just come back around to the front of the house, tool belt strapped around his waist, carrying a ladder. "Now, he looks like he's going to need some help before he kills himself. You just go inside and don't worry about it, okay? We'll take care of the window."

Penelope glanced at Zed as he set the ladder up against the house. She wasn't sure he'd welcome the help, but she thanked Jim and climbed the steps up to the porch, waving to Zed as she went in.

Surprisingly enough, Jim and Zed worked together to get the plywood nailed in place with only a minimal amount of swearing. After a while, Zed came into the office, wiping the sweat from his forehead with his arm. "Well, that's all done."

Penelope, who had been sweeping up the glass and splinters, leaned the broom against the wall. "Did Jim go?"

Zed nodded. "Said he had somewhere to be. He told me to tell you he'd talk to you later." He glanced at the envelope on top of the desk. "What's that?"

"The pictures from our third murder."

Zed held out a hand. "May I?"

She picked up the envelope and handed it to him. He opened the flap and slid the pictures out. As he looked through them, his face grew several shades paler. "This is demonic."

Demonic. She snatched the pictures back. "I think you might be right."

He looked at her, brow knit in confusion. "What? Well, I am, I'm sure. But I just meant that—"

"No, Zed. Can we go to your apartment?"

She glanced around the office, wondering what her dad thought of that question.

Zed shrugged. "I guess. What's up?"

"I don't know yet. I need to confirm something."

"Is that something going to be a problem for us?"

She was already headed for the door. "Isn't it always?"

———

Jim was a little surprised when Ephraim Brown answered the door himself, though he wasn't entirely sure who he expected. Ephraim was a tall man with a gray beard and a head full of gray hair. Jim was not so blessed. His own hairline had been retreating since the Eisenhower administration.

"Mr. Brown?" he said. "My name is Jim Everett. I'm a police detective. Do you have a few minutes to answer some questions for me?"

Without saying a word, Ephraim Brown nodded and motioned for him to come inside. The house was a nice colonial on Crescent Avenue, filled with expensive things to show off to other people, but Ephraim surprised him again when they passed by the formal living room, and he led Jim to the kitchen.

Ephraim pulled out a chair at the kitchen table for him. "I'd offer you a drink, but I believe you're not allowed to do that on the job."

Jim chuckled as he sat. "You don't know how tempted I'd be to take you up on that offer right now."

"Well, fortunately, there's no such prohibition for me." Ephraim retrieved a beer from the fridge and popped it open before he sat down across the table. "Especially since I'm assuming you're here to talk about the murders."

Jim nodded. "That I am."

"I suppose it's pretty suspicious—three of my employees die all within a month, and my whole business literally goes up in flames." He took a gulp of his beer.

"You might say that."

"I'm not sure I can give you the answers you're looking for, Detective."

"Please, it's Jim. And just try to answer as best you can. Rumor has it someone may be targeting you and your family. Any thoughts on that?"

He sighed. "Given everything that's happened lately, I can't say the rumors are wrong."

Jim leaned forward. "Have other things been happening, besides these murders?"

Ephraim started to peel the label off his beer bottle. "There have been ... threats against my wife and my son."

That was news to Jim, though somehow, he didn't think it would be news to Penny, if he asked her about it. "Why haven't you come forward before now?"

"If I thought it would do any good, I would have."

"Mr. Brown—"

"Ephraim."

"Ephraim, the police are here to help."

Ephraim took in a deep breath and let it out slowly. "I know. I'm sorry. That wasn't intended to be a slam on your abilities, but there are some things the police can't help with."

"And why do you say that?" Jim asked.

The corners of Ephraim's mouth turned up in a faint smile. "Let's just say these threats involve things outside the normal parameters of police work."

"With all due respect, Ephraim, that's not for you to decide." Jim worked his jaw from side to side. He was about to arrive at the point where he wanted to reach across the table and shake Ephraim until he gave a straight answer. "Do you have any idea who these threats are from, or why your family is being targeted?"

Ephraim shook his head. "I'm afraid not. I mean, tractor sales can be a cutthroat business, but not literally. This is all clearly the work of someone crazed and depraved."

Jim thought about each crime scene, about how there was no evidence of the killer. All that blood and no fingerprints, no footprints, not even a stray hair. No witnesses either. No one saw or heard anything. He had his doubts anyone crazed and depraved could pull that off. "One thing, though. If this is all just a plot to get back at you, why are your former employees the ones paying the price?"

"Current employees," Ephraim corrected. "We're going to rebuild the warehouse, and when we're ready, we're going to hire everyone back. As for your question, I don't know. I don't think like a serial killer." There was an edge to his voice, a warning not to continue down that line of questioning.

"Where is your wife, now?" Jim asked.

"She's in Virginia, visiting family."

"And your son?"

"Not certain. He left early this morning. He's been dealing with all the insurance companies, trying to hammer things out so we can start rebuilding."

"The inspectors haven't actually found the cause of the explosion yet, have they?"

"Not yet, but it was obviously just a freak accident."

Jim studied him. Did he really believe what he was saying? Ephraim Brown obviously had guile, but the trauma of losing his business could've had him in denial. "With threats to your family, don't you think the explosion might have been deliberate?"

Ephraim didn't flinch when their gazes met. "It was just an accident."

Jim decided he wasn't going to get anything more out of Ephraim. He leaned back in his chair. "Well, thank you for your time. When you talk to your son, let him know I'd like to speak with him as well."

Ephraim tipped his empty beer bottle toward Jim. "I'll convey the message."

Jim pushed his chair back and stood. "I can show myself out."

Ephraim Brown was hiding something, of course. Jim doubted he had anything to do with murdering his own employees, but that hint of a smile on his face was enough to send a chill down Jim's spine.

As Penelope drove to Ephraim Brown's house, she passed Jim Everett going in the opposite direction. She swore under her breath. Of course, it made sense Jim would want to talk to Ephraim, but she didn't know what kind of mood the elder Brown would be in after being questioned by the police.

Ephraim didn't act surprised to see her when he answered the door. He smiled and gave her a little hug, more affection than he had shown her in years, since before he and her father had stopped speaking to one another.

In the kitchen, an empty bottle of beer rested on the counter. That didn't stop Ephraim from getting another for himself. He offered one to Penelope, but she declined. She needed all her wits about her.

"So, Penelope, to what do I owe the pleasure of this visit?" He sat down at the kitchen table.

Penelope took the chair opposite. "I need to talk to you about something."

"Is it about Bertram?"

Penelope shot him a puzzled glance. "No. Why would it be about him?"

"The two of you are friends, right?" He took a swig and set the beer down on the table. "I mean, I know you're not as close as you used to be, but you still seem to have his confidence. I just thought he might have opened up to you about what's going on."

"We talked a few days ago. He's a little on edge about the recent murders, and I can't say I really blame him. The murders are actually what I came to talk to you about."

He grimaced. "You too?"

"So, Jim Everett *did* stop by."

His mouth twisted into a sly grin. "For a few minutes."

"I doubt he asked you about this, though." From her purse, Penelope pulled a photocopy of the drawing from her father's college journal.

Ephraim retrieved a pair of reading glasses from the pocket of his shirt. While he studied the drawing, she watched him for a reaction. As it turned out, his poker face was as good as Zed's.

He peered at her over the top of his glasses. "What's this?"

"It's a drawing of the pentagram that was on the floor of your warehouse." She wasn't lying.

"Is it safe?"

"It's as safe as anything. I have it on good authority this one is too small be used in a ritual. But I think someone is using the bigger version."

"But the warehouse was destroyed."

"The pentagram can always be redrawn."

He held up the paper. "And you think this is related to the murders of those two men?"

Penelope took an envelope out of her purse. She opened it and let the pictures from the scene of Lester Hayes' murder spill out onto the table. Jim would have blown a gasket if he knew she was showing them to Ephraim, but she couldn't think of a way around it.

Ephraim winced and shied away from the photos. "Why are you doing this, Penelope?"

"Because I need to show you something. You see the symbol carved into Lester Hayes' chest?" She placed a hand on top of the close-up photograph of the bloody sigil and pushed it toward Ephraim. "It's also at the end of one of the points of the penta-gram. The rest of the symbols on his arms are the ones arranged around the point. The last symbol, the one carved into the trunk of the tree, it's the symbol in the middle of the pentagram. Same thing with Lloyd Baker. He had the symbol from one of the other points of the pentagram carved into his chest."

"What are you trying to say?" Ephraim asked, making an attempt not to look too closely.

"That there are going to be three more murders."

"And then what?"

"I don't know, but whatever it is, it can't be good."

Ephraim sighed. "I'm going to tell you the same thing I told Jim. I wish I could help you, but I can't. I don't know why all this is happening. I don't understand any of it."

"But you know someone who might."

He looked at her sidelong. "Who?"

"The magic user you had come in and calm the spirit possessing Louise before we could get it out, the one who made the charm bracelet you're wearing right now, and the bracelet I've seen Bertram wear. I need help with this."

Ephraim glanced down at his beer bottle. "What about your friend Charles?"

"He's not … able to help as much right now."

"He went to Vietnam for a little while, didn't he?"

Penelope nodded. "He's been back for two years."

"But he came back a little different."

"How do you know that?" Penelope knew he was trying to distract her, but she was curious.

"Saw it a lot coming back from World War II. You experience horrible things, and they change you. They become a part of who you are. If you're not careful, they can eat you alive. He needs help."

"I try."

"Not from you. From someone trained."

"Charles will never agree to that."

Ephraim still wasn't looking her in the eye. "Then he's going to lose his war. Maybe not today, but eventually. I hope he changes his mind."

Penelope neared the end of her patience, but she managed to keep her voice even. "Ephraim, I appreciate your concern for Charles, but I really need help, or more people are going to die. Who is the magic user you employed?"

He shook his head. "I can't tell you. Besides, I doubt he could help you anyway."

She wanted to flip the table over. "Why? Why is it so important to protect this person?"

"Penelope, I'm not trying to protect anyone."

"Then just give me the name. Don't you understand? People are dying. Your people. People you claim to care about."

He took a deep breath and let it out slowly. "It's me. I made the necklace for Louise. I made the charm bracelets for all of us."

Penelope recalled something Zed said. At the time, she didn't think much of it, but Ephraim's confession made complete sense. As Zed explained it, the ghostly apparition of a toddler had been used to lure Bobby Parker to his accident in the warehouse. Because Patrick Wheeler needed a person with magical talent for his sacrifice, the illusion was specifically attuned to people with an aptitude for magic.

Penelope and Bertram couldn't even hear the boy's laughter the ghost hunters who stayed overnight in the warehouse captured on tape, but Zed could. Bobby's grandmother was a practitioner, and Zed suspected he might have dabbled. The fact that Ephraim had also seen and heard the apparition meant he had more of an affinity for magic than most.

"*You* can help, then," she said.

"No. I can't," he insisted. "I can only do simple things. Wardings, some minor healing spells. There's one that prevents a hangover I've used a lot. The ten-pound bag of ginger root was a little hard to explain to Louise. I didn't even know if the necklace I put around Louise's neck was going to work. I just knew I had to do something."

"But you could at least help us figure out how the spell using this pentagram works, right? What kind of ritual is the killer planning to perform?"

Ephraim let his shoulders slump. "Penelope, I don't have a library full of magic books. All I have is a diary from one of my grandmothers with pages full of her scribbled notes."

"Why didn't you say anything earlier?"

"I've kept it a secret so long, I didn't really see any reason to bring it up." He picked up the drawing of the pentagram again.

"Something about all this is vaguely familiar, though. Maybe I've seen it before. I guess it wouldn't hurt to root around a little."

Penelope reached across the table and grasped his hand. "Thanks, Ephraim. That's all I'm asking."

She left, still no closer to figuring out anything about the pentagram than when she had arrived. Either Ephraim was a regular Laurence Olivier or he really didn't know anything about the drawing in her dad's notebook. And that just raised more questions. Maybe she'd been barking up the wrong tree all along. Maybe what happened in the woods that night didn't have anything to do with the pentagram at all. Fortunately, she still had a few avenues to explore. If her dad and Ephraim couldn't tell her about the night excursion they had gone on, there were others who could.

4.

TUESDAY, AUGUST 1, 1972

"They're all dead."

Penelope stared at Carolyn Cole, mouth agape. "All of them?"

Carolyn nodded. "Every last one."

Penelope had met Carolyn for lunch, like she had promised to do forever, but she couldn't keep her promise not to talk business. She had asked Carolyn, a file clerk at the Division of Public Records—who in Penelope's opinion, could work magic every bit as mysterious as anything Charles could do—to see if she could track down her dad's college buddies who had ventured into the wilderness with him and Ephraim.

"What happened to them?" Penelope asked

"Well, as you already know, Geoffrey Wheeler committed suicide about twelve years ago. What you probably don't know is that he bit a gun in the bedroom of his house while the rest of his family was downstairs. I was able to track down his obituary. He lived in Columbia, and Patrick Wheeler was listed as his only child. Of the others, Bradley James apparently got drunk one evening about twenty years ago and drove his car off a bridge. It's the same story with Edward McDowell, except it was a truck, and he drove it into a tree. James was also from Columbia. McDowell was from Spartanburg. Jude Hall hanged himself with a necktie in the front parlor of his Charleston rowhouse. That was about five years ago." Carolyn took a sip of water, as if she had just casually listed off the winners of the church cake walk.

"None of them natural deaths I notice."

"Does that matter?"

Penelope moved her salad around on her plate with her fork. "Just an observation."

Carolyn shot her a dubious look. "You know, I'm used to all sorts of bizarre requests from you, and normally I know better than to ask, because I know I wouldn't like the answer, but this time I just have to. What's this for? Why are you looking for these men?"

"They all knew my father in college," Penelope replied. "I'm just looking for some information about him, to confirm some things I've found out recently."

Judging by the still suspicious expression on Carolyn's face, she didn't buy the half-truth, but fortunately, she didn't press. "Fair enough. Speaking of your dad, are you doing okay? I know it's been over a year, but I also know these things don't really have timetables."

Her appetite having left her, Penelope put down her fork and pushed away her plate. "Yeah. Life has to go on, you know. I miss him, but feeling sorry for myself isn't going to get the bills paid."

In fact, everything Carolyn had just told her put her father's death in a completely different light. Supposedly he was killed in the middle of a robbery gone wrong, but what if that wasn't the case? What if there was something more to his death?

"But what are the odds that none of them died of natural causes?" She asked the question more to herself than to Carolyn.

"You make it sound like they're related somehow."

Because they were. They had to be.

Penelope shook her head. "It's just surprising. That's all. Enough about this, though. I promised we wouldn't talk business. How is your life?"

Carolyn grinned. "You mean when I'm not looking things up for you? Same as usual."

Penelope's grandmother lived next door to Carolyn's family. They had moved in when Penelope was around nine or ten. Over the years, the two of them managed to stay in touch despite their lives taking differing paths, but Penelope had to admit she didn't really know very much about Carolyn. She had always been intensely private, shy even.

The day the moving trucks arrived at the empty house next to her grandmother's, Penelope found Carolyn under a tree in the front yard, reading a book while the movers unloaded all the furniture. It had taken a good hour to coax her to say more than two words, but after that, they quickly became friends.

"By the way, thanks for all the help you've given me lately," Penelope said. "I know I've asked for a lot, and I know it's seemed a little weird at times, but I do appreciate it. If you need anything, let me know. I owe you."

Carolyn was silent for a moment, studying her half-eaten club sandwich. "Well, there is one small thing."

Penelope sincerely hoped she wouldn't come to regret her next words. "Name it."

Carolyn reached into her purse and pulled out an envelope. She tipped it over, and a silver heart-shaped locket on a silver chain spilled out onto the table along with a note. "I want to know who sent me this."

Penelope picked up the note and read it.

Carolyn, I want to give you my heart.

The note wasn't signed. The handwriting was almost childlike. Penelope reached for the piece of jewelry but hesitated before she touched it, remembering what happened to Louise Brown. When her charm bracelet didn't raise any alarms, she picked the locket up and carefully opened it. There was nothing inside.

"Where did you find this?" she asked.

"It was left at my door a few weeks ago. I've been trying to figure out what to do ever since, but I'm at a loss. I know I should be flattered having a secret admirer, but something about this bothers me."

Penelope scrutinized the locket. It was not the cheap kind you could find at any K-mart. It had some weight to it, and though the heart itself was fairly simple, the hinge and the clasp were well-made. "Do you have any idea who could have left it? Any neighbors?"

Carolyn shook her head apologetically. "Not really. Honestly, I can't even remember the last time I talked to a guy my age, except for Zed, and I know he didn't do this."

"No, definitely not his style." Penelope held up the locket. "Mind if I take this?"

"Not at all. The fastener is broken anyway. Even if I wanted to wear it, I couldn't."

"I'll see what I can do." Penelope put the locket in her own purse.

She could ask Dan about it. Immediately, she got mad at herself for getting excited over the idea.

Carolyn grasped her arm. "Thanks. I know it's a long shot, but I'll sleep easier tonight."

After Carolyn left, Penelope remained for a few minutes. She took out the locket again and looked it over one more time. At least there was one person sleeping easy.

Martin Smith would've said he was close to Lloyd Baker and Lester Hayes during the time they all worked at the Brown Tractor & Farm Supply Co., but he'd be lying. So, while their deaths came as a shock—any God-fearing Christian would be horrified after all—he didn't exactly shed a tear for either of them.

Besides, Lloyd and Lester had made their beds when they trusted in Ephraim Brown. He and his son could talk all they wanted about loyalty and how everyone who worked for them belonged to one big family. They promised there would be a place for every last employee once the company got back on its feet, but everything they said was so much bullshit.

Martin had brushed the dirt off his sandals, so to speak, and never looked back. He didn't go a day out of work before he found a new job, and one that paid better at that. There had been a time when Martin would have done anything for Ephraim Brown, just like Lloyd and Lester, but that was before he started attending the Little Rock Baptist Church and Reverend Purdue opened his eyes to the truth.

Evil was real.

It was tangible.

Reverend Purdue said Ephraim Brown had made a deal with the Devil for his fortune. Now the Devil was coming for him to collect on his debt, and anyone foolish enough to side with the Browns would pay the price, too.

When Martin got home from work that night, he took off his muddy boots at the door and tossed his keys into the bowl on the table just inside. In the kitchen, he threw the remains of his take-out in the trash and grabbed a beer from the refrigerator. Reverend Purdue would have disapproved of his beverage of choice, but even the good preacher had to concede the simple pleasures were what made life bearable.

He turned on the television and sat down in his recliner. Angie, his girlfriend, was in Georgia visiting with her mother. She'd been doing a lot of that lately. He felt a little guilty he didn't miss her more, but to be honest, he was enjoying his days of freedom.

As Walter Cronkite droned on about something or other having to do with the presidential election, Martin's eyelids grew heavy, and soon he found himself nodding off. When he woke up, *Hawaii Five-O* was on TV, and Steve McGarrett was in the middle of telling Danno to book 'em. The noise that woke him, though, was someone banging on his door.

He pushed himself out of the recliner and accidentally kicked the empty beer bottle he'd dropped when he dozed off across the floor. Angie would have made him pick it up, but he didn't feel like it. He told himself he'd get it later.

When Martin answered the door, he found himself face-to face with the last person he ever expected to see standing there. "Mr. Brown? What are you doing here?"

"Can I come in, Martin?" his former boss asked. "I need to talk to you. I promise it'll only take a minute."

Martin shrugged. "Well, I guess so. Kinda late, though isn't it, Mr. Brown?"

"Please, call me Bertram," he said as he stepped over the threshold. "I'm sorry. I wouldn't be here if it wasn't important." His gaze wandered around the room, lingering here and there, as if he were making a mental catalogue of the room's contents. "Nice place you've got here."

"Um, thanks?" Martin ventured.

Bertram Brown had never said a friendly word to him the whole time he'd worked in the warehouse. Why was he trying to make small talk now?

"Bet you're enjoying your pass out with Angie out of town, aren't you?" Bertram walked around the recliner where Martin had been dozing, continuing to survey his home with a little too much interest.

"Yeah, I guess." Martin's gaze flitted to the overturned beer bottle as his unease grew.

"No one to order you around or tell you all the things you're doing wrong. You can be your own boss, eat what you want to eat, and drink what you want to drink." Bertram stooped to pick up the beer bottle on the floor. He placed it on the coffee table. "Must be pretty nice."

"She's coming back day after tomorrow," Martin muttered.

Bertram nodded. "Good to know. How's the new job treating you, Martin?"

Martin couldn't take it anymore. "Mr. Brown—Bertram—what

is it you needed to talk to me about? If this is to get me to come back to work for you, I'm afraid that ship has sailed. I'm grateful for the opportunity your family provided, but I have a new job now at the Milliken plant, a better one. They made me a shift supervisor."

"Oh, Martin," Bertram said, smiling and shaking his head. "I didn't come her to give you your job back."

Martin didn't like the strange gleam in Bertram's eyes, and only then did it occur to him what was making him so uneasy. "Wait, how did you know my girlfriend was out of town?"

He didn't see the glint off the blade of the knife until it was too late. It went into his side between his ribs with a squelch. He took a step back, knife still in to the hilt. He looked down to see a red stain spreading across his shirt. Searing heat radiated out from the wound, followed by cold, and then finally numbness. His heart, which had pounded in his ears for those first few awful seconds, began to slow. His legs got wobbly. He struggled to stay standing, but his legs finally gave way completely, and he stumbled to the floor.

Bertram's grinning face loomed over him. "That's three," he said as he removed the knife.

———

When Zed walked into O'Shaughnessy's, Jake was already there, sitting at the bar reading a book.

Zed took the stool next to him. "C. S. Lewis. *The Screwtape Letters*. Interesting choice."

Without looking at him, Jake closed the book and set it down on the bar. Zed flagged Russell, the bartender, and ordered his usual. The two were silent until Russell delivered Zed's beer.

He noted Jake's empty glass. "Been waiting long?"

"About an hour," Jake replied. "Today. Yesterday I went to the bookstore, but they told me you weren't scheduled to work, so I came here and waited for two hours. You never showed up."

"I was busy with my other gigs yesterday."

"I know. I listened to your radio show. All of it."

Zed sipped his beer. "We should talk about what happened."

"We should. I just don't know how."

Zed glanced at him. Jake sat huddled, arms crossed. Fear radiated off him, mixed with something else. Shame. "Why not?"

"Because I don't have any answers for you. I can't explain to you what I … what we experienced. I've never had that happen before. That's not how it usually works."

Zed raised an eyebrow. "That's not how *what* usually works?"

Jake shook his head. "You won't believe me."

"Try me."

"You'll just think I'm crazy."

Zed laughed. "I can basically guarantee that's not going to happen."

Jake scowled, clearly annoyed. "How can you say that? You don't know what I'm about to tell you."

"Look, Jake, if I told you all the weird shit I've seen, you'd be telling me to lay off the magic mushrooms." Zed finished his beer and flagged Russell for another one. "Besides, whatever happened, it happened to both of us."

"Okay, then. Just remember, you asked for it." Jake took a deep breath. "Sometimes I see the future."

Zed had premonitions from time to time, but they were little more than flashes of intuition that let him dodge a right hook at the last second. He'd never met a true seer before. This was going to get interesting. "So why aren't you rich from betting on the World Series every year?"

Jake drew his mouth into a thin line. "It doesn't work that way either. One, every time I have a vision, it's a lot like what happened at the bookstore. Just a rush of confusing sensations— sights, sounds, smells. Two, I only ever see *my* future, not anyone else's. And three, the visions give me seizures."

Shame and anger radiated off him. Clearly not the time for jokes.

When Russell came back with Zed's second beer, Zed stopped him before he could walk away. "Could I get another one for my friend here, whatever he was drinking." He glanced at Jake, who didn't protest. "How long has this been going on?"

"A while," Jake replied. "I was in high school the first time I had a vision. I was competing at a track-and-field meet, right in the middle of the 1500-meter relay. I was third and went down about halfway through my leg. That pretty much ended my athletic career, all so I could know two days in advance my grandfather was going to die. Since then, it's happened on and off. The last seizure cost me my job."

"When was that?"

Russell came back with Jake's beer. He took a gulp before he answered. "The day before I met you, actually."

"No wonder your mood was so black when you sat down."

"So, you could tell?"

"It was pretty obvious." At least to Zed it was. "What was the job you lost?"

"I worked in a legal aid office. They said I scared the clients, and they didn't want me to have another seizure there. They told me I couldn't come back until I had a note from a doctor saying I had the problem under control."

"A note you can't get."

His mouth twisted into a rueful grin. "You know a doctor who can prescribe something for seizures induced by visions of the future?"

"As a matter of fact—"

Jake held up a hand. "Don't say it."

Zed nodded. "What did you see in that vision?"

Jake shrugged. "Nothing special. A traffic light changing from green to red. Raindrops on my head. A blue car speeding by."

"Has that happened yet?"

"Right before I walked into this bar for the first time. I was waiting to cross the street just as it started to rain. When the light changed, I stepped off the curb, but a blue car ran the light and nearly hit me."

Zed frowned. "Doesn't that make it sort of a self-fulfilling prophecy though? You came here because you saw it."

Jake took another big gulp of his beer. "But I'd never been to O'Shaughnessy's before. And I didn't see the *name* of the bar in my vision. All I knew that day was that I needed to get out of the house. I had no idea I'd end up here, next to you. I picked this place at random, mostly because it didn't look like I'd get mugged the second I walked in the door."

"Does what you see always come true?"

"Always," Jake answered, almost in a whisper.

"Have you ever tried to change something?"

Jake shook his head. "I don't ever get enough detail to do that. Like I said, it's only a moment, a blitz of sensations, and then it's done. Generally, by the time I realize something's happened, it's already too late."

"And how far in the future do the visions go? Days? Weeks? Years?" Something in the pit of Zed's stomach told him the answers to all these questions would be important later.

"The furthest out has been about two months."

"So, in two months or so, you're going to be in a creepy grave-yard in the middle of the night, maybe bleeding."

"*We're* going to be in a creepy graveyard in the middle of the night, maybe bleeding. I can't tell if this vision was something from my future or from yours. Like I said, it's never happened that way before. I've never shared a vision by touching someone."

"You think we're together, wherever this graveyard is?"

"Yeah. That's something else I can't really explain. I could sense you somehow, your emotions. You were scared of some-thing, terrified even, but you were also angry, like 'wrath of God' angry." He finished his beer in one last swig. "Or maybe that was me and you were sensing what I felt. I don't know. I get a headache every time I think about it."

Zed hadn't considered the possibility before, but if Jake could share his visions by touching him, why couldn't Zed share his ability to read people's emotions? Of course, that made things infinitely more complicated.

Jake covered his face with his hands. "I'm just really confused right now. I don't know what to do."

Zed put a hand on Jake's arm. Jake tensed, but nothing happened.

"Whatever led us to that place we saw, we'll get each other through it. I promise." He raised his glass in salute. "Looks like we've got an adventure ahead of us."

5.

WEDNESDAY, AUGUST 2, 1972

Charles woke up to the sound of people talking loudly outside, happy banter, workers headed to the factories for the early shift. Cool air blew in through the open window. The stifling heat of August was finally gone. Now that fall had come to New York City, he could sleep with the windows open again. He turned his head to see Millie's form lying in bed next to him. Gradually, the events of the last few months filled in the gaps in his memory.

Thanks to Millie, he had gotten a job at The Blue Club as a waiter and had quickly worked his way up to manager. During that time, he and Millie had also grown much closer. He remembered early mornings together after the club closed, dinners in nice restaurants, walks in Morningside Park. He was happy when he was with her, away from the agitations of his other life, away from the constant state of near panic, the fear, the paranoia and anxiety, and away from the Shrouded Man. The malignant spirit couldn't get to Charles there in Harlem.

Next to him, Millie stirred and opened her eyes. She smiled at him and wrapped her arm around his chest. "What are you doing awake?"

He chuckled. "I could ask you the same question."

"You stopped snoring. The silence was jarring."

"I don't snore."

She shot him an incredulous glare. "You're asleep. How do you know?"

"I just do."

"Okay, sure. Now I answered. Your turn."

He gazed at her dark eyes looking back at him, full of intelligence and excitement and wonder, with just a twinkle of mischief. "Nothing special. I'm just lying here, thinking about how lucky I am that I found you."

She poked him in the side. "And don't you forget it either. There's something different about you, you know. I've known a lot of boys that have come back from the war—"

"You have now?"

Millie swatted his arm. "Not like that, you jerk. I mean as part of what I do as a singer. I've met a lot of people, but you, you're special. You seem like you come from a different time almost."

He tensed. "Why do you say that?"

"The way you act toward people. You're always putting what others want before yourself. You don't see that much anymore. It's old fashioned."

Charles let out the breath he had been holding. "I was just raised to believe we should look out for others who need our help."

"And that's why I'm lucky to have you."

She leaned in and kissed him. He relished the sweet and salty taste of her lips and the smell of lavender on her skin. He pulled her closer and wrapped his arms around her. He settled his own thoughts and memories in between the thoughts and memories of this person whose body he occupied. He let go of the old farm house out in the middle of nowhere full of old magical books waiting for him to repair. Right now, none of that mattered.

———

Charles woke up sitting at his worktable, needle and thread still in one hand. Daylight streamed through the window, open to let in the breeze. *The Beverly Hillbillies* was on television, and Millie was nowhere to be seen. He stood and stretched, and then looked down at the disassembled book and all his tools.

He didn't recognize anything.

He couldn't name any of the tools or remember how they worked. He turned his attention to the book itself. The text was all in Latin, in cramped handwriting. He flipped through the pages but couldn't understand any of it. Charles should have been more upset, he knew, but he couldn't bring himself to care. He wanted to sweep everything off the table, throw it all away.

He wanted to go back to Millie.

The knock at the door startled him. Charles froze. He thought maybe if he didn't make a sound, whoever it was would just assume no one was home and go away. But the knocking persisted.

"Charles!" a voice called, carried in through the open window. "I know you're home. If you don't answer the door, I'm coming in anyway."

Charles sighed. He trudged to the front door and yanked it open. Zed stood on his porch.

"Charles," he said. "I know you don't want me here, but we need to talk."

Charles stepped aside and motioned for him to come in. "Okay then. What's wrong, Zed?"

Zed turned to face him. "I should be asking you that."

Charles shut the door, but not before glancing outside to see if anyone or anything else was there. "Why? Nothing's wrong with me."

"Bullshit," Zed spat.

"Did you come here just to argue with me?" Charles asked.

He was tired of arguing with Zed, of listening to the self-righteous lectures, of being scolded for not living his life the way everyone else wanted him to live it.

"I came here because Penelope asked me to. She's worried."

Charles snorted. "She's worried I won't help her solve her little mystery."

"No, she's worried about you." Zed's expression softened, a little. "Look, I won't pretend you and I have seen eye-to-eye about anything, but Penelope's known you a lot longer than I have, and if she says you weren't always so stubborn and cantankerous, then I believe her. Why are you cutting everyone off again? The last time you pulled this crap was last summer, and we both know how that ended."

Charles shook his head. "This isn't the same."

Zed crossed his arms. "Pardon me if I'm skeptical."

"You didn't understand what I was doing."

"You were trying to kill yourself."

"You nearly killed us both by interrupting my spell. We had to rid the graveyard of those spirits. They were becoming dangerous."

"You had already lost control of the spell." Zed was yelling now. "It was going to kill you, and you didn't care. You wanted it to kill you. You were looking forward to dying."

"You don't know that," Charles said quietly.

"I do, actually."

Before Charles could ask Zed how he knew, a loud knock came from the back of the house.

Zed turned toward the door that led to the dining room. "What was that?"

Charles had heard it, too. He didn't know what made the sound either, but he didn't like any of the theories running through his head. "Nothing. The TV's on."

"That didn't sound like the TV."

Before Charles could stop him, Zed pushed open the door to the dining room and peered inside. The room was empty. Charles followed while Zed skirted around the dining room table toward the door opposite, which led to Charles' workroom.

Zed rushed into the workroom and skidded to a stop with

Charles still on his heels. Things were coming back to Charles now. When he glanced at the disassembled book on the table, he remembered what the Latin text said, and more specifically that it was a book from a monastery in the Spanish Pyrenees, another acquisition from Roy Arnold's collection. He had been sewing the signatures back together before he was sucked into Millie's world. He also remembered the names of his tools.

Zed scanned the room, though with the only furniture being the two folding chairs and card table, there really wasn't a place to hide. "No one's here."

Charles shot him daggers. If he'd had a spell handy, he might have shot real daggers. "Of course no one's here. Now, have you said everything you came here to say?"

Zed glared. "No, I haven't. There's been another murder. That makes three. Based on the symbols carved in the victims' chests, Penelope thinks the murderer is killing one person for every point on the pentagram, which means two more people are going to die soon. We need help to figure out when the next murder might be and what this Patrick Wheeler is trying to do, if he's, in fact, the one behind all this."

"I haven't found anything yet. That pentagram, it's not matching any of the systems I know. I can't promise anything."

"We've got to keep trying."

"I'll do what I can. Is that all, now?"

"Just one more thing."

"What?"

"Penelope puts up a good front, but she cares more deeply about everyone around her than anyone I've ever met. She's never going to give up on you, so you might as well quit fighting her."

Charles nodded. "I know."

Zed turned around and left. No sooner was he gone, than Millie's ghost appeared. She was crying, and her dress had the same red stain on the front as before. In her hand, she held a newspaper clipping. Charles stepped toward her. He was going to ask her what was wrong, but she vanished before he could. The newspaper clipping fluttered to the floor. Charles stooped and picked it up. It was an obituary for Millie Priest, dated March 19, 1920. She was shot to death, caught in the crossfire in a fight between two crime gangs.

———

Penelope's office phone rang.

She picked up the receiver. "Drake Detective Agency."

There was only silence on the other end of the line, but she could tell someone was there.

"Hello?" she ventured.

No response. She hung up only to have the phone immediately ring again.

"Drake Detective Agency," she said again, putting a little annoyance in her voice.

More silence. She was about to hang up for a second time when someone spoke finally.

"You ruined my life," a man said.

"Who is this?" Penelope asked.

"Who do you think you are getting involved in my business?" the man growled.

"I don't know what you're talking about." Penelope tried to keep the tremor out of her voice. "Who are you?"

"You know exactly what I'm talking about." His words were slightly slurred, as if he'd been drinking. "You took everything away from me. And now I'm going to take everything away from you."

He hung up. Penelope glanced toward the plywood boards covering her window. Someone was supposed to come the next day to replace the broken pane. The repair was going to take a big chunk out of her rainy-day fund, but what else could she do?

She jumped up from her desk and hurried to the foyer. She pulled the curtain back on the window by the door and peered out, half expecting to see the gold Ford parked outside her house.

The responsible thing to do would have been to call Jim. After thinking about it, she was almost positive the man glaring at her at church on Sunday was the man who rear-ended her car and threw a brick through the window. She could give him a description. She wasn't sure, though, she could bear any more judgment about her choice of careers or endure another lecture about how it was too dangerous for a woman. She could almost see the smug "told you so" look on his face. Instead, she went back to her office and called Zed.

6.

THURSDAY, AUGUST 3, 1972

The Value Motor Inn was the kind of place that made you want to take a shower just looking at it. The bright cotton-candy paint job couldn't make up for the crumbling concrete or the grime-covered walls or the burned-out neon sign alerting passers-by to the hourly rates.

"Another fucking fleabag motel," Officer Andy Barnes muttered under his breath as he pulled the patrol car into the parking lot of the motel on Townes Street, just north of downtown. "Who did I piss off to keep getting these shitty assignments?"

The night manager had called in a noise disturbance. Andy and his partner Mike were the lucky officers who got the privilege of checking it out. The night manager, an older woman in a lavender leisure suit, greeted them both outside the hotel office, cigarette dangling from her lips. Her name was Doris.

"Room 14." She pointed up to the second-floor catwalk with a bony finger that ended in an inch-long fire-engine red fingernail. A weak light on the overhang bathed the room number in a sickly glow. "Strange noises coming from in there all night. I've gotten lots of complaints from the other rooms. I knocked on the door, but no one answered."

Andy smirked. "You don't say." He elbowed Mike. "Care to describe these 'strange noises'?"

At a place like this, there were only two kinds of noise disturbances—couples in a screaming match with one another, or couples engaged in vigorous acts of intimacy. In either case, the parties involved didn't generally care if they were bothering their neighbors.

Doris scrunched up her face. "Weird moans and grunts, almost like an animal, but not any animal I've ever heard before."

Andy rolled his eyes. "Okay, well let's get this over with."

They walked upstairs single file to the second floor, Doris in the lead and Mike bringing up the rear. In his head, Andy counted off the room numbers. *10, 11, 12, 14.* Doris stopped outside. With a flourish, she motioned toward the door, ash falling from the end of her cigarette like dull gray snowflakes.

Andy listened for a moment. "I don't hear anything now."

"The noise stopped about ten minutes before you showed up," Doris explained.

Andy rolled his eyes again. "Of course. And it'll start back up again then minutes after we leave."

He knocked on the door.

No answer.

"Who's staying here?" Andy asked.

"The guestbook says his name is Patrick Wheeler."

Andy and Mike exchanged glances. Patrick Wheeler was the name of the person Detective Everett wanted them to try to find.

Andy knocked on the door again. "Mr. Wheeler, this is the police. I'm going to need you to come out of the room so we can speak with you."

Still no answer, but a noise came from inside, a low moan that made Andy's teeth rattle.

Doris jabbed a finger at the closed door. "See, there it is."

Andy knocked again, louder. "Mr. Wheeler, come out and talk to us or we're going to have to come in."

Another noise from inside, but it sounded more like words this time, and whoever was speaking wasn't saying wholesome things.

Andy sighed. "I was afraid of that. Why do they always make us go in?"

He nodded to Doris and stepped aside. She took his place and fiddled with the cluster of keys she extracted from her pocket. When she found the right one, the door unlocked with a click. Andy took hold of the doorknob, his other hand hovering over the gun at his side. Behind him, Mike rested his hand on his own gun, ready to draw also.

But before Andy could open the door, someone jerked the doorknob from his hand. The door flew open inward. Andy and Mike both drew their guns and aimed. Andy peered into the darkness inside the room. He thought at first the lights were simply off, but then he realized the light from outside wasn't penetrating the doorway. It just stopped at the threshold.

As Andy struggled to understand what he was seeing, the darkness inside Room 14 shifted. Another moan resonated from the room, but without the door muffling the sound, it moved through Andy's head and scraped across his consciousness. He took a step back and grabbed hold of the railing of the catwalk to keep from tumbling over the side to the parking lot below. Mike staggered back also. Doris dropped her cigarette. The darkness in the room continued to move and swirl, and as it did shapes formed—an arm, a leg, a hand ending in giant claws, and two glowing green dots. They bore into Andy like lasers, burning away his consciousness and leaving only fear. He was only vaguely aware of screaming. Then the thing in the dark rushed forward. His chest bloomed in warm, wet pain as blood spattered across his face. Then he was flying over the railing down to the pavement. His last thought before he hit the hard ground was *who did I piss off to deserve this?*

———

Penelope pulled her black Lincoln into the driveway of the small house near Mauldin. Everything about this situation set off alarm bells. Bertram had called her at about seven o'clock that morning and asked to meet her there. She confirmed the address with him twice on the phone, and as she climbed out of her car, she checked the house number on the door to make sure she was in the right place. A blue Buick was parked in the carport, but Bertram's red Camaro wasn't anywhere to be seen.

Penelope paused as she approached the front door. It was ajar.

She knocked anyway. "Bertram? Bertram, are you in there?"

She didn't get an answer.

She took her .22 out of her purse and pushed the door open. Inside all the shades were drawn, making it almost too dark to see, but a sliver of light came from a room in the back of the house.

"Bertram?" she called again.

The thought briefly crossed her mind that maybe he had left, but he was so insistent on the phone. She felt around until she found the light switch. The house was clearly a bachelor pad. The couch in the den didn't match either of the two chairs, and all three were very well worn. A television with aluminum foil on the rabbit-ear antennas sat on a table in one corner.

Penelope ventured down the hallway toward the source of the light in what she assumed was a bedroom. Through the gap in the door, she spotted someone sitting in a chair.

"Bertram, is that you? What are you doing back here?"

Still no answer.

She opened the door and covered her mouth to stifle her scream. Bertram sat in a chair, holding a knife. Blood covered his clothes. On the floor lay the body of a man, his shirt ripped open, more symbols carved into his chest and on his arms.

"I didn't do it, Penelope," Bertram said, tears running down his face. "I don't remember anything. I don't know how I got here. I swear I didn't do it."

Penelope couldn't say anything.

"Help me, Penelope," Bertram continued. "Oh, God, what am I going to do?"

Her hand shaking, Penelope pointed her gun at him. "First, you need to drop the knife and kick it away from you, toward me."

His eyes grew wide. "Penelope—"

"Just do it, please. I'm not saying I don't believe you, but if something is compelling you, how do I know you're not still being influenced?"

Or how do I know you're actually Bertram?

Bertram let go of the knife, which hit the hardwood floor with a clatter. He stood slowly, keeping his hands in Penelope's view. Then he kicked the knife like she told him. It skidded across the floor and stopped a few feet from her.

Penelope walked to the dresser against one wall and opened the top drawer, all the while keeping the gun on Bertram. She pulled out a white tee shirt and wrapped it around her hand before she picked up the knife.

"Thank you," she said. "Now what's the last thing you remember?"

"Last night. I was at my parent's house sitting out in the back yard, drinking a beer. My dad had just gone inside to bed. We had … not exactly a fight. A disagreement."

"About what?"

"The future of the company. He told me he wanted to be involved again. He said we could work together."

Penelope frowned. "You fought about that?"

"He wanted to move on with the rebuilding now, said we didn't need to wait for the insurance. I asked him where he was getting the money for that, but he wouldn't tell me."

"What do you think he meant?"

"I don't know. I was just pissed off and needed time to cool down. The last thing I remember really clearly was seeing two fireflies at the far end of the yard. I thought it was weird because it's so late in the summer, and also, they were the wrong color—

bright green. Then then the next thing I knew, I was here." Bertram glanced down at the dead body. "With George."

"Another Brown employee?"

Bertram nodded. "George Landry. He was a good guy. He didn't deserve this. Do you think … do you think I really killed him?"

"I don't know, Bertram, but I promise you we'll figure it out."

"How?"

She glanced around the small bedroom. Something she couldn't identify hung in the air, nothing that felt threatening exactly, but the residue of something sinister. She didn't really feel like pushing her luck, though. "We should continue this conversation somewhere else. I don't think it's safe for us to stay here."

"Where should we go?" asked Bertram.

Penelope considered the question. She could take him to Zed, but Zed lived in apartment complex. She didn't know if she could sneak Bertram in without anyone seeing. On the other hand, she could take him to Charles, but he lived in the middle of nowhere. If something went sideways on the way there, she'd be stuck alone with him, and she still didn't completely trust him.

She pointed with her chin toward the telephone on the nightstand next to the bed. "Is that the phone you used to call me?"

Bertram lowered his gaze to the phone, his bloody handprints still covering the receiver. "Yeah."

"I need you to make another couple of calls."

———

Zed met them at Penelope's house. They ushered Bertram inside as quickly as they could. After Bertram's call to Zed, Penelope had instructed him to pull some of George's clothes from the closet. She waited outside the door of the adjacent bathroom while he washed up and changed. George's clothes hung off him, but he and Penelope both agreed they'd attract a whole lot less attention than the smears of blood all over his old ones. Then they made sure to wipe the fingerprints off the knife, the telephone, all the doorknobs, and everything else Bertram might have touched. She made Bertram drive her car while she continued to hold the gun on him. It only took reminding him she had shot Roy Arnold twice in the forehead to stop his protesting.

"I swear I don't remember anything," Bertram said after he and Penelope explained to Zed what happened. "You have to believe me, Zed. Go on and tell her. I didn't kill George. It wasn't me."

Zed eyed him for a moment, and then nodded. "He's telling the truth, Penelope."

Bertram turned to her. "Did you hear that? You can put the gun down."

Reluctantly, Penelope lowered her .22. "Fine, but we still don't know what happened and whether or not it could happen again."

Zed shook his head. "Poor George. I liked him. He had some talent for magic. He saw the apparition in the warehouse. I thought he got lucky. He could have wound up mangled by that tractor instead of Bobby. Guess he wasn't so lucky after all."

"That makes four," Penelope said. "Only one more."

"What do you mean 'one more'?" Bertram asked.

"The symbols the killer carved into all the victims correspond to the symbols at the points of the pentagram that was drawn on the floor of the warehouse," Penelope explained. "One more, and all five points will have a dead body associated with them."

Bertram whistled. "And then what?"

Penelope glanced around, looking for any sign of her dad. "I wish we knew that."

———

Penelope paced the floor of her office. "I think we should call Charles again."

They had deposited Bertram in the guest bedroom in the

apartment upstairs with orders to stay put. When her dad was alive, that room had been hers. It was still painted pink.

"If he didn't pick up when you tried him earlier, what makes you think he's going to pick up now?" Zed asked.

Penelope shot him an exasperated look. "We'll just take Bertram there."

"And if he doesn't answer the door?"

"We make him. Charles will know what to do."

Zed shifted in the chair he occupied. "I wouldn't be so sure about that. Don't you think maybe you're relying on him a little too much?"

"Zed, this isn't the time."

"I'm not trying to be down on him, Penelope, not this time. But has it occurred to you that part of his problem might be how much you're relying on him? That's a lot of pressure when the stakes are literally life and death. Worse than death, actually. I got to thinking about it after I talked with him. He's not doing okay. I don't think it's a matter of refusing to help us. I don't think he can."

Penelope threw up her hands. "What other choice do we have?"

"We have to find another way."

"I'm open to suggestions."

Before Zed could reply, there was a knock at the door.

Penelope sighed. "Great. Could you go upstairs and check on Bertram? I'll try to deal with whoever this is."

"You going to be okay?" He cocked an eyebrow. "What if it's your secret admirer?"

She held up her gun. "I've still got this."

Once Zed was upstairs and out of sight, Penelope opened the front door to find Jim waiting on her porch. He wore a grim expression, one she'd seen only once before. Grief mixed with barely-contained anger and a dash of frustration.

She mustered a smile for him while she tucked the gun behind her back in the waistband of her skirt. "Jim, come in. What's going on?"

"What's going on is two more murders," he said as he stepped inside.

"Two?" Penelope reeled. Two more would mean Patrick had collected all five he needed for whatever he was planning. "Who? What happened?"

"One of ours last night at a motel just north of downtown," Jim answered. "You've met him, actually, Andy Barnes. Attacked and pushed over a second-floor railing. It was just a simple noise disturbance call. Or it was supposed to be. Whoever did it escaped."

"Was Officer Barnes there alone?"

Jim shook his head. "No, of course not, but the other officer isn't much use as a witness right now. All he can babble about is smoke and shadows. Here's the kicker, though. The room was being occupied by Patrick Wheeler."

Another blow. It didn't occur to Penelope that looking for Patrick might put the police in danger. She certainly never expected one of them to get killed. She had put poor Officer Barnes in the line of fire. Was what she had done any different than pushing him over the railing herself?

Penelope hesitated, dreading the answer to her next question. "Were there any marks on his body?"

"Not unless you count the giant gashes in his chest. They look like claw marks. The coroner's office thinks maybe a knife with some kind of serrated blade made the wounds, but even they're not sure."

Not the fifth sacrifice then.

Penelope winced, both relieved and appalled. She was pretty certain they were claw marks. She kept that opinion to herself. "He's getting bolder. He used his own name to check into that motel. He doesn't care if we find him. He doesn't think we can stop him."

Jim let out a nervous chuckle. "You make him sound like some sort of James Bond villain."

Penelope crossed her arms. "He sure seems to be acting that way."

He held up a finger. "*If* he's the one responsible for these other murders."

She eyed him. "It's him. I'm sure."

"Then he was busy last night. The second murder of the evening was all the way on the other side of town. Just liked the others, weird symbols everywhere."

"Tell me about that one." Penelope already knew everything, of course. She just wanted to see what Jim would actually share with her.

"The victim's name was George Landry. Three guesses where he used to work."

"The Brown Tractor & Farm Supply Co.," said Penelope.

Jim drew his mouth into a mirthless smile. "Sorry, there's no prize for getting it right on the first try."

"Who found him?"

"His sister," Jim replied. "She stopped by to check on him after he missed a big family birthday party."

She and Bertram couldn't have missed her by more than an hour. Penelope imagined the horror the woman must have gone through, walking in and finding her brother that way. Another thing for Penelope to feel guilty about. She hadn't wanted to just leave the body, but she didn't see any other option without turning Bertram over to the police, and she wasn't prepared to do that.

Before she could ask her next question, a bump from upstairs caught their attention.

"What was that?" Jim asked.

"Nothing," Penelope said.

Jim moved farther into the foyer. "Is there someone else here?"

Several someones, including her father's ghost, but Penelope wasn't prepared to go into that. "No. No one."

He eyed her. "Penny, what's going on?"

Just then Zed came bounding down the stairs. "Everything okay? I heard a bump."

Penelope blushed. Jim turned a shade redder, too.

"Detective Everett," Zed said without missing a beat. "How are you this afternoon?"

Jim sighed. "I've been better, Mr. McKay."

Zed's look of sympathy was so perfect Penelope wondered if he practiced it in a mirror. "Oh. Sorry to hear that."

Jim glanced back at Penelope. "I should get going. Got a long day and night in front of me. You both take care, okay?" He turned to go, but then he paused. "One other thing. Have either of you happened to see Bertram Brown in the last couple of days?"

Penelope and Zed traded looks.

"No," Penelope said. "Why?"

"I need to talk with him. I spoke with his father, and I just wanted to follow up on a few things. That's all. If you do see him, tell him to give me a call. Penelope, you know how to reach me."

"Well, that was close," Zed said after the door closed behind Jim.

Penelope walked back toward her office. "Was that you upstairs?"

Zed followed her. "Bertram. A lot of clutter in that bedroom. A lot of pink, too. Also, what's with the poster of Ricky Nelson I found under the bed?"

Penelope glared at him over her shoulder. "Don't judge. How's Bertram doing?"

"As well as can be expected."

"Did he remember anything else?"

Zed fell back into the chair in front of Penelope's desk. "Not really. Nothing that makes any sense."

Penelope perched herself on top of her desk and picked up her painted rock. "So, what exactly can he remember, even if it doesn't make sense?"

"He says he saw shapes in the dark. Smoke and shadows. And then he woke up with the knife in his hand. George was already dead and carved up."

Smoke and shadows. According to Jim, that's what the other policeman said he saw before Officer Barnes was murdered.

"Are you planning on hiding Bertram out here tonight?" Zed asked.

Penelope turned the rock in her hand. Its smooth, cool surface helped calm her. "I don't see that we have any other choice."

Zed straightened up in the chair. "Then I'm staying here, too."

Penelope's response came more or less automatically. "You don't have to do that."

Zed shook his head. "You said it yourself. We don't know if the thing influencing Bertram is gone or not. I'd rather be here just in case."

"I was just going to push a dresser in front of the bedroom door."

"I can help with that, too."

"I don't have any place you can sleep."

"You've got a couch in your living room," he persisted. "That's all I need."

"But you don't have a change of clothes. Or a toothbrush."

Zed arched an eyebrow and cocked his head to the side. "Penelope."

She sighed and put the painted rock down, resigned that she wasn't going to win this argument, but a little relieved at the same time. "Okay, fine. Thanks."

Zed's wicked grin made another appearance. "Now, who's going to break the news to Bertram that we're barricading him in your childhood bedroom?"

———

At about eight o'clock that night, there was another knock at the door.

Penelope, Zed, and Bertram, huddled in Penelope's office, all tensed as their gazes shifted to the foyer.

"Draw straws?" Zed offered.

Penelope rolled her eyes. "I'll get it."

She trudged to the door, Zed and Bertram following close behind. She found Charles on the other side. He held a satchel in front of him like a shield.

"Um, hello, Penelope," he said. "Can I come in?"

For a moment, Penelope was so startled she couldn't speak. She didn't remember the last time Charles had visited her. "Charles, of course," she finally managed to get out.

Charles stepped inside. He nodded to Zed and Bertram before returning his attention to Penelope. "I was doing some research on the pentagram you showed me. I need to talk with you." He held up his satchel.

Penelope noticed the slight tremor in his hands. "What is it?"

"Please tell me you've got something that can help us," said Zed.

Charles shook his head. "I wish I did. I looked everywhere I could think. There's no information on this particular set of inscriptions anywhere in any of my books. All I've been able to find are vague references to a lost ritual, one that may have been intentionally eradicated."

Zed frowned. "Eradicated? By whom? Why?"

"Who knows? It could have been the Catholic Church, or the Holy Roman Emperor, or the magical community itself. As for why, I think it's pretty obvious it's too dangerous and violent for anyone to know about."

"Well, someone obviously does," Bertram muttered.

Penelope swore. "What you're saying is that we're essentially helpless. We don't know what this thing is designed to do or how the ritual attached to it works. We don't know who Patrick Wheeler is going to kill next, or when, but if we don't stop the next murder, something really, really bad is going to happen. Is that it? Did I get all that right?"

Zed held a hand out toward her. "We'll figure something out."

Charles looked from Zed to Penelope. "What's going on?"

"There's been a fourth murder," Penelope told him. "That means only one more before we have a dead body for every point on the pentagram." She glanced at Bertram. "Also, we've run into a few other … complications."

Charles' eyes narrowed. "What do you mean by that?"

Penelope explained what happened to Bertram. While she was talking, Charles made a number of faces, none of them easy to interpret. When she was done, he put down his satchel and opened it up.

Hands still trembling, he took out a book. "Looks like I was right."

Penelope watched as he carefully leafed through the pages of the book, the faint blue glow she'd seen before dancing around his fingers. "I'm glad this makes sense to someone. Why all these murders now? Why did he kill Bobby Parker? Wasn't that the point? A sacrifice of someone with magical talent?"

Charles peered up at her. "I didn't say it made sense. What you showed me is the most complicated pentagram I've ever seen. Five different languages in as many alphabets, and all of them dead, at least the human languages anyway. Coming up with a coherent translation would be nearly impossible. It may be that Wheeler simply made a mistake."

Bertram grunted. "The tractor that attacked us didn't seem like a mistake."

"I don't think your killer tractor was the result of any demon called through the pentagram," Charles said as he continued to look through the book.

"Then what was it?" Bertram asked.

Charles turned the book to show them all a page with a drawing of a demon seemingly made of shadow and smoke.

Writing filled the margins of the page. The fluid letters looked like Greek. "The tractor was possessed by a daemon."

Bertram wrinkled his nose. "A daemon?"

"Daemons are low-level entities from beyond the Veil," Charles explained. "Some are good, and some are evil. This is one of the nasty ones if you hadn't figured that out. They're tools, basically, if you know how to call and control them."

Penelope craned her neck for a closer look at the illustration in the book. "Is that hard to do?"

"It's not a spell for a beginner," Charles replied.

Penelope clenched her fists. This wasn't getting them anywhere. They had to stop Patrick Wheeler somehow, but even beyond that, he was the only link she had to the truth about what her father and Ephraim Brown did all those years ago. Now, even as she watched, the opportunity to have her questions answered seemed to be slipping through her fingers. "Do you think Roy Arnold could have taught Patrick Wheeler? There has to be some sort of connection between the two."

Charles shook his head. "Roy Arnold wasn't all that experienced either. I don't think either one of them could have taught the other."

"So, what you're telling me is we have a third magician to worry about." Penelope buried her face in her hands. "That's just great."

Zed cleared his throat. "Let's deal with one evil wizard at a time, shall we?" He looked toward Charles. "So, these daemons. We already know they can kill. What else can they do?"

"A lot of things." Charles closed the book and put it back in his satchel. "They can create illusions, alter memories, even possess a person. They also enjoy spreading despair, hopelessness, misery."

Zed stood, stroking his chin. "You're right. That's pretty nasty."

Bertram leaned in close to Zed, lips curled in a caustic sneer. "Try having one of them inside you. Then you can talk to me about how nasty it is. Jesus, you guys make this sound like a goddamn college lecture."

Zed held up a hand. "No one's trying to downplay what happened to you, Bertram. We're just trying to understand it. You have to admit these daemons explain a lot about how our friend Mr. Wheeler has been able to do all the things he's done—creating the ghost boy in the warehouse, concealing himself and others, erasing Lloyd Baker's memory, not to mention what he made you do."

"Except we don't exactly know *what* he made Bertram do," Penelope interjected. "Can you account for where you were when the other murders happened, Bertram?"

Bertram shrugged. "I was asleep? I've been burning the candle at both ends lately. There's been a couple of times in the past week I've woken up at the kitchen table drooling all over an insurance claim form, but I just figured I'd dozed off. Besides, my dad would have noticed if I tracked in blood everywhere." He pointed to Charles' satchel. "Okay, Professor, I've got a pocket knife, and Penelope's got a gun. I figure that's enough to handle any flesh and blood humans. Got anything in there we can use to stop these fucking daemon things?"

If Charles was offended, he didn't show it. "Not exactly. We can't fight them directly. We stop them by stopping Patrick Wheeler." He reached into his pocket and pulled out more charm bracelets. "These should protect us specifically from the daemons, though. That way we'll at least have a fighting chance."

Penelope took one of the bracelets from Charles and slipped it over her hand. Bits of silver and copper were woven into the leather straps as well as colored glass and other artifacts she took for pebbles at first, but soon realized were pieces of bone. "What good are these going to do if we don't know where Patrick Wheeler is? The Brown Tractor & Farm Supply Co. had dozens of employees. The last sacrifice could be any one of them."

"But all the ones killed so far were working the day Bobby

Parker had his accident in the warehouse," Zed noted. "That narrows it down a lot."

Penelope blew a piece of stray hair out of her face. "That doesn't narrow it down enough, though."

"True," Zed replied, "but we have one thing Patrick Wheeler doesn't have at the moment."

"What's that?" she asked.

Zed pointed at Bertram. "Him. If a daemon has been possessing Bertram to commit these murders, then we just need to make sure he can't go anywhere."

Penelope glanced around the foyer where they were all still gathered. Her father had been quiet so far during the conversation. She wondered if he was there, what he thought about everything they had discussed. "What makes you think he won't come for Bertram here?"

"If he does, he'll just have to go through us first, then," said Zed. He looked at Charles. "Are you in?"

Charles nodded, though his eyes darted toward the door. "One hundred percent."

Zed grinned. "Great! It'll be just one big happy slumber party."

7.

Penelope opened her eyes and glanced at the clock on her nightstand. One-thirty in the morning. She rolled over in bed and tried to go back to sleep, but something tickled the edges of her consciousness, like someone whispering her name. She threw off her covers and sat up. Silence pervaded her room, but not the usual quiet of nighttime. She listened for any sound at all, but heard nothing, not even crickets chirping outside. The air seemed stale, moldy almost—strange since she left her window cracked open, a must in the summer. But even stranger, as she looked around her room, it seemed darker, like she was wearing sunglasses. She climbed out of bed and threw one of her father's old sweatshirts on over her pajamas. She got her .22 out of the top drawer of her dresser and crept to the door.

As soon as she put her hand on the doorknob, the cold crept up her fingers. Something was seriously wrong. She opened the door, and cool air brushed her face. The second floor of the house had been converted into an apartment at some point in the distant past, complete with its own kitchen and living area at the top of the stairs. Penelope's bedroom was on one side. The guest room was on the other.

Charles had volunteered to keep watch outside the guest room while Zed stayed with Bertram inside, but even in the darkness,

Penelope could see that Charles wasn't there and the door to the guest room was open. She rushed across the living room, only to trip over something lying in the floor. When she looked down, she saw it was actually Charles. He moaned softly and tried to sit up.

"What … what happened?" he asked.

She shushed him and pointed to the open guest room door. "Where are Bertram and Zed?" she whispered.

Charles eyes grew wide. "I don't know. I thought I heard a noise downstairs. I stood to go look over the railing, and then, I don't remember."

Penelope jumped up and ran to the guest room. Inside Zed lay on the floor, in about the same shape as Charles. Bertram wasn't anywhere to be seen. She helped Zed up, and together they joined Charles in the living room.

"Sorry, Penelope," Zed said. "I don't know what happened. He tore through all our wards like they were tissue paper."

"Penelope!" a voice called from downstairs.

Bertram.

They rushed downstairs to find Bertram in the office, but he wasn't alone. He knelt while a man in ragged clothes held the blade of a knife to his throat. Beneath them, a pentagram had been drawn on the office floor. No, not a pentagram, *the* pentagram. The man wielding the knife lifted his head to look at them, mouth twisted in a malevolent grin. Penelope gasped. Zed swore under his breath, and Charles said something in a language Penelope had never heard before.

The man holding the knife had Bertram's face, too.

Penelope took a step into the room. "Patrick Wheeler, we know who you are. You can drop the illusion now."

The Bertram with the knife laughed. "How do you know that, Penelope?" He even had Bertram's voice. He could have been the one to call out to them. "How do you know I'm not the real Bertram, and this is just some other poor victim I've given my face? You remember Gerald Holloway, don't you? He was the manager on duty the day Bobby Parker had his accident. Maybe this is him."

The Bertram with the knife at his neck grunted, but that was pretty much all he could do without the blade slicing into his throat.

"You're lying," Penelope said.

"Am I? Does it bother you to consider someone you thought you knew so well could do such horrible things? That a man you considered a friend—and maybe thought of as more than a friend—could gain your trust so completely and then turn on you?"

Penelope's cheeks burned. "Stop it."

"I liked you, Penelope, back when we were in high school. I thought you were the most amazing girl I'd ever met. Smart, pretty, funny. But you weren't interested, no matter what I did, what I tried."

"You—Bertram never told me he liked me like that."

"I did tell you, over and over. You just never paid attention. All serious all the time. All about your grades so you could go to college and be a police detective, just like your dad. How's that working out for you, Dreadful Penny? How'd it work out for him?"

Penelope raised her pistol. "I said stop it!"

He laughed again. "I'm just getting started. Are you gonna shoot me? Really? Go ahead. I dare you."

"Why? Why would Bertram do all this?" Tears welled up in her eyes.

"Because I'm tired of being nobody. Just another tractor salesman in a long line of tractor salesmen. I was never going to be a star athlete or a brain or be good looking enough to get the girls. So, one day I decided that if I'm always going to be in the shadows, I might as well make friends with them."

While he was focused on Penelope, the other Bertram, the one with the blade at his throat, painstakingly fished his pocket knife out of his pants. He flicked it open and stabbed his evil twin in the thigh. The evil Bertram's scream echoed through the small room, and he released his hold on his doppelganger. As he did, his features changed, shifting into the ones Penelope recognized from Reverend Lowell Purdue's protests as well as Clay MacDonald's ghost hunters—Patrick Wheeler, his face contorted in pain and rage.

What light there was in the room disappeared, replaced by billowing darkness. Shapes loomed at Penelope—glowing green eyes and claws and mouths full of sharp teeth. The darkness reached out for her, but never quite touched her. No matter how she moved, it always stayed a few feet away. Then suddenly it flew up toward the ceiling and hovered there just over their heads. She looked to Charles and Zed, who both nodded that they were okay. The bracelets had protected them, just like Charles said.

The daemons had done perhaps what they were supposed to do, though, by distracting the three of them. Patrick had Bertram at knifepoint again, the blade ready to slide across his throat. The daemons hovered overhead whispering in some forgotten language. Their words were vile, Penelope knew, even if she couldn't understand them.

She fired her pistol at Patrick, but the bullet curved abruptly and embedded itself into the wall next to Zed's head.

"Do that again, and I can move the bullet a few more inches to the right," Patrick snarled. "Neat trick using charms to stop my daemons. You're going to have to show me how you did that."

"Like hell I will," muttered Charles.

Patrick sneered at him. "We'll see. It must have been one of your charms that drove the daemon out of Bertram after he killed George Landry. He was supposed to go home and forget it all happened, just like the others."

Charles glared at the other magician. "Not one of my charms."

Patrick cocked his head to the side. "Then whose?"

"George's," said Zed. "He could see the ghost boy you conjured up at the Brown warehouse. He had magical talent. Killing him must have somehow monkeyed with your spell."

Patrick shrugged. "Just as well. Bertram still got the job done, didn't you? And now you're going to be the final sacrifice."

Bertram, sweat pouring down his face, pleaded with his eyes. He still didn't dare speak for fear of the knife blade. His own pocket knife lay useless a few feet away.

"You've had plenty of time to kill him, but you haven't yet," Penelope said. "Instead, you called us down here. What do you want?"

"I want you to be here when I finish this."

"Is this about your father?" she asked. "We know what happened to him, Patrick."

The rage on his face intensified while the mass of darkness at the ceiling roiled. "Do you? Do you really know what happened to him? His own parents wouldn't even look him in the eye after he was expelled from school. But that wasn't the bad part. Do you know what it's like to spend your entire childhood waking up every night to your father screaming? Do you know what it's like to watch your father numb himself with booze and medication until he's so fucked up he doesn't know what day of the week it is? Do you know what it's like to live with the knowledge that he wasn't stronger than the nightmares, that in the end, they got him? Your father and Ephraim Brown did that to him."

Penelope did know what it was like waking up to her father's nightmares, and now she just wanted answers. "What did they do, Patrick?"

"What do you think they did? They tried to call a demon."

Penelope's face flushed with anger. "My father would never do anything like that."

"Are you sure?"

Despite a warning from Zed, Penelope ventured farther into the room, her hands balled into fists. "You don't know the faintest thing about him."

The corners of Patrick's mouth curled up in an altogether unsettling smile. "Is that so? Too bad you can't ask him yourself."

He didn't know. There's no way he could.

"Did you kill my father?" The question escaped her lips before she could reconsider.

Patrick laughed. "No, that was just luck. Or maybe he was cursed like all the rest of them, and it came time for him to pay."

Penelope took a step closer, stopping just short of the pentagram's perimeter. "What makes you think you'll be successful where they failed?"

Patrick looked at her like she just told him she believed in little green men from Mars. "What makes you think they failed? I'm just finishing what they started."

"I don't think you have any idea what you're doing. Whatever you were trying at the warehouse, it didn't work."

His smile grew wider. "Didn't it?"

Charles swore. "Double meanings. The words around the pentagram have double meanings. Parallel spells. Bobby Parker was the first part. This is the second."

The smile on Patrick's face faded. "I'm kind of tired of talking right now."

Patrick's hand tensed around the handle of the knife. Bertram gritted his teeth and shut his eyes. Penelope, Zed and Charles all called out and rushed forward, while at the same time, daemons descended from the ceiling in a dark maelstrom. The shriek that passed through the malevolent spirits threatened to shatter Penelope's reality. Faster and faster they swirled around, creating a wind that nearly lifted her off her feet. She lost sight of the others. The spirits still couldn't touch her, but they could taunt her, whispering horrible things in her ears and reaching toward her, claws swiping and teeth gnashing.

She flailed her arms, trying to open a path through them toward Bertram, or at least where she thought Bertram should be. The daemons had her disoriented. They leered and swooped, howling and crying.

"Go away," she screamed. "Stop it. Be quiet."

She was met with hoarse laughter and more shrieks. Penelope

stumbled to her knees, but a dark-skinned hand reached through the blackness and grabbed hers.

"Don't let go." Charles' voice was distant, as if he were speaking to her from another room.

Someone else took hold of her other hand.

"I've got you," said Zed.

The hairs on the back of Penelope's neck stood on end. Immediately, the daemons slowed their frenzy. Their screams died down to a low murmur, and then, one by one, they vanished. When the darkness dissipated, Bertram knelt on the floor, clutching his neck. Patrick Wheeler lay nearby, face frozen in shock and streaked with blood. The painted rock from Penelope's desk rested next to his body.

Penelope let go of Zed and Charles and rushed over to Bertram, throwing her arms around him. "Bertram! Oh, my God. Are you okay?"

"I … I think." Bertram took his hand away from his neck to reveal a slender red line. "It's just a small cut. Barely broke the skin."

"What happened?" Penelope asked.

Bertram shook his head. "I don't know. One second, I was bracing myself for the end, and the next, he just let go and fell to the floor. Then all hell broke loose. Literally."

Zed knelt next to Patrick's body and felt for a pulse on his neck. "He's dead." He glanced up at Charles. "Looks like this rock somehow flew across the room and bashed him in the side of the head."

Charles held up his hands. "Wasn't me."

"Rogue daemon maybe?" Penelope suggested, but she knew who threw the rock. Silently, she thanked her father.

Bertram's gaze fell to Patrick's glassy-eyed stare. "What do we do now?"

———

After saying good-bye to Zed and Penelope, Charles leaned the shovel against the side of his house next to the back door. The sky in the east glowed in shades of pink and orange, heralding the sunrise. Soon the light would hit the freshly turned earth by the tree line at the edge of his property, the final resting place of Patrick Wheeler, though Charles had his doubts about how peaceful Patrick Wheeler's eternal rest would be.

He wasn't concerned about any part of the rogue magician returning. Beheading Patrick Wheeler made his body useless. Charles was the one who insisted they do it, though Zed actually performed the deed. And if anything was left of Wheeler's spirit, the offerings they'd buried with the body would keep it on the other side of the Veil.

Sweat dripped from Charles' chin. The day was already starting out hot. He opened the back door and all but stumbled through the tiny laundry room, an addition put on the house in the 1940s, into his workroom. He stripped out of his shirt and turned on the fan. Millie sat in a chair, waiting for him. This time there was no red stain on her dress.

"I don't think I can do this anymore," he said, tears streaming down his cheeks. "It's too much."

She smiled and held her arms out to him. He collapsed into her embrace, curling up like a child and resting his head in her lap while she stroked his hair.

8.

MONDAY, AUGUST 7, 1972

Jim Everett tapped his fingers on the table while he waited in a windowless room in the basement of the police station. He hummed an old hymn that midway through somehow changed over into a song he'd heard on the radio. Some band called the Eagles singing about Winslow, Arizona. Soon, though, the door opened, and a young officer—Parks according to his nametag—brought in a cardboard box.

"Sorry that took so long, Detective Everett." He set the box down on the table. "We had the darnedest time finding this thing. For some reason, it wasn't where it was supposed to be. Pretty cold case. Stumble on some new lead?"

Jim wasn't really paying attention. He was busy looking over the box. "No, I just want to check on something."

Several moments of awkward silence passed while Jim waited for the kid to leave. He apparently expected more of an explanation. Jim wasn't in the mood to provide one.

"I'll, uh, let you know if I need anything else, okay?" Jim said.

The young officer's face fell. "Right, well, I'll be outside. Just let me know."

Jim nodded. "Will do."

He waited until the door shut behind Officer Parks before reaching into his coat pocket for a pen. He signed the paper attached to the top of the box on the first available line and jotted down the date—part of the protocol for preserving the chain of custody. Then he used his pocket knife to cut the pieces of tape sealing the box's lid.

Inside he found a set of dusty files and old photographs. This was the case that the most recent string of murders reminded him of, the one Jonathan Drake had handled. It was almost ten years old and had never been solved.

Linda Howard was found nude in the middle of the woods not far from the campus of Furman University. Her body was unmarked except for a strange symbol carved into the skin on her left arm. In fact, the coroner had a tough time figuring out a cause of death, other than she had simply stopped breathing.

Jonathan interviewed dozens of people about the woman and had even done research into the symbol, but the more Jim dug through the evidence in the box, the more troubling things became. Pages from the interview transcripts were missing. Several photographs were unaccounted for as well, and while there were more than a few descriptions of the symbol carved into the woman's arm, there were no images of it, neither photos nor drawings, though it was clear that at one point those images existed. A little ball of dread formed in the pit of Jim's stomach when he realized that a few of the transcripts had been outright doctored, especially one of an interview with a professor from Furman. Whole sections were taken out, substituted with phrases lifted from other interviews.

Someone had gone to a lot of trouble to cover up something about this murder. Jim glanced at the top of the box and the sheet of paper affixed there. Just as he feared, the last signature before his own was in the flamboyant looping hand of Johnathan Drake, the date a few months after the body was discovered.

Jim shook his head. Only a few years after this murder, another officer had accused Jonathan of tampering with evidence at a crime scene. Nothing was ever proven, but his reputation was shot to hell. He resigned from the police force and started his own private detective agency. Jim never did believe the allegations. He'd been one of Jonathan's biggest defenders, but after seeing with his own eyes the tampered evidence in the open box on the table in front of him, he couldn't help but think he'd been wrong.

What would Penelope think if she ever found out the truth about her father?

Jim was replacing the lid, trying to figure out what to do with his newfound knowledge, when he spotted something in the corner of the box. It appeared to be a small slip of paper tucked in between the box's cardboard panels. He pulled it out slowly. When he unfolded it, bits of dried leaves crumbled to dust between his fingers. He held his hand to his nose and sniffed. Sage. On the scrap of yellowing paper were a few words Jim didn't recognize and a pentagram with odd symbols at each point, a lot like the symbols carved into Lloyd Baker and the other murdered warehouse workers.

"What were you up to, Jonathan?" he muttered to himself.

LEGEND TRIP

A DREADFUL PENNY NOVELLA

1.

MONDAY, OCTOBER 23, 1972

Death is not the end the preacher tells you at the funeral. You'll see your loved one again someday, in the Sweet By-and-By. It's an easy thing for him to say. He says it a lot at a lot of funerals.

But you—you're the one who has to believe it. You're the one who has to look at the unnaturally beautiful face of your mother, or your brother, or—God forbid—your child, and have faith. And as the days wear on and as that faith begins to fade, where is he? Where is that son-of-a-bitch preacher with his empty platitudes and hollow promises?

But what if you didn't need faith? What if you had the chance to know for sure that the person you loved more than anything was okay and that someday you would see them again? How far would you go for that certainty? What would you give up?

———

Penelope set the rock down on her desk. She had managed to get most of the blood off. She accidentally took off some of the paint, too, but not much. She'd made the paperweight for her father when she was eight. It had a yellow and orange sun on one side and a green tree on the other. He'd used it every day until the day he died.

She stared at it hoping it would move, just a little, to prove he was still there. Ever since the night his ghost had flung it across the room to save her and her friends from Patrick Wheeler—a magician with a grudge and some heavy firepower—she hadn't had any sign of her father at all, nothing, not even the usual knocks he used to communicate with her. One for *no* and two for *yes*.

Penelope sighed. "Dad, I miss you. I wish you could talk to me. Can you hear me? Please do something to let me know you're still here."

But she was met with only silence.

———

Once he unlocked the door, Zed and his companion slipped quickly inside the bookstore.

"Isn't this against one of Mr. Keller's rules?" Jake Dempsey asked as Zed grabbed his hand and pulled him through the darkened maze of bookshelves.

Mr. Keller, the owner of the bookstore, posted a set of rules that included such things as no religious discussions and no excessive browsing. Everyone thought the rules were amusing, but no one dared break them when Mr. Keller was around.

"It's absolutely against one of his rules," Zed called over his shoulder, "but he's out of town, and you have to admit this is as safe a spot as we're going to find."

He'd suggested the bookstore on a whim. He didn't know exactly why, other than he wanted to talk to Jake alone, away from other people, afraid they might overhear. And he was a little drunk. Zed took a seat on the floor in the history section and leaned his back against a bookshelf.

Jake sat down next to him. "So now what?"

Zed rested his head on Jake's shoulder. He caught a whiff of the subtle cologne Jake wore. "I don't know. I hadn't thought that far."

"You're awfully comfortable with this."

"With what?"

"With this. Being close."

Zed made to move away. "Well, if it's a problem for you …"

"No, not at all," Jake said hastily. "It's just that when you told me you'd dated women before, I just figured—"

"That this was just some sort of attempt to satisfy my curiosity?"

Jake shrugged. "Well, a little. Hope you're not offended."

Zed chuckled. "It's going to take more than that to offend me. I've just always been attracted to people as people. Man or woman, it's never made a difference."

Jake lowered his voice almost to a whisper. "Does your family know?"

"I don't have any family besides my mom. And she knows. I told her a long time ago."

"And she's okay with it?"

"I don't think she completely understands, but she always taught me to be myself, no matter what. What about you?"

Jake shook his head. "Oh, no. I've never told anyone. My family would never speak to me again, not that I'm really talking to them now. It might have been easier to tell them I'm a faggot than I'm volunteering for McGovern's presidential campaign."

"Sorry about that."

Jake sighed. "It's hard when you don't know who to trust. One careless move and you're out of a job, or worse. Although, I guess I don't have to worry about the job thing right now, not like you. You have to worry about three."

Zed kept quiet about his relationships at work. Jake was right. He'd be fired in a heartbeat from the radio station, and Mr. Keller had no trouble making his opinions on the matter known. But Penelope, that was different. He considered her a friend. He didn't think she'd really care who he dated, but even so, he'd never told her. He could try to convince himself the topic had just never come up, but that would be a lie.

He grasped Jake's hand. "I guess it's good to find people we can trust, right?"

Maybe the few beers he'd had were giving Zed some fortitude, or maybe it was because he could sense Jake's anticipation, but either way, Zed leaned over and kissed him. Jake returned the favor while running his fingers through Zed's hair.

Then suddenly Jake's body went limp.

"Jake?"

Zed didn't have time to say anything more than that, though, because a bolt of lightning ran through his body. A flash of white light blinded him, and when his sight cleared, he wasn't in the bookstore anymore. Just like the last time he and Jake shared a vision, he found himself alone in the forest on a chilly night. Pale moonlight filtered down through the canopy. Stepping over tree roots and pushing back branches, he moved through the woods with a purpose, though he didn't know what that purpose was. He hadn't noticed before the palmetto trees among the oaks and pines and beech trees. He must have been somewhere in the Low Country.

A howl rose up that sent a chill down his spine. He had heard that sound before. Shadows rolled and rippled at the edges of his vision. He picked up his pace, but the shadows followed. They grew and multiplied, taking on form—long, loping limbs and heads with canine snouts and glowing green eyes—daemons— just like the ones Patrick Wheeler compelled into his service, but he and Charles and Penelope had stopped Patrick Wheeler, hadn't they? Suddenly, the shadows surged toward him, and he took off running through the woods.

Branches scraped his hands and face. He stumbled more than once, but he didn't dare stop. He knew what those things could do. They called to him in his head, telling him awful things, trying to make him despair and lose hope. He focused on putting one foot in front of the other, but even he couldn't run forever. Eventually he'd get tired, and the things would get him.

He stumbled over what he thought was just another rock, but it had a flat face and sharp edges—a gravestone. He'd found the graveyard from the first vision. He struggled to his feet, but it was too late. The shadows overtook him.

And then Zed was back in the bookstore, lying on the floor, staring up at the ceiling. He pushed himself up. Jake lay next to him. He didn't move when Zed nudged him. Zed felt for a pulse and found a thready one. He shook Jake a little harder, calling his name and working what little magic he could to get Jake to wake up. When that didn't work, he looked around frantically, trying to figure out what to do. He'd carry Jake to the hospital if he had to.

"Happiness," Jake croaked.

Zed knelt down over him. "Jake?"

The other man opened his eyes and sat up slowly. "Man, what…"

Jake met Zed's gaze. Fear came off him in waves. He scrambled to his feet.

Zed grabbed his arm. "Wait. Don't run this time, please. Can't we just talk?"

"There were … things in the woods, with green eyes," Jake said.

Zed nodded. "I know."

"And you knew what they were."

"Yes, I did."

Jake was silent for a moment. When he spoke, his words had a hard edge. "I was honest with you. I think the least you can do is be honest with me."

Zed nodded. "You're right. I'm sorry. My detective work is a little more interesting than I let on."

———

Morning sunlight streamed into Charles' bedroom. When he pushed back the covers and sat up in bed, he shivered. It had gotten chilly overnight, the first really cold night in a long time. He crossed bare wood floor to close his bedroom window.

The scene outside the window was a busy street in Harlem in 1919, far from Greenville, South Carolina, in 1972. Here he was Isaiah Jenkins, a former World War I soldier and now the manager of a jazz spot called the Blue Club.

And he had a breakfast date.

Half an hour later, freshly showered and dressed, Charles stepped outside into the crisp air. Everyone he passed wore coats and scarves not seen since April. The leaves on the trees in the park were edged in orange and yellow and red.

He saw her before she saw him. Wearing a dark red dress with a fur coat and stole, she sat at a table at a sidewalk café while sipping a cup of coffee and nibbling on a pastry. Not only was she beautiful, but Millie Priest had the most remarkable voice Charles had ever heard. She was whip-smart, too. Millie had always managed her own career. She knew how to pack a house and make sure she got her cut of the take.

When their eyes met, he smiled and waved. She smiled back, and his heart skipped a beat. He slipped into the seat opposite her. They talked about easy things for a little while. Charles drank his coffee and watched people go by. Isaiah's memories were all there, right next to his own. As they chatted, it was easy for him to think of himself as Isaiah.

Charles was the bad dream.

"I was thinking about wearing the dark blue dress tonight," she said after taking a sip of her coffee, "the one with the white rose on the sleeve. What do you think?"

"You know that's one of my favorites. You trying to distract me from my job? Hard enough as it is when you're up there."

She smiled, but it seemed strained somehow. "There's going to be some important people in the audience tonight. We need to impress them."

Charles frowned. "Important people? Who are you talking about?"

She hesitated. "You know how the Blue Club has had a couple of lean months."

"Yeah, but they've been just that. Lean months. We'll bounce back."

"Lewis isn't so sure." She glanced down at her half-eaten Danish and lowered her voice. "He's worried about what happens when we can't serve booze anymore."

Lewis was the owner of the Blue Club, and he wasn't wrong to be worried. Charles, too, wondered what would happen when Prohibition stopped the liquor from flowing.

Charles leaned forward and waited until Millie met his gaze again. "You know the drinks aren't what brings people out. It's you they're coming to see."

"Some people are thinking about investing. That's all."

Charles leaned back again. "Who?"

She shook her head. "I don't know their names. Only Lewis does."

"How come you know before I do? I'm supposed to be the manager."

"He pulled me aside last night, told me to pick out my best dress and my best songs."

Charles' ire rose. "He should tell me himself rather than leave it up to you to do it."

"I'm sure he'll talk to you tonight."

"He'd better, or there's going to be hell to pay."

She placed a hand on his and made him unball his fist. "Isaiah, behave now. All you have to do is make sure everything runs smoothly, just like you always do, okay?" Her smile returned. "Stop by the dressing room tonight after the set when you get a chance. I have a present for you."

"A present? What is it?"

She laughed. "It's a surprise."

The tension in his shoulders eased somewhat. "What if I don't want to wait?"

She stood, but her hand lingered. "Just be patient. I promise you'll like it."

He watched her walk away and vanish into the throng of people.

———

That evening, as he always did, Charles oversaw the last-minute touches before the patrons were let into the Blue Club—making sure the tablecloths were straight, the silverware polished, and the glasses clean—but he couldn't shake the nagging worry at the back of his mind.

The worry eased somewhat as the club filled up. Everything ran smoothly at first. The Bill Porter Three—piano, bass, and trumpet—played their low-key set as everyone drank their cocktails, but about ten minutes before Millie was supposed to go on stage, a small commotion erupted at the door. A group of people entered the club, a dark-skinned man dressed in a midnight blue three-piece suit leading the way. Even the Blue Club bouncers gave the heavies on either side of him a wide berth.

A ripple of murmurs ran through the crowd. The man was Andre Lestrade, who styled himself a businessman. Charles had learned about him while working at the docks. Nothing went on in Harlem without Andre having a finger in it, legal or not.

What's he doing here?

He can't be the investor Millie was talking about, not him.

Charles knew better than to tell him he wasn't welcome at the Blue Club, but the least he could do was make sure Andre understood trouble wouldn't be tolerated. Before he could get to Andre, though, Lewis intercepted the businessman, an ear-to-ear grin on his face. The club owner took Andre's hand and shook it enthusiastically, then led him and his entourage to a group of tables near the stage. Several waiters came over immediately.

For the moment, Charles retreated. He'd have a talk with

Lewis later. No good could come from throwing in with a man like Andre Lestrade.

The lights dimmed, and Millie came on stage, dazzling as always. This was Charles' favorite part of the day, but he couldn't enjoy her set. He kept glancing at Andre and his entourage. Millie, too, looked Andre's way more than once. Usually Charles could imagine she was singing only to him, but that night it was obvious she was singing to someone else.

To make matters worse, after Millie's set was over, she didn't retreat backstage like she normally did. She went over to Andre's table and sat in the chair next to him, recently vacated by one of his bodyguards. Charles watched as Andre crept closer, putting his arm on the back of her chair, placing a hand on top of hers. She smiled and laughed occasionally as the Bill Porter Three played their second set. Eventually, she stood and took her leave, but not before accepting a kiss on the hand from Andre.

In the small hours of the morning, after the club closed and all the patrons had gone home, Charles went to Millie's dressing room. He knocked three times like he always did.

"Come in," a muffled voice called from inside.

Charles opened the door. Millie sat at her dressing table.

Her smile faded as soon as she saw the expression on his face. "What's wrong?"

"What's wrong? Do you know who was at the club tonight? That was Andre Lestrade."

"I know who he is." Her expression became a little more guarded.

"Why was he here?"

"I think you can figure out why."

"Why didn't you tell me before?"

She gestured at him. "Because of this. Because of how you're acting now."

"But he's dangerous," Charles said. "We can't take money from him."

"We have to do something."

Charles shook his head. "No. There's got to be another way."

"Trust me, Isaiah. If Lewis thought there was another way, he would do it. We can't lose the Blue Club."

Charles took a deep breath. "You let him put his arm around you."

"Yes, I *let* him." She squared her jaw. "And that's all I let him do."

"What if he wants to do more next time?" Charles asked.

Unbidden, the image of Millie in her blue sequined dress stained with blood came to his mind. Her ghost had revealed to him that she died on March 18, 1920, in the real world, less than six months away. He'd spent a lot of time thinking about how he could stop her death.

"There's not going to be a next time," she replied. "He was just coming over tonight to check out the place and talk to Lewis."

"And if he invests? Don't you think he'll be here a lot more?"

She glared. "What kind of girl do you take me for, Isaiah Jenkins? I am a singer. I am a professional."

"I'm not talking about you. I just know that sometimes men in his position don't take no for an answer."

"Well, he will take it from me."

Charles wiped a hand across his face. "Millie, this is a bad idea."

"It's not your decision to make, Isaiah."

"I just worry."

"Too much." She stood and came across the room and placed a hand on his chest. "Nothing is ever going to separate us. Do you understand?"

He covered her hand with his. "I want to believe that."

"Then believe."

He leaned down and kissed her. She melted into his embrace.

———

Charles woke up in his own bed in his own house, surrounded by his books. The moonlight shown through the curtains that moved like ghosts in the breeze. He sat up, buried his face in his hands, and sobbed.

———

Ephraim Brown turned on the television and fell into the recliner. His clothes still held the faint whiff of the blackberry root he'd burned as part of the ritual, but at the moment, he didn't care. He was tired. Louise was still in Virginia, and Bertram was on a camping trip somewhere in North Carolina, so no one was there to question him about it. He'd take a shower later.

The news was full of reports that a truce had been reached in the fighting between North and South Vietnam. At least they weren't talking about the break-in at the Watergate Hotel anymore. He was sick of hearing about that, just the news making a big deal out of nothing. There was also a small update about the murder of the Israeli athletes at the Munich Olympics. Everyone always acted shocked when such evil things happened, but Ephraim knew you only had to look at your own back yard to find evil—just look at his.

His company destroyed, his family attacked, his employees murdered. The police hadn't caught the murderer, but Bertram told him the person who did it had been taken care of. Bertram didn't offer any more than that, and Ephraim didn't ask any questions. But now it was time to take charge of things again. He was going to make sure no one could harm his family any more.

Ephraim awoke to the test pattern on the television screen. He must have dozed off. He stood and turned off the television, figuring he ought to get things cleaned up. Bertram was supposed to come home the next day, and he didn't want to have to answer any awkward questions. Some small part of him had hoped to reconnect with his son after he moved back to Greenville, but those hopes had been dashed also. Everything would be sorted out soon, though, he told himself. He just needed a little more time, and he'd get his family back. He'd get everything back.

The back door opened and closed. Bertram coming home early, Ephraim's groggy brain told him, though that didn't exactly make sense. He expected to hear footsteps on the stairs or the clatter of cabinets from the kitchen as his son rummaged for something to eat, but there was only silence. Ephraim glanced over his shoulder. The silhouette of a figure stood in the doorway.

"Bertram? Is that you?" he called out.

The figure entered the room without taking a step. In a blink, it simply stood a few feet closer. Ephraim grasped the charm he wore around his neck. It didn't do any good. Another blink, and the dark thing was on top of him, two green glowing dots where its eyes should have been.

"No, not—"

Ephraim never got a chance to finish the sentence before he was lost to the darkness.

———

Bertram eyed the cute blonde at the other end of the bar. Their gazes met briefly before she smiled, tucked a piece of stray hair behind her ear, and turned away. Any other night he would have ambled over and introduced himself, but not that night.

He slid his empty glass over and flagged down the bartender for another beer. He came into the bar just off the highway near Asheville intending to muster up some courage to go home. Otherwise he didn't know if he'd have the guts to talk to his dad the next day and tell him he was leaving.

He didn't have any reason to stay in Greenville. Not anymore. He'd come back to help his dad run the company, but the warehouse for the Brown Tractor & Farm Supply Co. was destroyed in a freak explosion, one helped along by a demon-possessed tractor. There was no company to run. He'd tried to help pick up the pieces, but lately his dad seemed to want to take care of things himself.

He didn't like how secretive his dad was being. Something strange was going on, and given everything he had learned over the last several months, Bertram knew strange. But he couldn't stay. He'd never had a better chance to figure out what he wanted for his own life, away from the family business. He hadn't worked out exactly where he'd go. Maybe back to Atlanta. Or Knoxville even. He had some buddies up there. Someone had to know about a job he could take.

When he looked up again, the blonde was gone. A scan of the room revealed her near the door on the arm of another guy. Just as well. He wasn't really in the mood, because there was one other reason he didn't want to stay in town.

Her name was Penelope.

He still cringed every time he thought of the words Patrick Wheeler had said when he was wearing Bertram's face, when he was holding Bertram at knife-point, ready to sacrifice him for whatever ritual he planned. About how he'd basically thrown himself at Penelope when they were teenagers. About how he wanted to be more than friends. About how she'd never noticed. It was all true. Everything he'd said was true, but Bertram had never told anyone else how he felt. How did Patrick Wheeler know?

He just wanted to get as far away from magic as he could. As he stared at the bottom of yet another empty glass, he wished he'd never come back.

2.

TUESDAY, OCTOBER 24, 1972

Penelope pulled her black Lincoln onto Church Street. In front of her, the city spread out, brown and gray against the bright blue sky. She could count about a half dozen church steeples reaching heavenward. She wondered how many people knew there was a whole other world underneath the one they saw. Of course, her pastor would say that there were other realms of existence. Heaven and Hell were real places. Angels and demons were real beings, fighting every day over people's souls. She'd never met any angels, though, only demons, and it seemed like she and her friends were the only ones fighting against them. Her father had fought too, until he was shot and killed in a botched robbery. She missed him. She really could have talked with him right then.

When Penelope stepped into the Grayson & Sons antique shop, she nearly turned around to see if she'd accidentally walked into the wrong shop. She expected the usual tidal wave of furniture, paintings, lamps, china, and a thousand kinds of knickknacks. But that day, she found everything meticulously arranged in perfect vignettes, as all the things might look in a real home. In fact, Penelope was reminded a little too much of all her older relatives' houses. There was an unwritten list of acceptable furnishings for a Southern home of a certain stature, and Dan

Kowalczyk, owner of the shop, had everything on that list in spades.

Dan came from somewhere in the back of the store. When he saw her, his face broke out in a wide smile. "Penelope. How are you?"

"Great, Dan. And you?" She continued to gape at all the neatly arranged antiques.

He followed her gaze. "It's a big change I know. Do you like it?"

"It's certainly different."

"It was Barbara's idea. She said it might help people to envision things in their own homes if we arranged the inventory in a more natural way."

Barbara was Dan's new assistant. His former assistant, Mary, was murdered by the magician Roy Arnold. The part Penelope never told Dan was that a demon Roy Arnold controlled actually committed the deed.

Penelope frowned. "It just seems so … orderly. Don't you think it takes away some of the sense of adventure?"

Dan shrugged. "Maybe, but it also increased sales by fifteen percent. Barbara was definitely onto something."

Barbara, in addition to being friendly and attractive, was frighteningly competent, and she annoyed Penelope.

"Is she here?" Penelope asked.

He shook his head. "Not today. It's her day off. What brings you by? Better circumstances than the last time I hope."

The last time Penelope had visited Dan, she had just been rear-ended by someone driving a gold Ford, the first of a few threatening incidents, including a brick thrown through her office window. Nothing new had happened for a couple of months, though, and Penelope hoped whoever it was had gotten it out of their system.

"Thankfully, yes. I have a question for you."

"Sure. Ask away."

Penelope opened her purse and pulled out an envelope. Inside was a silver locket in the shape of a heart. "I have a friend whose grandmother just passed away. She found this locket and wanted to know if it was valuable."

Dan grinned. "Back to the dead grandmother line?"

The first time they met, Penelope had tried to get information out of him by making up a story about her recently departed grandmother. To her dismay, he saw right through that lie.

"It's true this time," she lied.

The locket came from her friend Carolyn Cole, who worked at the Division of Public Records. A secret admirer left it at her door. She gave it to Penelope so Penelope could try to figure out who had given it to her.

Dan smirked as he held out his hand. "May I?"

She handed over the locket.

He squinted and held it up to the light. "Does your 'friend' know anything about it at all?"

Penelope pretended she didn't notice the stress on the word *friend*. "Not really. She never saw her grandmother wearing it. She told me she just found it in the back of a drawer."

That last lie she was particularly proud of.

Dan opened the locket and examined the inside. "Wow, it's a shame it stayed hidden."

"What do you mean?"

He leaned forward and pointed to the inside surface of the locket. "See these markings here? That's the hallmark of the silversmith. This locket was made by a Swedish silversmith named Lars Dahlberg around 1870."

"So, it's over a hundred years old."

He nodded. "I'd say it's probably worth about twenty dollars, even with the broken clasp. Not a huge amount, but nothing to sneeze at either. That's what your friend wanted to know, right?"

Not exactly.

Penelope tried not to let her disappointment show. "I think she was hoping for more of a story. This Lars Dahlberg, are a lot of pieces by him still around? How likely would someone here have something by him?"

Dan shrugged. "I don't know a lot about him. I've run by more than a few of his pieces since I've been in this business, though. It wouldn't be unheard of for someone around here to have a piece or two by him."

"Well, thanks, anyway. I'll let her know what you said."

Dan handed the locket back to Penelope. "It's beautiful work. A little polish and it would be stunning. Tell her she should wear it."

"I will. Thanks again. I should let you get back to work. It was nice talking to you." She turned to leave.

"Penelope."

She paused. "Yes?"

He took a deep breath. Everything he said next came out in one long exhale. "Maybe you could stop by one day, you know, after the shop closes, and we could go out for dinner somewhere?"

She stared at him, a little shocked. Was he asking her out on a date? The words tumbled out of her mouth before she could stop them. "Sure. That sounds great. When?"

"How about Thursday?" He pointed to the store window. "Store closes at five."

She nodded. "I'll be here."

She turned to leave again, this time with her stomach tied in knots.

———

Detective Jim Everett stared at his desk. In front of him rested a neat stack of files. He'd gone through each of them at least a dozen times, hoping for some other explanation than the one he arrived at again and again. Evidence tampering. Fourteen cases spanning more than ten years. And the only person who could have done it was Jonathan Drake, Penny's father.

Jonathan had once been a close friend. It was bad enough to think he could have been a dirty cop, but something truly weird was going on with these cases, something that raised the hairs on the back of Jim's neck, like a quiet whisper in a dark room. Strange circumstances surrounded each one, whether it was a murdered woman with an odd symbol cut into her arm or a missing person who seemingly vanished from a moving car. Also, every evidence box was misplaced in a unique and creative way, and when Jim opened each of them, he discovered a small scrap of paper inscribed with a five-pointed star and other symbols, plus a cache of dried herbs.

Jim was a good Christian. He'd gone to church his entire life. He knew just about every hymn in the hymnal by heart, at least the first, second, and fourth stanzas. He believed the Bible was the literal Word of God, and the Bible said the Devil was real. The drawings on those pieces of paper looked Satanic to him, but Jonathan Drake didn't exactly fit the profile of a Satan worshipper. He was a good man from a good family. Penny Drake was like Jim's own daughter.

Nothing made sense.

Jim never told anyone that when Jonathan left the police force, he'd kept Jonathan's rolodex. Now he thought going through Jonathan's old contacts might help him get to the bottom of things. He had to start somewhere, after all. Flipping through, he found a lot of the same names in his own rolodex, but a few stood out as unusual—a professor of anthropology at Furman University, a self-styled psychic with an office address in Greer, a pastor at a small AME church.

As he reached for the phone to give the college professor a call, the rolodex flipped on its own, to a card he hadn't seen before. All it contained was a name, an address, and a phone number, no job title or other information. The name, Margaret Delacorte, he didn't recognize, but the smell that rose from the card—sage and ash and something slightly coppery, like blood—was familiar. The same aroma hit him when he opened each of the evidence boxes.

Jim dialed the phone number.

————

Charles' phone rang. He let it go. He was busy. He smoothed out the leather he had just glued to a piece of cardboard that would become the new cover of a book. After the glue dried, he'd stamp the name into the leather and add gold leaf. Normally, he wouldn't go to so much trouble for one of his books. He didn't need them to be fancy. He just wanted to repair them. This one was special, though. It belonged to Millie.

His jaw dropped when he saw it on a shelf in her Harlem apartment. He recognized it as one of the books he got from Roy Arnold. It must have fallen into the rogue magician's hands somehow. When Charles leafed through it, he discovered it was a book of everyday folk magic, written in a peculiar French patois. Millie told him the book had belonged to her grandmother. When she died, she wanted Millie to have it. Millie thought it was just an old recipe book. She didn't understand the true meanings of the "recipes" written down in it.

The book could very well have been tethering Millie's spirit to the present, but he hadn't worked out exactly why or how he was being drawn into her world of Jazz Age Harlem. All he knew at the moment was that he wanted her book to be perfect.

————

Libraries made Zed nervous. He and Jake sat in a stiflingly quiet room on the second floor of the Greenville County Public Library, looking through every book and record they could find about graveyards in the Low Country.

The library outing was Jake's idea. He figured if they looked at enough pictures, one of them might trigger something, enough to identify the place they saw in their shared vision of the future. Given the sheer number of dead people who had accumulated in the last several hundred years, though, there was a lot of ground to cover, and so far, they'd come up empty.

Zed slammed shut the book on the table in front of him a little too hard, earning dirty looks from the only other person in the room, an older man with wisps of white hair surrounded by a fort he'd built from books about the Civil War.

Jake glanced across the table at Zed. "Something the matter?"

Zed rested his chin in his hands. "I don't know. I just can't help but feel like we're wasting our time here."

"What would you suggest we do instead?" Jake shut the book he'd been looking through. "I don't want to wait for what I—we —saw to happen this time."

Jake was right. At least they were doing something. Zed just hated feeling so toothless against the bad guys. He'd been beaten senseless by Roy Arnold, even if Arnold did have a demon inside him at the time, and he hadn't been much help against Patrick Wheeler either. Charles deserved the credit for that one, mostly, although he claimed the rock that bashed in the side of Patrick Wheeler's head wasn't his doing.

And now here was Jake, all curly brown hair and square jaw and tight polo shirts. He didn't ask to get tangled up in Zed's business. If anything happened to him …

After a glance at their elderly companion, Zed leaned across the table. "I've been meaning to ask you something."

Jake raised an eyebrow. "What?"

"When you were coming to last night, it sounded like you said, 'happiness.' Do you have any idea what that was about?"

Jake shook his head. "Not at all. I don't even remember saying anything. What do think that means?"

Zed shrugged. "I don't have a clue. I didn't see anything to be happy about. That's for damn sure."

Jake opened his book again. "I've been thinking. The cemetery we saw seemed overgrown and neglected."

"So, it probably isn't attached to a church, at least not an active one. Another thing, too. The markers themselves were pretty plain. Some of them didn't even have names."

"What does that mean?" Jake asked.

"Have you ever seen some of the fancy gravestones in the Christ Church cemetery? Some of those mausoleums are bigger than my apartment. We're not looking for a place where rich people are reposing in their eternal slumber—a family plot maybe, or a graveyard for blacks."

After the Civil War, blacks were still buried separately, not fit even in death to share the same space with whites. It made Zed's blood boil every time he thought about things like that. Racism was such a stupid, evil, vile human invention. After all, boiling or otherwise, everyone's blood was the same color.

"That narrows our search down a little," Jake said.

"But not nearly enough."

Jake's gaze went to the stack of books on the table. "It's going to have to be enough."

———

Never in a million years would Penelope have guessed who decided to come calling that afternoon. When she answered the door, she was met with the frowning face of the Reverend Lowell Purdue. Despite his best efforts to appear quite literally holier than thou, the dark circles under his eyes and his slumped shoulders betrayed him. He was tired, and maybe a little afraid, and also angry.

"Miss Drake, may I come in?" he asked.

She eyed him warily, but stepped aside so he could enter. "Of course."

She ushered him into her office and offered him a chair.

"What can I do for you today, Reverend Purdue?" she asked as she sat down behind her desk, putting a physical barrier between her and the preacher.

She had the feeling they would both be more comfortable that way.

He looked around, scowling as if he might lose his salvation just by being there. "You said you were friends with a member of my congregation, Patrick Wheeler."

Reverend Purdue had been a thorn in her side during their initial encounter with Wheeler. Somehow Wheeler had weaseled his way into the congregation of the Little Rock Southern Baptist Church, and Penelope was more than certain he had a lot to do with the protests the church had staged at the Brown warehouse, even if the good preacher was the one barking Bible verses into a megaphone.

Penelope nodded. "I did say that."

A lie, a necessary one at the time. She just hoped she remembered all the details.

"He hasn't been in church in some time now, since you paid us a visit, actually. I was just wondering if you'd heard from him at all. I—we miss him and are a little worried." He paused between words, choosing them carefully.

"Sorry, I haven't heard from him in a while," Penelope replied.

Because he's buried behind an old farmhouse out in the middle of nowhere.

Reverend Purdue sighed. "Well, if you do, let him know we all at the Little Rock Southern Baptist Church miss him and would love to see him back in the pews."

He motioned to get up. Penelope remained in her chair.

"Reverend Purdue," she said, "with all due respect, you didn't pay me a personal visit just to ask me about Patrick Wheeler. You could have done that with a phone call. And it must be something truly important if you're willing to risk a visit to the house of an unmarried woman without a chaperone."

The preacher pursed his lips and slumped back into the chair. "How well did you know Patrick?"

Penelope didn't see any other choice but to keep the lie going. Bearing false witness to a preacher should have made her feel guiltier than it did. "Well, I can't say we were close, but I cared about him as a friend."

He glanced down. His hands rested in his lap, palms pressed together. When he looked back up at her, he smiled, clearly uncomfortable. He really must not have wanted to ask the next question. "Would you say he is a person quick to anger?"

"If I recall, you described him as a fine Christian young man," Penelope responded.

The preacher's nostrils flared, but otherwise, he kept his anger in check. "I stand by what I said, but Patrick did struggle with his own personal stumbling blocks, like all of us do."

"His father did commit suicide when he was a teenager," Penelope said. "That had to have left some scars. I may have seen him get angry once or twice, but nothing out of the ordinary. Why do you ask?"

He took a deep breath. "Miss Drake, are you familiar with 1 Peter 5:8?"

She barely managed to keep from rolling her eyes. "Why don't you refresh my memory?"

"'Be sober, be vigilant; because your adversary the devil, as a roaring lion, walketh about, seeking whom he may devour.'"

"So, you believe the Devil devoured Patrick?"

His eyes narrowed. "I have the sense you're mocking me, Miss Drake, but there is a lot of truth in what you say. I think Patrick's anger may have allowed Satan to influence him, and our church."

"So, you admit your publicity stunt at the Brown warehouse was wrong?"

Reverend Purdue shifted in his seat. "That was no stunt, and that is not what I meant."

"What do you have against the Browns, Reverend Purdue?"

"They do not make their money honestly."

Penelope let out a chuckle. "Neither do lawyers, but you're not protesting any law firms from what I've seen."

"They made a bargain with Satan, Miss Drake, and it appears he's come to collect."

"What do you mean by that?"

"I come from a long line of farmers. There have been stories about the Browns going on three generations now. Their good fortune has at times been … improbable, and people who cross them have a habit of coming to bad ends."

"That hardly means they've made a pact with the Devil."

He took another deep breath. "There is more to this story, Miss Drake. Patrick told me his father's suicide had to do with something Ephraim Brown did to ruin him financially."

That was a lie. Patrick's family wasn't even from Greenville.

"When I heard about the Satanic activity at the Brown warehouse, I knew it was no coincidence Patrick had joined our congregation," Reverend Purdue continued. "God was calling us to take action, but in the end, Patrick's own anger may have blinded him to our mission as a church."

"Spreading God's love?" Penelope offered.

He looked at Penelope like an indulgent parent. "Spreading God's whole message. Love and mercy, yes, but also His judgment."

"I'm pretty sure the judgment part came through loud and clear."

If he picked up on her sarcasm at all, he ignored it. "Patrick wanted us to do more than show light on the Devil's work, though. In his last conversation with me, he talked about wanting to do more to the Browns to hurt them. He mentioned breaking into the warehouse. Naturally I counseled against that."

Penelope did her best to keep her temper in check. "You knew this when we talked before. Why didn't you tell me any of it then? Or go to the police?"

Reverend Purdue held up his hands. "It wasn't my place. He spoke to me in confidence."

"So, what's happened?" Penelope asked. "What has changed since then that you're coming to me now?"

"You know how the Holy Spirit endows those who believe with spiritual gifts."

"I believe I had a Sunday School lesson about that at one point."

"Such a shame your church doesn't put more emphasis on such things, given that we are called to use our gifts to fight against the darkness every day. Spiritual gifts are not to be taken lightly, Miss Drake."

Penelope was getting tired of these games. "What is your point, Reverend Purdue?"

"One of those gifts is the gift of prophecy."

She raised an eyebrow. "Prophecy? Is that one of your spiritual gifts?"

He nodded. "Over the last several weeks, I have been plagued with dreams. I've asked about you and your family, Miss Drake, and I've discovered quite a bit—more than I expected. I don't believe you'll as easily dismiss what I'm about to say as the police might."

"So, what have you seen in these dreams?"

"I can see Patrick standing somewhere in the woods. His clothes are all black. Somewhere nearby there's a house."

Penelope took in a quick breath. She hoped the Reverend didn't notice.

"I can feel his pain and anger," the Reverend continued. "He's trying to tell me something, but I can't hear. It gets dark, but not like it does when the sun sets. The darkness instead comes rushing through the woods. It overtakes Patrick, washes over him like a giant wave. I run, but there's nowhere to go. Somehow, I know that even if I can reach the house, the person who lives there won't let me in. In the end, it doesn't matter, though. I don't get to the house in time. The darkness surrounds me. I can't see anything. It's cold, and I know I'll never know the warmth of the sun again. In that darkness I can hear one word being whispered over and over again. *Happiness.*"

While he talked, the mask fell off completely. Gone was the arrogant preacher, certain in his faith, sure of his salvation and his moral superiority, replaced by someone scared of something he couldn't understand, couldn't control.

Unfortunately for him, Penelope wasn't in the mood to offer reassurances. She was too busy trying to guess the meaning of the dream and how much trouble they were in if any part of Patrick Wheeler's spirit had managed to linger.

"Did you come here to hire me, Reverend Purdue?" she asked.

He glanced down at his hands in his lap again. "I want you to find Patrick."

"And who would be paying me? You or the Little Rock Southern Baptist Church?"

"Your fee would be paid entirely by me personally."

She shook her head. "I'm sorry, but that's not a job I can take right now."

His face contorted in an angry scowl. "Why not?" There it was again. The pride. He jutted out his chin. "I'm sorry, I thought you cared about your friend. Did I get that wrong?"

"You didn't get that wrong at all. I care. I just don't have the resources right now to dedicate to the case. Finding people takes a lot of effort."

She considered taking his money for a fraction of a second, but she couldn't do it in good conscience. There certainly needed to be an investigation, just not the one the preacher thought.

"The dreams need to end." His voice trembled.

Penelope held her ground. "I'm sorry. I can't help you with that."

The Reverend's expression hardened. "Thank you for your time, Miss Drake. I won't trouble you anymore. You have a blessed day."

With a curt nod, he stood and left. Penelope glanced down at the painted paperweight on her desk. Her father would have known how to handle that situation better. Maybe he could have helped, too, to figure out the meaning behind the Reverend's dreams. The daemons in Patrick Wheeler's service took pleasure is spreading hopelessness and despair. Why would the voices in the darkness whisper the word *happiness*?

———

All the lights were off when Bertram pulled into the driveway. He didn't think anything about it. After all, it was almost midnight. He hadn't meant to get home so late, but he'd run into an old college buddy on his way out of Asheville. He'd invited Bertram over to his place for a beer, which turned into several, and, well, there he was.

After he managed to get his housekey in the lock on the fourth try, Bertram pushed the door open and stumbled inside. Everything was still. Sometimes his dad stayed up late, but he'd apparently decided to go to bed early that evening. Bertram's talk with his father would have to wait. Again.

As he shambled toward the stairs, though, a flicker of something from the back of the house caught his attention. His left hand automatically went to the charm bracelet circling his right wrist, his fingers seeking out the comfort of the bracelet's texture. Strands of leather wove around small stones, silver charms, and other objects Bertram preferred not to think about. The bracelet was supposed to protect him from malicious magic. He hoped it hadn't lost any juice.

Silence smothered the house like a blanket. Bertram moved down the hallway toward the family room. The air grew stale, oppressive, bad-tasting even, like rotten fruit. He glanced into the kitchen as he passed. Dirty dishes filled the sink, and empty beer bottles littered the counter. That was a little unusual. He'd never considered his dad a slob.

Bertram paused in the doorway to the family room. The television was on with the volume turned all the way down. The screen showed only static. Could that have been the flicker of movement he saw? The dancing gray light threw an eerie glow onto his dad's leather recliner.

Bertram stepped into the room. "Dad? Dad, did you fall asleep watching TV?"

He went to turn the television off, expecting to see his dad slumped over in the recliner, but the chair was empty. Bertram scanned the room. Nothing else seemed amiss, until he noticed the back door ajar. A shaft of moonlight spilled into the room through the gap.

Bertram's heart pounded in his chest. He crept toward the door. When he reached it, he placed a tentative hand on the door knob. He glanced back over his shoulder at the dark and empty family room before he pulled the door open just enough to peer out into the back yard. The moon gave off enough light to see the whole thing—the kidney-shaped pool, the patio with the grill and the fire pit—everything for a child's dream summer.

But he wasn't a kid anymore.

And summer was over.

His dad wasn't in the back yard either, but the feeling something was wrong intensified. Without thinking about it too much, Bertram slipped through the door and outside onto the patio. The eerie silence struck him there, too. Normally he'd be hearing crickets and owls and the rustle of leaves in the breeze, but there was nothing.

The fire pit attracted his attention. All the patio chairs normally around it were shoved to one side. As Bertram approached the pit, he caught a faint whiff of herbs like sage and rosemary and mustard, and he wondered why his dad was using the fire pit to cook instead of the grill, but then other aromas assaulted his nose—the smell of tar and something distinctly coppery.

When he saw the rim of the fire pit he finally understood. All around it symbols and words were drawn in chalk. The bile rose in his throat. Bertram backed away so fast he nearly tripped over his own feet. His thoughts went to the pentagram drawn on the floor of the warehouse before it was destroyed. Daemons had been responsible for that, and back in August daemons had come for him in that very back yard. At the edges of his vision, the shadows moved. He turned and broke into a run. He practically dove through the back door, slamming it shut behind him.

A search upstairs confirmed his fears. His dad wasn't there.

But something else was.

While he stood in his parents' room, a figure appeared in the mirror, leering at him with green eyes and a grinning mouth full of pointed teeth. He bolted down the stairs and out the front door. He swore he heard laughter and felt sharp fingernails scrape down his back as he burst outside. The tires screeched as he pulled his Camaro out of the driveway. He wasn't sure where he was going. All he knew was that he had to get away from there or he wasn't going to see another sunrise.

––––––––

On December 31, 1919, the Blue Club threw one hell of a New Year's Eve party. It would be the very last one before Prohibition went into effect in January 1920. Lewis pulled out all the stops. Oysters, steaks, whole roasted pheasants, and everything in between, and of course, buckets of champagne. Despite the cold weather, the room was burning up. The band played, and people danced, and for just one night, they forgot all their cares.

Charles couldn't afford to forget, though. He never stopped moving, making sure the night went off without a hitch. Whenever Millie came on stage, he always managed to steal a moment or two to listen to her sing, but that night he couldn't spare even a second. He took comfort in the fact that he could see her later, after the turn of the new year and all the revelers stumbled home.

It was almost two in the morning before he got a chance. Charles approached Millie's dressing room and was about to knock when he heard talking on the other side. Millie's melodious voice was easy to pick out. The other voice was lower—a man. Charles stepped back and retreated to the main room where he sat down at the bar. The clatter of dishes and glasses from the kitchen told him the dishwashers were still cleaning up, but otherwise everyone had gone home, even Lewis.

Soon the door to the backstage opened, and Andre Lestrade, Lewis' new business partner, emerged. He had purchased a share of the club about a month earlier. Charles didn't like it. Already he was making changes—firing long-term employees and bringing in his own people, reserving tables for "important" friends with unsavory reputations. Not to mention the checks Charles saw made out to names he didn't recognize.

Lewis said everything was above-board, and it was all good for business, but Andre's business was crooked in every way. Most of all, though, Charles really didn't like the way Andre looked at Millie. Millie, for her part, said she could take care of herself, and under any other circumstance, Charles would have agreed, but no one said no to a man like Andre Lestrade. If he wanted something, he got it, one way or another.

Andre waved to Charles. "What are you still doing here, Isaiah? Go home. Get some sleep. You deserve it after the night we just had. Everything went off without a hitch thanks to you, and no one who was here tonight can say they didn't have a blast."

Charles forced a smile. "Given the amount of liquor we went through, I'll say. I suppose we won't be having any more nights like that."

He slapped Charles on the back. "Oh, I wouldn't worry too much about that. We've got big plans for the Blue Club."

Charles eyed him. "What sort of plans?"

Andre wagged a finger. "Not just yet. When the time is right, Lewis and I are planning to bring you on board. You'll see, then. It'll knock your socks off."

"Yeah, Andre, we'll see. I don't plan on going anywhere anytime soon."

Andre laughed as he left through the front door, letting in a blast of chilly winter air. Briefly, Charles thought about going to see Millie, but he changed his mind and left himself, walking the few blocks to his apartment in the cold January night.

———

Millie came by his apartment at about four o'clock the next afternoon. She didn't say anything when he opened the door. She didn't need to. He just stepped out of the way as she came inside.

"You didn't stop by my dressing room to see me," she said.

Charles closed the door. "I did, but you already had company."

"Nothing happened, Isaiah. You know that."

"I know. But why was he there? Why was he talking to you? Why are you keeping me in the dark about things?" He sighed and pinched the bridge of his nose. "I'm the manager. I should know about what's going on before you do."

She glared. "Why? Because I'm just a singer?"

"I didn't say that."

"But you meant it."

He reached over to caress her shoulder. "Millie, you are amazing, and I don't doubt you could be President of the United States if you set your mind to it, but *my* job is managing the Blue Club, and I can't do *my* job if I don't know what's going on."

She placed her hand atop his. "Andre just wanted to talk to me about a party he's throwing in a couple of weeks for some friends of his. He wants me to give a little private performance and asked me to sing some of his favorite songs. That's all. I promise."

Charles jerked away. "Is this party going to be at the Blue Club? Are we going to have to close down again? That's the fourth time in two months. Do you know how much money we lose every time he does that? We can't afford to lose anymore, especially with all the liquor drying up. People don't get all dolled up to come out and drink water."

She blinked, clearly stung by his words. "I thought you said people would come out to hear me sing in an empty warehouse. Now you're saying all they want is to drink?"

Charles silently cursed himself for letting his temper get the best of him. "I didn't mean it that way."

"Then why did you say it that way?" she asked. "Besides … I don't think you need to worry."

He snorted. "Now you sound like Andre."

But the downcast expression on Millie's face told him what he already suspected.

"Wait," he said. "Lewis and Andre aren't planning to stop selling liquor, are they?"

She shook her head.

Charles threw his hands up. "What are they thinking? That's crazy."

"See, they knew you'd be this way. That's why they didn't want to tell you at first." She cocked an eyebrow. "Really, you think it's just the Blue Club? Every jazz joint in Harlem is doing the same thing."

"How do they plan on not getting caught?"

"There's a big room in the basement," Millie replied. "It was just used for storage. They made it into a secret bar."

Dozens of odd little things that had happened over the last month suddenly fell into place. "Those workers I let in a few weeks back—"

"You thought they were just here to work on the accountant's office on the floors above the club?"

Charles felt stupid for not adding things up sooner. "So, you've got a secret bar. How are you getting the liquor there? And who's making it if it's illegal?"

She shrugged. "I'll leave that to Lewis and Andre. I would suggest you do the same."

He shook his head. "This isn't right, Millie."

She frowned. "Why are you so opposed to this? Why do you care so much?"

"I told you, Millie. Andre is bad news. Nothing good is going to come from getting mixed up with him."

"You're just overreacting. I can handle him."

He shook his head. "But that's not all I'm worried about. You get mixed up in the things he's mixed up in, you're bound to make enemies, not to mention what happens if the police get on his tail. Or the FBI. I don't want to see anyone hurt, especially not you."

"Why would I get hurt?"

Because the obituary your ghost showed me says you're going to die three months from now.

But he couldn't say that.

"I keep telling you I can take care of myself." She took a step closer. "And whatever I can't take care of, I know you can, now that you're here."

Now that you're here.

What did she mean by that?

"You act like you were expecting me to show up or something."

She pulled at his shirt collar. "Maybe I was. Maybe I've been waiting a long time for you to come into my life, Isaiah Jenkins."

He smelled the sweet roses of her perfume, and for just a moment, his anger faded. When her lips met his, he leaned into the kiss, never wanting it to end.

3.
WEDNESDAY, OCTOBER 25, 1972

Penelope woke up to someone banging on her front door. The clock next to her bed said it was a little after three in the morning. She got up and hurried down the stairs, pulling on a robe as she went and clutching the Louisville Slugger she kept at her bedside. Her charm bracelet didn't give off any warnings, so no dark magic was at play, but neither was there when a brick smashed her office window.

Whoever was on the other side of the door was getting more panicky by the second, calling for her by name. She recognized the voice.

"Penelope. It's Bertram. Please let me in."

When she opened the door, Bertram nearly ran her over trying to get inside.

"Bertram, what—"

"Shut the door. Hurry. Shut it!"

She did as she was told. "Bertram what's going on?"

Bertram stood in the middle of the foyer, wild-eyed, hands shaking, struggling to catch his breath. His gaze darted around the room. "They followed me here."

"Who?"

Bertram gestured frantically toward the door. "Those things. The daemons. They were following the car."

"Daemons? You saw them."

"I didn't have to see them. I know they were there." His words had a hard edge to them.

A daemon had possessed Bertram's body in order to commit at least one murder, something they'd managed to cover up so far. It was all part of Patrick Wheeler's evil plan. Seeing Bertram so agitated made Penelope wonder just how much of a toll being possessed by one of those dark creatures had taken on him.

"Bertram, what's going on?"

"Dad's gone. Missing."

An icy ball of dread formed in Penelope's stomach. "When?"

He ran his fingers through his hair. "I don't know. I've been out of town for a couple of days. I got home kind of late. The house was dark. The door was open to the back yard. I found some ... upsetting things there. The daemons were there, too, waiting. They must have taken Dad."

"Upsetting things? What kind of upsetting things did you find?"

"One of those spells like Charles does. There were weird symbols drawn all around the fire pit, and it smelled like when we got baked at parties back in college, only about a thousand times worse."

Penelope shook her head. "I never got baked in college."

He shot her a dirty look. "You know what I mean. When the daemons showed up, it scared the shit out of me. I didn't know where else to go, so I came here. Sorry I woke you up."

"It's fine." She put on what she thought was a reassuring smile. "We can go back over there when the sun comes up and take a look around. Charles and Zed might be able to help, too."

Chewing his lip, Bertram stared at the baseball bat Penelope still held. "So, does that mean I can ..."

She set the Louisville Slugger down by the door. "Stay here? Of course. Guest room is all yours if you want to try to get some sleep."

His whole body slumped in relief. "Thanks."

Penelope grasped his hand. "We'll find your dad, Bertram. I promise."

———

Bertram staggered out of the bedroom at around ten in the morning, still looking like he'd been run over by a truck. Penelope was sitting on the couch, reading a trashy true crime paperback. She shut it quickly and stuffed it between the cushions.

"Coffee's in the kitchen if you want some," she said.

Long ago, the old house had been divided into two apartments, one upstairs and one downstairs. Her father had converted the downstairs apartment into his office when he became a private detective. They lived together in the apartment upstairs until he died. Now Penelope lived there alone.

Bertram yawned. "It's going to take a lot more than coffee to get me through today, I think."

"Got plenty of bourbon, too."

"I might take you up on that." He walked into the kitchen, scooped up the mug Penelope had set out for him, and poured himself a cup of brown sludge.

"How are you holding up?" she asked.

"Been better. I used the phone in the bedroom to call my mom just now. She's still in Virginia, staying with a cousin of hers. I promise I'll pay the long-distance charge."

"Did you tell her about your dad?"

"No. I'm not going to do that unless I absolutely have to. There's no point in upsetting her more." He threw himself down on the couch next to her. "I did ask her about the last time she talked to Dad, though."

"And?"

Bertram stared into his coffee mug. "She said she hasn't spoken with him in more than a week."

"So, nothing helpful there."

He shook his head. "You don't understand. They've never

gone more than a couple of days without talking to each other. They're not estranged. My mom has just been staying with relatives because she still has problems with our house, you know after what happened."

Louise Brown had been possessed by a spirit trapped in a cursed brooch, part of Roy Arnold's elaborate scheme of revenge. They had saved her and taken care of the rogue magician, but then the trouble with Patrick Wheeler started up. Penelope didn't realize it at first, but she had spent the last couple of months waiting for the final shoe to drop. The story of the Brown family wasn't over yet.

"Maybe they had a fight," she offered.

"No, Mom was as puzzled as I was. Dad just stopped calling, and he didn't pick up whenever she called him."

"Any idea why?"

Bertram took a sip of coffee, made a face, and took another sip anyway. "He's been acting strange the last few weeks. He had this weird glint in his eyes, and he talked about fixing everything, making things even better than they were before."

Knowing what she knew about Ephraim's secret talent for magic, Penelope didn't like the inferences to be made there. "How so?"

Bertram shrugged. "Hell if I know. He never would tell me anything when I asked. He just said he was taking care of things. I can't imagine how. We don't have the funds to rebuild the warehouse and replace what we lost, and the insurance company's been dragging their feet. I think they suspect the explosion that blew up the warehouse wasn't exactly an accident, but I really don't believe they'd be willing to accept a demon-possessed tractor as an explanation."

Just then there was a knock at the front door. Muttering under her breath about Grand Central Station, Penelope went to answer. She found Zed on her front porch. He didn't look like he'd gotten much sleep either. He raised an eyebrow when he came upstairs and saw Bertram in the kitchen pouring himself a second cup of coffee, but he didn't say anything. He simply nodded in Bertram's direction. Bertram saluted back with his coffee mug.

"Coffee?" Penelope asked.

Zed shook his head. "No, thanks."

"You sure?" Bertram took a big gulp and grimaced. "You're missing out."

Zed ignored him. "Penelope, there's something we need to talk about. This business with Patrick Wheeler, I don't think it's over yet."

Penelope exchanged glances with Bertram. "You don't say?"

Zed frowned as his gaze passed between the two of them. "What's going on?"

Penelope turned toward Bertram. "You want to tell him? You were there."

Bertram sketched out the events of the night before for Zed, from discovering his father was missing to being chased by daemons through the streets of Greenville. As Zed listened, he grew a shade paler.

"Funny you should mention daemons," Zed said when Bertram finished, though he wasn't smiling. "I've been having dreams about them chasing me through the woods, and I don't think they're your average run-of-the-mill nightmares."

"What makes you say that?" Penelope asked.

Zed scrunched up his face. "I don't know. They just seem like more. They're too real to be just dreams."

Penelope had the impression he was holding something back.

Bertram set his empty mug down on the counter a little too hard, the noise echoing through the tiny kitchen. "I thought we'd taken care of Patrick Wheeler. Charles said he couldn't come back." He tried to hide his trembling hand behind his back.

Penelope noticed. "Why don't I call Charles? Hopefully he can meet us at your parents' house, and we can all put our heads together to figure out what's going on."

Zed huffed. "Let's all just hope Charles decides to answer the phone."

———

Upon hearing a knock at his door, Charles' first thought was that he needed to strengthen the wards again. Maybe this time he'd do more than just shore up the barriers protecting his property from anyone—or anything—that might wish him ill. He'd recently stumbled upon a book written by a hermit monk who lived in the mountains of Lombardy in the fifteenth century. The book's spine was damaged, and when Charles picked it up, it fell open to an intriguing spell. The incantation scribbled out in cramped Latin could put the notion in a person's head that they just didn't want to pay him a visit at all. Charles found the idea tempting, but messing with people's heads could have all kinds of unforeseen consequences.

The knocking persisted, and despite his better judgement, Charles went to answer the door. An older man dressed in a suit stood on the porch, maybe in his early sixties, not fat but well-fed.

"Can I help you?" Charles hoped his frown would do what magic failed to accomplish.

The man smiled, not a genuine smile, but one calculated to put Charles at ease, one meant to make him let his guard down. "Good morning. My name is Jim Everett. I'm looking for someone named Margaret Delacorte. Does she happen to be home?"

Charles shook his head. "She doesn't live here anymore."

The man seemed taken aback, as if he hadn't considered that possibility. "Do you know where she might have moved to?"

"She's dead."

Again, that same confused look. "Oh, I see. I'm so sorry. Are you … are you her son?"

Charles nodded. "More or less."

The furrow of his brow deepened, and the corner of his mouth twitched. Everett's confusion was growing, and so was his annoyance. "What does that mean?"

"My name is Charles. Margaret adopted me when I was small. She raised me. Any particular reason you're looking for her?"

Everett glanced past him, into the front parlor. His gaze took in the bookshelves lining all the walls, laden with books. Charles had recently rearranged them to accommodate the acquisitions from Roy Arnold's hoard. There wasn't any other furniture in the room. Most people would consider the arrangement curious, even suspect. No doubt Everett was making his own judgments.

"Have you ever met anyone by the name of Jonathan Drake?" he asked.

Drake. Penelope's father. It hit Charles where he had heard the man's name before. Jim Everett was a police detective. No good in lying then.

"I've heard of him. What's this about?"

Everett shifted his weight. One foot crossed the threshold. "Can I come in?"

Charles met his gaze. "Is there a reason you need to?"

Detective Everett raised himself up, the color rising in his face. He probably wasn't used to being talked to that way by someone like Charles. He could see the indignation in the detective's eyes, but Charles refused to look away.

The next few moments seemed like hours—enough time for Charles to wonder if he'd pay for exercising his rights—but then the detective's shoulders slumped, and he sighed. "Thank you for your time. I'm sorry to have bothered you. You have a nice rest of your day."

Charles shut the door without replying. He listened to Detective Everett's footsteps on the porch as he retreated back down the steps and through the overgrown yard. Finally, when the crunch of tires on the gravel drive faded into the distance, Charles went to grab his leather satchel. He didn't have time to think about why a police detective would be looking for Margaret after all these years, and asking about Penelope's father, too. That would have to wait for later. He had his own appointment to keep.

As he was leaving through the back door, his telephone rang. He let it go. More and more that spell seemed like a good idea.

When Charles didn't answer the phone, Penelope, Zed and Bertram went ahead to the house on Crescent Avenue without him. Penelope hated that Zed was right. She wanted so desperately to believe Charles had come around finally, that he was ready to include people in his life again, but every time it seemed like he was better, he retreated back into his old habits, isolating himself in that falling-down farmhouse in the middle of nowhere, surrounded by his books, pushing everyone away.

The oversized brick colonial stood silent and dark, unexceptional among the other mansions on Crescent Avenue, revealing no hint anything out of the ordinary had ever happened there. *If the neighbors only knew,* Penelope thought. Bertram led them all straight to the fire pit in the back yard.

"If I didn't know better, I would think the neighborhood teenagers were pulling some kind of prank." He pointed to the lines drawn in a practiced, methodical hand around the fire pit's rim. "But tell me if those don't look like the same symbols as the pentagram from the warehouse."

Zed leaned over and studied the chalk markings, wrinkling his nose at the lingering smell. "Just because some of the symbols are the same doesn't mean this circle was intended to summon a demon."

Bertram frowned. "Then what was it used for?"

"It's hard to tell." Zed pointed to one of the symbols, which looked like an arrow crossed with three diagonal lines. "There are lots of spells that might use these elements. Shapes, symbols, letters, words—they're all just used to focus energy in different ways, depending on how they're combined, depending on where the energy comes from."

Penelope frowned. "Probably safe to say this isn't a cure for a hangover, though, right?"

Zed raised an eyebrow. "If it is, it's major overkill."

"What are you talking about, Penelope?" Bertram asked.

She clenched her fists. "He lied to me."

Bertram crossed his arms. "Who?"

"Your dad, Bertram." She grew more irritated by the second. He should have told her. None of this had to happen. "He practiced magic. He was the one who made the first charm bracelet for you. And the necklace to try to save your mother, or at least keep her calm. He told me he didn't really know how to do much more than cure a hangover, that all he had was a book he inherited from his grandmother. Obviously, he wasn't telling the truth."

"And if he lied about that …" Zed mumbled.

Bertram scowled. "That's impossible. I've only known about this magic bullshit for a few months. How could he have hidden something like that from me my whole life?"

Zed shook his head. "It's not that hard really. Remember he hid it from your mother, too, and for a lot longer. People don't want to believe in magic, so they ignore or rationalize things. All he would've had to do was tell a few little lies here and there. Your brain just did the rest."

If he had only told the truth, maybe they could have avoided everything that happened. Penelope was mad at Ephraim for lying, but she might have been angrier with herself for taking him at his word. "He's a lot more powerful even than what he admitted to me."

Bertram looked pained as he massaged his temples. "Do you think whatever this is had something to do with the company and all Dad's talk of trying to make things right again?"

Zed dragged his finger through the soot on the lip of the fire pit and brought it up to his nose. He seemed a little on edge. He was sensitive to magic, even if he wasn't a magician himself. Penelope's father had been sensitive to the world beyond the Veil, too. She didn't inherit that trait, so she'd learned to trust Zed's instincts. She was just waiting for him to tell them all to run.

Instead, he wiped his hand on his jeans. "Charles could tell you for sure what this spell was supposed to do, but it doesn't seem like a prosperity spell to me."

Bertram's eye grew wide. "You mean a spell that brings you money? Those things work?"

"Sometimes," Zed replied. "They're not the easiest to pull off. The magic user's motives have to be crystal clear, and when it comes to money, our motives are always so mixed up. But there's a touch of darkness here I'm not so sure about."

Bertram's gaze went to the bushes at the edge of the yard. "The daemons—"

Zed held up a hand. "No, not them. Something else. There's something dark about the spell itself."

Bertram's scowl returned. "Are you telling me my dad was out here practicing some kind of black magic?"

Zed winced at the phrase *black magic*. "I wouldn't throw that term around if I were you, and no, I'm not telling you that at all. A lot of spells intended for good have dark histories and ... questionable requirements."

"Care to get any more specific than that?" Bertram inched away from the fire pit.

"I can't. There's definitely something off here, though. I don't like it." Whether consciously or not, Zed also had taken a step back.

The breeze picked up, scattering dead leaves around the yard and stirring the ashes in the fire pit. The wind carried voices— faint whispers.

"Do you have a place to stay, Bertram?" Penelope asked while fixing Zed with her gaze. "I'm not sure you should be here until we figure out what's going on."

Bertram shrugged. "I can find somewhere to crash, I guess."

"You can crash with me," Zed said with a sigh as he glared back at Penelope. "All I can offer is a couch, though."

Bertram glanced back toward the house, as if he expected to see a face staring out at them from one of the darkened windows. "Give me ten minutes to pack a bag."

———

It seemed to Ephraim as if they'd been walking for hours. Overhead the stars peeked through a web of bare tree branches, black against the indigo blue sky. Leaves crunched under his feet. He shivered. The air was crisp, brittle even, chilly enough to need a jacket, but he didn't have one.

Six of them marched single-file through the woods. He brought up the rear. Up ahead, the light from a flashlight bobbed up and down, dancing like a will-o'-the-wisp from his grand-mother's stories of growing up in the mountains, leading them farther into the woods. The light didn't help much with the path directly in front of him, though, and more than once he stumbled over the uneven ground.

He didn't know where he was or what they were all doing there, only that he needed to get control of his growing unease and face down his fear. Otherwise he wouldn't get what he wanted.

But what did he want?

Eventually, they came to a clearing—no, not a clearing. Here and there stones jutted up out of the ground at odd angles. Grave markers. They had arrived at a graveyard, an old and neglected one. Something waited for them there, something ancient, some-thing that wasn't human. A single word echoed through Ephraim's brain.

Happiness.

The fog in Ephraim's head lifted, if only for a moment. He found himself in his bedroom at his grandparents' house. Every-thing was exactly as he remembered it the last time he'd been there. A patchwork quilt made from old scraps of cloth covered the four-poster bed. A few of his grandmother's cross-stitch samplers hung on the walls. A secretary desk was tucked into one corner, and in another corner, a low chest of drawers stood with a vanity mirror on top. Ephraim paused, shocked at his reflection. Looking back at him was not a gray-haired, middle-aged man with dark circles under his eyes, but a golden-haired boy about ten years old.

Outside the room heavy footsteps made the hardwood floor creak and groan like someone in pain. Ephraim scrambled for somewhere to hide. He had just managed to wriggle himself under the bed when the footsteps stopped directly outside the door. The cut crystal doorknob turned, and the door opened. At the same time the fog returned to Ephraim's brain, and he didn't remember anything else after that.

—————

A general store had stood on the corner of Edgeworth Street and Greenacre Road almost as long as there had been a Nicholtown community. Generation after generation of the Rose family served the mostly black community by stocking things you couldn't get at the Winn-Dixie down the road. Uncommon spices, more unusual cuts of meat, harder-to-find vegetables—any odd ingredient one of your grandmother's recipes called for, Rose's General Store had it.

Charles pulled into the store's tiny parking lot a little before noon. The tailpipe of his pickup truck barked and choked out a plume of black exhaust as he killed the engine. He grimaced. The last thing he wanted to do was deal with that, but he mentally added it to the already long list of things he had to take care of.

Inside the store an older black man sat on a stool behind the counter. The voice of Lena Horne spilled out of the radio by his elbow. She was singing some lazy blues tune. Charles tried not to think about Millie.

The man, Benjamin Rose, glanced at the clock on the wall behind him. "You're a little late today, Charles."

Charles hoisted his satchel up onto the counter. "Had an unexpected visitor."

"A visitor? You?" Benjamin chuckled.

"Yeah, I wasn't happy about it either."

Benjamin pointed toward the door. "Heard your pickup truck

griping again just now, too. You know I got a brother-in-law can—"

"Thanks for the recommendation, but I think I got it covered."

In all honesty the truck was beyond what any mechanic could do for it. Magic held it together more than the rusty nuts and bolts. Charles just needed it to last a little while longer.

"Probably for the best." Benjamin leaned over the counter with a conspiratorial grin. "He's a good-for-nothing SOB anyway. I was just saying something to be nice to my sister."

Charles smiled and shook his head. "You tell Addie I said hello."

"Will do." Benjamin glanced over at Charles' bag. "So, you got anything specific you need today, or are you just looking to resupply?"

"A little bit of both." Charles reached into his satchel, pulled out a notebook, and turned to the page where he'd scrawled out a list of everything he needed to get. It was longer than normal. "I'm looking for some yarrow root. Having the damnedest time finding it anywhere."

Benjamin stroked his chin. "I may have some in the back. Let me go check."

Rose's General Store also catered to those with grocery lists less mundane and more magical, something the Rose family didn't see as anything unusual.

"Magic bleeds through into everyday life," Benjamin told Charles once. "You can't draw a line and say, 'This is magic,' and 'This isn't magic.' People practice magic all the time. They just don't call it that."

All those recipes for tinctures, balms, salves, and teas passed down from generation to generation had a touch of magic in them, and it wasn't really a giant leap from brewing a cure for a headache to mixing up a tonic to make nightmares go away.

While Benjamin was in the back of the store, Charles gathered up the rest of what he needed and brought everything to the counter. Benjamin reemerged from the storeroom holding a small glass jar.

"It's your lucky day." He handed the jar of coarse, brown powder to Charles. "I've only got a little, though. Will that do?"

Charles held the jar up at eye level. "That should be perfect."

"Not a lot of folks around here use yarrow root much. What are you planning on doing with it?"

"It's for something to help me sleep better," Charles answered. "That's all."

Benjamin eyed him. Charles knew what he was thinking. You could go to the drug store to get something to help you sleep better. You didn't need a magic elixir for that. But Charles was telling the truth. He *did* need the yarrow root to help him sleep, just not the way he said it.

Benjamin motioned for Charles to come closer. "Come here. I want to show you something I found. I've been waiting for you to pay a visit."

Benjamin took a package wrapped in brown paper from under the counter. He carefully unfolded the paper to reveal a small wooden box with a hinged top decorated in a pattern of inter-locking vines. He opened the top of the box to reveal a deck of tarot cards, the backs emblazoned with the same pattern as the top of the box.

"Like it?" Benjamin took the deck of cards in his hands, thumbing through them to show Charles the illustrations on the faces. "It's from New Orleans, probably printed around 1902."

Charles reached toward the deck. "It's beautiful."

Benjamin gave the deck a quick shuffle and fanned out the cards face down on the top of the counter. "Why don't you pick one?"

"What?" Charles jerked his hand back like he'd gotten an elec-tric shock.

"Pick one," Benjamin repeated. "When was the last time you had any kind of reading done?"

It had been about five years, when Charles was in Vietnam.

That reading didn't go well for anyone involved, but he didn't tell Benjamin that. "I don't think this is a good idea."

But Benjamin persisted. "Come on. Just one card."

One card. Not really enough to get a good reading. One card could mean anything at all depending on how you chose to interpret it. How much could Benjamin really find out about Charles from one card?

He sighed. "Okay, fine."

Charles let his fingers hover over the deck for a second, trying to pick up on any malicious magic, but nothing jumped up and tried to bite him. He pulled a card out of the middle and turned it face up on the counter. The card depicted a smiling man seated on a bench in front of a wall. Resting on top of the wall were nine cups.

It was the last card he'd ever expect.

Benjamin started laughing. "The Nine of Cups. The Lord of Happiness. Looks like all your dreams are going to come true."

Charles wasn't in the mood to join in on the laughter. "Maybe not. It's reversed."

Benjamin held up a chiding finger. "Now you know as well as I do the Lord of Happiness is the only card in the deck that's just as lucky reversed as it is right-side-up. Maybe even luckier. That just means you need to look inside yourself for contentedness."

Charles glared. "I think your deck is defective."

"Oh, come on now, Charles. Don't be that way." Benjamin tempered his glee, but the smile never left his face. "Even you've got to let a little happiness into your life sometime. Don't you want your dreams to come true?"

Charles was pretty sure he didn't.

———

Bertram passed out on Zed's couch around eight o'clock. Zed tried to read a book, but the snoring distracted him. He was about to give up and go to bed himself when there was a knock at his door. He glanced at Bertram sprawled out before he went to answer. Probably Penelope checking on things. Instead, he found Amy Parker, Bobby Parker's sister.

"You decided to knock this time," he said.

The last time Amy visited him, he had found her in his kitchen drinking his coffee, having let herself in. That time she wanted assurances Zed would do his best to get who killed her brother. Zed had kept that promise, after a fashion. He told her the person responsible for her brother's death had been dealt with. She understood what "dealt with" meant and had enough common sense not to ask any more questions. They hadn't talked since, and Zed didn't see any reason they would.

She bit her lip. "I … need to ask you a favor."

Bertram let out an obnoxious snort before rolling over.

Amy tried to peer past Zed into the apartment. "Is this a bad time?"

"No, it's fine. Just an unexpected houseguest." Zed took a step back. "Come on in. We can talk in the kitchen."

"I don't know anyone else to go to," Amy said once they were both seated at the kitchen table. "Anybody in my family would have me committed."

Zed fished a Winston out of his pocket for himself and offered one to her, too. "What's the problem?"

"I'm getting rid of my grandmother's stuff. I'm tired of tripping over it all the time." She took the cigarette and accepted Zed's light as well. "Bobby was the one who insisted on keeping everything anyway."

When Zed had visited the trailer Amy shared with her brother, uninvited and unannounced, he'd found it crammed to the gills with antique furniture and other things. Their grandmother, who had a touch of magic, died in a housefire that spared Amy and Bobby by some miracle. Zed suspected Bobby had some magic talent himself. In the trailer Zed also discovered their grandmother's old books of folk magic, recipe books as Amy called them, and at least one of them had been used recently.

"It's the books. You don't know what to do with the books."

Amy nodded. "I don't want them. I don't have any use for them, but I know I can't just sell them to anyone."

"No, that wouldn't be a good idea."

Zed watched Amy's internal struggle play across her features. He didn't need his special talent to see her emotions. Anger, embarrassment, and guilt darkened her eyes and wrinkled her forehead.

She abruptly let out a string of expletives. "I hate this. I'm the last person to ask anyone for anything, but will you take them? Please?"

Zed leaned back in his chair. "You want me to take the books?"

"You would know what to do with them."

He gestured toward his tiny living room where Bertram still snored. "In case you hadn't noticed, I don't really have a lot of room."

"But you know people. Surely you can think of someone to give them to. They need to be kept safe."

Zed didn't want the books, but Amy was making it really hard for him to say no. A lot of people disparaged folk magic, saying it wasn't "real" magic just because the people who practiced it didn't have any formal training. Most didn't know Church Latin from Pig Latin and didn't care to learn the difference, but folk magic could be powerful and dangerous. Just like recipes passed down from generation to generation, how things were written down didn't always match how things were actually done. Only, in unpracticed hands, folk magic could create a lot more problems than biscuits that didn't rise right.

Zed took a long drag and blew a stream of smoke out of the side of his mouth. "Okay, I'll take them."

"Great." She smiled, relief radiating off of her. "They're in the car. I'll just go get them."

She had already brought them. Of course.

4.

THURSDAY, OCTOBER 26, 1972

s the last notes of the song played out, Zed switched on his microphone. "You were just listening to 'Black and White' by Three Dog Night. Coming up next, I've got a song from the Eagles that's pretty appropriate for this time of year, if you ask me, but first here's something to think about on this chilly October morning. I know I've got at least a few listeners who care what I say, God only knows why."

Three days a week, from midnight until five in the morning, Zed deejayed at WRXQ, playing whatever he wanted and saying whatever popped into his head. It was a wonder the station owner hadn't fired him yet, except they'd probably never be able to find anyone else willing to take his job.

"I've been thinking a lot lately about fate or destiny or whatever you want to call it," Zed continued. "Just consider the people you meet every day, the ones you pass in your cars, or walking down the street. Most of them you'll never see again, but all it takes is one random event—you turn left instead of right, or leave your house five minutes later than normal—and you cross paths with someone who becomes more than just a stranger. Maybe they become the most important person in your life, and you have no way of knowing who or when or how that will happen. Or why. I certainly don't have all the answers, but I do know this. We were not meant to walk the world alone, any of us, even on a cold October morning when no one has any business being awake."

———

Amy Parker certainly didn't have any business being awake. She had to be at work by seven, but she couldn't sleep, and so she found herself listening to the radio, telling herself it was just by chance she happened upon Zed's show.

Amy knew she wasn't alone, even though it felt like it at times. She'd known ever since the angels saved her and Bobby from the fire that killed her grandmother. She'd never been much on going to church, but she always believed the angels watched over the two of them.

Until what happened to Bobby.

Maybe what her mother always said was true. Maybe she should have listened to the preachers sooner. Maybe fiddling with magic was against God's will. Maybe that's why the angels didn't protect Bobby from … the thing that killed him.

That was the real reason she wanted to get rid of the books. Since Bobby was gone, the angels were all she had. She didn't want them to leave her too. Strange how thinking of them made her think of Zed McKay. What was it about his voice that caused her to think of the angels? And what was she doing even thinking about a man she'd spoken to a grand total of four times like that? It was ridiculous. Still, she listened until she finally drifted off to sleep.

———

Penelope pulled up to her grandmother's house at half past two, just as the ending credits of *The Guiding Light* would be scrolling on the television. She knocked and listened as her grandmother got out of her chair in the den and slowly came to the door. That walk became longer and longer as the years went by, but Edith

Drake would never ask for help. She'd lived on her own for over two decades. She wasn't about to stop now.

She ushered Penelope in with a smile and made her sit at the kitchen table while she cut a piece of pecan pie and poured a glass of sweet tea. Penelope was content to let her grandmother talk for a while as she enjoyed her pie and sipped her tea. She learned all about the controversy over the election of the current Junior League president, which led to an essay on exactly what her grandmother thought of *those people* who had broken into that office in Washington, D.C., which somehow segued into her recipe for lemon icebox pie.

The biggest news, though, was her ongoing feud with the music minister at church, who continued his efforts to modernize the Sunday morning worship service. While the guitar had been bad enough, apparently the tambourine was a bridge too far.

She shook her head and clicked her tongue, which growing up had always been Penelope's signal to duck and cover. "And all the while that beautiful pipe organ sits unused."

She did have a point there.

She reached across the table and placed her hand on top of Penelope's. "Listen to me, going on about things you don't care anything about. Tell me about you. What has my favorite grand-daughter been up to?"

Too much.

"Not a whole lot," Penelope answered.

Her grandmother eyed her. "Oh, surely that's not the case. You're always going on about how busy you are. Mrs. Atkinson talks about running into you in the library all the time. Mrs. Redding could have sworn it was your car parked across the street from her neighbor's house for several hours last Thursday. And Mrs. McGee saw you just the other day downtown. She would've said hello, but you were going inside that antique shop on Coffee Street."

The CIA had nothing on Edith Drake.

"That's Grayson & Sons," Penelope said. "I know the owner. He's been helping me with a case."

"Oh, yes, I know exactly the one, but if I recall the Graysons don't own the store anymore, do they? It's the boy with the funny last name. When poor Mrs. Styles passed on a few months ago, her daughters sold some things to him. From what I gather, he's very nice, you know, for a Yankee." Her grandmother said the last word at almost a whisper.

"His name is Dan. Dan Kowalczyk." Penelope took a sip of her iced tea, hoping her grandmother wouldn't notice the flush in her cheeks.

"Yes, that's it. And how is your other gentleman friend? Zed McKay, is that his name? Is that short for Zedediah?"

Penelope wasn't sure exactly. He'd always just been Zed. "Zed's my assistant. He helps me with work."

"Well, in any event, he's awfully handsome."

Even her own grandmother ... Penelope couldn't help but roll her eyes. "He's also good at his job. And it's nothing like that. Zed and I are friends. He's ... not exactly my type."

Her grandmother pursed her lips. "Well, I'm sure you're the best judge of that."

She did not approve of Penelope's job, and unlike everyone else, she was not afraid to speak her mind. The two of them had recently managed to come to an understanding, though. Penelope believed what she did was important, and not just the supernatural cases, but the normal ones, too. People, mostly women, came to Penelope who were afraid to go to the police, or even to other private detectives. Her grandmother disapproved because she worried for Penelope's safety, not because she thought Penelope's job was a waste.

"Although you weren't always such a good judge of things," her grandmother continued, chuckling.

"What do you mean?" Penelope asked.

"Bertram Brown used to follow you around like a lost puppy

dog when you two were in high school," she held up a finger, "but you would barely give him the time of day."

Penelope shook her head. "I don't remember that."

Her grandmother looked at her like she'd just said she preferred store-bought pie crust. "You had your head in the clouds all the time. It was obvious to everyone else he had a liking for you."

Penelope thought back to those years, to the interactions she'd had with Bertram in high school, trying to figure out what she'd missed. Could she have been that oblivious? "That can't be right. Bertram? Really?"

All the things Patrick Wheeler said when he invaded her home disguised as Bertram came to mind. Maybe he didn't make it all up. Maybe when the daemon got inside Bertram it saw his secrets and told them to Patrick. Penelope shuddered at the idea.

"Have you talked to Bertram recently?" her grandmother asked. "You used to be such good friends. I'm happy you two were able to reconnect. I just wish it was under better circumstances."

Penelope weighed lying, but given the way the conversation was going, thought better of it. "I talked to him just a few days ago. He seems okay."

On the other hand, a little fibbing might be in order.

Her grandmother frowned. "That's just a nasty business all around. Those poor men who were killed all worked for the Browns, you know. Someone's out to get that family."

Penelope stared across the table. It wasn't a closely held secret that all the men murdered by Patrick Wheeler were Brown employees, but at the same time it wasn't a fact shared widely in the news. Her grandmother would have had to do some more-than-casual digging to find out that information. It seemed Edith Drake was still able to surprise her granddaughter.

"Is there a reason someone might be out to get them?"

Reverend Lowell Purdue said the Browns' good fortune at times seemed improbable, and people who crossed them had a habit of coming to bad ends. Roy Arnold. Patrick Wheeler. Was it so far-fetched someone *else* could be set on revenge against the Browns? Someone who conspired with the others? Penelope didn't like where her thoughts were taking her.

"Well, I don't like to repeat idle gossip, but you don't get to be successful like that without stepping on a few people. I've heard stories. You know I'm not Ephraim Brown's biggest fan, but he's an absolute angel compared to his father. That man was a piece of work. And don't even get me started on Ephraim's grandfather. They're both dead and buried, though. I'm not sure why anyone would go after Ephraim for something *they* did."

Penelope asked herself that question, too. But magic was one topic she knew far more about than her grandmother. Ephraim wasn't as innocent as he made himself out to be, and neither was her father. She couldn't shake the notion that somehow everything was tied to whatever happened in the woods outside Columbia all those years ago, and the only people who could tell her the truth were gone.

———

Zed didn't know what to expect when he walked into the tiny McGovern for President office. It was barely big enough to fit the furniture—a folding table, two folding chairs, an old leather couch, and a red and orange recliner. Campaign signs took up most of the rest of the space.

That afternoon, three people had also managed to cram themselves into the office, two men and a woman. They all looked up at Zed in unison as soon as he entered. He seemed to have interrupted some heated debate between the two men, one of whom was perched on the arm of the couch while the other sat cross-legged at the opposite end. The woman sat in one of the folding chairs at the table, stuffing envelopes.

"Can I help you?" the man balanced on the arm of the couch asked.

He had shaggy black hair and thick-rimmed black glasses. He was probably younger than Zed. They were all probably younger.

"I'm looking for Jake Dempsey," Zed said. "I thought he might be here."

"He had to step out for a minute," the man replied. "He should be back soon." He gestured to the recliner near the door. "You're welcome to wait if you want."

Zed nodded and took a seat. "Sure."

The two men continued their debate, though a little more subdued. They were arguing about the Watergate scandal. Zed had read a few stories in the newspaper about possible links between the Nixon Administration and the break-in at the Democratic National Headquarters, but he didn't know what would come of it, if anything. As the minutes passed, Shaggy Hair and Glasses got more and more animated, jabbing fingers in every direction and declaring at one point that the President needed to be thrown in jail. The other man, a red-head with a line of freckles across the bridge of his nose, accused him of jumping to conclusions.

The woman seemed oblivious as she took pamphlets off a stack, carefully folded each in thirds, and stuffed them into the envelopes in front of her. Zed caught her eye.

"Are those guys always like this?" he asked.

She twisted her mouth into a wry grin. "Most of the time. Usually it's worse. I'm Linda, by the way."

He saluted. "Zed."

She waved a hand over the pamphlets. "We've got plenty of reading material for you if you're looking for something to pass the time."

Zed shook his head. "No thanks."

"Have you thought about who you're going to vote for in November?"

He laughed and immediately regretted it.

Linda's smile melted. "What's so funny?"

"Nothing. Sorry. I wasn't making fun. It's just, so many people pin so much hope on who the President is, but there are a lot of things even the President can't fix."

"There are a lot of things he *can* fix, though," Linda replied, "like this stupid war. McGovern's promised to get us out of Vietnam entirely. So many of our boys have died, and for what? Don't you think it's time to bring all the soldiers home?"

Tears threatened to spill over onto her cheeks, and the grief radiated off of her so intensely it physically pained Zed. She'd lost someone close to her in some nameless jungle half a world away. He agreed about the Vietnam War, but as horrible as the war was, some things were even more terrifying. He doubted very much McGovern knew how to banish a higher-level demon back to Hell. He smiled weakly and picked up a pamphlet. Linda tucked a piece of her long, straight black hair behind one ear and went back to stuffing envelopes, but Zed spied her looking at him more than once.

After a few more minutes, the door opened, and a shadow appeared over his reading material. He glanced up to see Jake standing there, but he wasn't looking at Zed.

Instead, he glared at the two men. "Hey, Allen, Jeff, aren't you supposed to be helping Linda stuff envelopes?"

The two men both sighed loudly as they reluctantly gave up their places on the couch to join Linda, who cheerfully handed each a stack of envelopes to seal and stamp.

Only then did Jake turn his attention to Zed. "Want to talk outside?"

"Your friends seem nice," Zed said once they were out of earshot of everyone else.

Jake still wasn't smiling. "What are you doing here?"

Anger and fear. The last two emotions Zed expected. "I ... I needed to talk to you."

"No one is supposed to know about you," said Jake through a clenched jaw.

So that's what this was about. "You don't have to tell people the truth. You could just introduce me as your friend. I'm not going to say anything. I promise."

Jake bit his lower lip. "Are you saying we're more than friends?"

"I wouldn't have ..." Zed glanced through the window of the campaign office just to make sure Linda, Allen, and Jeff were still busy stuffing envelopes. "I wouldn't have done what I did in the bookstore if I didn't want to be more than just friends."

Jake sighed. The anger subsided, but the fear remained. "You're right. I'm sorry. It's just that this is new territory for me, not just with ... what's going on between us, but with my 'medical condition,' we'll call it. I've only shared the first secret about myself with a few other people. I've never shared the second one. I'm trying, but it's hard."

Zed wanted more than anything to reach out and put a hand on Jake's shoulder, but he stopped himself. "Look, I get it, but you can trust me. Okay?"

Jake took in a deep breath and nodded.

"Your 'medical condition' is what I came to talk to you about, though," Zed continued. "I came home this morning from my shift at the radio station and collapsed into bed like I normally do. Usually I'm so tired I go right to sleep, and I don't remember my dreams. Today I did. I was there again, in the woods, wherever we were the other times. You didn't happen to have any weird dreams last night, did you?"

The look on Jake's face told Zed the answer to his question. "Yeah, I had another vision this morning. Full-body spasms. Banged my knee pretty good. Woke up on the bathroom floor."

Again, all Zed wanted to do was touch Jake, to wrap his arms around him and cradle his head on his shoulder. He shoved his hands in his pockets. "You all right?"

Jake shrugged. "I'm fine. I've been hurt worse. What did you see?"

"Lots of trees. Gravestones. Demonic shadows. And something else I hadn't seen before. A sign. It said—"

"Happiness," Jake finished.

"So, you saw it, too."

"Yeah, but I still don't understand what it means."

"I'm beginning to, and I don't like it. I have to find out where this graveyard is."

Jake cocked an eyebrow. "You mean *we*. Wherever it is, we're both there."

Zed absentmindedly twisted his amethyst ring around his finger. "I've been thinking about that. Maybe we try to change the future. You can't protect yourself from the things we've seen. I don't want you to get hurt."

Jake crossed his arms. "And what makes you think you're going to be okay?"

"I don't, but I'm more experienced in dealing with this stuff."

"You don't really have a choice here."

Zed shook his head. "I can't put you in danger like that."

"That's not what I mean, Zed." Jake pressed his palms together. "Please listen to me. I've been dealing with this most of my life. No matter what you try to do, what we both saw *is* going to happen. I can't stop it, and neither can you."

Zed understood. He almost believed Jake, but what good was he if he couldn't protect the ones he cared about? "I still have to try."

Jake threw up his hands. "Suit yourself, but don't be surprised when I say I told you so."

He stepped past Zed.

"Where are you going?" asked Zed.

"Back to work," Jake answered as he kept walking. "Someone's got to save Linda from Allen and Jeff."

"I'm just doing what I think is right," Zed called after him.

Jake paused and turned. "I know. I think you're wrong."

———

"I need to tell you something," Zed said as he threw himself down in the chair opposite Penelope's desk, "and I need you to trust me and not ask a lot of questions, okay?"

Penelope smirked. "So a normal Thursday around here then."

Zed frowned. "I'm serious."

Penelope did her best to reign in her facial expressions. "Okay, what is it?"

"I think I know where Ephraim is. I mean, I don't exactly know where, but you remember the graveyard I told you I was having dreams about? Where I was being chased by daemons? Find that graveyard, and I think we'll find Ephraim. It's old and neglected, and based on the grave markers, it could be a cemetery meant for black families. I think it might be somewhere in the Low Country."

"Any particular reason you can think of why you're getting these dreams now?" Penelope asked. "I can think of a couple of cases where that trick would have been helpful."

Zed's gaze went to the floor. "You promised not to ask questions."

Penelope regarded him for a moment. Was he afraid? She probably would be, too, in the same situation. "Okay, fine. Just one more question. Why do you think this graveyard is in the Low Country?"

"The woods around it don't look like the woods here," he replied. "I remember there being palmetto trees, for one."

Her father's reassuring knocks still hadn't returned, but Penelope could almost hear them in her head, rapping off replies to her silent questions as she worked through what Zed was telling her. "You know, palmetto trees don't grow just in the Low Country. They grow in Columbia, too, because of the sandy soil. If this is all tied to what happened in college with Ephraim and my dad, then I'll bet you this graveyard is there."

Zed shook his head. "Still, that's a lot of ground to cover. And as neglected as this graveyard looked, it might have been forgotten completely. How would we find it if that's the case? Unless ..."

"Unless what?"

Zed lowered his voice, almost to a whisper. "Happiness."

Penelope's blood ran cold. *Happiness* was the word the Reverend Lowell Purdue heard in his nightmare vision of Patrick Wheeler. "What are you talking about?"

"I saw the word on a sign in my last dream. It must mean something. There's no way it doesn't, right?"

"I think it means everything." Penelope jumped out of her chair and beckoned for Zed to follow her. "Come on. We don't have a lot of time."

"Where are we going?" Zed asked.

Penelope was already headed for the door. "To see a friend of my father."

———

Zed wasn't exactly sure what he expected. The owner of an occult shop maybe. Or a psychic who did readings for people out of her living room. When they parked behind a classroom building on the Furman University campus, Zed shot Penelope a puzzled look. A few minutes later he found himself in a cramped office, face to face with a small woman wearing large, round glasses, her long gray hair plaited in a braid. The brass nameplate on the door said "Dr. Evelyn Boyd."

"I haven't seen you since your father's funeral, Penelope," said the professor. "I hope you're doing okay."

Penelope nodded. "I'm doing fine."

"Well, good. I'm glad to hear it. So, what brings you here today? I assume this is more than just a social call." The professor eyed Zed, who leaned on the wall next to the door, trying to casually hide his discomfort over the number of magically charged artifacts cluttering the space.

Penelope hesitated before she replied. "I know you helped my father in the past with some of his cases."

Penelope was being cautious, unsure how much Professor Boyd knew about the kinds of cases her father had handled, but among the notebooks and papers strewn on her desk, Zed noticed a working *gris-gris* bag. He also spotted an earthenware pot like the ones he'd seen in houses up in the mountains, meant to contain water from the last snow of the season, and a twist of dried tobacco leaves bound with a white string. Zed was pretty confident Professor Boyd understood more about the unseen world than most, and she knew exactly what Jonathan Drake's cases involved.

The professor chuckled. "Your father certainly did make some unusual requests over the years, but then again, there was a reason he had a … certain reputation. I have it on good authority you've followed in his footsteps."

Penelope's face turned red. "You could say that."

Professor Boyd was a folklorist, specializing in the folklore of the American South. Judging by the small arsenal at her disposal, as well as the titles of the books on the shelf behind her desk, she was well prepared for anything Penelope's father could have thrown at her.

"So, what strange question can I answer for you today?" she asked.

Penelope glanced at Zed. "We're looking for a graveyard near Columbia, probably one for black families, possibly abandoned. I know it's not a lot to go on, but there might be a sign or some-thing with the word *happiness* on it. You wouldn't know about such a place, would you?"

Professor Boyd scrunched her nose and tilted her head, then stood and pulled a book down from her bookshelf. "Are you plan-ning on going legend tripping?"

Penelope frowned. "Legend tripping?"

"A visit to a place where some tragic, horrific, or supernatural event supposedly happened," Zed said, "usually at night, usually by a group of young people wanting to get all hot and bothered."

Penelope twisted her mouth into a wry grin. "You mean like college students."

"Exactly. You don't want to know the number of students who've gotten in trouble for trespassing over the years." The professor opened the book and began thumbing through it. "Graveyards especially. Seems it never occurs to anyone that most cemeteries are on private property."

Penelope leaned forward, craning her neck for a better look at the book. "So, you think you know where this graveyard is?"

Professor Boyd nodded and pointed to a picture in the book. A wrought-iron sign half covered in vines stood above a broken gate. It said, "Happiness Community Cemetery." Zed stiffened and hoped the professor didn't see his reaction.

"Happiness was the name of a community founded by freed slaves after the end of the Civil War," she explained. "It's abandoned now, and it's hard to find, on purpose. For decades there have been ghost sightings in the area, but they bulldozed over the road leading to the community after a number of serious accidents put some curious legend trippers in the hospital."

"Why was it abandoned?" asked Penelope.

"A curse if the stories are to be believed," replied Professor Boyd. "One of the members of the community was a root worker originally from the Sea Islands just below Charleston. According to the stories, her daughter was assaulted and killed. She accused one of her neighbor's sons, but the neighbor was well-liked, so no one believed her. So, on a night without any moon, she took justice into her own hands. She walked into the center of the graveyard and cursed them all, sealing the hex with her own blood."

Zed grunted. "A blood curse. That's serious. I'm afraid to ask what it was."

The professor eyed Zed again, suspicious, and curious. "She declared no one in Happiness would ever find their rest as long as her daughter's killer went unpunished. And they didn't. Anytime someone died, their ghost came back to haunt their living relatives. The more people died, the more ghosts, until the town became uninhabitable. Everyone who could, moved away. After the last resident died, nature reclaimed Happiness. A lot of the buildings are still there, but they're falling apart. That's how people get hurt, going into places that aren't safe. Of course, afterward they say something lured them in, or pushed them, or tripped them."

There were other photographs, of the cemetery, of some of the falling-down buildings, including a church. If Zed wasn't mistaken, someone stood in the doorway of the church, though the front of the building was in shadow, and it was hard to tell. The figure was only halfway there—if there at all—fading out just below the waist.

Penelope caught her breath. She saw it, too. "If, hypothetically, one were to want to visit Happiness, how would one get there?"

"It's just north of the city, off Highway 321, near the intersection with Cedar Creek Road. Like I said, it's hard to find, but you should still be able to see the remnants of the old road if you look hard enough."

"Thank you. That helps a lot." Penelope stood. "I'm sure you're busy. We won't keep you any longer."

"You're very welcome. I'm glad to help. Any time." Professor Boyd closed the book and put it back in its place on the shelf. "If, hypothetically, one were to go looking for Happiness, though, I'd recommend waiting until tomorrow. If you leave now you won't get there until after sunset, and it's easy to get lost in the dark."

Zed nodded. "We'll be sure to heed that advice. Hypothetically."

Penelope threw him a sidelong glance. She probably would have elbowed him if the professor hadn't held up a hand.

"Wait, one more thing before you go."

Penelope turned her attention back to Professor Boyd. "What is it?"

"It's interesting you should stop by now. I had a visit from a police detective yesterday. He wanted to know about some of the cases I helped your father with while he was on the police force."

Penelope glanced at Zed again, this time with a wary look. "Really? What did you tell him?"

The professor shrugged. "I told him what I remembered. I mostly helped your father build criminal profiles. Even though I'm not a psychologist, a great deal of my work is based on how people think about the world around them. He seemed satisfied with that answer. He politely thanked me for my time, and then left." She scanned her desk and picked up a card. "Here, he gave me his card."

Zed read it over Penelope's shoulder.

Detective James Everett

"What's Detective Everett doing asking questions about your father's old cases?" Zed asked once they were back in Penelope's Lincoln.

"I don't know," Penelope replied as she started up the car and threw it in reverse, "but we can't deal with that right now. We've got other things to worry about."

"True. This graveyard sounds like a perfect place to summon a high-level demon. The boundary has to be pretty thin there, what with all the ghosts."

"If you believe the stories."

Zed looked at Penelope in surprise. "You don't?"

"Sometimes stories are just stories, Zed."

"You saw the ghost in the picture, too, Penelope."

"But that still doesn't mean the story Professor Boyd told was true."

"There has to be a reason your father and Ephraim went there in the first place."

Penelope gripped the steering wheel until her knuckles turned white. "I know that."

"Then what's the problem?" Zed persisted.

Penelope sighed and let her shoulders slump. "Do you honestly think my father would actually go along with a plan to summon a demon? I won't believe it, even if he was young and reckless."

There it was. That was the reason the visit to Professor Boyd had her so upset.

"There's another possibility you might consider," Zed prodded gently.

"What would that be?" She wasn't bothering to hide the annoyance in her voice.

"Maybe he was only pretending to go along with it. Maybe he knew how dangerous it was to be summoning a demon like that, and he went there that night to stop it."

She snorted. "That's insane. He could have gotten himself killed."

Zed wagged a finger at her. "Hey, you're the one who called him reckless."

The rest of the trip back to Penelope's office passed in silence. Zed watched outside the window as they traced their way through neighborhoods with tree-lined streets, past cozy little houses where no one worried about ghosts or demons or failing to protect the people they loved.

"Can you let Bertram know we're taking a road trip?" Penelope asked when they pulled up in front of the old converted house that served as her home and her office. "I'm going to go talk to Charles. Regroup here in an hour?"

Zed frowned. "What about what Professor Boyd said? About waiting until tomorrow?"

Penelope shook her head. "We can't afford to do that. We don't know how much time Ephraim has left, if it isn't already too late."

Zed studied her profile. Penelope was right, of course. The longer Ephraim Brown went missing, the less of a chance they had of finding him alive, but Zed could see another motive written in her tensed jaw and also hear it in her strained voice.

She was desperate to find out what happened to her father, and she'd do just about anything to get to the truth.

———

Charles turned another card over. By now he imagined the grinning man who stared back at him from the card's face was mocking him. He'd performed close to a dozen readings, using three different decks, but every time, the Nine of Cups—the Lord of Happiness—turned up. The odds of that happening by chance were close to zero.

What the card foretold, Charles had no idea, but he knew for damn sure it didn't mean he could expect any happy news in his future.

He shuffled the deck again for another reading, but before he could turn any more cards over, he heard a noise from behind the house. He glanced out the window, his gaze going immediately to the place where they had buried Patrick Wheeler, near the tree line about fifty yards from the back door.

It was the best they could do at the time, though Charles wasn't thrilled with the idea of making his back yard into a private cemetery for dark magicians. Patrick wasn't coming back—not in body and not in spirit. He had made sure of that. Still, the shadows around the burial place seemed a little bit darker than they should have been, taking the shape of a man covered in a burial shroud. He blinked, and the illusion was gone.

Charles turned his attention to the damaged book on his work table. He took a deep breath in an effort to slow his racing heartbeat. No more Patrick Wheeler. No more Brown family. No more Lord of Happiness. No more Shrouded Man. He wanted to lose himself in the work of repairing the old book. It was the only time he ever found any peace.

He turned up the radio before he sat down. Instead of the soulful sounds of Mahalia Jackson or another gospel singer, though, Dizzy Gillespie's trumpet blared from the speakers as Charles picked up his X-Acto knife.

A knock on the back door immediately derailed his plans. Swearing under his breath, he went to answer and swung open the door to reveal Penelope standing on his back steps.

"Hi, Charles," she said. "You busy?"

Charles glanced back over his shoulder at his work table and the half-dismantled book lying among his tools. "A little."

Penelope chewed on her lower lip. "Sorry, but this is kind of important. Can I come in?"

Sighing, Charles stepped aside.

"I knocked on the front door, but you didn't answer," Penelope said as she entered. "I heard music coming from around the back of the house, so I figured you'd be back here." She pointed to the radio. "That's not Mahalia Jackson."

"No, it isn't."

She narrowed her eyes. "It's just, you don't normally listen to—"

"Don't assume you know everything about me," Charles snapped. "You said it was important. What's going on?"

A hurt expression crossed her face, but vanished as quickly as it appeared. "Ephraim Brown is missing. He disappeared two days ago."

"You want me to help find him? You got a lock of his hair for me?"

"Actually, we think we know where he is. Have you ever heard of a place called Happiness?"

Charles' blood froze. "Is that supposed to be a joke?"

"No, it's a real place. Or it used to be. It's an abandoned community near Columbia, founded by freed slaves." She waved a hand. "It's really a long story. I can explain all of it on the way."

Charles crossed his arms. His feet remained where they were. "Who says I'm going anywhere?"

Penelope frowned. "We need you, Charles."

"You always need me."

She pursed her lips. "Look, I get it. We've asked a lot of you lately, more than we probably should have. But we don't have a prayer of stopping whatever is going on without you."

"You don't have a prayer of stopping it with me either."

"What are you saying?"

"I'm saying I don't have the first clue about that pentagram you gave me, and I'm not going to miraculously find the answer in one of my books this time. If I don't know what it is, I don't know how to stop it. In all likelihood, Ephraim Brown is dead. Let him go."

"What if it doesn't stop with him?" she asked.

"Let them all go, the whole Brown family."

She shook her head. "They don't deserve that."

Charles stifled a laugh. "Don't they? Are they really worth sacrificing yourself, Penelope?"

"This isn't like you, Charles, to not care." Her voice trembled in frustrated anger.

"I have cared, Penelope, more than you know," he said, "but did you ever stop to think that maybe the Browns brought this on themselves? My … Margaret heard stories about them."

"But what if this goes beyond the Browns? What do we do then?"

"Find a hole to hide in," he replied.

She glared. "Fine. Do what you want. Zed and I are going regardless. We're not just going to stand by and let any more innocent people die."

"There you go using that word again."

Penelope spun on her heels to leave without saying anything else. Charles glanced down at the deck of tarot cards resting on the edge of his work table. As he watched, the entire deck skewed sideways until the top card tipped over and fell to the floor, landing face up. Once again, the Lord of Happiness leered up at Charles with his mocking grin.

"Wait," Charles called after Penelope, who paused with her hand on the doorknob to the back door. "I need to take care of some things first. You go on. I'll meet you at your place in a little bit."

Penelope smiled. "Don't be too long."

———

When Penelope arrived back at her house, she noted, with no small amount of annoyance, that she'd beaten Zed and Bertram there. She thought for sure they'd be there already. They'd wasted so much time.

Time they didn't have to begin with.

Time they needed to save Ephraim.

Time she could have used to find out the truth about her father.

As she climbed the steps to the porch a sickly-sweet smell assaulted her nose, like flowers beginning to die, but it was almost November, and the flowers were long gone. She had just put her housekey in the door when the shadow fell over it. A rough hand reached around and covered her mouth with a wet handkerchief. The sickly-sweet smell filled her nostrils.

"Don't try to struggle," he growled.

But she couldn't struggle even if she wanted to. He was bigger than she was, and his arms held her like a vise. She recognized his voice from the threatening phone call she'd gotten a few months back, after a gold Ford tried to run her car off the road and someone threw a brick through her window. She wondered briefly if this was the same man she'd caught staring at her at church the day she'd visited her grandmother, but she didn't have much time to consider the possibility. Her head became fuzzy. It got harder and harder to think. Black dots formed at the edges of her vision, multiplying and growing until everything went dark.

———

Zed didn't see Bertram's red Camaro in front of his apartment building when he pulled up. That was going to put a kink in Penelope's plans. Bertram hadn't told Zed he was going out. Then again, Bertram was a grown man and didn't need Zed's permission to leave the apartment.

When Zed walked through his front door, he didn't find the apartment empty, though. Jake sat on his sofa, next to the pillow and folded-up blanket Bertram had been using to crash there.

"Jake?" Zed said. "How did you get in?"

"Through the door," Jake replied.

"Through the *locked* door? Don't tell me Bertram left it unlocked. I mean, granted he's had a lot on his mind, but I did give him a key."

"Bertram? Is that his name?" Jake pointed to the pillow and blanket on the sofa. "Is that who's been staying here with you?"

Zed didn't like the strange tone in Jake's voice. "Well, yeah. I'm just letting him crash here for a few days. He's … uh … going through some things."

"Are you sure that's all there is?"

"What more would there be?"

Jake stood. "What are you hiding, Zed? Why didn't you tell me?"

"What? You mean you think me and Bertram … Oh, trust me that would never happen, for so, so many reasons. What's wrong, Jake? Are you okay?"

"I'm fine," he replied, just a little too calmly.

Zed saw the flash of metal in Jake's hand almost too late. The knife came inches from slashing Zed's throat, but fortunately he was faster than Jake and sidestepped the attack. Jake spun around to face him again, clumsily lunging with the knife.

Zed did his best to stay out of reach in the small room. "Jake, what the fuck do you think you're doing?"

Jake didn't reply. He instead hurled himself at Zed again. Zed dodged the knife blade, pushing off of Jake and sending him headlong into the wall. Jake let out an animal cry of frustration.

"What's wrong with you? Stop! I don't want to hurt you."

While backing up, Zed stumbled over his recliner. Jake pounced on top of him, bringing the knife down in a deadly arc. Zed clutched Jake's forearm with both hands, stopping the knife's descent, but Jake was strong, stronger than he should have been. An unnatural green light flashed in his eyes, and for just a moment his shadow moved slightly out of sync with the rest of him.

A daemon. Jake was possessed by a daemon.

"Get out!" Zed screamed. "Get out of him now."

He threw all the willpower he could into the charm bracelet Charles had made for him and tried to channel some of his own magic as well, raw though it was. Blue and violet energy crackled around his arm, and the next thing he knew, Jake went flying backward across the room. He hit the wall and dropped the knife from his hand. Jake's body slumped to the floor while a dark, shadowy form rose up, taking up most of the space in the room, making it hard for Zed to breathe.

Two green points of light fixed on him, their malice impossible to escape, but Zed stood his ground. He held his arm up in front of his face, the charm bracelet encircling his wrist still sparking. He recited the Lord's Prayer and the Twenty-third Psalm and the *Vade Retro Satana* at the top of his lungs. The thing shrieked and moaned, but when Zed lowered his arm again, it was gone.

Zed rushed over to Jake, relieved to find him still breathing. Zed tried to rouse him. Jake groaned and his eyes fluttered, but Zed couldn't wake him up. He took the charm bracelet off his wrist and put it on Jake's.

Still nothing.

Zed paced the floor for a couple of minutes trying to figure out what to do. There was no way he was going to take Jake along with them to find Happiness, not if the visions were true and they were all headed into a forest teeming with daemons. Zed would never forgive himself if anything happened to Jake.

But he also couldn't leave Jake alone in the state he was in.

Who to leave him with was the problem. Jake had never exactly introduced him to any family or friends, not that Zed really blamed him. Their relationship could easily put both of them in harm's way, as Jake had reminded him. And then it dawned on him that he *did* know a few of Jake's friends. He picked up the phone and dialed the Greenville headquarters of McGovern for President.

"Hi, Linda, thank God you're the one who answered the phone," he said. "This is Zed McKay. We met yesterday. I'm Jake's friend. Listen, Jake's … sick, and I need someone to look after him. I can't do it because I have to go out of town. Last minute trip. Dealing with an emergency of my own. … No, no, he doesn't need to go to the hospital. He just needs someone to stay with him until he sleeps it off. … Thanks, Linda, you're a lifesaver. Let me give you my address."

———

When Penelope opened her eyes, she found herself in a dark room. A thin line of light traced the edges of heavy curtains drawn over a large window. The bright white sliver was just enough for Penelope to make out the other shapes in the room. A bed. A desk. A dresser. A television.

She was in a motel somewhere.

One by one, her other senses returned. The muffled sounds of a television vibrated through the wall from the next room over, the smell of stale cigarettes and musky cologne assaulted her nose, and a dull ache rose from her arms and legs. She tried to stand, but found she couldn't. Only then did she realize she was tied to a chair, with her wrists bound together behind her back. Someone had ripped up the bed sheets to use as rope.

Fortunately, she still had some range of motion in her arms, just enough to work at the knots at her wrists. Her father had insisted on teaching her a number of useful life skills, like how to change a flat tire, how to make a deposit at the bank, how to pick a lock with a hairpin, and how to get out of being tied up. It took about twenty minutes to work one of the knots halfway free, but she stopped when a metallic click drew her attention to the motel room door. Someone put a key in the lock.

The door opened, and light flooded into the room, blinding Penelope for a moment. When her eyes adjusted, she saw an older man with black, thinning hair standing in the doorway. In his hand he held a brown paper bag. He wore a flannel shirt and a pair of jeans, and at least a day's worth of stubble covered his face, but he glared at her the same way he had that Sunday when she met his gaze from across the church sanctuary. Then, he was clean-shaven and in a three-piece suit. She couldn't say she was surprised. If she had to guess, he'd left a gold Ford parked just outside.

When he saw her, his lips spread in an unpleasant smile. "Oh, good. You're up."

"Who are you?" Penelope asked, continuing to work at the knots around her wrists.

He feigned a hurt expression as he shut the door, plunging the room into near darkness again. "You know who I am, Miss Drake. You and your little lackey took enough pictures of me, and then you handed them over to that bitch."

Of course. How could she forget? "Ronald Gaines."

He turned on a lamp. The nasty grin returned, even more unsettling with his features thrown into sharp relief by the lamp-light. "That's me."

Penelope had been hired by his wife Joyce to spy on him because she suspected he was seeing another woman. As it turned out, Mrs. Gaines was right.

His mouth curled into a snarl. "She took away everything I had because of you. I lost my house. I lost all my money. My kids won't look me in the eye. My former friends cross the street to avoid me. You destroyed my life."

She refused to look away as he leered at her. "I think maybe you did that when you decided to have an affair."

He spun around and raised his arm. Penelope braced herself for the back of his hand across her face, but the blow never came.

"You don't know anything about me," he yelled, angry tears welling in his eyes. "You don't know anything about my life. All you did was sit across the street and take pictures of something that was none of your business. Who are you to pass judgment on me?"

"I was just doing my job," she said quietly.

"No, you don't get to use that excuse." He set the bag he had brought with him on the desk next to the door and pulled out a gun. "I'm going to make sure you pay for what you've done."

He retrieved the magazine from the bag. His hands shook as he tried to load it into the gun, and it took him several attempts. It was obvious to Penelope he'd never held a firearm before.

She just needed to keep him talking.

"You don't have to do this."

"What choice do I have?" he asked as he looked down at the loaded gun in his hand.

"Seems to me you've got a lot of choices. You could try to put your life back together."

He let out a dry, bitter laugh. "Why? I'm a middle-aged insurance salesman. Some life there. I come home from work, heat up a TV dinner, and fall asleep to the eleven o'clock news. Then the next day I get up and do it all over again."

Just a little bit longer. "You can't possibly think you'll get away with it. You're not even wearing gloves. And you don't have a silencer. Everyone will hear the gunshot."

"Who said anything about getting away? This is going to be all over the news for months. Every time she turns on the television, she's going to have to deal with me."

The last knot slipped from her wrists, and suddenly Penelope's hands were free. For the time being, though, she held the makeshift rope behind her back.

"Now it's not going to do any good for you to try to spoil things," he continued. "No more talking for you."

He put the gun down and picked up the ruined bedsheet, which lay in a heap on the floor at the foot of the bed. He tore off another strip and came toward her, but as soon as he leaned down to tie it over her mouth, she grabbed his arm with both hands and bit down as hard as she could, enough to break the skin. He shrieked and jerked away.

"What the hell is wrong with you?" he screamed as he surveyed the bloody set of teeth marks on his forearm.

She shook her head. "Nothing. I'm just trying not to get shot."

She really didn't have much of a plan, though. Her legs were still tied to the chair, and she didn't think she could untie herself before Gaines reached the gun. So, she did the only thing she could think to do. She pitched forward onto her feet and threw herself at him, chair and all. Together, they toppled to the floor, knocking the lamp off the desk. The lightbulb shattered with a pop, and the darkness returned. Her weight combined with the chair pinned Gaines to the ground while she struggled to work her legs free.

"Get off me, you crazy bitch!" Gaines yelled.

He flailed his arms and legs until he managed to shove her off. He scrambled up from the floor and made a reach for the gun, but Penelope hooked an arm around his leg, and he went down hard, banging his head against the desk. While he was still dazed, she slipped out of the knots around her ankles, and before he could get back to his feet, she slammed the chair down on top of him. Then she dashed for the door. She threw it open and ran out into the dazzling light of the motel parking lot. She had no idea where she was, but she didn't stop.

She was halfway across the parking lot when the gunshot rang out. She threw herself to the ground, expecting another, but no second shot came. She glanced back over her shoulder. Ronald Gaines leaned against the frame of the open motel room door. A giant red hole marred one temple. The gun fell from his hand, and he crumpled to the ground.

Penelope jumped to her feet and kept running.

———

Zed was still standing outside his apartment building when Bertram's red Camaro pulled up. He had just seen Linda off with a still half-conscious Jake stuffed into the passenger seat of her VW. She'd given them both a lot of odd looks, especially after Jake started mumbling in something that sounded like Latin, but she promised she'd take Jake back to his apartment and stay with him there. The charm bracelet would keep them safe, Zed hoped.

"Everything okay?" Bertram asked as he climbed out of his car.

"Not exactly," Zed replied. "Where were you?"

"I was just driving around, doing some thinking, trying to clear my head." Bertram glanced down at his shoes. He wanted to say more, Zed could tell. He was just looking for the words. "Those books, you said Bobby Parker's sister left them with you? I was looking through some of them. They … look a lot like books my dad has. I never knew what they really were. It's just a weird place to be in, you know, having to rethink your whole life."

Zed knew exactly what he was talking about.

Bertram sighed. "So, anyway, what did I miss?"

Zed pasted on a crooked grin. "Where do I start? For one, we're going on a road trip."

———

Penelope didn't answer the door when Zed and Bertram finally made it to her house, even though her car was parked outside.

"Maybe she's gone somewhere with Charles to get something he thinks we might need," Bertram said.

Zed shot him a dubious look. "You don't really believe that."

Bertram shook his head. "No, I don't."

About that time Charles pulled up in his wreck of a truck. Alone. Now Zed knew something was really wrong. He and Bertram waited for Charles to join them on the porch.

"She left my place a couple of hours ago," Charles said after they told him Penelope wasn't answering the door.

"Why didn't you come back with her?" Zed asked, his tone a little more accusatory than he intended.

"I had some things to take care of," Charles replied with ice in his voice.

Zed put his hands on his hips. "Well, where the hell is she?"

Bertram stared at the door. "She could be in there, unable to answer."

Zed and Charles looked at him, and then each other.

"Only one way to find out, I guess." Zed backed up, preparing to kick the door in.

Before he could, though, someone called his name. They all turned to see a black and yellow checked taxi parked in front of the house. Penelope was climbing out of the back seat. The look on her face told him something really wasn't right.

Zed rushed down the steps and over to her. "Penelope, what happened?"

She didn't say anything. She just collapsed against him, wrapping her arms around his midsection and burying her face in his chest. He hugged her as her whole body convulsed in sobs.

"What happened, Penelope?" he repeated.

She still didn't answer, so he stood, quietly embracing her, until she stopped crying. Finally, she took a deep breath and let go of him, reaching up to wipe the tears away from her cheeks. "I'll tell you on the way." She looked over her shoulder at the taxi, still waiting. "Could ... could you pay the cab driver? I don't have my purse."

Zed was going to argue with her about leaving right then, about how they could wait until the morning to confront whatever was waiting for them in Happiness, South Carolina, but he couldn't. They were out of time. They had to go. They had to deal with it, for Ephraim, for Jake, for all of them. He reached into his back pocket for his wallet.

———

When Ephraim opened his eyes, he was ten years old again, hiding underneath the dining room table in his grandparents' house. Everything was quiet, except for the ticking of the grandfather clock in the entryway. He didn't know why he was hiding, alone in the darkened house, only that he needed to. He hugged his knees and tried to push down the rising panic, but that was a losing battle.

Suddenly the grandfather clock rang out the hour. The shadows grew darker, and from inside the walls came sounds of scratching and shuffling, as if something was trying to break through. The front door opened, and heavy boots made the hardwood floors shake. Ephraim scrambled out from under the table between the chairs and ran upstairs to his grandparents' bedroom.

A giant four-poster bed dominated the center of the room. He ducked behind it, up against the wall, away from the door, but there was no use trying to hide. The door opened. Ephraim put his hands over his head in an effort to get as small as he could, but a rough hand grabbed him by his shirt collar and yanked him up. Soon he was looking into the angry face of his father.

"Boy, what are you doing up here?" he snarled. "You know you can't hide from me."

Before Ephraim could answer, the scene dissolved. His father, the four-poster bed, the house, it all vanished, replaced by overgrown gravestones in the middle of the woods and the sounds of the night.

Ephraim remembered. All of it.

He sat cross-legged on the cold ground. Jonathan Drake sat to his left, Geoffrey Wheeler to his right. Torchlight threw dancing shadows over the faces of Bradley James and Edward McDowell who sat facing him. Together the five of them formed a circle, or—although it didn't occur to Ephraim at the time—the points of a star. Jude Hall, the sixth member of their delinquent band, stood in the center, holding the torch.

They had trekked through the woods to the abandoned grave-yard for a ritual, an initiation. If they got caught sneaking out of their dormitory, they'd all get expelled, but it would be worth the risk if everything went well that night—or so Ephraim and the others had been told. Pass the test, and everything they ever wanted would be theirs.

Except it was all a lie.

Jonathan figured out the truth. Ephraim's first instinct when Jonathan told him was to back out and refuse to go, but Jonathan argued they'd just find others to take their places. He convinced Ephraim they had to go along so they could stop the ritual. Now Ephraim was rethinking that plan.

Jude held the torch high over his head and began to chant. On the ground around his feet glowing lines flared to life, radiating outward toward each of them, connecting them all in a giant pentagram. Strange symbols wove around the lines. They hurt to look at. Ephraim and Jonathan played along when the others let out muted gasps and traded nervous glances. No one dared move from their spot, though.

Jude's chanting grew louder, and the dark figures Ephraim had seen before emerged from behind the gravestones. Made of pure darkness, they oozed their way toward the pentagram, until they formed a wall of shadows around the group. Genuine panic spread around the circle, but still none of them moved. It was all part of the test surely. If they got up and ran, they failed.

A giant raven landed next to Jude, bigger than any Ephraim had ever seen. Silently, it walked around the circle staring at each of them in turn. When it turned one beady, black eye toward Ephraim, he felt all his secrets laid bare. The black disc of its eye grew, expanding until the empty nothingness blotted out the fire-light. It drew Ephraim in, enticing him to come closer, to reach out to it and be lost forever. No more worries. No more cares. No more pain. Just ... nothing.

The giant bird cawed, and Ephraim blinked, the illusion shat-tered. The raven spread its wings, and with a single flap, it perched on Jude's shoulder. He didn't even seem to notice. His eyes were closed. His mouth still moved, but his words were barely audible.

Ephraim glanced at Jonathan, who gave a subtle nod. Ephraim removed a rosary from his pocket. A silver cross dangled from the string of beads.

"*Vade retro, Satana,*" he cried.

Step back, Satan.

Ephraim's performance was mostly a distraction, though. They needed something a little more primeval than a Latin rite to stop Jude. While Ephraim continued to recite the Prayer of Saint Benedict, Jonathan took out a pocket knife. He slashed the palm of his hand and made a fist, squeezing until the blood seeped through his fingers.

As soon as the drops of blood touched the ground, the whole forest screamed. The wind whipped up around them and blew out the torch in Jude's hand. The black shapes that had been standing sentry wailed and moaned and lashed out with clawed hands, tentacles and mouths full of sharp teeth, but they stopped short of crossing the pentagram's perimeter.

Jude had stopped chanting. Instead, he stood facing Ephraim and Jonathan, his hair wild, his face contorted in rage. In that moment, the giant raven swooped down on Ephraim, knocking him to the ground. It tried to rip the rosary out of his hand with its claws while it pecked at his face with its beak.

Jonathan attacked the bird, stabbing it with his knife. The raven squawked and flew off. Ephraim struggled to sit up. Scratches covered his hands. Something wet and warm ran into his left eye. It stung.

Jonathan turned toward Jude. "Banish the demon back to where it came from."

"You don't have any idea what you're doing," Jude snarled. "You could have had anything you wanted."

Jonathan held out his bloody hand. "Not this way. Banish the demon, or I will."

Jude glared. "You don't know how."

He resumed his chanting. The lines of the pentagram glowed anew, and the shadow demons went back to their vigil at the pentagram's edges. At the same time, new words tumbled out of Jonathan's mouth, the same as those Jude recited, but in a different order, like a song sung in a round. It seemed as if they were going to settle into a prolonged duel, until Jonathan threw his knife at Jude. It pinwheeled through the air, and the blade stuck in Jude's arm. Jude cried out. With an infuriated roar, he pulled the knife out of his arm and tossed it aside, but he'd lost the rhythm of the incantation.

Jonathan's words overpowered him. Jude clutched the sides of his head and screamed for Jonathan to stop, but Jonathan continued, a look of determination on his face. The wind picked up again, and the shadows screeched, fleeing back to wherever they had come from. Somewhere above, the lonely call of a raven echoed.

When Jonathan stopped and the wind died, Jude lay in the middle of the broken pentagram, alive but unmoving. The others had all run away. Ephraim wanted to leave Jude there, but Jonathan said they couldn't do that. He had been their friend once. Maybe he wasn't completely responsible for his actions that night. And so they picked him up and carried him through the woods, back toward civilization.

In the days that followed, Ephraim couldn't get the raven out of his head. It spoke to him in a hoarse voice all day and all night, drowning out nearly every other thought, beckoning him to return to the darkness, to embrace the nothingness.

It would all be over.

It wouldn't hurt anymore.

When he couldn't stand the voice any longer, he told Jonathan, and Jonathan … did something to make him forget. Ever since, Ephraim had only a vague idea of what happened that night. Jonathan told him he'd just gotten drunk.

When Ephraim's eyes opened for the final time, he was still in the cemetery. He couldn't move. He could barely even feel his arms and legs. He looked up to see the branches of a tree rising above him and the coils of rope around his outstretched arms. The same rope bound his legs to the tree as well. The bark scoured his back. His mouth was dry, and his lungs were on fire. He had no idea how much time had passed.

Something stirred in the underbrush at the edge of the clearing. Ephraim barely had enough energy to turn his head. A man emerged from the trees, long gray hair in tangled knots and pale blue eyes crazed. Nearly forty years had passed, but Ephraim recognized him right away.

Jude Hall.

He rushed toward Ephraim, the blade of the knife he held gleaming in the moonlight. Ephraim could only watch as he swung his arm in a wide arc and slashed open Ephraim's throat. As the warm blood spilled out of the gash, and with it, Ephraim's life, a smile spread across his face. At least he had remembered.

————

Bertram woke with a start. He glanced around. He was in the back seat of Penelope's Lincoln. Charles sat next to him, cradling his leather satchel in his lap. Penelope sat in the front on the passenger's side. Zed drove.

"What … what happened?"

"Nothing," Charles said. "You dozed off."

Bertram glanced out the car window, but it was too dark to see anything. "Where are we?"

"We just passed Chapin," Zed answered. "Almost there."

"That is, if we can even find this place," Charles added.

"We have to find it," Penelope said. "We don't have a choice."

"I think I might be able to help with that." Bertram stared back at three pairs of skeptical eyes. "What? I'm not allowed to have weird dreams, too?"

———

Charles glanced sideways at Bertram. He'd been adamant when he told Zed to pull over, pointing to a patch of darkness by the side of the road. To Charles, it was indistinguishable from all the other patches of darkness they'd passed by in the last half hour, but Bertram insisted it was the old road to Happiness.

Zed parked the car as far off the road as he could, and they all climbed out. Each of them had a flashlight. Zed shined his into the woods. Sure enough, there was a gap in the trees, easy to overlook, but plain to see if you knew what you were looking for.

Dry leaves crunched under their feet as they made their way single-file through the forest. Zed took the lead. Charles brought up the rear. None of them had much to say. Even Zed was uncharacteristically quiet, for which Charles was grateful.

A few dozen yards from the road, the path widened and flattened out. Before too long, they came to the stone foundations of long-gone buildings, and beyond that a few structures with walls still intact, though overgrown with vegetation.

It would have been easy for Charles to imagine things in those half-collapsed buildings watching them, waiting for them, but Charles knew better. He didn't have to imagine. They were there. All the ghosts of the people of Happiness, doomed never to find rest.

Soon voices came to his ears, people talking, not in hushed whispers as he might have expected, but loud, boisterous conversations. They seemed to come from every direction. Then the music started, low at first but gradually getting louder. None of the others seemed to hear anything. As Charles looked around for the source of the noise, a flash of blue in the woods caught his eye. And then another.

Out of nowhere a trumpet blared. The strings of a bass thrummed, and a piano set down a staccato rhythm. Charles recognized the tune. It was a favorite of the jazz trio from the Blue Club. With his next step, Charles walked out of the woods near

Columbia, South Carolina, in 1972 and back in time more than fifty years, into Isaiah Jenkins' Harlem.

———

The Blue Club was hopping. Every table was full, and so was the dance floor. But no one was there for the Bill Porter Three, as good as they were. When they finished their set, a hush fell over the room as Millie Priest took the stage, stunning as ever. From the very first note she sang, she owned the place.

Charles smiled as Isaiah's memories of the months since he'd been gone filled in—lazy mornings huddled under warm blankets in bed, walks in the new-fallen snow, nights in Millie's dressing room after the club closed. There seemed to be fewer of those, though. Despite Prohibition, the Blue Club was busier than ever, and it wasn't uncommon for Charles to be busy until three or four in the morning after a packed night.

Of course, the reason for that was the speakeasy in the basement selling bootleg liquor. Charles had been cut out of that part of the business, but he knew all too well about it, especially the number of times Millie disappeared down there for private performances.

His eyes fell on Andre Lestrade at the best table in the place, watching Millie sing. Charles didn't like the smile on his face. He wasn't just enjoying Millie's beautiful voice. His grin was possessive, as if he were enjoying something from a collection he owned.

And Millie's gaze, more times than not, was on him. Charles knew she was just putting on a show, but it still bothered him.

After her set, she returned backstage. By then Andre was gone from his seat, too. On an impulse, Charles decided he needed to check on Millie. He went to her dressing room, but she didn't answer when he knocked on her door.

He went to the speakeasy next. There was a hidden door just past the stage, out of sight from the rest of the room. A secret knock and a password let special patrons in. The password changed weekly, as did the knock. Charles rapped on the door with his knuckles—three quick taps, a pause, and then another tap.

When the door cracked open, Charles whispered the password. "Azure."

The bouncer, the same one who had tried to stop Charles from seeing Millie in her dressing room on his first night at the club, let him through. A short flight of stairs led to another door and another bouncer. He opened the door for Charles, who stepped inside. This room wasn't any less packed than the room upstairs. A piano player in the corner hammered out an upbeat tune, and cigar smoke hung heavy in the air. Here, the bar was fully stocked, and the liquor flowed. Charles scanned the room. He found Millie quickly, seated at a table with Andre and his entourage. He had his arm around her. She was laughing at something someone said.

When they made eye contact across the room, though, her smile faded. She turned to Andre and whispered something in his ear. He nodded, and she stood up. She circled the room before approaching him, speaking with some of the other patrons along the way. When she reached him, she grabbed him by the arm and pulled him aside.

"What are you doing here?" she asked.

"I could ask you the same question," he snapped.

She crossed her arms. "I'm working."

Charles glanced at her empty seat at Andre's table. "Doesn't seem like you're doing any singing right now."

"That's not all of my job."

"Really? That's news to me."

Millie ran her fingers down his arm. It was as much of a display of affection as they risked, but her touch still made him tingle. "Listen, we can talk about this later. I need to get back."

He cocked an eyebrow. "And do what?"

"Andre likes me to sit with him when we have VIPs. He says it makes the room more attractive." She added in a low voice, "Nothing has happened, and nothing is going to happen."

Charles didn't get a chance to say anything else. The door flew open, and the body of the bouncer fell into the room. Over it leapt three men, all with guns drawn. They immediately started firing.

The gunshots sent the room into chaos. People shouted, trying to get out or dive for cover somewhere. The bullets missed Andre, but one of his men when sprawling across the table, an angry red bloom on his forehead. The bullets would have hit Millie had she been sitting next to him. Andre's men had their guns drawn now too, and they were returning fire.

Charles pulled Millie down behind the bar. His stomach turned in knots as he remembered the date. March 18. The day Millie was supposed to be shot and killed.

He looked at her, panic on her face as they crouched down. He had saved her before. Maybe he had just saved her again. Maybe that's why he was there.

"Can we get to the other door?" he asked as bullets shattered the glasses above the bar.

"What other door?"

Charles risked a glance around the side of the bar but ducked back when a bullet splintered off a chunk of it just next to his head. "You and I know full well there's another door for situations just like this. I'm sure Andre's used it already."

Millie shook her head. "It's clear across the room. I don't know if we can make it."

"We've got to find a way."

As he peered around the bar again, his training from Vietnam came back to him. He noted where all the shooters were. He could see a pathway through the chairs and tables. They could make it if they kept moving.

He took her hand. "Come this way. I think I can get us out of here."

She hesitated. "Are you sure?"

"Yes, just trust me. I can do it." Charles looked in time to see another one of Andre's men go down. "Come on. Let's go."

Millie pulled her hand back. "Wait, Charles."

He looked at her. "What did you call me?"

"I called you by your name."

"You called me Charles. I'm Isaiah."

She didn't say anything.

It was as if all the color drained from Charles' vision. "None of this is real."

"But it can be." Millie offered him her hand again. "We can leave here. Find somewhere else to go. Maybe Chicago. We can be together."

He shook his head. "No, it still won't be real. This has all been a set-up, in case I got hold of those books, to keep me busy, distracted."

Her expression hardened. "You don't have to do this."

"Yes, I do." He kissed her on the forehead and wiped a tear from her cheek. "I love you, Millie Priest. I've enjoyed our time together more than you will ever know, but I have other people who need me."

He stood up over the bar, and not a second later he caught a bullet in his chest. The pain was more than anything he ever imagined. As he fell backward, Millie screamed.

———

Charles woke up staring at the night sky.

"Hey, I think he's awake," someone said.

Suddenly Penelope's face appeared in his field of vision.

"Charles? Are you okay?" she asked.

He managed to push himself up into a sitting position. His head pounded. "Yeah, I think so."

Penelope crouched down beside him. "What happened?"

"I'd rather not talk about it." Penelope opened her mouth to protest, but he held up a hand. "Someday, I promise. Right now, I think we've got bigger problems. Where is this cemetery?"

Bertram offered him a hand in getting to his feet. "It shouldn't be much farther."

As Charles retrieved his satchel and his flashlight, he glanced up to see not only Penelope, Bertram, and Zed, but also two other men. They were both black, dressed in clothes from the late 1800s, and neither of them was completely there. The moonlight shone through them. One of them smiled at Charles and tipped his hat. Then they both turned around and disappeared among the trees.

Zed's heart pounded as they entered the clearing. This was the graveyard from his shared visions with Jake. There was no doubt about it. Thankfully, Jake was a hundred miles away and safe, or at least safer than he would be if he were here. As they ventured farther into the cemetery, his apprehension grew, though, wondering if he had done the right thing, if maybe Jake was needed here somehow. His thoughts were interrupted by a cry from Bertram. They had found Ephraim. He was tied to a tree, his clothes in tatters, dripping in blood.

"Dad?" Bertram ran toward the tree. "Dad, it's me."

Ephraim didn't answer.

Bertram stopped just a few feet away from him. "Dad? Oh, God."

When Zed and the others joined him, they could all see what Bertram saw. Ephraim's throat was slit open. He stared ahead with sightless eyes, an odd smile frozen on his face. The blood was already drying.

"He's gone," Bertram whispered. "We're too late."

"Did you think this was going to have a happy ending?"

The voice came from behind them. They turned around to see a man holding a knife, the blade caked in brown-red blood. A giant raven perched on his shoulder. With a flick of his wrist, all their flashlights went out, replaced by an eerie glow under their feet. The outline of the pentagram spread out across the ground, just the same as the floor of the Brown warehouse and Penelope's office, and the drawing she found among her dad's things.

"Malphas," Charles said.

"What's that?" Bertram asked.

"It's the name of the demon he's summoning. The raven is Malphas' emissary."

Bertram glanced back at the body of his father. "How bad is this demon?"

"We're fucked," Charles replied. "It won't be the end of the world tomorrow. Malphas doesn't work that way, but we're still fucked. He's a corruptor. Things will happen by increments. People will care a little less about their neighbors. It won't look bad, not at first, but eventually we won't be the good people we see ourselves as anymore. We won't be the kind-hearted heroes who stand up for what is right. We'll be the villains."

The man rolled his eyes. "A little dramatic, don't you think?"

Bertram took a step closer to Charles and the giant satchel of magical things slung over Charles' shoulder. "Is this Malphas here now?"

Charles closed his eyes. Zed had seen that expression on his face countless times, as he reached out beyond his five senses. Even Zed could feel the charge in the air, just like the moments before a thunderstorm.

"Not yet, but he's coming," Charles said when he opened his eyes again.

"Who are you?" Penelope asked the man.

He sighed. "I suppose I shouldn't be surprised your father never told you about me. He probably just wanted to forget the whole thing happened. I can't say I blame him. I'd want to forget too, but the difference between us is that he could move on with his life. I couldn't."

"Jude Hall," Bertram said.

Penelope raised an eyebrow. "Jude Hall? But you're supposed to be dead. You hanged yourself."

Jude laughed. "I *am* dead, for all intents and purposes. After tonight, though, it won't matter anymore. I'll have what want."

"Why now?" Penelope asked. "You've had forty years."

"Because I couldn't." His mouth curled up into a bitter scowl. "After what your father did to me that night, I was an invalid. I could barely move. I was bedridden for years, but then one by one, the others died, and I got better, stronger. I started making plans. I faked my death to rid myself of any obligations. On the night your father died, I knew my time had come."

Charles scanned the symbols and words arrayed around the lines of the pentagram. "You tried to summon Malphas back then, too, didn't you? Penelope's dad disrupted the spell and banished him back to the other side of the Veil, but you had to extend your own spirit out as a beacon for the demon. When everything went sideways, part of your soul must have been ripped away, and shards of it clung to everyone who was there. As the others died, those pieces came back to you."

Jude nodded. "Go on, magician, tell them the rest."

"I've studied these symbols for months, trying to pry all their secrets out," Charles continued, "but I've come up with nothing. Now things are beginning to make sense. This pentagram is a work of genius. Evil, twisted, malevolent genius, but genius all the same. It's a circle without a beginning or an end. Recite the spell one way, and you summon a demon. Recite it another way, and you call on that demon to grant you power. That's why you killed Bobby Parker and the rest. They were sacrifices."

"And ultimately so were Roy Arnold and Patrick Wheeler, once you'd gotten them to do your dirty work for you," Zed added.

Penelope looked to Zed, a silent communication passing between them. *Keep him talking. Buy Charles time.* "What do you gain from all this?"

Zed grunted. "Same as every other jackass who tries to summon a higher-level demon. Knowledge, power, money."

"Shows how much you know. You don't understand anything." Jude jabbed the knife in his hand toward the body of Ephraim Brown still tied to the tree. "They didn't understand, either. Malphas can show those who summon him things that lie beyond the Veil, including people who have passed. If they had just let me finish, they could have talked to anyone they wanted to."

Penelope's eyes narrowed. "All this happened because you wanted to talk to someone you lost, didn't you?"

"That's not your business," Jude spat.

Penelope persisted. "Who was it?"

"You don't deserve to know."

"Then it was someone."

Jude gripped the handle of the knife tighter. "That's enough."

"It was his sister," Bertram said quietly. "She died the year before. She was only sixteen."

Jude regarded Bertram icily. "How do you know that?"

Bertram seemed equally surprised. "I … don't know."

Penelope took a step forward. "He's right, though, isn't he?"

Jude was shaking. His grief was real, and deep, and it was all he had left. He'd burn everything down before he let go of it. "So, what if he is? Malphas would have let me see her again, just one more time."

"In return for what?" Zed asked.

"What does it matter to you?" Jude worked his jaw, eyes darting from Penelope to Zed. Holding onto the demon was taking its toll. The last bit of his sanity was fraying.

"An awful lot if you're going to invite that kind of evil into the world," Zed replied.

Jude let out a humorless chuckle, and odd smile on his face. "What's a little more evil in a world like this?"

"Malphas lies," Charles said. "It's what he does."

"No, I could see her before Johnathan ruined everything, just as beautiful as the day she died." Looking at something that wasn't there, he extended his free hand up into the air. "She was reaching out a hand to me. I came so close to grasping it, and then she was ripped away from me again."

Charles shook his head. "It wasn't her. That was just a trick."

"No, it was her," Jude screamed. "I know it was her. And I'm going to see her again. Tonight."

"I wouldn't count on it." Charles pointed to Ephraim. "He gave us the key. I don't know how he did it, but before he died, he gave his son the memories of what happened here before. We know how to stop you. Like I said, this spell is a circle, with no beginning or end. Say the words in the right order and it'll send Malphas right back where he came from."

"You're bluffing."

"Try us," said Penelope.

Jude's lips pulled back in a sneer, showing his teeth. Howls rose up from the forest all around them as the shadows billowed up and daemons descended on the graveyard, but before they could attack, Zed held up the rosary Charles had given him—one of the trinkets he carried in his satchel. Zed recited the *Vade Retro Satana* just like he had before to drive the daemon away from Jake. At the same time, Penelope made a cut in the palm of her hand with Zed's pocket knife and let a trickle of blood fall on the pentagram to deflect its magic. She had to be the one, Charles said, because she carried her father's blood.

The daemons shrieked and swooped down on them, but none of them came any closer than the pentagram's perimeter. Charles began chanting, the words unfamiliar to Zed's ears, *wrong*, somehow. They physically hurt him, but he dared not stop chanting himself. Charles needed time to finish the spell.

Jude didn't seem to be bothered. "Idiots. I'll admit it, I was angry when the traps I set for each of you didn't work, maybe a little irrational even, but now I see I shouldn't have gone to the trouble."

With another flick of his wrist, Charles was lifted in the air and thrown back down to the ground. As soon as he stopped chanting the daemons doubled their screaming, and Zed couldn't hold them back any longer. The charms Charles gave him, Penelope, and Bertram meant the daemons couldn't harm any of them directly, but they could hurt in other ways.

Bertram huddled with Penelope. The shadow demons surrounded them, hissing and shrieking. As Charles tried to push himself up off the ground, they tormented him, swooping down over him until he was reduced to swatting at them, unable to get up. Zed fared a little better. They shied away from the rosary, but still they flew around him, obscuring his vision and whispering their vile lies of hopelessness and despair.

"Malphas is coming," Jude said, his voice different, not entirely his own.

He commenced his own incantation, and this time, the words tore through Zed like knives, until he could barely stand. The daemons moved in concert along the lines of the pentagram, faster and faster. The wind picked up, carrying Jude's voice up into the night sky.

Just then a figure stumbled out of the forest into the graveyard. The bottom fell out of Zed's stomach when he recognized the mop of curly brown hair.

Jake.

Zed fought through the swarm of daemons to get to him. "Jake? How did you get here?"

"I waited for Linda to fall asleep," he replied. "Then I snuck out."

"But how did you find us?" Zed's gaze went to Jake's hand clutching his side.

He had a cut over his right eye, and his clothes were torn in more than a few places.

Jake shook his head. "I don't know. Something in my head just told me the way to go."

Zed grasped him by the shoulders. "You shouldn't have come here."

"I had to, Zed. I told you. I'm supposed to be here. I ran into those shadow things in the woods. I got away from them. Mostly." Jake held up his arm. "This bracelet you gave me. It helped."

He pulled his other hand away from his side with a sticky sucking noise. Both his hand and his shirt were covered in blood.

"Oh, my God, Jake. You're hurt."

He looked down at himself dispassionately. "Am I? I can't really feel anything."

Then his eyes rolled back into his head and he collapsed on top of Zed. Zed lowered him to the ground as gently as he could.

He took Jake's hand in his. "Hang in there. It's going to be okay."

Charles tried to stand again, but a flick of the wrist from Jude sent him flying once more. He crashed into a toppled gravestone. Jude never even broke his rhythm. Bertram and Penelope weren't faring much better among the horde of screaming shadows. Finally, a great howl rose up, one that scraped across Zed's brain. The daemons parted briefly to reveal Jude in the center of the pentagram.

"He's here," Jude said, his voice low and gravelly.

In that moment, Zed made a decision.

His abilities didn't stop at being able to sense the emotions of others. He could project them, too, make people feel things he wanted them to feel. Usually he pushed positive emotions—hope, confidence, contentment—and even then, never too much, just enough to give others whatever they needed to work through the problems in their lives. That's what he'd done with Annie, but he could make people feel other emotions, too. That day he focused all he had at Jude. One word passed his lips.

Fear.

———

Penelope couldn't see through the thick, black cloud of screaming daemons. She and Bertram were separated from Charles and Zed.

Between the daemons' shrieking and Jude's chanted words echoing in her head, she could hardly even think. When the daemons had come, Bertram took her by the arm and pulled her behind a gravestone, though it proved to be an imperfect shelter. Bertram shielded them both as best he could. Charles' bracelets kept the daemons from hurting them, but there were so many. Penelope didn't know if their magic would withstand the barrage. And if Jude succeeded in calling Malphas, it wouldn't matter anyway.

Through the swirl of daemons, she caught a glimpse of Zed ... and someone else. The newcomer said something to Zed, and then the man collapsed. Zed knelt over him, grabbing his hand.

A cry loud enough to shake the gravestone she and Bertram hid behind reverberated through the cemetery, and the daemons stopped. Jude stood in the middle of the pentagram, or so Penelope thought until she realized his feet weren't touching the ground. Though the air had stilled, his clothes and his hair still moved as if blown by the wind.

"He's here." Jude's lips moved, but the voice didn't belong to him.

Zed glared at him, an expression on his face Penelope had never seen before, and one she hoped to never see again. For the first time since she'd known him, she was afraid of him.

———

Jude wavered as the emotion overtook him. He clutched the sides of his head and screamed. The giant raven on his shoulder took flight, and with it, the daemons rose into the sky. Jude staggered a few feet, swiping at imagined foes, until he collapsed to the ground, curled into a ball, with his hands over his head.

"Keep chanting, Charles," Zed yelled.

Charles, still gathering his wits after the abrupt end to his second flight through the air, began his spell again. This time, Jude, crazed with fear, couldn't stop him from banishing Malphas back to the other side of the Veil. The daemons' shrieks and the call of the raven faded away until Charles' words were all that was left. When he stopped speaking, the woods were absolutely still and quiet, as if the whole world had just paused.

It didn't last.

Jude screamed, a wail of pure anguish and rage. The emotion knocked Zed to the ground. He almost blacked out from the intensity of it, but then Jude's cry was cut off abruptly. The magician collapsed, the handle of the pocket knife Penelope had used to cut herself sticking out from the back of his neck.

———

The two ghosts appeared to Charles again at the edge of the graveyard. The one who had tipped his hat before did so again. This time he spoke, and though he made no sound, Charles had no trouble understanding the words he mouthed.

"We'll be seeing you again, soon, Mr. Delacorte."

5.

MONDAY, OCTOBER 30, 1972

Penelope set the rock paperweight back down on her desk and stared at it. She'd taken the stone with her to Happiness, hoping, maybe stupidly, that somehow her father would be there with her. She still wasn't ready to let him go.

He was there in a way, she supposed, smiling sadly. The time he'd spent teaching her how to properly throw a knife hadn't gone to waste, though she still didn't quite understand what happened when Jude lost control. Zed had … done something to him, that she was sure of. He was vague about it afterward, his focus more on getting his friend help.

Zed said his name was Jake. He confessed to her the truth about their relationship while she waited with him in the emergency room of the hospital for word about Jake's injuries. The two of them were the only ones awake. Bertram and Charles had both long since fallen asleep.

She asked him why he hadn't told her sooner. He said he was afraid of how she'd react. She'd grasped his hand and told him he was her friend, and she just wanted him to be happy. After everything they'd been through together, she couldn't really say much else.

A knock at the door brought her back to the present. She found Bertram on her porch.

"I can't stay long," he said as he stepped inside. "I just stopped by to say good-bye."

She nodded. "I figured this was coming. Where are you headed? Back to Atlanta?"

Bertram shook his head. "Virginia. I need to spend a little time with my mom. I owe it to her after everything she's been through. Things are going to be tough for a little while. It's going to take some time to wind down the business. And then there's the other stuff that needs taking care of. There are a lot of things my family's done, a lot of dark secrets that need to be brought into the light of day. I just need a little time to sort through what's in my head."

They had buried Ephraim in Happiness. They'd never be able to explain his death to anyone without raising questions none of them were prepared to answer. As far as anyone else was concerned, Ephraim Brown would forever be just another missing person.

The package arrived for Penelope the day after their return from Happiness—Ephraim's magic book, and a letter, explaining what he had done. He knew there was a chance he might die sooner rather than later, and so he bought himself a little insurance by casting the spell they'd discovered the remnants of. It was supposed to transfer his memories of the ritual in college to Bertram if and when he passed on. Those memories helped them defeat Jude Hall, but, as often happened with magic, the effects spilled over. Bertram found himself in possession of a little more knowledge than he necessarily knew how to handle.

As for the book itself, it was a lot more than the simple recipe book Ephraim led Penelope to believe. Many of the spells dated to before the Civil War, and some were even older, going all the way back to the Brown's ancestors in Wales.

Despite the general pain in the ass Bertram could be, Penelope had to admit she hated to see him leave. "You'll come back to visit?"

He leaned over and kissed her on the cheek. "I'll be back. I promise you. You're not getting rid of me that easily, Dreadful Penny."

———

Zed was working near the front of the bookstore when the bell jingled and Jake entered, still limping, still with a bandage above his right eye.

Zed smiled. "Hi, there."

Jake smiled back. "Hi."

Zed pointed to the bandage. "How are you feeling?"

"Like I got mauled by a horde of shadow demons," Jake replied, "but well enough to at least leave the house."

"I hope I didn't cause you too much trouble with Linda."

Jake chuckled. "Are you kidding? She wants to know who my dealer is."

Zed had stayed away to avoid any more questions about their relationship, but it hadn't been easy. Not a minute passed that he didn't fight the urge to check in on Jake.

Even at that moment Zed just wanted to throw his arms around him. "I'm really glad you're doing better."

Jake peered over Zed's shoulder. "Is … ah … Mr. Keller here?"

"He had to step out for an hour or so. We can talk."

"Look, I—"

Zed held up a hand. "You know, I understand if you want to call things off. You didn't sign up for this. I mean, evil magicians calling forth Dukes of Hell from the netherworld isn't usually what we deal with, but I can't say it's the first time we've had a run-in with the things that go bump in the night. And I can't ask you to stay for that."

Jake stood silent for a moment. "Do you want me to stay?"

"What?"

"Do you want me to stay?" Jake repeated.

"Of course," Zed replied.

"Then I want to stay."

Zed sighed. "Jake—"

This time Jake held up a hand. "No, you don't get to unilaterally make decisions. We share something special, and I'm not ready to let that go."

Zed started to say something else, but then the door opened, and a slight, bald man wearing a pair of round glasses entered the store.

Zed nodded at him. "Mr. Keller."

He barely acknowledged Zed as he strode to the back of the store.

"We close at six today," Zed said to Jake.

Jake grinned. "I'll be here at six-thirty."

———

Charles held the book up to the light. When he found it, the leather had been worn off the corners of the cover, exposing the crumbling boards underneath. The spine was cocked and frayed. Some of the signatures were loose, and a lot of the pages showed signs of foxing.

But now it was perfect.

The new leather cover glistened and the gold leaf gleamed. This was Millie's book. Making it beautiful was the least he could do for her. He hadn't seen Millie since coming back from Happiness, nor had he traveled to her version of Harlem again. Isaiah Jenkins' memories were fading away bit by bit, everything except Millie's voice and the sight of her in her blue sequined dress. He didn't know if what he had encountered was really her ghost or just an elaborate illusion. In one sense, it didn't really matter.

Charles put the book down and turned his attention to one that still needed a lot of work. He carried it to his work table, but before he sat down, he turned on the radio. An old spiritual, "Mary Don't You Weep," poured out. Charles picked up his X-Acto knife and began to cut away the book's old cover.

———

Penelope was headed upstairs to her apartment when someone else knocked on the door. This time, Dan waited for her on the front porch.

"Dan? Hi. Come in," she said. "What can I do for you?"

He seemed anxious. He didn't know exactly what to do with his hands, putting them first in his pockets, then by his sides, and finally behind his back. "Well, truth be told, I was a little worried about you. You didn't show up at the shop on Thursday. Is everything okay?"

Penelope suddenly felt sick. Thursday. They were supposed to have dinner. "Oh, God, Dan. I'm so sorry. I had a case blow up and wound up having to go out of town."

He raised an eyebrow. "Nothing too serious I hope."

By "serious" he clearly meant "dangerous."

Penelope dodged the question. "It's … been taken care of."

"Good. I'm glad to hear it. And I understand. I know being a detective isn't exactly a nine-to-five job." He paused, still obviously nervous. "So, I was wondering if I could also ask you a favor."

"Sure. What is it?"

"Do you think you could have your friend bring by her locket, the one you showed me before?"

"I think so." Penelope didn't tell him she still had the heart-shaped locket from Carolyn's secret admirer in an envelope in her desk.

"Great," Dan said. "I actually got in some pieces by the same silversmith, and I'd like to compare them to see if I can narrow down the year they were made."

"I'll talk to her tomorrow. Maybe I can bring the locket by the shop myself."

Dan managed a smile. "Yeah, I'd like that. I mean, if it's not too much trouble."

An awkward silence settled between them. Dan didn't make a

move to leave, and Penelope didn't necessarily want him to go, though she wasn't sure what else to say, other than to apologize again. "Look, I'm really sorry about blowing you off. Is there any way I can make it up?"

He shrugged. "Why don't you have dinner with me tonight?"

Penelope glanced upstairs. She wasn't really looking forward to the TV dinner waiting for her in the freezer, and after everything that had happened, Dan's company sounded awfully appealing. "Sure. Just let me get a jacket."

As she passed by the door to the office, her gaze went to her desk. Her paperweight wasn't where she'd left it.

ACKNOWLEDGMENTS

I would like to thank Darin Kennedy and Caryn Sutorus for reading early versions of these novellas and offering their helpful critiques, Melissa McArthur not only for her editing skills but also her cheerleading, and John Hartness for his quiet mentoring. As always, I would also like to thank my wife Lara for her support.

In addition, I want to offer special thanks to my family members who put up with all my questions about "how things used to be" and *The Greenville News* for making their entire archive of old editions available online. Without them I would never have been about to bring the world of Greenville, S.C. in 1972 to life.

ABOUT THE AUTHOR

J. Matthew Saunders is the author of the Daughters of Shadow and Blood trilogy inspired by the Brides of Dracula, the Dreadful Penny occult detective series, and numerous published fantasy and horror short stories. He is a member of the Horror Writers Association.

A native of Greenville, South Carolina, He received a B.A. in history from Vanderbilt University and a master's degree from the School of Journalism at the University of South Carolina. He received his law degree in California and practiced there as an attorney for several years.

Matthew is an unapologetic European history geek, enjoys the Celtic fiddle, and makes a mean sun-dried tomato-basil pesto. He currently lives near Charlotte, North Carolina with his wife and two children. To find out more or to sign up for his newsletter, visit www.jmsaunders.com.